The Takers

ISBN: 1-4196-0958-0
Library of Congress Control Number: 2005930591

To order additional copies, please contact us.
BookSurge, LLC
www.booksurge.com
1-866-308-6235
orders@booksurge.com

R.W. RIDLEY

THE TAKERS

BOOK ONE OF THE OZ CHRONICLES

The Takers

For Mom, Dad, and Marianna

ONE

We killed the retarded boy. He took his own life, but we killed him just the same. Everybody should have the right to go through life unnoticed, and we took that right away from him. We reminded him that he was different every chance we got. It was harmless fun, harassing the retarded kid, thrusting disgrace upon him everyday. We were kids. What did we know? He was like a dumb animal to us. He didn't absorb the abuse. He shed it like a snake sheds its skin, or so we thought. We didn't know that with each degrading remark and act of humiliation that we forced him to perform, a sense of tangible worthlessness was building up inside of him. He put the horrific pieces of his seemingly useless life together in his damaged mind. Slowly he saw that he was less than human, not because God made him that way but because we saw him that way.

His name was Stevie Dayton, and I think about him almost every minute of every day. In fact, it's pretty much all I think about since the world ended.

***

On October 10, 2006, I had a fever of 104. I was 13 and the kissing disease, mono, had claimed me as one of its latest victims. Because I had never done more than kiss a girl on the cheek, the doctor was fairly certain I contracted the disease some other way, which to a 13-year-old boy, not quite interested in girls yet, is splendid news.

I don't remember much that following week. I was in and out of consciousness. You'd be surprised how much your brain shuts down when your body is fighting for your life. But I do remember bits and pieces. The first day or so my mother was constantly by my side, feeding me broth, keeping me cool with a cold compress, putting her soft cheek against my forehead and whispering, "Mamma's little baby," over and over again. If I had had full use of my faculties, I would have protested. But when you're sick, and helpless, you desperately want to be somebody's "little baby."

By the third day, my mother's presence by my bedside had become sporadic. I heard her talking with my father in the distance, but their voices were like distorted radio signals. I couldn't make out a word they were saying. I could sense a panic in their voices. I assumed it stemmed from their concern over my well being, but looking back it may have been because of what was happening in the outside world.

On day four, I could feel my father lifting me out of my bed and carrying me a short distance. Where he was carrying me I don't know because my vision was shot. I could only make out the simplest shapes of objects. When he put me down, I felt him stand and then my world suddenly went completely dark. I never felt the touch or heard the voices of my mother and father again.

Days later, I don't know how many, I broke the fever. I was still in total darkness. When I first opened my eyes, the only thing I could immediately determine was that I was buried under mounds of clothes. I sat up and realized that I was on the floor of my parents' walk-in closet. Finding yourself in such a place, after several days of a semi-conscious state, you tend to be beset by confusion, and if I did not have the almost intolerable urge to pee, I may have stayed in that closet forever.

I pushed the door open and peered into my parents' bedroom. It was still. The air was dry and stale. I inhaled and could smell my mother's perfume. As I stepped out of the closet, I heard the familiar tap, tap, tap of my dog Kimball's claws on the hallway floor. The door leading to the hallway was shut. My need to piss trumped my desire to see Kimball's friendly face so I bolted to the bathroom as fast as I could.

I can't tell you how long it had been since I peed, but I can tell you I have never felt such relief in my entire life. It felt like I was making up for at least a week of missed opportunities to empty my bladder.

I flushed and stepped back into my parents' bedroom, anxious to see my old friend Kimball. The door leading to the hallway was locked. As I put my hand on the doorknob, I could hear Kimball's deep penetrating growl. Kimball was a good-natured old pup. I had only heard him growl a few times in my life, mostly at other dogs. So to hear him growling at that moment, when I felt confused and vulnerable, was very disturbing. Part of me didn't want to open the door, but a bigger part of me knew that Kimball would never hurt me. He certainly could if he wanted to. He was a 90-pound German shepherd with paws as big as dinner plates, but he was as sweet as a six-week-old kitten. With deep, deep feelings of doubt, I unlocked the door and slowly turned the knob. The door open just a crack, I peeked into the hallway. Kimball was crouched down, the hair on his back raised. His teeth were bared, and he was ready to attack, but not me. He was looking down the hall toward the entrance of the house.

I opened the door but could not will myself to look at what was making Kimball so upset. He was fixated on it. He gave no indication at all that he was even aware I had opened the bedroom door. "What is it, Kimball?" I asked. With that,

Kimball barreled down the hallway. The growl was replaced by a rapid series of barks. I turned to look at what he was chasing, but I could only make out a fast moving shadow. I heard the front door open. A sudden splash of sunlight reflected on the wall. Kimball's bark faded as he pursued the unknown intruder out of the house.

I was paralyzed by fear. With great hesitation, I moved down the long, dark hallway. The walls were decorated with family photos and framed inspirational passages from the Bible. My mother was a religious woman who endlessly sought to negate my father's blasphemous behavior with Biblical knickknacks throughout the entire house.

At the end of the hallway I turned and saw the open front door. Kimball was already making his way back. I could see the scowl was gone. He was grinning with his tongue dangling from his mouth. His ears were pinned down and his tail was wagging back and forth a million miles a minute. He leapt through the open doorway and nearly tackled me to the ground. He whined and covered my face with kisses. I had never seen him so happy.

I had awakened from a long sickly slumber, and as a result I was thin and gaunt. Getting a closer look at Kimball, I could see he was in the same condition. He had not eaten for a while. I suspected the source of his happiness was that my presence meant he would eat.

"Where are Mom and Pop?" I asked. He, of course, did not answer. They obviously had been gone for some time by the looks of his emaciated body. He was the best-fed dog in the county. Pop never let him miss a meal. Something was definitely wrong.

I didn't notice the electricity wasn't working until I tried to open a can of dog food for Kimball. The electric can opener was dead. I tried the light switch in the kitchen. Nothing. I retrieved a screwdriver and hammer from the utility drawer and pounded on the top of the can until I eventually opened it wide enough to stick a spoon in and dig the contents out. Mom would have killed me if she saw me use one of her good spoons like that.

While Kimball inhaled his food, I looked for something that I could keep down. My stomach was a gurgling volcano that I knew would accept only bland and light food that possessed little to no smell or taste. I found a can of broth with a pull back tab on the lid and considered it. Without electricity, I couldn't heat it up. The mere thought of cold broth almost made me vomit. I settled for some saltines and warm ginger ale. As I ate, I noticed that the kitchen was as clean and organized as my mother always kept it.

The rest of the house was in order. Not one stick of furniture was out of place. My clothes were still neatly folded in my drawer and hanging in my closet. My Pop's office was as messy as usual. There was nothing to indicate that my parents wouldn't be home soon, that they hadn't just gone to visit the neighbors or driven to the store to do some shopping. I couldn't quite reconcile the fact that they left me, their extremely sick son, home alone. Was there some sort of emergency that required both of them to be present? There was no time to get a sitter, and I was obviously too sick to travel. Waking up in the closet was easy enough to explain. I had been known to sleepwalk. I must have gone on one of my nocturnal excursions and ended up in the closet.

Kimball was harder to explain. Why had he gone so long without food, and what or who did he chase out of the house? The more I thought about it, the more frightened I became. I deadbolted the back and front doors of the house, and made sure every window was locked. I then sat in the den and tried to convince myself my parents would be home soon.

I sat there and listened to the ticking of the grandfather clock in the front foyer. It ticked away while Kimball and I sat there waiting for my parents to come home. The clock struck one. An hour had passed, and I had accomplished nothing except making myself more convinced that something was horribly wrong. I soon realized that sitting there wasn't the answer. Calling my parents' cell phone was out of the question because the phones were out of service. I had to do something.

The first order of business was to change out of my clothes. They reeked of sickness. I entered my room with Kimball following close behind. Neither one of us wanted to be out of the other's sight. We were both scared out of our minds. I grabbed a clean pair of jeans and a t-shirt and moved to my bathroom. I took my first good look at myself in the mirror. My face was pale and drawn. My brown hair was matted and disheveled. My frame was built out of more bone than muscle. I wasn't the same Oz Griffin I was before I got mono. I must've shed twenty pounds.

I turned on the faucet and splashed water on my face. To my surprise, the water warmed up. That meant the water heater was working. Later I would determine that it was because the water heater was gas operated, but at the time, it didn't occur to me. I considered a shower, but concluded finding my parents was far more important than going out into the world clean and refreshed. I dressed as quickly as I could. I was still suffering some of the effects of the fever. My equilibrium was off and my head felt light. Doing anything quickly was a rather difficult task. When I finally finished dressing, I was weak-kneed and out of breath.

When I regained my energy, I ventured outside, uncertain,

and unsteady. I carried a baseball bat with me, but given my physical state I had no confidence I'd be able to swing it with any kind of authority. Kimball was with me, but most of his strength had been zapped as well. We were two pathetic explorers entering a world of unknown dangers.

The neighborhood was vacant. There were cars in the driveways. A wind blew through the trees. Piles of leaves were scattered throughout the neighborhood. But there were no signs of life beyond Kimball and me. When the wind stopped, the silence set in, and the neighborhood felt less than empty, it felt dead.

I walked to the Mueller's. Their house was what my grandmother called a shotgun house. If you opened the front door, you could see the back door. It was small, but functional. The Mueller's, an older couple, were the unofficial overseers of the neighborhood. We had no neighborhood association or rules, but they let you know when they felt your yard was out of control or your house wasn't up to their standards. I figured if anyone knew where my parents were, they did. They knew everybody's business.

Their front door was open. Kimball and I slowly stepped up on their front porch. "Mr. Mueller?" I said. There was no answer. I looked at Kimball. He looked at me. "I don't like this." Kimball wagged his tail in agreement. "Mrs. Mueller?" I said, as if she would not have answered when I called out Mr. Mueller's name.

I entered the house. My heart was racing. I was sweating despite the cool fall temperature. Kimball was panting like he had just chased a rabbit for a mile and a half. It seemed neither of us wanted to enter the house, but we felt compelled to.

It was in shambles. Wallpaper was ripped from the walls. Furniture was torn apart. Garbage was strewn throughout the entire house. There were stains on the carpet that my imagination immediately identified as blood. Whether it was or not is still a mystery to me, but given what I know now, it most likely was.

Kimball and I inched our way down the hall. Common sense told me to turn back at the first sign of trouble, but curiosity drove me farther into the house. I reached the bathroom. It was in the same condition as the rest of the house. The ceramic tile floor was cracked and the toilet was ripped from its molding and lying in the bathtub. I could see all this from the hallway. There was no reason to go inside, but I did. Till this day, I wish I hadn't because once inside I turned to my left and saw written in red on the shattered mirror, *Beware the Takers.*

The message jolted me and I backed out of the bathroom. I whispered the slogan to myself trying to make sense of it. "Beware the Takers." The front door slammed shut. I told myself it was a gust of wind, but tightened my grip on my bat just in case. Above me, in the attic, I heard what I thought were heavy footsteps. Thump. Thump. Thump. Kimball began to bark. Chaos was breaking out all around me. I dashed down the hall and through the kitchen. "C'mon, Kimball," I shouted. "C'mon!" He ran after me. I opened the back door, and we exited the house like runners out of the starting blocks.

The backyard was enclosed by a six-foot wood fence with a padlocked gate on the side of the house. I could scale it with some difficulty, but Kimball was another story. I couldn't get him out, and I wasn't about to leave him. I pushed on the gate to see if there was any give. To my surprise, the gate pushed back. Kimball's fur on his back stood straight up and he began to growl just as he had done before. The gate shook violently. I looked around me. We were trapped.

"We've got to find a way out, Kimball."

He looked at me as if he understood me and then took off towards the back of the fence that lined a patch of woods. There was an area where the ground dipped and left a small crawl space underneath the fence. Had I not been sick and just shed twenty pounds, I would never have been able to fit, but given my new slimmer build, I followed Kimball through the crawl space with no problem. Safely on the other side, I heard the gate to the fence crash open.

I was exhausted but knew that we could not hang around to find out if whatever was on the other side of the fence could fit through the crawl space. Kimball and I quickly navigated our way through the thick mass of trees and bush until the fence was out of sight. I fell to my knees gasping for air next to a large fallen oak. Kimball made a small circle around me, panting, his legs wobbly and unstable. He could have collapsed at any moment, but he remained vigilant.

I rested for no more than two minutes. When I pulled myself up on my feet, my thighs burned and itched. My legs were getting exercise for the first time in more than a week, and they were protesting.

There are sounds deep in the woods that don't exist anywhere else on the planet. Traversing the dead pine needles and leaves, I heard crackles, crunches, pops, snaps, and thwacks coming from every direction. As long as Kimball wasn't alarmed, I remained relatively calm. He would know if real danger was afoot.

We reached the vacant lot at the back of our neighborhood, which put us about three blocks from my house. I wanted to lie down and take a nap. I wanted to be back in my parents' closet, still asleep, oblivious to what was happening outside. I wanted to be lying in my bed with my mother sitting next to me saying "Momma's little baby." I closed my eyes and hoped against hope that when I opened them I would be back in my house awakening from a bad dream.

I opened my eyes and found myself still standing in the vacant lot. Kimball was looking up at me with a curious tilted gaze. He barked as if to tell me to get myself together and keep moving. He was right. I was standing in an open field like a sitting duck. I moved to the house next to the lot and stooped down behind the front bush. A quick scan of the immediate area told me the coast was clear, I moved to the next house and then the next and the next, each time stopping and hiding behind the biggest bush I could find.

When I got to the Chalmers' house, just two houses down from mine, I did as I had done at all the others, I found a bush and bent down. I was about to move on when a noise caught my attention. It was a scream; a high-pitched squawk that at once chilled and confused me. I didn't want to even think it, but it sounded human. It came in waves and every once in a while would end with a horrible breathless cough. I lost track of Kimball while I sat and listened to the sound. It wasn't until I heard him scratching on the Chalmers' front door that I realized he was trying to get in their house. "Kimball, no," I whispered emphatically. He didn't listen. He continued to scratch at the door. "Kimball."

He worked his paw between the door and frame and finally got the door open enough to fit his body through. I jumped up and reluctantly moved up the porch and into the house. The Chalmers' house was in disarray, too, though not nearly as much as the Mueller's. The screaming was louder inside the house.

Kimball was at the top of the stairs by the time I walked through the door. With a great deal of difficulty I followed.

The screaming grew more intense. Kimball galloped down the hall and stopped. When I reached him, he was calmly sitting at a door at the end of the hall. The screaming was clearly coming from the other side. I looked at Kimball. "A baby," I said. Before I had gotten sick, Mrs. Chalmers was pregnant. Had she had the baby while I was fighting my fever?

The door was locked. There was no way I could break it down. I ran into the bathroom and retrieved a bobby pin and straightened it out. I ran back to the door at the end of the hall and stuck it in the hole and jimmied the lock open. Kimball and I burst through the door only to find another flight of stairs. Kimball climbed them with ease. I did not. At the top of the stairs, I found a finished attic that had been turned into a recreation room. It had a pool table, a big screen TV, and a gaming computer.

Kimball's tail was sticking out from behind the big sectional sofa. The screaming had subsided. I walked over to investigate. I found what I was afraid I would find, a baby, and Kimball was licking its poor puckered little face.

I bent down and examined it. It was small, even small for a baby. I estimated it weighed maybe six pounds. It was wearing a diaper and blue shirt. A black crusty stub stuck out where its belly button should've been. I suspected the kid was hungry. A hungry, screaming baby is all I needed to worry about. I stood and scratched my head. I had no idea what a baby eats.

I turned to make my way down to the first floor of the house to find some baby food when I caught a fast moving blob rushing towards me out of the corner of my eye. I didn't even have time to raise my bat before it was on top of me. The weight of it sent me flying over the sofa. I lost my grip on the bat and it sailed over my head. Kimball started barking.

"Keep away from my baby," I heard.

I scrambled back and tried to find the bat. The thing that attacked me stood with the baby in its arms and I saw for the first time that it was Mrs. Chalmers. "It's me, Mrs. Chalmers. It's Oz Griffin."

She looked at me. "Oz?" She moved around the sofa. "Oz Griffin, is that really you?"

"Yes, ma'am."

She fell to her knees still holding on tight to her baby. "Thank God. I thought we were the only ones left. Oh, thank the heavens above." She began to cry.

Kimball moved around the sofa and sat beside her. "What's going on, Mrs. Chalmers? I can't find my parents."

She gave me a strange look. "You don't know?"

"No, ma'am. I woke up this morning and nobody was home. Something..." I didn't want to say it.

"Something what?" she asked.

"Something chased me and Kimball at the Mueller's house."

She quickly stood and moved to the window. "It didn't follow you here, did it?"

"No, ma'am, I don't think..."

"Listen, to me, Oz," she interrupted. "This is very important." She was panicked which didn't do much for soothing my already fragile state. "Did you see this... thing that was chasing you?"

"No, ma'am. It was practically breathing down our necks, but I never got a good look at it."

"A good look at it or a look at all?"

"At all, I suppose."

She raced back to my side. "Listen to me, you have to be certain. Did you see it at all?" Her voice was soft but demanding.

"No, ma'am," I said.

She collapsed on the sofa. "Thank God."

"What's going on, Mrs. Chalmers?"

To my surprise, she unbuttoned her blouse and began breast-feeding the baby. "I wish I knew, Oz. I wish I knew." I turned away in embarrassment.

"Where is everybody? Where are my parents? Where's Mr. Chalmers?"

She began to cry again. "I don't know." She wiped the tears from her eyes. "How are you still here?"

"I don't know. I was sick. I don't remember much."

"That's right. You had mono. Your mother was so worried." The baby lay content in her arms. "The last time I saw her was when I went into labor with little Nate."

"How long ago was that?"

"A week ago, I guess. I don't know. It's been hard to keep track of time. The clocks don't work. The baby keeps me up most of the time. I think he's colic. I'm exhausted. I don't know if I'm coming or going half the time." She spoke as if it took all her strength.

"What was chasing me, Mrs. Chalmers?"

She looked at me as if I had asked some horrible state secret. "Oz, you mustn't speak of them. They... they know you when you know them." She said it as if it made perfect sense. "The less you know the better off you are."

"But I have to find my parents..."

"They're gone," she yelled. "Everybody's gone. There is not one single soul left in Tullahoma or in Tennessee or in the world besides us. They got everybody."

"I don't understand," I said.

"You don't need to," she said with a disturbing darkness in her voice. She had the look of someone who had gone completely mad. I remembered her as a beautiful woman, but now her face was a horrid combination of red and gray. She had heavy bluish bags beneath her eyes, and she had broken out with an awful rash on her forehead. Asking her further questions was pointless. She lay back on the sofa with the baby still suckling at her breast. "I have to get some sleep," she said. "You'll watch over me, won't you, Oz?"

"Yes, ma'am, Kimball and me will keep watch."

She almost smiled. "The baby should sleep, too. He won't be any trouble." She barely could finish the sentence before she fell asleep. The baby continued to feed.

I wandered over to the window to see if anything was happening outside. The streets were still deserted. I couldn't comprehend what was happening. Mrs. Chalmers only confused the matter more. She gave me more questions than answers. How could everyone be gone? Where did they go? This entire thing was insane. It occurred to me that this all could be a dream. That maybe the fever had driven me crazy. Maybe I was strapped to a bed in a hospital somewhere and this entire thing was just some demented fantasy of a brain that had been cooked by an abnormally high temperature.

I looked around the room. It was all too real to be a dream. This was happening. I couldn't deny that. I didn't know why or how, but it was real, and wishing it weren't wasn't going to get me anywhere. Mrs. Chalmers may have been right, my Mom and Pop were gone, but that didn't mean I couldn't find them or at the very least find out what happened to them.

I plopped down on a beanbag chair and watched Mrs. Chalmers and the baby. The little guy had zonked out just as she said he would. Kimball lay down beside them on the floor. His ears erect and scanning the immediate area for any unusual sounds. As my eyelids grew heavier and heavier, I struggled to stay awake and keep watch over Mrs. Chalmers and the baby as I had promised, but my desire to sleep grew more intense with each passing moment until finally, I slept.

***

I awoke to the sound of a door slamming. I shot out of the beanbag chair as quickly as I could. Mrs. Chalmers and the baby remained asleep. Kimball was up at the ready. The slam came again. It was coming from outside. I ran to the window and looked out. The door to the Wentleys' house across the street was opening and closing on its own. The trees were not swaying in a strong wind, and the piles of leaves on the side of the street remained intact. There was no wind. It was as calm as I had ever seen it.

Mrs. Chalmers woke up. "What is it?" she whispered. She carefully lifted the baby and gently laid him on the sofa. She stood with some difficulty.

"The Wentleys' front door," I said. "It's opening and closing... on its own."

"Get away from the window," she demanded, running in my direction. I didn't comply quickly enough so she yanked me aside. "They're trying to get you to notice them."

"Who?" I said. This time my voice was raised. I left no room for doubt. I was tired of the cryptic references. I wanted some answers.

"Never you mind," she said. "You have to stop thinking about them."

"Who..." I suddenly remembered the shattered bathroom mirror in the Mueller's house. "The Takers, is that what they're called?"

The gray and red coloring of her face was replaced by a pale shade of white. "How do you know their name?"

The slamming stopped.

She looked out the window. "They know we're here. They're coming." She ran to get her baby.

I turned to see who "they" were. I saw a shadow zip across the tree line in front of the Wentleys' front lawn. I could not see what or who cast the shadow, but judging by the trees, it was big, eight or nine feet tall. "What do we do?" I asked.

"Why did you say their name?" Mrs. Chalmers cried. "Why?" She held her baby and paced back and forth. "I won't let them get my baby. I won't let them," she said.

"We need a place to hide," I said. I had the bat back in my hand and nervously tightened my grip on it.

We heard a noise coming from the first floor. Kimball let out a short heavy "woof."

"They're in the house," Mrs. Chalmers said.

"We have to hide," I insisted.

"It's no use." She held out her baby. "Take him." A sudden calm had come over her.

"Mrs. Chalmers..."

"Take him," she said, her voice steady and forceful.

"But I don't know how to hold a baby."

She walked over to me. "Make a cradle with your arm."

I did as she said.

"Now, support his head in the crook of your arm."

He fit in my arm like he was made to go there. "Like this?"

"Perfect." She smiled and kissed him on the forehead. "His name is Nate," she said. "There's formula in the pantry in the kitchen." She backed away. "You stay here. I'll lock the door behind me."

"No, Mrs. Chalmers..." I started to cry. "Don't go down there. I don't want to be alone. I'm scared."

She stopped and smiled again. "Oz, take care of my son. He's your responsibility now."

"No..."

She moved to the stairs. "Once they've taken me, they'll leave. They always do. No matter what you hear, don't open the door." She started down the stairs and stopped. "Oh, and Oz, remember they can't see you if you don't notice them." With that she hurried down the stairs. I heard the door open and shut. Minutes later, all I could hear were the sounds of Mrs. Chalmers screaming.

TWO

Hours passed after Mrs. Chalmers's last scream before I dared to leave the attic. Had it not been for the baby crying and throwing a general fit, I probably would have waited even longer. As it was, he was in desperate need of a diaper change, and I suspected he was hungry again.

With Nate in my left arm, the baseball bat in my right hand, and Kimball at my feet, I descended the stairs as frightened as I have ever been. Mrs. Chalmers said they would leave after they took her, but I couldn't be absolutely sure she knew what she was talking about. She wasn't exactly firing on all cylinders.

Standing in the hallway of the second floor, I knew she was right. I don't know how exactly, but I could sense that they were gone. They brought with them the stench of terror, a sharp sour effervescence that seeps into your bones and sends a horrible sense of doom up and down your spine. If they'd remained in the house, I would have smelled them. Instead all I smelled was the kid's foul and disgusting diaper.

I moved into the Chalmers' master bedroom where they had set up a changing table. I had never changed a diaper before, but I had seen my aunt change my cousin's diaper when we visited them the Christmas before last. Until I woke up from my bout with mono to find that everybody in the world had disappeared, I counted that experience as my most horrible ever.

I set my bat down on the bed and laid Nate down on the flat cushioned top of the changing table. Kimball looked at me as if I were insane to even attempt to change the kid's diaper, but my only other option was to let him keep his soiled diaper on and learn to live with the awful, awful smell. It wasn't an option. I pulled back the adhesive tab on the diaper and lifted Nate's feet to get his hindquarters high enough to slip the diaper out. I was absolutely appalled at the milky green deposit Nate had made. Its consistency defied reason. I quickly wrapped the diaper up tight and tossed it in the nearby trashcan.

Nate kicked and thrashed about on the changing table. His eyes were closed tight. I cleaned his bottom with about a hundred baby wipes, and after several attempts, successfully put a clean diaper on him. Then before picking him up and heading down the stairs to the kitchen, I prayed that I would come across an adult before the kid crapped again. I was through with diaper-changing duty.

The kid gulped down his formula like he hadn't eaten in a month. After he finished the last drop, I soon learned that Nate's favorite thing to do after downing a bottle of formula was vomit. The little brat threw up all over my shirt. I was absolutely convinced he was the most disgusting baby ever born.

As Nate lay on the kitchen floor with Kimball watching over him, I washed my shirt out in the kitchen sink, and watched out the window as the sun sank in the sky. It would be completely dark soon. I decided that I would spend the night in the Chalmers' rather than slink through the neighborhood in the dead of night carrying a squirming baby the short distance to my house.

I raided the pantry for whatever looked edible and stuffed everything into a plastic garbage bag. My appetite was slowly returning to its old form. Much to my delight, the Chalmers were really into junk food. It seemed like they had every kind of chip, chocolate, and soda known to man. There was no dog food, but they did have a lot of canned tuna and chicken. Luckily, they all had pull-up tabs so no can opener would be needed.

The bag full, I scooped up the little kid and headed back up to the master bedroom where I would hole up for the night. I didn't like the attic. It made me feel trapped and boxed in. The master bedroom connected to Mr. Chalmers's office through a large walk-in closet, which gave me two exits. Besides, the baby was set up to sleep in the master bedroom. I figured if he was in familiar surroundings he might have an easier time of it.

By nine o'clock that night (I knew the correct time because I found Mr. Chalmers's watch on the desk in his office), it was obvious I was wrong. The kid howled and wailed from the moment I set foot back in the master bedroom. Mrs. Chalmers said he was colic. I wasn't exactly sure what that meant, but if it meant an enormous pain in the ass, he was definitely colic.

I paced the floor of the bedroom rocking the kid back and forth so long that my arm went numb. It was then that I found something that was labeled a baby sling. It was a device that hung around my shoulder and across my belly and had a pocket big enough to lay the kid in. As soon as he was inside, Nate went out like a light. From that moment on, that baby sling was always in my sight. As far as I was concerned, it was the most miraculous invention ever made.

I stretched out on the bed and drifted to sleep as Kimball took a spot next to me and closed his eyes.

***

At two in the morning, Nate woke up hungry. I fed him some formula and fought hard to stay awake. He was an annoying little bugger. There was a time when I was five or six years old that I begged my Mom to give me a kid brother. Lying there with one eye open, propped up on the Chalmers' bed feeding a flailing little blob some crap that he was going to throw up about two seconds after he got done, I was glad she didn't listen to me.

Despite my best efforts, I dozed off and let my head drop. I quickly jerked awake and breathed out deeply trying to will myself to stay alert. I stood and immediately froze as I looked out the window and saw a large pair of green eyes staring back at me. They were back.

Nate fed unaware of the danger. Kimball hopped out of the bed and charged the window. The eyes didn't move. Nor did I. We were locked in a stare. Mrs. Chalmers's words came back to me. "They can't see you if you don't notice them."

How could I not notice them? All I could see in the darkness were the eerie green eyes. They were there. I couldn't deny that. A tapping came at the window, then I could hear scratching. I looked closer at the green eyes. The thing turned its head, and they disappeared only to reappear seconds later. Kimball barked. I heard a hiss and a low raspy meow. I let out a sigh of relief. The glowing green eyes belonged to a cat. Kimball lunged at the window and the cat took off. I laid back down and Nate and I were asleep before Kimball returned to the bed.

***

I woke up the next morning thinking about Stevie Dayton. Six months earlier, he was found in his basement with a noose around his neck hanging from some pipes. My Mom told me like she expected me to crumple over in a grief-stricken heap. I could sense her disappointment when my only reply was, "Okay," and I went on about the important task of playing Madden on my Xbox.

Stevie was on my mind at that particular moment because I remembered his stories. He was retarded, or "mentally challenged" as my mother used to correct me, but he had an incredible imagination. He wrote comic books about bizarre worlds where people had three heads and eighty-six toes or potato peelers for fingers. It was crazy stuff that never made any sense. He worked on them constantly at school. His drawings were surprisingly good, but his handwriting was barely legible. The stories meant something to him. We, of course, teased him mercilessly about them. Looking back, it was perhaps the cruelest thing we did to him, making fun of his stories. To him, they were the only places he felt real solace, and we set out to destroy them.

There was one story that haunted me this particular morning, a story about a group of creatures that hunted people. The details were vague to me, but I seemed to recall that they were invisible until you could see them. That was Stevie's logic, "invisible until you could see them." At the time, I thought it was the rambling reasoning of a retarded kid, but at that moment, hearing Mrs. Chalmers's voice in my head saying, "they can't see you if you don't notice them," I was beginning to wonder if Stevie knew something the rest of us didn't.

I put a fresh diaper on Nate, and packed up all the baby supplies that would fit in the garbage bag. With a great deal of hesitation, I exited the Chalmers' house with Nate in his sling and Kimball by my side. We made the short trip to my house without incident.

I struggled to come up with a plan for survival. I was

thirteen, and I felt like I didn't know anything about anything that was important. Put me in front of a video game and I could tell you how to defeat the invading Xoran army on planet K-Zap and save the Chalathiun race from extinction. But I couldn't tell you squat about how to pack only the most essential food and other items to keep you alive on planet Earth when it appears you and a baby were the only humans left. I say appears because I had made up my mind that Mrs. Chalmers was wrong. Everyone wasn't gone. After all, what were the chances that three people in the same neighborhood were the only ones that survived? Somebody else had to be out there. I could either wait until they came to me, or I could go out and find them. I never was much for waiting.

I could not drive. I didn't know the first thing about the mechanics of making a car go and more importantly stop. I knew cars had a gas pedal and a brake pedal, but when I tried to imagine how much pressure was the proper amount to apply to either, I convinced myself that not knowing the exact answer to that question would result in a horrible wreck that would leave me either dead or badly injured. So, taking my parents' car was not an option, and since carrying a lot of equipment and Nate on my bike was impossible, I was left with my only mode of transportation being my feet.

I loaded my mom's garden wagon full of supplies; food, clothes, diapers, tools, kitchen knives, flashlights, matches, anything I could think of that would be useful. At one point, the wagon was so full I could hardly pull it. I unloaded it and eliminated whatever I could to make the load lighter. It was a process I repeated several times, until I got it down to a weight I was comfortable with.

With Nate in his sling and dangling from my shoulder, I made one last pass through my house. I stared at the family photos as long as I could, burning them into my memory. They were pictures of happy times, and I wanted those memories to be the ones I carried with me on my journey. I took the photo of my Mom and Pop's last anniversary, all three of us at Baskin Robbins eating our weight in ice cream, and stuffed it in my pocket. That's when I realized that I had not taken a picture of Nate's parents with me. It would be our first stop before we headed out of town.

Just in case, I left a note for my parents on the refrigerator. "Gone looking for you. Love, Oz." I think it was the first time I ever signed a note to my Mom and Pop with the word "love." It saddened me that they would probably never see it.

I took a picture from Nate's father's office. It was a picture of Mr. Chalmers, Mrs. Chalmers, and Nate at the hospital. Mr. Chalmers had the biggest smile I think I had ever seen. They all looked tired and on the verge of collapse, but I felt like it was their happiest moment. Nate should know that he made them happy.

As I was about to leave Mr. Chalmers's office, I noticed that he had a sword hanging on his wall. According to its plaque, it belonged to a Union Officer in the Civil War by the name of James J. Petty. I pulled it off the wall and was surprised at how heavy it was. It looked as if it were brand new. I dubbed the sword J.J. and brought it with me.

I positioned myself in the middle of the road. The temperature hovered somewhere in the high 50s. I put on my Tennessee Titans sweatshirt and made sure that Nate was bundled up tight in his blanket. I figured my body temperature would keep him warm. I gave my house one last look over my shoulder and then started pulling my wagon down Harper Street.

We crossed over to Collinwood and then Freemont Avenue

where I made my next stop. I stood in front of Stevie Dayton's house, and felt a chill race through my bones. I avoided this house like the plague whenever I went bike riding for fear Stevie would see me and come running out after me, begging me to come in and read his latest story. It was the only time I was polite to him because his mom was always within earshot, and I didn't want her to know how I really treated her son.

I walked inside and like all the other houses it was empty. It was left intact like my house, but it was just as disturbing as all the other houses that had been ransacked. The faint odor of terror was in the air. I quickly made my way to Stevie's room and found his collection of stories in a series of boxes underneath his bed. Amazingly, they were all neatly filed away. I overturned the first box and rifled through the mound of monster and mutant stories. Stevie had written hundreds of comic books. I dumped the next box, and then the next. It wasn't there. All the boxes empty, I stood and backed out of his room.

At the end of the hall, I saw the door to the basement. "That's where they found him," I told myself. "He had it with him." I said it with a knowing that made no sense to me. How I thought I knew that he had the comic book I was looking for with him the day he killed himself, I don't know, but I was sure of it. I took a step toward the door and stopped. It was foolish to go down there without protection. I ran back to the wagon and got J.J. and a flashlight.

A rush of cold air struck me when I opened the door to the basement. Nate must have felt it too because he squirmed in his sling. I took one step down and looked at Kimball. He backed away from the door. "Kimball, c'mon," I said, but he backed away even farther. He would not make the trip downstairs with me.

Each stair creaked and sagged as I stepped on it. The beam from my flashlight created a bent tunnel of light surrounded by total darkness. I felt as if I were entering hell.

My feet touched the cement floor. I scanned my flashlight back and forth. It was an unfinished basement that served as the Dayton's laundry room. A basket of laundry sat on top of the dryer. I turned to my right. A series of pipes snaked across the ceiling to the far corner of the room. To the left, there were six metal shelves that contained tools and spare parts for various household items.

Back to the right, I followed the pipes to the corner of the room. J.J. shook in my trembling hand as I approached the area where I was certain Stevie had taken his own life. A musky smell grew stronger and stronger as I got closer. A group of fast moving spiders scurried in front of the beam from my flashlight. I followed their frantic journey and stopped when my light illuminated an overturned chair. "It was the one he was standing on," I told myself. The guilt that I had been, in part, the cause of his death started to boil inside of me. The chair represented to me his last stand. It was where he gave in to the constant bombardment of abuse from my friends and me. We caused the pain he wanted to end. As I looked at the chair, I knew that worse than never recognizing my culpability in his death was recognizing it too late.

I shined my flashlight up at the ceiling and was relieved the noose wasn't there. I imagine Stevie's parents ripped it down the first chance they got.

I bent down and examined the immediate area. The floor was damp so I didn't hold out much hope that the comic book would survive in that environment. I zipped the flashlight to the left wall. A man, crouched down on the floor was looking at me. I screamed and fell back. Nate screamed along with me. I looked at the man closer. He was holding a sword and a flashlight and had a sling across his shoulders. The man wasn't a man. He was me. I was looking in a full-length mirror.

I stood. My pants were now covered in the muck from the damp floor. I stepped to the mirror. That's where I saw it. In the mirror, I saw a stack of paper on the washing machine. I turned and hurried to retrieve it. My blood ran cold as I read the name of the comic book, *The Takers*. Without thinking, I whispered the name out loud.

As I looked up from the homemade comic book, the mirror crashed to the floor. Kimball began to bark. Nate kicked and cried. I felt the ground begin to shake. I stuffed the comic book in Nate's sling and held tight to J.J. and the flashlight as I sprinted up the stairs only to have the door slam shut in my face.

I whipped my flashlight around to face the bottom of the stairs. I could hear something digging its way through the concrete floor. I rammed my shoulder into the door. Kimball barked frantically. He scratched at the door. I turned and grabbed the knob. The flashlight fell out of my hand and bounced down the stairs. It landed with the beam facing into the room. I threw my shoulder into the door again. This time it gave way. As if someone were pushing against me, I forced the door opened wide enough so I could fit through. I gave the basement one last look and saw the shadow of a hand breaking through the floor. It was all the impetus I needed to dash down the hallway and out of the house.

I grabbed my wagonload of supplies and bolted down Freemont Avenue until my lungs felt as if they were going to burst. Whatever was in the basement had not followed me. Without looking at the comic book, I took it from Nate's sling, rolled it up tight and buried it in the wagon under the supplies.

***

Before leaving Tullahoma, I went to all my friends' houses, Gordy Flynn, Larry Barr, and Tim Sanders, just to check if by chance any of them had survived. They had not. I was tempted to take Gordy's dad's hunting rifle, but I could not bring myself to do it. The truth is it intimidated the hell out of me. It was long and shiny, and by the looks of all the deer heads on the wall was a very efficient killing tool, but I had never fired a gun. I was convinced if I took it, I would end up shooting myself before I shot one of the creatures.

I left the only hometown I had ever known behind me. It was a peculiar little Southern village that was for the most part a great place to grow up. There wasn't much to it, but it was my world, and I would miss it.

By eight o'clock that night, I had reached Manchester, a small town located off of I-26 that was only fifteen miles from Tullahoma, but considering my weakened condition and sizeable load my progress was severely impeded. Once I was on the interstate I would head east toward Chattanooga. I decided to head east because I had an uncle in Charleston, South Carolina. I had no idea if he was alive, but there was only one way to find out.

The sky had been overcast all day, but now the sun was completely gone, and the moon didn't provide much light. I pushed on until I reached a Kroger's grocery store, an ideal place to set up camp for the night, or so I thought. As it turns out, meat doesn't keep too well when the refrigeration system fails. It stunk to high heaven. I covered my mouth and nose with my hand, grabbed a couple of plastic bags at the end of the first register, and went from aisle to aisle taking what I thought were useful supplies, including five packages of Oreos.

I was tearing open a box of chocolate frosted Pop Tarts when I heard a noise from the other end of the aisle. I turned and was greeted with a bright light in my eyes.

"What'cha doing in my store, boy?" I heard a thick hoarse voice say.

Kimball growled.

"Sir?" I tried to sound unafraid.

"I said, what'cha doing in my store?"

"Nothing." The light hid him from my view.

"Nothing? Looks like you're eatin' my food." I heard him suck in a huge gob of snot through his nose and spit it out.

Kimball stalked toward him.

"Call your dog off."

"Kimball, stop," I yelled. He obeyed. "Listen mister, I don't want any trouble. I didn't know this was your food."

A small grubby hand snuck in under my nose and ripped the Pop Tart out of my grasp. I turned to see a girl, maybe twelve-years-old, gobbling up the chocolate breakfast food. Her clothes and face were filthy, and her hair was wild and unruly.

"Ignorance of the law ain't no excuse," the man said. "That there's Lou. Don't bother saying nothing to her. She can't talk. She's mute or something."

Lou noticed the sling around my shoulder moving. She stepped closer and reached out. I backed away. "Me and Kimball will just go."

"Where you going?" The man asked. He started to walk down the aisle.

"Headed east," I said.

"What's east?"

"I got an uncle in Charleston."

"Charleston?" He started to laugh. "You figurin' on getting there tonight?" He took the flashlight from my eyes, and I could finally see him. He was in his forties. He had more belly than anything else. He wore a rough three-day old beard that spread across both his chins. He had a name patch on his shirt that read "Wes." By the looks of his uniform and oil-covered hands, he was a mechanic by trade. I could see now that he was holding a large hunting knife.

"I was going to camp near the interstate."

Lou stepped up again and peeked inside the sling. She let out a gurgled scream of joy.

"What'cha got there?" Wes asked.

"Supplies." I said.

He chuckled. "Lou don't get that excited about supplies."

Lou reached for the sling. I slapped her hand away. She wailed.

"Watch it, boy!" Wes reached around me and opened up the sling. "Good lord almighty, boy. That's a baby. Newborn from the looks of it." Kimball watched him suspiciously. "You best come with us."

"I don't want any trouble."

"And you ain't going to get none either, unless you brought some of them damn Greasywhoppers with you."

"Greasywhoppers?" I said.

"Them ugly buggers," he said. "The ones that done all this." He waved his knife around to indicate the devastation that surrounded us.

"No, sir, I didn't bring any Greasywhoppers with me."

"Well, c'mon then," he said. "We're holed up at the mattress store down the way." He moved past me, grabbing a box of breakfast bars as he headed for the exit.

Lou stood in front of me eating the Pop Tart. She looked like a wild animal tearing into its prey. I wondered if she had always been like that or if she had just gone crazy because of what was happening to the world. I carefully moved around her and followed Wes. As I passed her, I saw her break off a chunk of her Pop Tart and try to give it to Kimball. I quickly grabbed her arm. "Don't do that," I said.

She ripped her hand away and screamed so loud I thought she was going to puncture my eardrums.

"I didn't mean anything by it," I said. "It's just that dogs aren't supposed to have chocolate. It could kill him."

She threw the remaining Pop Tart at me and took off towards the door, screaming all the way. It must have been a regular occurrence because Wes had no reaction to it at all. I could see him through the window calmly walking toward the mattress store at the end of the shopping center.

Kimball and I looked at each other. We were both confused by what had just happened. The thought of going outside, grabbing the wagon and pulling it all the way to the interstate crossed my mind. These people were strangers after all, and they didn't exactly make a great first impression. In the end, I decided my opportunity to spend time with people might be limited over the course of my journey. I might as well take advantage of it whenever I could. I exited the building, grabbed the wagon, and headed towards the mattress store.

When I got there Wes was sitting on a mattress at the back of the store. "Take whichever you like," he said. "Lou sleeps on the floor."

There were probably twenty mattresses to choose from. I picked one at random and put the grocery bags on it. Kimball jumped up on top of it and lay down.

"I figured this is good as place as any to hole up," Wes

said. "Got a nice place to sleep. Food store right next door. Hell, I got enough stuff over there to go a year or more without a peep from my old hungry stomach."

I lay Nate on the bed and started to change his diaper. Lou popped up from behind the bed and watched with great interest. She moved around the bed to stand next to me, never taking her eyes off Nate.

"You related to that little fella?" Wes asked.

"No, sir," I said. "He belonged to my neighbors, the Chalmers." I said it like he may have heard of them.

"That's a big job, taking care of a little one like that. You up for it?" He asked.

"Got no choice," I said. Without prompting, Lou handed me a diaper from the wagon. "Are you Lou's daddy?"

He laughed. "Me? No. Found her in an RV off the interstate, bout a week ago. She was hiding in the toilet. Her parents must've got took." He leaned forward. "I figure they's alien or something."

"Lou's parents?" I said.

"No, the Greasywhoppers. They's aliens."

"Why do you call them Greasywhoppers?"

"Cause that's what they is," he said. "They're big hairy whoppers covered in grease and grime, and they're all kinds of foul smelling." He leaned down and picked up a can of beer from the floor and popped it open. "Greasy-whoppers," he said just before he took a sip of beer.

I looked at him in disbelief. "You've seen them?"

"Damn right I did," he said. "Killed one of the suckers."

"You did?"

"Hell, yeah. One of them come into my shop while I was working on Mrs. Jervey's Olds 88's brakes. Had me by the neck. Claws diggin' into me." He pulled his shirt collar away to show me four puncture wounds on his neck. "He was a big ugly fella'. Dead red eyes. Long sharp teeth. He was slobbering and foaming at the mouth."

"How'd you kill him?" I asked, enthralled by his story.

Wes pulled his hunting knife from its sheath. "I had this on me. I always do. Used to creep some people out, but by God, where are them people now? They got took, that's where they is. I stuck this in that Greasywhopper's belly and gutted the sucker."

"Wow," I said, unable to contain my amazement at his bravery.

"They took everybody else that same day. You and Lou's the only ones I've seen since." He took another sip of beer.

"Where do you suppose they take everybody?"

"Don't know," he said. "But this whole thing is a military operation. You can count on that."

"Military?"

"Yes, sir. They cut power and communications first. Isolated everybody. Our chain of command didn't have no way to get instructions to our soldiers. Then they done something to the guns. Won't none of them fire."

I filled a bottle with formula. Lou was hovering over Nate. I reached around her, picked him up and started to feed him. Lou stood inches away from me watching every move the baby made.

"Saw a few planes from the air force base down the road fly over in the beginning," Wes said. "I guess jet fuel worked for some reason or another. But I ain't seen one in about five days now. I reckon there ain't nothing left of our military."

I tried to move away from Lou, but she followed me wherever I went. A thought came to me. "How do you know her name's Lou if she can't talk?"

"I don't," he said. "She looks like my sister Louise." He stretched out on his mattress. "You missed dinner. Lou and me cooked us up some beans and rice."

"Cooked?" I said, surprised.

"We got us a propane deluxe grill from the Wal-Mart across the way. He closed his eyes. "Can't fire it up, though. Not 'til tomorrow morning. We're rationin' the propane." Within seconds I heard him snoring.

Nate finished his formula, and I put him on the bed. Lou quickly walked over, picked up the baby and gently put him over her shoulder. She started to pat his back. Nate let out a loud belch. Lou looked at me and smiled. "You've got to burp him," she whispered.

I raised an eyebrow. "You can talk?"

She nodded.

"But Wes said..."

"They can hear you talk," she whispered even lower.

I looked out the front window of the store. "You mean..."

She nodded. "They don't hear screaming or laughing or dogs barking or cats meowing or most anything else, but they can hear people talk."

I sat down on the bed. "Why can't they hear us now?"

"I don't know. I guess they're not looking for us." She started to rock Nate back and forth.

"They took your parents?" I asked.

"My Mom and Stepdad. We were going to Disney World." She sat next to me. "I don't know about the rest of my family. My little brother and grandparents were going to meet us there." A sudden sadness covered her eyes. "What about you?"

"I'm not sure," I said. "I've been kind of out of it with a fever for the last week or so. I woke up and everybody was gone."

Kimball jumped off the bed and started sniffing the wagon. I knew that meant he was hungry so I opened one of the grocery bags and retrieved a pouch of wet dog food and tore it open. I dumped the contents on the floor and Kimball devoured it.

I looked at Lou. "What is your name, by the way?"

She frowned and looked at Wes. "Call me Lou. I think it makes him feel better."

I looked down and much to my delight she had rocked little Nate to sleep. "Thanks, Lou," I said.

She looked at me with tears in her eyes. "I miss my family."

"Me, too," I said.

She stood and handed me the baby. "You should get some sleep while you can. He'll be awake in a couple of hours ready to eat again." She stood and moved to the back corner of the store. She disappeared behind an adjustable bed.

I lay down and tucked Nate between my arm and body. Kimball jumped up and lay at the foot of the mattress. I did not fall asleep immediately. I thought about Wes's story. I wondered if it was a load of crap or if he really had killed one of the Greasywhoppers, as he called them. I had only seen a few shadows. I hadn't seen the actual creatures. I had no idea if his description was accurate. As I drifted off to sleep, I thought about Stevie's comic book in the wagon. It was possible the answers I needed were in there, but Mrs. Chalmers had told me the less I knew the better off I was.

"Hey," I heard Lou whisper.

I carefully sat up. She was peeking over the adjustable bed. "Yeah?" I said.

"What's your name?"

"Oz Griffin."

"The baby?"

"Nate."

"Good night, Nate, good night, Oz Griffin," she said. "Try not to dream about the Greasywhoppers. They can get you there, too." She disappeared behind the adjustable bed again.

I closed my eyes and tried not dream about the Greasywhoppers.

THREE

As promised, Wes fired up the grill behind the mattress store the next morning and roasted half a dozen corn-on-the-cobs. They tasted fantastic. We each took two and ate them in record time. Wes warmed himself a pot of coffee on the grill. Had somebody seen a snapshot of us they may have guessed we were on a camping trip having the time of our lives.

"Sure could go for a steak right about now," Wes said, corn stuck between his teeth. "Meat in the store's done turned on me."

"What about a generator?" I asked. "Doesn't Wal-Mart have one of those?"

"Course it does," he said. "But they don't work."

"They don't?"

"No, sir," he said. "They run on gas and the gas ain't no good no more. Them Greasywhoppers ruined just about everything."

Nate let out a cry from inside the mattress store. I started to stand, but Lou beat me to it. She ran inside the store.

Wes burped and threw his stripped corncob behind him. "You still figurin' on heading east?" he asked.

"Yes, sir."

"It ain't gonna be easy. You got Monteagle to cross. It could take you two, three days to make it to the other side. Temperature's about twenty degrees cooler up there. You get stuck up there, that baby's liable to freeze to death."

"I'll just stick to the interstate. We'll be fine."

"Maybe," he said. "Course you could just stay here. Me and the girl will help you with the baby."

He said it casually, but I had a feeling he really wanted me to stay. "Maybe a day or two."

"Suit yourself, but the girl ain't going to be none too happy..."

A crash came from the other end of the building. Wes and I jumped to our feet. Kimball stood point, sniffing the air, his ears straight up. Wes held his hunting knife in front of him. I thought about running to get J.J., but I decided there wasn't time. I searched the immediate area and found a board from a broken palette. We waited. Another crash came. This time Kimball took off like a shot towards it.

"Kimball," I shouted. "Stop!" He didn't obey.

"We best get inside," Wes said.

"I can't..." Before I could protest a large fast moving animal with black fur burst out from the corner of the building and charged Kimball. Kimball didn't waver. I moved in closer. Wes grabbed my arm. "Get inside," he insisted. I ripped my arm from his grasp and chased after Kimball.

Suddenly the animal and Kimball stopped. They faced each other. I got within ten feet of them and finally could tell what the animal was. I could recognize it, but I couldn't explain what it was doing in Manchester, Tennessee, about 150 miles from the closest zoo. It was majestic, powerful arms, an enormous head that came to a point, black eyes underneath a prominent brow ridge. It was a gorilla. Correction, it was an angry gorilla. It beat its chest, displayed its three-inch fangs, and let out an earth-shattering roar. Kimball barked.

I moved in slowly. "It's okay," I said. "It's okay." I grabbed Kimball's collar and pulled him back. The gorilla paced and let out the occasional grunt.

I looked at the gorilla. We made brief eye contact. It was as scared as we were. It growled and lunged forward. I pulled Kimball back some more. The gorilla turned and slowly walked back to the corner of the building where it picked up a doll and a blanket and disappeared behind a dumpster.

Wes joined Kimball and me. "That weren't no Greasywhopper," he said.

"It was..." I hesitated. "It was a gorilla."

"A go-rilla?" he said, emphasis on the first syllable. He chuckled. "I wondered where that thing went."

I looked at him like he was crazy.

"C'mon, I'll show you," he said.

We headed back toward the grill. He stopped and yelled inside to Lou. "Back in a minute, Lou. Keep a watch over the baby and mind the go-rilla out back." He laughed. "A go-rilla. Lordy, the end of the world sure do make for some interesting times."

***

Wes took Kimball and me to a convenience store about a mile and a half from the mattress store and about a half mile from the interstate. Parked on the side near the diesel pumps was a large customized bus. The bus had pictures of a gorilla and the words "AJAX, The World's Only Talking Silverback" painted on the side.

"I figured they stopped for gas when the Greasywhoppers got 'em," Wes said stepping up inside the bus. Kimball and I followed. The inside of the bus was torn apart. "You can see they put up a pretty good fight." The bus was obviously a home to Ajax and his owners. It had a kitchen, a bathroom, a bedroom with a double-sized bed, and a large cage in the back. The keys to the cage were still in the door. He picked up a book off the floor and handed it to me. "The go-rilla can't really talk. He just knows some of that sign language stuff. The kind deaf people use."

The book was about Ajax. It was a detailed account of his upbringing and training. I flipped through it. It had pictures of Ajax from a baby all the way to an adult, working with some dark haired woman named Dr. Alice Fine. She loved Ajax. You could tell that from the impossible smile she had in every picture. According to one of the captions under the pictures, Ajax knew over 1500 words in American Sign Language.

"All this set me to wonderin'," Wes said. "They's a lot of zoos and such all across this country. What do you reckon happened to all those animals?"

I shrugged my shoulders. "Maybe the Take..." I stopped myself. I did not want to say that name again. "I mean, maybe the Greasywhoppers took them."

He shook his head. "They got no use for animals. I seen dozens of stray cats and dogs since this all started. I'm bettin' there's lions and tigers and monkeys of every kind runnin' around this country free as field mice."

"Maybe they're still locked up in the zoos." The thought of those animals starving to death behind their enclosures sickened me, but it was probably the unpleasant truth.

"Some of them," he said. "But I bet you dollars to donuts some of them got out some how some way, and they's out there looking for something to hunt."

I thought about what he said, and concluded that he was probably right. That meant that the Greasywhoppers weren't the only danger we had to cope with. With no guns or fast moving vehicles, my journey to Charleston was looking more and more perilous with each passing moment.

***

Back at the mattress store, I went through the book about Ajax. He was an amazing gorilla. Dr. Fine believed that he had a real understanding of the world and could even hold conversations about great works of art, music, and war. He watched movies and had a monthly article in a national magazine reviewing the latest releases. Dr. Fine wrote the articles, of course, but they were all Ajax's opinions. He was something of an artist, too. His paintings had actually sold for thousands of dollars.

Lou had taken over Nate duty and was busy walking him around the store. Kimball was snoozing away on one of the mattresses. Wes was nowhere to be found. I continued to flip through the book. I discovered that Ajax's favorite food was peaches. I excused myself, exited the mattress store, careful not to disturb Kimball, and headed for the grocery store.

Inside the store, I found a couple dozen peaches in the produce department. I grabbed as many as I could and went out the back door. I made my way to the area I had last seen Ajax and dumped the peaches on the ground. I found a hiding spot behind a stack of empty boxes and waited to see what would happen.

Minutes passed and nothing. Just as I was about to give up, I saw a long arm covered in black fur reach out from behind the dumpster and grab a couple of peaches. I could hear Ajax gobbling up the juicy fruit.

I inched my way out of hiding. I could make out half of Ajax's face behind the dumpster. He saw me and hoot-growled in attempt to shoo me away, but I didn't move. He continued to eat the peaches. I watched him for about ten minutes and then got up and walked back to the mattress store, feeling Ajax's eyes on me the whole way.

Back in the mattress store, I lay down on one of the beds.

Lou had gotten Nate to sleep. She was standing guard over him like he was a lost treasure. "What do you think happened, Lou? I mean with the Greasywhoppers. Why are they here?"

She looked at me for a long time before answering. "I think we made God mad," she said.

I thought about her answer. "How do you figure?"

"This is what happens in the Bible, isn't it? Jesus comes down and takes everybody way, all the good people anyway."

"I'm a good person," I said, a little offended by her assessment.

"Maybe Jesus doesn't think so."

I turned away from her. "I liked it better when I thought you didn't talk." I didn't want her to be right, but I considered the possibility. I thought about Stevie Dayton. I wasn't such a good person to him. If he had any kind of vote in who Jesus took back with him, then I surely wouldn't have made the list. But then again, neither would've Gordy, Larry, or Tim.

I looked at the wagon and considered getting the comic book out and reading it, but I couldn't bring myself to do it. If I notice them, I thought, they will notice me. I closed my eyes and fell asleep.

***

I woke up with Lou sitting on the bed next to me, staring holes through me. I wiped my eyes and sat up. "Can I help you?" I said.

"What do you think happened?" she asked.

I looked at the wagon. "I don't know."

"I think we're supposed to do something," she said. "I think there's a reason they didn't take us."

"It's not for a lack of trying," I said. "They've come after me a couple of times." I stood up and stretched.

"Yeah, but they never got you. Most everybody else didn't have a chance to get away, but you and me and Wes and Nate, we all found a way to escape."

"So."

"So, I think there's a reason for that," she said. "I think we have a mission."

"A mission?" I laughed. "You watch too many movies. We just got lucky, that's all. Truth is, it's just a matter of time. They'll get us all sooner or later."

She gasped at the thought and bowed her head. I suddenly felt bad for dismissing her theory and providing her with such a prediction of doom. I looked at the wagon. What if she were right? What if we were supposed to do something? Maybe Stevie Dayton wrote about more than just the creatures. Maybe he wrote about... our mission.

"Look," I said. "Don't pay any attention to me. Right now our mission is to survive. We'll figure out the rest as we go along."

I grabbed the book on Ajax and left the store. Lou put Nate in his sling and followed. "Where are you going?" she asked.

"To make a new friend," I said.

We walked to the grocery store, grabbed as many peaches as we could carry, and headed out the back to pay Ajax another visit. Now that I knew he was open to accepting food, I was hoping he would be open to accepting our friendship.

I instructed Lou to take my previous position behind the stack of boxes while I put the peaches a little farther away from the dumpster than I had placed them the first time. I sat about ten feet away in the open. After several seconds, Ajax poked his head out from behind the dumpster. I opened the book to the section on American Sign Language and searched for the sign for friend. Ajax stretched his body out and grabbed a peach.

The book was a little difficult to decipher, but I did my best and interlocked my right index finger over my left index finger and then switched their positions. Ajax ignored me at first, but when he reached out for his second peach he saw what I was doing and huffed. I didn't know if he was telling me I was doing it wrong or to get lost. He took the peach and peered out from behind the dumpster as he ate it. I lightly touched my fingers to my cheek and pulled my hand away, the sign for peach. I did it over and over again until Ajax responded by throwing his half eaten peach at me. I felt I had won a small victory.

I was looking for another word to sign when Nate let out his usual afternoon wail. Ajax stopped in mid stretch for another peach and howled in anger. I turned to Lou signaling for her to get Nate to shut up, knowing full well there was nothing she could do. I turned back to Ajax and to my surprise he was now sitting just three feet away from me. I was shocked and felt myself having difficulty breathing. Ajax looked in the direction of the stack of boxes and then back at me. Nate continued to cry. Ajax looked back and forth from me to the baby, and then to my astonishment he put his arms together like he was forming a cradle and rocked them from left to right, the sign for baby.

He put his right hand to his mouth and then brought it forward to his left hand. I searched through the book to find the gesture. I learned it meant good. "Baby good," he was telling me.

I looked up the word yes and signed it to him.

He responded by signing, "Baby good," and then he added another sign, his hands locked in a defensive motion in front of him. I scrambled to look up the word. After flipping through several pages, I found it, protect. "Baby good protect."

I searched through the book to find the signs for my question. I made the sign for "protect" and then pulled my right index finger away from my left index finger for the word "from" and then struck my right index finger across my left palm for the word "what." "Protect from what?"

He grunted, frustrated. He backed away. I asked again. "Protect from what?"

He made a gesture with his right hand as if he were grabbing for something and then moved it across his body. He did this several times adding the signs for "protect," "baby," and "from." After repeating the message several times, he turned to the peaches, sat with his back to me and ate. I looked up the sign. My heart skipped a beat when I found it. Ajax had just signed, "Protect baby from take."

I stood up and silently urged Lou to follow me. We made our way back to the mattress store with little Nate crying the whole way.

"That was cool," Lou said.

"Yeah," I said, not wanting to let on that the whole thing had freaked me out. "Cool."

"What did he say?"

"Just something about the baby. Never could really get all of it." I lied not to protect her, but to protect me from having to repeat the message.

She lay Nate on the bed and prepared to change and feed him. She periodically interrupted her preparations by mimicking Ajax's message. "Protect baby from take," she signed several times without realizing what she was signing.

"Would you cut that out?" I finally asked.

"Why?" she said just a little annoyed.

"It's getting on my nerves, that's all."

"So don't look at me," she said.

"I thought you were afraid to talk?"

She pursed her lips together and shot me a death glare. She returned her attention to Nate.

We spent the next couple of hours in silence. I looked out the back door occasionally to see if Ajax would re-emerge, but he never did. Around mid afternoon, Wes returned, and he wasn't alone.

"Got something to show ya'," he said.

Lou (with Nate in his sling) and I followed Wes out the front of the store. Tied to a support column to the left were two horses.

"Meet Phil and Ryder," Wes said. They were beautiful, enormous animals, sturdy and tan with blonde manes and tails. The only difference between the two was that Phil had a white diamond patch between his eyes. "They's Belgian's. Good work horses."

Lou walked up and started to stroke Ryder's nose. I was a little more hesitant. "What are they for?" I asked.

"Your trip," Wes said. "Got 'em off Frank Greeley's farm 'bout six miles north of here."

"I can't ride a horse," I said.

"Ain't nothing to it, sides these horses ain't really for ridin'. They's for pulling." He walked over and patted Phil's back. Phil blew air through his nose and mouth and stomped one of his back hooves. "Easy now. Easy now," Wes said.

"Pulling what?"

Wes laughed. "A wagon, what else?"

"A wagon?"

"Greeley had a couple but they're in need of repair something awful. I figure we could high tail it on over to Archie's Seed and Feed tomorrow and see if there's one in better condition."

I maintained my distance from the horses. "I don't know the first thing about driving a wagon."

Wes gave me a curious scowl. "The horses do all the work. You just nudge 'em in the right direction and give 'em a little slap with the reins. Off they go."

I didn't want to come out and say I was afraid, but I think he was beginning to get the idea. Horses, especially these, were big animals that always seemed to me to have minds of their own. I wasn't all together confident that I would have any kind of control of them once I was behind the reins.

"Look," Wes said. "It beats walkin', and it'll give poor ol' Phil and Ryder something to do. They's work horses who are just itchin' to pull a wagon."

I wasn't thrilled with the idea, but I felt if I protested any further, Wes would start to get the idea that I was a sissy. I shrugged my shoulders and tried to look indifferent about his proposal. "Yeah, sure. I'll give it a try." I said it without an ounce of meaning.

"I'm workin' on something else, too," Wes said.

"What?" I asked.

"Can't say just yet. Ain't sure it's going to work. I don't want to get your hopes up." He slapped Phil on the rump and headed for the grocery store. "Whatcha' want for dinner?"

I shrugged my shoulders. "I don't know."

"I'm in the mood for something different," he said as he reached the entrance of the Kroger's. "I'll surprise ya'." With that he disappeared inside.

A few minutes later he emerged with an armload of candy bars. "The candy man has arrived. Hope you like chocolate and caramel 'cause it feels like a Snickers night tonight." He stopped a few feet away from the horses and dropped the entire load of candy on the sidewalk. Dozens of Snickers bars in their brown wrappers decorated the concrete walk. He reached in both pockets and pulled out two red Macintosh apples. "Here." He handed one to me and one to Lou. "Give these to Phil and Ryder. You best make sure they like you 'cause they're going to be your feet for the next 500 miles or so."

Lou and I took the apples from him and proceeded to feed the horses. Lou was more excited by it than I was, but I was surprised how gently Phil took the apple from my hand. I half expected him to gnaw my hand off in his attempt to grab the apple with his enormous teeth, but he very deftly snatched the fruit from my hand and gobbled it down.

Wes sat on the sidewalk and tore open a Snickers bar and started eating it. Lou and I joined him. We ate the chewy chocolate bars and watched the sun dip down behind the horizon.

"If it weren't for that fact the world was going to hell in a hand basket," Wes said. "This would be downright fun. Kind of nice not having to worry about money and such." He looked at us. "I guess you two wouldn't know anything about that. Paying bills is rough. I worked close to 60 hours a week trying to keep up with my mortgage, my credit card bills, my utilities, you name it. I pert near had to work my fingers to the bone tryin' to pay for it." He grabbed another candy bar and opened it.

"Don't you miss your family?" I asked. I was nibbling on my Snickers bar.

"My sister's the only one I had left. Everyone else passed. Louise was a special gal, but I didn't see much of her once she got married and started a family. Her husband didn't care much for me."

Kimball sat beside me and started whining. He was ready for his dinner. I got up and went back in the mattress store where I opened another pouch of dog food and fed him. As I was headed back out to join Wes and Lou, I happened to glance out the back door and saw Ajax sitting along the back of the lot. He was holding his blanket and doll and rocking back and forth. I moved to the back door and crouched down in the doorway.

He looked at me and pointed to himself and then hunched his shoulders with his hands balled in fists as he shook them back and forth. I didn't need the book to interpret what he was saying. "Me cold." I stood and quickly moved to my bed and picked up the book. Back at the door, I looked up the sign for "inside" and invited Ajax into the mattress store.

He grunted and moved his hands in front of himself as if he were protecting himself. According to the book it meant "afraid."

I made the sign for friend again.

He gave me the same grunt, waved his hand in front of his hand, and then motioned both hands down in front of him. "Stranger."

I repeated the friend sign.

He repeated the stranger sign.

I shook my head and pushed my hand out in front of me with my fingers together, "your," and then spread the fingers on my left hand and acted as if I were picking things from my fingers with the index finger and thumb of my right hand, "choice." "Your choice."

He waved his hand at me and turned away. I didn't need the book to tell me that meant leave me alone. I laughed and walked away.

Later as Lou, Wes, Nate, Kimball, and I lay in our respective beds (Lou's still being on the floor behind the adjustable bed), Ajax quietly entered and maneuvered through the maze of mattresses. Kimball was the first to notice him. He sat up and watched the great ape with a keen interest. I smiled as Ajax hopped on a mattress next to mine. He sighed and collapsed with his back to me, still shaking from the cold.

Wes lifted his head up and chuckled. "I'll be damned," he said. "A go-rilla."

With that I could hear Lou start to giggle. I followed, and unless my mind was playing tricks on me, I even saw little Nate smile at the prospect of a 400-pound silverback lying in the bed next to us. Kimball jumped off my mattress and jumped up on Ajax's mattress, and as if the two had been best buddies forever, he lay next to the gorilla to help keep him warm.

***

Lou was the first one awake the next morning. She woke me to let me know she was taking Nate from me to change and feed him. I was happy to let her do it. She was growing really attached to the kid, which worked out great for me. I hadn't changed a diaper since the first day I arrived. I looked over to my left and saw that Ajax and Kimball were still asleep. In fact, Ajax was snoring so loudly I'm surprised I was able to sleep at all.

I stood and stretched. My head ached from the over-consumption of candy bars the night before. It was a tasty indulgence that I deeply regretted at that moment.

I made my way to the bathroom in the back of the store and washed my face in the sink. When I walked back into the showroom, Wes was just waking up. He stretched, groaned, and yawned.

"I swear," he said. "I ain't never slept so good." He sat on the edge of the bed. "We best get movin' on to Archie's and see if we can find a wagon. I think I remember him having an old farmer's wagon." He stood and moved to the bathroom. "Just give me a minute to do my mornin' business." He stepped inside and closed the door.

I walked over to Lou. "I wish he would forget about those horses."

"They're beautiful."

"Yeah, well they're big and smelly, too." I looked out the window at them. "I don't know anything about taking care of a horse."

She smiled. "Sounds like you're afraid of them more than anything else."

"What do you know?" I snapped.

"I know we'll make it to Charleston a lot faster on a wagon pulled by horses than we will on foot." She had Nate cradled in her arm feeding him his formula.

I looked at her. "What do you mean 'we'?"

"We," she said. "Me, you, Nate, Kimball, and I'm guessing Ajax. I don't think Wes will come."

I looked at Kimball and Ajax sound asleep in their bed. "I got enough to do looking after Nate. I don't need you or... that gorilla making it any harder on me."

"I thought you told Ajax you were his friend." She gave me a look of disdain.

"I did, but..."

"But you didn't mean it?"

"No," I said. "I was just trying to get him to come out."

"Why?"

"Because..." I couldn't come up with an answer. "Just because. You're not coming and that's that."

I started to walk away when I heard her say, "Protect baby from take."

I turned to her. "What did you say?"

"Protect baby from take. That's what Ajax said to you yesterday."

Ajax stirred on his bed.

"How do you know that?" I asked.

"I looked it up in the book. I could tell you were lying yesterday, so I wanted to see for myself."

"You should learn to keep out of other people's property."

"That book's not your property," she said. "You took it from Dr. Fine."

"Dr. Fine doesn't exist any more, so I couldn't have taken it from her."

"Whatever," she said. "The point is Ajax knows something. He knows what our purpose is."

"What purpose?"

"The reason they didn't take us. It's Nate."

I looked at the baby in her arms. "Nate?"

"He's special."

"A special pain in the ass, maybe..."

"No, listen, he's our purpose. We have to protect him."

"There you go with that we stuff again..."

We heard the toilet flush and ended our conversation as Wes exited the bathroom. "I wouldn't go in there for a while," he said, smiling from ear to ear.

Ajax sat up and looked at Wes.

"Hello, Mr. Go-rilla," Wes said. "How 'bout we head on down to the Kroger's and get us a bunch of bananas."

Ajax grunted in agreement and climbed off the bed.

"Don't that beat everything," Wes said. "He really does understand what I'm saying." He laughed as he followed the lumbering ape out of the mattress store. Kimball took off after them. Wes turned to Lou and me. "Two weeks ago, I would've thought you were crazy if you told me that I was going to have breakfast with a go-rilla and a dog one day. But I'll be damned if that ain't just what I'm doing."

When he was out of earshot, I turned back to Lou. "You can't come."

"I can and I will," she said. "And Ajax is coming, too."

I sighed. "I don't see why you're so set on it."

She looked at me, tears forming in her eyes. "Because," she said. "It's my mission."

***

What Wes didn't tell me about going to Archie's Seed and Feed is that in order to bring the wagon back with us, we would have to ride the horses, a prospect that did not sit well with me. I argued until I was blue in the face that I could walk the horse, but Wes didn't see how that made sense. He was right. It didn't make sense. It was apparent that my mode of transportation to Charleston was going to be a horse-drawn wagon. I might as well get used to the animals.

After several aborted attempts to mount Ryder, Wes finally was successful at setting me on top of the huge, snorting beast. My legs spread across the animal's back so wide that there were times I felt as if I were being pulled apart. Wes easily mounted Phil and we set out.

After a mile or so, my anxiety started to wane. Ryder was a gentle old horse that moved slowly and smoothly across the paved terrain. There were times I even thought I could detect just a hint of gratitude from the old horse. He seemed to enjoy having me on his back.

As we journeyed on, I couldn't help but look at my surroundings with a measured level of sadness. Manchester was dead. The buildings remained intact and the roads were in good condition, but the heart of the little town had been ripped out. The cool October wind blew through its winding streets and alleys without notice. There was no one there to comment on the cold day or the coming holidays. It was a shell with nothing inside.

When we arrived at Archie's Seed and Feed the first thing I noticed was the odor. There was the sharp pungent smell of rot. The building was surrounded by it. We stepped inside and stood among the rows of sacks full of seed and feed. The smell grew stronger. Wes led me to the counter and stepped behind it. He looked on the floor and recoiled "Stay back," he said, trepidation in his voice. He covered his mouth with his hand and opened a drawer. He frantically rifled through it and pulled out a key. As quick as he could, he stepped from behind the counter and headed for the door.

I couldn't resist. I stepped around the counter and saw what made him draw back, the bloated, decaying body of an old man. The skin was gray turning brown. The eyes were milky and blank, and the belly looked as though it would pop. I fought the urge to retch and ran out of the building.

Once outside I placed my hands on my knees and doubled over. "What was that?" I said, fighting hyperventilation.

"Archie," he answered. He was breathing in deeply trying to flush out the odor of death. "I told you to stay back."

"I thought..." I was struggling to breathe. "They killed him."

"They didn't kill him," he said. "Old man probably dropped dead of a heart attack. They got no use for a dead man."

I stood up straight. We moved to the back of the building. Wes used the key he retrieved from the drawer to open up a large shed near a huge silo. He pulled back the double doors and, just as he had surmised, there was a medium-sized farm wagon. He smiled. "This will do. Old-timers used to use it to haul hay. Let's hook Phil and Ryder to it and get the hell out of here."

"What about..." I looked at the seed and feed store. "Shouldn't we bury him?"

"What the hell for?" Wes snapped.

"It doesn't seem right..."

"You want to go back in there and drag his old rotting body out back and bury him, that's fine by me, but you can count me out." Wes moved past me to fetch Phil and Ryder from the front of the store.

"I thought he was a friend of yours."

"He was a cranky old man that would sooner spit on me than say a kind word to me."

"Yeah, but..."

"But nothing." He disappeared behind the front of the building.

I went into the shed and found a shovel hanging from the wall. As I was exiting the shed, Wes was approaching with the horses. He stopped and looked at me.

"You're going to do it, aren't ya'?"

I didn't say anything. I found a spot of soft dirt next to the silo and started digging. It wasn't long before Wes joined me with another shovel. "You're some kind of stubborn, kid," he said.

I smiled and we dug the hole together.

***

By two o'clock in the afternoon, we were back at the shopping center. Phil and Ryder pulled the wagon like they'd been doing it their whole lives. We pulled up in front of the mattress store like we were cowboys in an old Western movie.

We jumped off the wagon and walked inside the store. Ajax and Kimball were sitting near the front. They were playing tug of war with Ajax's blanket. They had become fast friends.

Lou was sitting in the back with Nate in his sling around her shoulder. Her head was down and I could see that she was reading something. I didn't think much of it.

I had worked up a hunger burying Archie, so I retrieved a package of Oreos from my supply wagon and started chomping on as many as I could fit in my mouth. It took a while to notice that something wasn't quite right. I looked at the garden wagon. Something was out of place. I went through the wagon and gasped when I realized what that something was. Stevie's comic book was missing.

I stood in a panic. "Lou," I shouted. "Give that back!"

She looked up from Stevie's comic book. "They're called the Takers," she said, her eyes red from crying.

"Who's called the Takers?" Wes said entering the store. "And since when can you talk?"

I ran over to Lou and took the comic book from her. "Don't say their name."

"Where did you get that comic book?" she asked.

I ignored her question and ran back to the wagon and grabbed J.J. They were coming.

"What's got you all jumpy?" Wes asked. "And answer my question, little miss, since when can you talk?"

Kimball was the first to sense them. He let go of Ajax's blanket and ran to the front door. The fur on his back stood up straight. Ajax was next. He stood next to Kimball and let out a short series of hoots. With the hair on his shoulders and back puffed out, he looked twice as big.

Wes looked at the pair at the door and then me. "Damn."

He pulled out his hunting knife. "I was beginning to think they was gone." His hand was trembling and sweat began to form on his brow. "Looks like I'm going to have to gut me another one of them suckers." He nervously chuckled.

"We should hide," I said.

Wes looked around the small mattress store. "Our choices are kind of limited here. Our best bet is to move down to the Kroger's."

"Shut up!" Lou whispered frantically. "They can hear us talk."

Wes and I looked at each other. She was right. I motioned for her to join me, and we all slowly made our way to the front door. Ajax and Kimball were firmly ensconced in their positions. It was hard to get their attention. "Kimball, go," I whispered. He darted out the door.

Ajax looked at me with a wide-eyed look. "Protect baby from take," he signed.

"I will," I whispered. I pointed to the Kroger's. "Hide." Still clutching his blanket, he turned back into the mattress store, ran to his bed, grabbed his doll and kissed it. He quickly moved past us and followed Kimball to the Kroger's.

"Don't that beat everything," Wes said.

Lou punched him in the stomach and shushed him.

Wes exited the mattress store first, followed by Lou with Nate in his sling, and then me. We were huddled together. J.J. was at the ready and Wes had a firm grip on his hunting knife. We stepped slowly, expecting the Takers to appear at any moment.

We were almost in a state of disbelief when we made it to the front door of the Kroger's without incident. Inside the grocery store, we scanned the area for out best vantage point.

"Frozen foods," Wes whispered leading the way. I grabbed

Lou's hand. She was shaking. I pulled her along, and we all ducked down behind a row of waist high open-air refrigerator units with hundreds of boxes of spoiled frozen foods stuffed inside them. Kimball paced with his tongue hanging from this mouth, and Ajax sat clinging tightly to his blanket and doll.

Minutes passed and nothing happened. We were almost ready to let ourselves believe we were out of danger when we heard the front door open and slam shut. Before we could tell ourselves it was the wind, we heard a low clicking chatter, like locusts swarming a field.

Kimball immediately crouched down. He crept forward ready to attack. Ajax moved in front of us. His hair was standing on end again. They were two warriors ready for battle.

Lou squeezed my hand so tightly I thought she might break my fingers. She was biting her lip to prevent herself from screaming, and rocking little Nate back and forth trying to keep him calm. I was too scared to breathe.

We followed their motion through the building by the chattering. They moved to the opposite end at first. It was obvious they knew we were in the store. It was just a matter of time before they found us. Slowly they made their way toward us. It was torture listening to them go up and down every aisle as they made their way to the frozen foods section. The chattering grew louder and louder.

Wes couldn't take it anymore. "I can't take that awful noise," he said, his voice low and shaky.

Lou suddenly screamed. They had found us. At the end of the aisle, there stood a Taker or a Greasywhopper, whichever name you prefer. I estimated it to be at least eight feet tall because it was taller than the shelves that housed the food. And just as Wes had said, it was covered in a thick coat of greasy black hair. Its eyes were a blazing red, and it had a short snout with a wide nose and mouth. Its ears were big and pointy and stood on top of its head like a wolf's. The chattering came from it clicking its rows of nail-sized teeth together. It had long fingernails on the ends of its long fingers that dangled from long arms.

Ajax beat his chest and bluff charged the monster. It retreated a step or two. Kimball joined Ajax and began to bark. The Taker backed away even more. They advanced some more on the creature and it gave a little more ground each time. As I was about to let out a sigh of relief, I turned to my left and saw another Taker standing just six feet away from us. I stood with both hands holding on tight to J.J. Wes followed my lead. The Taker spread his arms out and let out a screeching roar. Lou was paralyzed. I tapped her with my foot, "Stand up."

She didn't move.

"Lou," I said. "Stand up."

She looked at me, her mouth agape, tears freely falling down her cheek.

"We have a mission, remember," I said.

With that she attempted a smile and slowly stood up.

I looked at the other end of the aisle. Ajax and Kimball had the other Taker surrounded. The creature was more than double their combined sizes, but it retreated like it was under attack by a huge advancing army.

The Taker that stood just feet from us was another story. It crept toward us, opening and closing its mouth, gnashing its teeth. It was almost as if it were playing with us. Huddled together, we backed away. It skulked after us. Wes lunged forward with his knife, hitting nothing but air, and retreated.

"Get away from us, you Greasywhopper sucker!"

The Taker flailed its arms and chattered madly.

Behind us I heard the other Taker scream in horror. I turned to see Kimball tearing a chunk of flesh from the monster's thigh. Ajax pounded the beast's back with his powerful fists. The Taker swung its arms wildly, but never laid a hand on either Ajax or Kimball. It was then that I realized the Taker couldn't see them.

Ajax grabbed the Taker's right leg and yanked it out from under him. The creature crashed to the ground, screaming for its life. Kimball dashed in and out on the fallen monster extracting a piece of flesh each time. It was as if Ajax and Kimball understood the Taker could not see them. They began to tear into it with reckless abandon.

Our Taker had no problem seeing us. It snapped its powerful jaws at Wes and managed to catch his shirt in its mouth. Wes thrust his knife forward and stuck the beast in the shoulder. It did not flinch. I swung J.J. and caught the Taker on the hip, leaving a gaping wound. Still the creature advanced on us.

Nate let out a gurgled cry. The Taker was momentarily distracted. It sniffed the air. Nate cried again. The creature leapt forward with a fury, tossing Wes aside and pushing me into the open-air freezer. Grease dripped from its protruding jowls as it bent down and sniffed Lou. It was looking for the baby. Its large hand ripped Lou up by her neck and held her out in front of it. It examined her with its red eyes.

A roar echoed throughout the store. Ajax and Kimball, having disposed of the other monster, were now focusing their attention on our Taker. The creature retreated. It was struck with a sudden rush of fear. Holding tightly to Lou, it backed away. Ajax stood and pounded his chest, pock-pock-pock. He was claiming his territory. The beast tried to run with Lou in tow, but it was tackled by Ajax. The Taker released Lou to fight off its attacker. Lou scrambled away. Within seconds

Kimball had joined Ajax in the assault. A cacophony of growls, screams, and hoots filled the air.

I crawled out of the freezer and helped Lou to her feet. Wes lay dazed under a pile of 2 liter plastic bottles of soda that had collapsed on him when the Taker tossed him into the shelf. It wasn't long until Ajax and Kimball ceased their bloody assault on the creature. They stepped away as it lay there motionless, obviously dead.

I looked Lou and Nate over. Lou was a little shaken, but she would survive. Nate was howling away, but that was normal for him. I turned my attention to Wes. He was regaining his senses and trying to sit up. I helped him to his knees.

"Goodness knows," he said. "That was ugly."

"Are you alright?" I asked.

"Not hardly, but I reckon I'll live." He breathed in deeply through his nose and blew air out through his mouth. "Whoa, sure don't want to do that again."

I looked at our troops. Ajax was pacing and breathing heavily. Kimball was sitting calmly, licking his paws. Lou had a pained look on her face. We were all battle-fatigued, but we were not beaten. I gathered up the others, and we headed out of the Kroger's.

Once we were back in the mattress store, I found Stevie's comic book, rolled it up, and stuffed it back in my supply wagon. "You shouldn't have gone through my stuff," I said to Lou.

"That book's about us," she said. She had Nate out of the sling and was cradling him in her arms. He was fussy and on the verge of having an all out crying session.

"What are you talking about?" I said.

"It's about us," she insisted. "I saw my name. I saw Ajax. I saw the..."

"Don't say their name," I said.

"Just what in the hell is going on here?" Wes asked, irritated.

"Nothing. Lou just shouldn't have gone through my things."

"Make him show you the book," Lou said.

"No," I said emphatically.

"Let me see it," Wes insisted.

"I can't," I answered.

"C'mon, boy."

"No," I shouted. "Don't you see? They're invisible until you see them."

"That's just plain crazy talk," Wes said. He walked over to my supply wagon and started looking through it.

"No!" I grabbed his arm.

"Boy, you better let go of my arm."

Kimball came to my defense. He didn't growl at Wes, but he let him know with a look that he didn't like Wes's tone. Wes heeded the warning.

"Listen, we can't look at the book. It brings them out. I wasn't sure of that until just now, but if we read that book, they'll come back, and my guess is they'll be more of them this time."

Wes sat down on a nearby mattress. "Let's burn it then."

"We can't," Lou said. "It's about us. It might show us how to beat these things and bring back..." She stopped herself. She didn't dare say it out loud.

"Bring back, what?" I asked.

"Our parents," she said. "Maybe there's a way."

"You're dreaming," Wes said. "I say we burn it." He reached for the wagon, but before he could lay a hand on it, Ajax pulled it away and grunted. "What the..." Wes leaned over farther, and Ajax pulled the wagon farther away. Wes leaned over even farther, but this time Ajax slapped his hand hard. Wes pulled back. "Ow!"

"Doesn't look like Ajax thinks we should burn it," I said.

Ajax snapped his forefinger and middle finger on his thumb. I scrambled to find his book. It lay underneath the bed. I hurriedly opened to the chapter on American Sign Language and found the sign, "No." He then held his palms up and wiggled his fingers. "No burn." He laid his hands out and mimicked the opening of a book. "No burn book." He made a V shape with his forefinger and middle finger and waved them over the palm of his other hand. I flipped through the pages, and could not believe my eyes when I found it.

"What'd he say?" Wes asked.

I hesitated. "He wants us to read the book."

FOUR

L ookie, here," Wes said. "You do what you want, but I wouldn't listen to no go-rilla if I was you." He hoisted a case of beans up on the wagon. "You best burn that comic book."

With great difficulty, I lifted a box filled with trail mix bags onto the back of the farm wagon. "I don't know, something tells me I better listen to Ajax for now."

He turned and looked at Lou sitting inside the mattress store. She was making sure Nate was fed and changed before we took off for the interstate. The run-in with the Greasywhoppers the day before had convinced me I didn't want to make the trip by myself. "She say anything else about what she saw in that book?"

I shook my head. "She hasn't said much of anything since... You know."

"Yeah," he said. "I know." He looked over the well-stocked wagon. "Okay, you got food, first aid kits, blankets, sleeping bags, warm clothes, water. They'll be plenty of places to re-supply along the way."

"You think we'll run into anyone else out there?"

"Bound to," he said. "They're not all going to be friendly either, so take extra care."

"Sure you won't come with us?"

He rubbed his grizzled chin. "Working on something."

"You said that before," I said.

"Still working on it. I may be able to catch up with you." He patted Ryder. "Don't push the horses too hard. They'll let you know when they're ready to stop. Stick to the interstates, 24 to Chattanooga, 75 to Atlanta, 20 to Columbia, 26 to Charleston. It's the long way, but it's the safest route."

"I know," I said. "You've only told me about a hundred times."

"It's important." Kimball chased Ajax down the sidewalk. They were playing like they didn't have a care in the world. "You're going to have a go-rilla, a dog, a baby, Lou, and two horses on this trip. Might as well call you Noah."

"I guess we better get going." I stepped toward the store. "Saddle up, Lou. We're going to hit it."

Lou picked up Nate and put him in his sling. She gathered up as many baby supplies as she could carry (even though we had plenty on the wagon) and exited the store. Kimball leapt onto the wagon with no problem. Ajax hesitated and then pulled his huge frame onto the back of the wagon.

I shook Wes's hand. "Wish you were coming."

"We'll see each other again," he said. "You can count on that."

I wanted to cry, but I didn't feel like it was the manly thing to do, so I didn't.

Wes bent down on one knee in front of Lou. "Thanks for..." He started to cry. I guess he thought it was the manly thing to do. "For letting me call you Lou. It sure was nice to have my little sister around again." He hugged her, careful not to smother Nate.

Lou began to bawl. All she could manage to say was, "I'm going to miss you."

Wes picked her up and lifted her onto the wagon seat. I gave the supplies one last look and then walked around the wagon and climbed up on the other side of the seat. We both gave Wes one last goodbye, and then, with a flick of the reins, we were off on our journey.

***

Lou and I didn't speak much that first day. We were scared to. Not because we were afraid the Greasywhoppers would hear us, but because we were afraid we would talk each other into turning back and staying with Wes for the rest of our lives. It's funny, if everything was normal, if my parents were still alive, and all I had to worry about was school and the Titans next game and anything else a thirteen-year-old boy spends his days thinking about, I would have never given Wes another thought. He would have been just some hick mechanic who needed a bath. I would never have taken the time to get to know him. I guess normal times aren't all they're cracked up to be.

We stopped at the Days Inn on top of Monteagle. The horses had pulled us up a long and winding mountain road, and they were badly in need of a rest. Luckily the motel still used real keys, not key cards. We located two keys to adjoining rooms on the first floor and set up camp for the night.

I unhitched Phil and Ryder and wiped them down with some towels from the motel. They were soaked in sweat. The temperature was somewhere in the 40s on top of the mountain. I was sure they were going to catch colds and die. Lou and I both had two double beds, so I ripped the covers from each of the extra beds and placed them over the horses. It wasn't much, but I hoped it would do.

Lou prepared a meal for everybody, formula for Nate, fruit cocktail for Ajax, Alpo's finest for Kimball, and water and canned beans for her and me. We had a small propane camping grill, but we decided we would use it sparingly, so we ate the beans cold.

After dinner I got up and walked around the motel a few times. My butt was killing me from sitting on the badly cushioned wagon bench all day. I was hoping I would be able to walk out the kinks.

As I walked around the complex, I recalled my family's last vacation. Pop took us to Charlotte so we could watch the Titans play the Carolina Panthers. We stayed in a motel a lot like the Days Inn. It may have even been a Days Inn. I can't remember. What I do remember was having the time of my life. The Titans won in overtime, so that made it even better, but the funnest part was being with my Mom and Pop, watching a football game, eating hotdogs and popcorn. It wasn't much and it only lasted three days, but it was the best time I think I ever had in my life.

Back at the rooms, I checked in on Nate and Lou. They were fast asleep, as were Ajax and Kimball. I lay down on my bed, closed my eyes, and tried to will myself to dream about the Titans' overtime victory and the best vacation I ever had.

The next day Lou and I had some trail mix and cokes. The caffeine, sugar, and protein woke us up. Nate was his usual cranky self. Ajax and Kimball had awakened earlier and were outside exploring the grounds of the empty motel. Lou and I sat on her bed dreading the day of travel ahead of us.

"My butt's killing me," I said.

"Mine, too," Lou said, fighting with Nate to get him to take his bottle. "How much farther?"

"About 450 miles."

She rolled her eyes. "Don't suppose you got an uncle in Chattanooga." She chuckled.

"Hey, you wanted to come," I said.

"I had to." She made a point not to look at me.

"Okay," I said. "Let's hear it. You've been looking at me like I've got a third eyeball and some horns ever since you looked through that comic book. What gives?"

She hesitated. "You were mean to him?"

"Who?" I asked even though I knew the answer.

"Stevie Dayton. The boy who wrote the comic book."

I cleared my throat and shook my head. "He put that in there?"

"He called you Ozzie the Titan." She pointed to the Titans sweatshirt I was wearing. "You made him do things."

"I wasn't the only one."

"Yeah, but you were the only one that he cared about."

I looked at her like she had just shot an arrow through my heart. "What's that supposed to mean?"

"He liked you. He looked up to you."

"What makes you so sure?"

"Because," she said, "he made you the hero of his comic book."

"Yeah, right," I said, feeling more and more ashamed the more she told me.

"It's true. You're this mean boy most of the time, but when there's an emergency you always save the day."

It was all a little overwhelming. I never felt more like a rat than I did sitting there listening to her tell me what Stevie Dayton had written about me. "You get any ideas how to beat these Greasywhoppers in that book?"

"I only got through the first couple of pages, but I got a pretty good idea what they want," she said.

I gave her a befuddled look. "What's that?"

She looked down at the wriggling baby in her arms. "Nate."

I furrowed my brow and almost laughed. "What in the name of Vince Lombardi would they want with that little crap factory?"

"Vince who?" she asked.

"It's something my Pop used to say. He's an old-timey football coach for the Green Bay Packers."

"The Green Bay what?"

"Never mind," I said. "Why do you think they want Nate?"

"I don't know why," she said. "But I do know when that Take..." "She stopped herself from saying Taker. "When that Greasywhopper in Kroger's yesterday saw Nate, he didn't waste his time with you and Wes anymore. He went right for the baby."

"That doesn't mean anything," I said. "Maybe..." I regretted starting the sentence.

"Maybe, what?" She asked, insistently.

"Nothing," I said.

"Finish what you were going to say," she said.

"Maybe they like the taste of babies better." As soon as it came out of my mouth I regretted it. It was hateful and insensitive, but I feared it was as close to being the truth as anything else. Her jaw dropped and she looked at me with utter disdain.

"You think they eat people?"

I couldn't believe that thought had never crossed her mind. "What do you think they did with everybody?"

She struggled to come up with an answer that was as plausible as mine. We both saw the hunger and hate in the creature's eyes when it tried to get us in the grocery store. Its gnashing teeth, its vicious attack, how could anyone not think it wanted to eat us?

"I don't know," she finally said. "But I do know where we can find out." She looked at me waiting for my protest.

"The comic book?" I stood up. "Not going to happen." I gathered up my empty Coke can and empty bag of trail mix.

"We have to read it," she said.

"As soon as we look at that book those things will be on top of us."

Carrying Nate, she followed me to the trashcan at the front of the room. "I got through four pages before they showed up yesterday. I could have read more if you hadn't interrupted me. It takes them a while to find us."

"So," I said.

"So, we read three or four pages at a time."

I walked into my room with her on my heels. "That's crazy. They'll find us."

"We can be ready for them," she said. "Ajax and Kimball will be there. You saw what they did to those things."

"We can't count on that happening again."

"They can't see animals. You saw how they were scared to death of Ajax and Kimball."

I turned to her. "It's too risky."

"But..."

"No. Now, if you bring it up again, I'm burning the comic book."

She huffed in anger. "Fine, but let me ask you something. Why did you bring that comic book with you?"

I couldn't answer the question. The truth is I didn't know why I'd brought the comic book. Something drew me to Stevie's house. Something told me I needed that comic book, but if I told her that, she would take that as a sign we should read it. And she may have been right, but I was not ready to deal with the consequences. "Get your stuff together," I said. "I'll hitch up the horses."

***

Coming down Monteagle was just as hard on Phil and Ryder as going up. At the bottom of the mountain, we stopped and let them rest. I jumped off the wagon and stretched my legs. I noticed Ajax signing something. He had his hands in fists together in front of him and then he burst them apart. I retrieved his book from the back of the wagon and searched for the sign.

"Explode?" I said.

He repeated the sign over and over again.

I signed, "What explode?"

He pointed to a billboard down the interstate. It was for a Crazy Jay's Fireworks in South Pittsburg, Tennessee. It depicted several fireworks exploding in midair. "Explode," he signed again.

I looked up the word fireworks; both index fingers shooting off like sparks. "Fireworks," I said as I signed it. I heard myself say the word and it suddenly occurred to me that he was right. Fireworks explode.

"Fireworks," I said absentmindedly.

"What?" Lou asked.

"Ajax just gave me an idea," I said. I signed, "Smart gorilla," to Ajax. He grinned and pounded his chest.

I got back on the wagon, and we headed for Crazy Jay's.

***

South Pittsburg, Tennessee, was nestled next to the interstate with Crazy Jay's less than a mile off the exit. It was an enormous metal fabricated warehouse full of every kind of firework you can imagine. It all looked spectacular, and in theory a well-placed firecracker could provide us with some line of defense against the Greasywhoppers, but the question was, did they work? After all, Wes had said that they did something to the guns so they wouldn't fire. Had they done the same thing to the fireworks? There was only one way to find out. I found a box labeled "Warning: Explosives," full of fat M-98 firecrackers. I retrieved a lighter from behind the checkout counter and stepped outside. With Lou, Ajax, and Kimball looking on, I lit the firecracker and tossed it toward the road. Within seconds it let out an explosion that sent Ajax and Kimball into a state of panic, but it was just the result I wanted.

"Yes!" I screamed.

"What's the big deal?" Lou asked.

"Don't you see? We have a way to fight back."

She thought about it. Slowly a smile began to form on her face.

We spent the next hour carefully repacking the wagon and loading as many fireworks as we could. We stuck with mostly firecrackers like Hydro Crackers, Black Cats, 16,000 count Wolf Pack strips, Thunder Bombs, Silver Crackling Crackers, and virtually anything else we could light and throw. When we finished packing and discovered we had room for more, we went back for the bottle rockets. If it said "The Loudest Available by Law" on the package, we loaded it on the wagon.

Had it been different times, I would have allowed myself to enjoy the little shopping spree. My Pop and I used to have a blast shooting off fireworks on the 4th of July and New Year's. But these fireworks weren't for fun. They were going to be used to inflict harm.

As I lifted the last box of fireworks into the wagon, I saw

some movement under the highway overpass to our right. I quickly grabbed the horses' reins and hid the wagon on the other side of Crazy Jay's metal building. I instructed Lou to stay near the wagon and keep Ajax and Kimball occupied while I checked it out.

I hid myself from view behind signs and deserted parked cars as I moved in closer to the overpass. At about thirty feet, I could make out a half dozen people on bikes, four boys and two girls. I estimated the youngest to be a boy about eight or so and the oldest a girl that was 17 or 18. They were all smoking, even the youngest one. I could see by their ragged appearance they had traveled long and hard. Remembering Wes saying that I should take extra care when it came to dealing with strangers, I stealthily made my way back to Lou and the others without being spotted by the bicycle gang. They may have been perfectly fine, but I wasn't in the mood to find out. Instead, we waited until they got on their bikes and rode away. Unfortunately, they were headed in the same direction we were. We decided that we would spend the night in South Pittsburg and let them have a day's ride on us.

There were motels up and down the street, but we elected to spend the night at Crazy Jay's for no other reason than we were already there. Our two days of travel had really taken their toll on us. We wanted nothing more than to just stop, sit, and not move for the next several hours, and that's exactly what we did. We sat in the middle of Crazy Jay's and didn't make a sound. Exhaustion had set in on all of us. Ajax was the first to conk out. He curled up in a ball and started snoozing away. Kimball lay down next to him, let out a worn-out grunt, and fell fast asleep.

I was so tired I don't remember falling asleep, but I do remember waking up to the sounds of Phil and Ryder whinnying, snorting, and throwing a general fit. We all rose up. Our minds immediately kicked into defense mode, I grabbed J.J. and slowly moved toward the front door, Ajax and Kimball flanking me on the left and right. The horses whinnied some more, and I could hear voices. Lou picked up Nate and headed for the back of the warehouse.

Looking out the glass door, I could see what had the horses so upset. The bicycle gang was back, and they were trying to steal the horses and wagon. Relieved they weren't Greasywhoppers, I breathed easier. It did not occur to me that I still had a crisis on my hands. It only occurred to me that I would not have to face another one of those slobbering ghouls for the time being.

I looked at Ajax and then Kimball. "We can handle this," I said. With that I opened the door and stepped outside. Ajax and Kimball remained hidden behind me. "Can I help you?" I asked the thieves.

The older girl turned to me first. She was tall, skinny, and covered in road dirt. "That's all right," she said with a thick country accent. "We're just going to help ourselves."

A boy, about 15 and shorter than the girl, positioned himself in front of her. He was wearing a Hixon High School hat and a heavy flannel jacket. He held a thick, four-foot length of chain and twirled it around at his side. "You don't have a problem with that, do you?" he asked.

Another boy, maybe 13 years old, stood beside him. He was a chubby kid with a broken pair of glasses and a pair of Converse high tops that had seen their share of mud puddles. He laughed. "Nah, he ain't got no problem with that."

The youngest boy, a small kid wearing only a t-shirt and a baggy pair of blue jeans had hold of Phil and Ryder's reins. He looked petrified. A girl about his age stood next to him.

She wore a tattered dress that was at least two sizes too big for her. She held a handful of sugar cubes in her hand trying to get the horses to calm down. At the end of the parking lot near the bicycles, another boy stood in the darkness guarding their belongings.

"As a matter of fact, I do have a problem with that," I said. I stepped out into the open. I motioned for Ajax and Kimball to stay put behind me.

The fifteen-year-old stepped forward. "We got us a hero, Reya."

The older girl answered. "Show him what we do to heroes, Miles."

The fifteen-year-old howled and stepped forward. He raised his hand high above his head and started swinging the chain. "Whatcha' gonna do, boy?" he shouted with a look of unbridled insanity.

"Me?" I said calmly. "Nothing."

The chubby thirteen-year-old chimed in. "Then how you going to stop us?"

I smiled. "I'm not."

Reya snorted. "That's what I thought." Phil snorted and whinnied. "Tyrone, I told you to get them horses calmed down," she said.

"I'm trying," the small kid said.

"Let go of those horses, Tyrone," I said. "They're more likely to give you a swift kick on the noggin than calm down. They're tired and fussy."

"Shut up," Miles said.

"Devlin, go help Valerie and Tyrone keep them horses under control," Reya told the chubby kid.

"What about him?" Devlin asked, gesturing to me.

"He ain't going to do nothing," Miles said.

"It's not me you have to worry about," I said.

"Oh yeah," Reya said. "Then who do we have to worry about?"

I stepped back and motioned for Kimball and Ajax to come outside. They burst out the door and stood in front of me, Kimball with his teeth bared and tail bent down and Ajax beating his chest.

Valerie screamed and the horse reared up. Tyrone went tumbling to the ground. I ran over quickly and pulled him to safety. Reya stood like a statue while Miles and Devlin were already half way to the bikes.

I heard Devlin yell out, "Monster," as his fat legs carried him to the end of the parking lot.

"Still want to help yourself to our horses?" I asked Reya.

She turned to me, the color drained from her face. "We didn't mean nothing by it. We was just tired of riding our bikes."

"Well," I said, "I hope you're not too tired to ride on out of here."

She started to back away. "Valerie, Tyrone, come on, let's get."

Tyrone looked up at me. "I didn't want to do it," he said. "They made me."

"I just wanted to give the horses some sugar," Valerie said.

I looked at them and felt guilty that I had scared them half to death. "That's alright."

They followed Reya. She shifted her gaze back and forth from me to Ajax and Kimball. She was angry because she had been beaten.

The bicycle gang mounted their bikes and disappeared

into the night. I turned to Ajax and Kimball and smiled. "Man, did I pick the right friends," I said.

* * *

Needless to say, I didn't get much sleep that night. Kimball and I took up residence in the wagon, while Ajax watched over Lou and Nate in Crazy Jay's all night. Besides being cold, I drove myself crazy by reacting to every little noise that I heard in the darkness. I was convinced Reya and her mob were going to return and finish what they had started.

But by daybreak, they had not reappeared. I wasted no time getting the horses hitched up and coaxing Lou, with Nate, and Ajax on the wagon. I wanted to hit the road and get as far way from South Pittsburg as I could.

I didn't see any signs of the bicycle gang until we crossed Nickajack Lake. Just over the bridge, I spotted Devlin trying to hide his pudgy frame behind a car parked at a truck stop just off the interstate. The others were nowhere in sight. I didn't like seeing him. It meant one of two things. We were either headed in the same direction by chance, or they were deliberately following us. Either way it increased our odds of having another run-in. I turned and looked at Ajax. As long as I had him with me, I felt relatively safe from Reya and her group. I wouldn't worry about them for now. I gave Phil and Ryder a tap with the reins, and they went from a walking pace to a slow trot.

"What's the hurry?" Lou asked.

"No hurry," I said. "Just seeing how fast this thing will go." I smiled.

She smiled back and opened the sling on her lap. Nate's red face peered out. He was in an unusually good mood. Lou goo-gooed and gaw-gawed him. She gently tapped his nose with the end of her finger. "I sure hope we're doing everything right," she said.

"What do you mean?" I asked.

"With Nate. I was around when my baby brother was born. I kind of watched my mom, but that was three years ago. I don't know if I'm doing everything right."

"You're doing great," I said.

She shrugged her shoulders and continued to play with Nate. "You ever notice Nate's ears?" she asked.

"His what?"

"His ears. They look kind of funny."

I leaned over and looked at the little guy. "They look okay," I said. "They're kind of small and funny shaped, but he's a baby. He'll grow out of it."

"They just look weird," she said.

"Yeah, well we've all got our burdens to bear."

"What?"

I looked at her and laughed. "It's something my Mom used to say when I complained about something. 'Yeah, well we've all got our burdens to bear, Osmond. Get over it,' she used to say."

"Osmond?" She laughed.

"Family name. Now you know the burden I have to bear."

"It's not so bad," she said still laughing.

"Yeah, right," I said. "How 'bout you? Any words of wisdom from your parents you want to share?"

"Words of wisdom?"

"I figure we might as well teach each other as much as we know. Doesn't look like anyone else is going to."

She furrowed her brow and tried to think of something she could pass along from her parents. "My parents were always too busy fighting to really teach us anything."

"They didn't get along?"

"They hated each other. That's pretty much why they got divorced. Although my Mom meeting my Stepdad didn't really help things much."

"How long ago?"

She thought about it. "About four years ago, I guess."

"Tough?"

"Scary," she said. "My parents fought a lot, but they were always around. It was weird not having my Dad around any more."

"I guess that was your burden to bear," I said.

She thought about it. "Until now."

"Yeah, until now."

Her eyes suddenly brightened. "My grandmother Kate used to tell us something that might count as words of wisdom. She was kind of a loon, but she usually meant well."

"What was it?" I asked.

"She used to say that God put us on this planet to see the magic in everybody."

I looked at her. "I like that."

She smiled. "Me, too."

Gray clouds started to form above us. A crack of thunder echoed in the distance. "Looks like a storm is headed our way," I said. I saw a sign for a rest area ahead. "We should probably wait it out." I looked behind us and saw no signs of the bicycle gang. Relieved I tapped Phil and Ryder again with the reins, and shouted, "Get up, boys." They responded and barreled toward the rest stop.

***

The rain came in torrents for hours. We (Lou, Nate, Kimball, Ajax and I) took shelter under one metal-canopied picnic area, while Phil, Ryder and the wagon rested under another. We ate lunch and relaxed as best we could. The sound of the heavy raindrops pounding the metal cover was deafening at times, but the noise somehow soothed little Nate into a peaceful slumber. Lou tucked him away in his sling and approached me.

"We should do it now," she said.

"Do what?" I asked.

"Read the book?"

"What?"

"We've got the fireworks. We're out in the open. We can see them coming from every direction."

"No," I said, my tone sharp and serious.

"Why not?" Her tone was just as resolute.

"Because we don't know how many will come this time. I'm not saying you're right, but let's say they are after Nate, they're liable to send a whole army to get him. We can't do much against an army even if we do have Ajax and Kimball."

"They won't send an army," she said.

"How do you know?"

She couldn't answer.

Ajax heard our conversation. He knuckle walked through the rain to the other picnic area and climbed on the wagon. He rifled through some stuff until he found what he was looking for. He returned with the book written by Dr. Fine.

"What?" I signed.

He handed me the now wet and muddy book.

"You want to talk?"

He nodded. He formed his arms in a cradle and rocked back and forth.

"Baby," I said.

He put his fingers together, thumbs up, palms in, and then pulled his hands into his body.

It meant, "Have."

He then held his hands like he was a soldier marching and carrying a rifle across his body. "Army."

"Baby have army," I said out loud. "I don't understand."

"Baby have army," he signed again.

I looked around the picnic area. "Us? We're not an army."

Ajax shook his head furiously. "Baby have take Army," he signed.

I looked at Lou and told her what he said. "That just doesn't make any sense."

She thought about it. "Ask him how he knows," she said.

I asked him and he replied, "Gorilla always know."

"How?"

He pulled down from his chin like he was pulling on a long beard and then he made his hand into the shape of the American Sign Language letter 'F' and moved it in steps ahead of his body. "Old future." He repeated the signs for "Gorilla always know."

I turned to Lou. "He's not making any sense."

"Maybe we're the ones not making any sense," she said. "I think he's telling us it's safe to read the comic book."

Ajax grinned and nodded. He signed, "No take army."

"I'm supposed to take an ape's word for it?" I said, frustrated. "Old future? Gorilla always know? I think you're nuts, Ajax."

He grinned wildly and shook his hands above his head as if to show me what crazy really was. When he calmed down, he signed, "Baby sentence tell."

"Well, now he's just lost it," I said. "'Baby sentence tell' doesn't make any sense at all."

"What do we have here?" a voice said. "Horse-boy is talkin' to the monkey." Reya and her gang had snuck up on us while we were talking. They lined up outside the picnic area. Devlin, Miles, and the kid who stood in the dark the night before held fast to the leashes of four pit bulls. The dogs had not barked but there was a raw bloodlust in their eyes that let everyone know they were killers.

Tyrone and Valerie stood back. They were soaked to the bone and shivering. It was obvious they did not want to be there.

Miles stepped forward with his pit bull. The chain link he had brandished as a weapon at Crazy Jay's was wrapped around his left hand and arm. "We got us some killer pits to take care of your stinkin' ape," he said proudly.

"Yeah," Devlin shouted. His pit bull pulled on its leash and nearly knocked him to the ground.

The other kid held on calmly to his two pit bulls. "These are fightin' dogs," he said. "They'll tear your gorilla and German shepherd apart." I could tell from his tone he was older, and he looked a lot like Reya. My guess was they were twins.

I looked at the four dogs. They were stout fierce animals, and they probably could kill Kimball with no problem. But I had my doubts they could put much more than a scratch on Ajax.

"All we want is the horses," Reya said.

"Get your own," I said.

"I'm going to snap your neck, horse-boy," Miles said.

"Seriously," I said, "there are probably hundreds of horses around here. Their owners certainly don't have any use for them anymore."

I could see Devlin scratch his head. "He's right. Why don't we just get our own?"

"Shut up," Reya screamed. "We're bandits. We take what we want. And we want your horses... and the gorilla, too."

Ajax stood on the table. He roared and pounded his chest.

"What are we going to do with a gorilla?" Devlin asked.

"Yeah, I don't know about that," Miles said.

"Shut up!" Reya was so mad she could hardly see straight.

"Tell you what," I said. "You figure out what it is you want and come back when you get it all straightened out."

Lou giggled, and Nate gurgled from his sling.

Reya stepped forward. "You got a baby in there?"

"What if we do?" I said.

She smiled. "We'll be takin' that, too."

Now they were starting to piss me off. I signed to Ajax, "Protect baby." He leapt forward with his fangs displayed. Kimball followed his friend into battle.

Devlin released his dog, which promptly ran as far away as it could. The other pit bulls cowered as the great ape approached on two legs, pounding his chest. They were fighting dogs, but they were also smart enough to know when they were outmatched. The remaining three dogs ripped free of their leashes and sprinted out of the area.

Reya and her gang stood dumbfounded. The rain drenched them as they struggled to come up with a dignified exit strategy. Ajax and Kimball stopped advancing, but they remained poised and ready to attack at a moment's notice.

"You're not very good bandits, are you?" I said.

"Call off your monkey," Miles said, arms raised, afraid to move.

"He's not a monkey. He's an ape same as you and me." I was starting to enjoy myself.

"Whatever," Devlin said on the verge of tears. "Just don't let him hurt us."

I thought about his request. "You've tried to steal my stuff twice now. Seems to me that it might make my life a whole lot easier to let him just rip you bandits to shreds. It would keep me from having to look over my shoulder all the time."

"Mister," Tyrone said. "Please don't let him rip us to shreds. Me and Valerie didn't want to come..."

Reya turned to him and screamed, "Shut up, you traitor!"

I stood and walked to the edge of the canopied picnic area. "Tell you what, I'll let you go on your merry way on one condition."

The kid whose name I didn't know cleared his throat. "What's that?"

"Tyrone and Valerie come with us." I looked at the two little kids. "You wouldn't mind that, would you?" They looked at each other and then me. They shook their heads.

Reya snarled. "No way. They're part of our gang."

"Ajax," I said. "When I count to three you start ripping these bandits apart." He looked at me and it was clear he had no idea what I was talking about, but Reya and her gang didn't know that. "One."

"C'mon," Miles said, pleading now.

"Two."

"Let him have the kids," the older boy said to Reya.

Reya hesitated and then relented. "Okay, okay, you can have them." She motioned to them to join us under the canopy.

I called Ajax and Kimball off and they quickly joined us under the shelter.

The remaining bandits turned to mount their bicycles when Reya stopped. She looked at me with pure hatred and said, "We'll be back." With that the four bicycle bandits got on their bikes and disappeared in the rain.

"You hungry?" I asked Tyrone and Valerie. They nodded enthusiastically. I ran to the wagon and got them some food, which they gobbled up like they hadn't eaten in days.

"What do you reckon on doing with us?" Valerie asked.

I shrugged my shoulders. "I don't know."

"You ain't going to feed us to your gorilla, are ya'?" Tyrone asked.

"He's not my gorilla," I said. "He eats what he wants."

Lou shook her head. "Gorillas don't eat people."

Valerie and Tyrone sighed in a moment of unified relief. Their faces were dirty, and their clothes were drenched. They looked like refugees. Kimball sat next to them and started licking the mud from their faces.

"Your dog's crazy, mister," Tyrone said between giggles.

"Don't call me mister," I said. "I'm only 13." I squatted down at the edge of the canopied picnic area and watched the rain pound the rest area grounds. "How'd you two end up with Reya and the others?"

"They found us in the hospital," Valerie said.

"Hospital?"

"In Chattanooga," Valerie said. "I had my tonsils out. See." She opened her mouth wide to show me her tonsil-less throat. "Anyway, that's where they found us."

"What were you doing there, Tyrone?" I asked.

"Visiting my granddad. He had a brain tutor."

"You mean 'tumor'?" I said.

"I guess," he said.

I stood and thought about my next question very carefully. I didn't want to traumatize the little kids by making them relive what they may have seen the Takers do, but in the end my need to know trumped my concerns for their mental well being. "Do you know what happened to everybody else at the hospital?"

They thought about it. The pained expressions on their faces verified they were drudging up some unwanted memories.

"The monsters got 'em," Tyrone said.

"Swallowed 'em up," Valerie said.

"How did you two get away?" Lou asked.

Valerie hesitated. She seemed to be studying Lou's question carefully, as if she was afraid that her answer might sound crazy. "An angel helped us."

Tyrone rolled his eyes, "He weren't no angel. He was the janitor."

"He was too an angel. I seen him fly." Valerie seemed hurt by Tyrone's protest.

Tyrone huffed. "How many angels you know named Stevie?"

The name struck me like a fist to the gut. "What did you say his name was?"

"Stevie," he said.

I avoided looking at Lou, but I could feel her looking at me. I knew what she was thinking. But she was wrong. She had to be. Stevie was a fairly common name. Just because this janitor was named Stevie doesn't mean he was Stevie Dayton. Besides it was impossible. Stevie Dayton was dead. I thought about that word "impossible" and how little meaning it had any more.

***

The rain continued into the evening. By the time it stopped it was too late to carry on with our travels, so we settled into the rest area for the night. The plan was that Lou would stand watch the first half of the night and I would take over the latter half. Although I could have volunteered to stand watch the whole night because there was very little chance I was going to get any sleep. And I wish it were because I was concerned about the bicycle bandits returning.

The truth of the matter is that as soon as the sun fell, I could feel the presence of the Takers slithering in the darkness. They were in the picnic area. They were in the restrooms. They were on the highway. They were everywhere, waiting to be noticed, to hear their name. I could feel their desperation. The wind carried the chattering of their teeth. Looking back over my life, I know now they had always been there. They were that unexplained noise whenever I was left home alone, that misplaced shadow on the wall of my bedroom that I would notice just as I was about to drift asleep. They were the disembodied cool breeze that caused the hair on the back of my neck to stand up straight. They had always been around, and they were harmless until somebody said their name, or until you read Stevie's comic book.

We heard the bathroom doors slam around midnight. The Takers' desperation had turned into frustration. They could smell us, but they couldn't find us until we found them.

The night air was cold. Valerie and Tyrone were buried under mounds of blankets. I couldn't see their faces, but I was sure they were awake, praying for God to make the monsters go away. Lou's posture told me all I needed to know about her state of mind. She held J.J. firmly with one hand and Nate's sling with the other. She was ready to fight to the death. Kimball and Ajax sat attentive but calm. They were soldiers waiting for their orders.

"The Music City Miracle," I said. "January 8, 2001. The Titans played the Buffalo Bills in the AFC wild-card playoff game." This drew a strange gaze from Lou. Tyrone and Valerie peeked out from under their blankets. "The Bills had just kicked a 41-yard field goal to go ahead of the Titans, 16 to 15. There were only 16 seconds left on the clock. Everyone in the Titans hometown stadium thought the game was over. I know. I was there with my Pop. I thought for sure that was the end for the Titans." All eyes were on me. "But what none of us knew was that the Titans had been practicing a play all year called Home Run Throwback. It was made just for situations like they were facing, down by less than a touchdown with just seconds left on the clock. The Bills were expected to squib kick on the kickoff to keep it out of the hands of the Titans return men." I got more and more excited as I relived the memory. "The Titans were waiting for them. The key to the play is to get the ball to Frank Wycheck, the Titans tight end. He would then take the ball and backwards pass it to Derrick Mason, their best return man. Mason would then follow a wall of blockers down the field and either get them into field goal range or take it all the way in for a touchdown. The only problem was Derrick Mason had left the game with a concussion. So they called on Kevin Dyson to take his place. Dyson had never run the play in practice. Well, what do you think happened?" I asked.

Tyrone was sitting up on his elbows now. "What?"

"The play worked to perfection," I said. "Steve Christie with the Bills kicked off to Lorenzo Neal with the Titans. Neal took the ball and handed it off to Wycheck on the 25-yard line. Wycheck lateraled the ball across the field to Dyson who ran 75 yards for the game-winning touchdown. Have you ever heard 67,000 fans screaming their heads off?" I was standing now. The elation of the memory swirled all through my body. "It was the most incredible thing I have ever seen."

"Not if you ask my granddad," Lou said.

"What do you mean?" I asked.

"He's a Bills fan. He says the lateral was an illegal forward pass." She smiled. "I don't know what that is, but he hates the Titans because of it."

"Your granddad's nuts," I said. "It was legal all the way." Neither one of us noticed that we had used the present tense in referring to her grandfather. We were so caught up in the story that we talked as if everything was normal, as if we were old friends back home talking about one of the greatest moments in NFL history.

Something else happened as I told the story. The Takers had gone away because we refused to notice them. I had successfully turned their frustration into futility. They had moved back into the shadows and seeped into the surrounding nothingness.

FIVE

Riding into Chattanooga the next morning, we passed a billboard for a car dealership that had the word "Takers" spray-painted over it. We tried not to focus on it, and to a certain extent we were successful. But seeing the word written in such a public place made me curious. Was that how they did it? They write the name in enough public places so people see it, eventually read it out loud, maybe catch the eye of a TV station or a newspaper. They take pictures and run it as a news item. Suddenly the word "Takers" is in every home in every community. Hell, if you write it on the side of Air Force One or the White House it becomes national news. Pretty soon everyone in the whole country – the whole world for that matter – is seeing it, hearing it, and saying it. Who would have thought that something as innocuous as vandalism would cause the end of the world?

Under the shadow of Lookout Mountain, we passed a small one-foot by one-foot blue sign with a white letter "H" on it – Hospital. The details of Tyrone and Valerie's story came rushing back. An angel named Stevie saved them. Logic told me that it wasn't the same Stevie, but my mother once told me there is no such thing as a coincidence. A billboard for the hospital was a half mile ahead of us. Giant smiling doctors, nurses, and staff looked down on I-24 and welcomed the infirm to pay them a visit while they were in Chattanooga. A closer look at one of the staff members in the advertisement made me do a double take. A man, in a gray uniform and holding a mop, looked very similar to Stevie Dayton. I pulled back on the horses' reins and stopped. I stared at the billboard. Valerie and Tyrone peered from the back of the wagon.

"Is that your angel?" I said pointing to the billboard.

"Yep," Valerie said.

"That's him," Tyrone added. "'Cept he ain't no angel. He's a janitor. See, he's holdin' a mop."

"So," Valerie said a little perturbed. "Angels can mop."

"What's wrong?" Lou asked.

I flicked Phil and Ryder with the reins. "Nothing a trip to the hospital won't fix."

***

The hospital was not far off the exit, so it wasn't that difficult to find. The parking lot was full of cars. If I hadn't known better I would have thought that it was bustling with people inside, scurrying from floor to floor, visiting loved ones, or administering care to the sick.

Once inside though, it became apparent that the eight-story building was abandoned by the crowds long ago. Lou, Nate, and Ajax stayed with the wagon while Tyrone, Valerie, Kimball, and I entered the darkened hallways of the hospital. I held J.J. in one hand and a flashlight in the other. I also stuffed a dozen or so firecrackers in my pockets. I didn't know what I was going to find, but I wanted to be prepared if it was unfriendly.

Tyrone and Valerie guided me through the maze of hallways to the stairs at the back of the building. I opened the door. It was a pitch dark stairwell. I shined the light around revealing the jagged pattern of a seemingly endless number of zigzagging stairs.

"He took us down there," Tyrone said.

I shined the light to the set of stairs leading down. "Of course he did," I said sarcastically.

We stepped inside the stairwell and slowly made our way down three flights of stairs to the landing. The sign above the heavy steel door said, "Basement: Records, Morgue, Boiler Room, Authorized Personnel Only." I swallowed hard. "Morgue," I whispered.

I pulled on the door with all my strength to get it open. Once we were on the other side, the heavy door closed with a thud behind us. The putrid smell of rot, the same as I encountered at Archie's Seed and Feed, only ten times stronger, slapped us in the face as we stood in the wide cold hallway. It didn't take a genius to figure out that the smell was coming from the morgue.

Valerie pointed at the morgue door. "That's where the angel hid us."

"It's full of..." Tyrone started, but I stopped him.

"I know what's in there," I said. "There's no need to talk about it."

As I stood there staring at the door, I could hear Wes's voice in the back of my head saying, "They ain't got no use for dead people."

Suddenly I heard a tap, followed by another and another. Then a cool breeze raced through the passageway. I turned the flashlight in the direction of the breeze and nearly collapsed to the floor in fright as I saw the door to the boiler room closing. Tyrone and Valerie were clinging tightly to me. Kimball was sniffing the ground near the door.

"Let's go," Tyrone said. "Let's get out of here."

I should have listened to him, but instead I moved to the boiler room door, took a deep breath, and opened it. "Hello," I said hoping for a friendly salutation back. I heard nothing but a quick succession of footsteps traveling deep into the bowels of the boiler room. Kimball barked. The bark echoed through the empty chamber, bouncing off the dead machinery that once powered the huge hospital.

"Stevie!" I yelled.

The footsteps stopped.

"Stevie, I want to talk to you."

"Who dat?" asked a voice from the darkness.

"We're friends."

"Stevie fends gone," the voice said. "Monstas take away."

"We're new friends." There was a long silence. "I have Valerie and Tyrone with me. They said you helped them hide from the monsters."

"Valley?" Stevie said. "Ty-lone?"

"Say something," I said to Valerie and Tyrone. They were still holding me tightly.

"Hey, Stevie," Tyrone said. "What's up?"

"You got away," Stevie said with obvious glee.

"Me, too," Valerie said.

"Valley," Stevie said. "I told you the monstas wouldn't find you in the mo'ga."

I pinpointed the direction of his voice and shined the light towards him. I saw Kimball saunter up to a pair of feet sticking out from behind a metal construct of some kind. His tail began to wag.

"Hello, doggy," I heard Stevie say. His head appeared out of hiding as he bent down to pet Kimball. He turned his face toward the light. "I like doggies."

***

After some gentle coaxing we convinced Stevie to come

with us upstairs. He agreed but he refused to leave the hospital. Instead he took us to the fifth floor to the hospital's chapel. A stained glass window provided a source of light that ranged in colors from yellow to purple as we sat on the front pew and talked.

I learned his name was Stevie Spangler. He had a flat facial profile, a depressed nasal bridge, and a small nose. His eyes had an upward slant. He obviously looked similar to Stevie Dayton because they both had Down syndrome.

"Are you here by yourself, Stevie?" I asked.

"No, I'm with you, silly," he said. This drew a laugh from Tyrone and Valerie.

"No, I mean, were you here by yourself before we came?"

"Yes," he said. "Eveebody's gone."

"Have you left the hospital since they went away?"

"No, monstas out they." He pointed toward the outside world.

"How do you know?"

"I hea' dem."

"You hear them? The monsters?"

He nodded his head. "They lookin' fo sto-weetellas"

"Sto-weetellas?"

"Sto-weetellas," he repeated.

I didn't understand. Valerie tugged on my shirt and whispered, "Storytellers."

"Storytellers?" I said, perplexed.

Stevie nodded.

"What storytellers?"

Stevie shrugged his shoulders. "All of dem."

"How do you know all this?" I asked.

"I he' dem."

"You hear them? They talk?"

"No," he said. "They say it to my bain." He pointed to his head.

"Brain? They're telepathic?"

He shrugged his shoulders.

I rubbed my chin. "What do they say to your brain?"

He thought about the question. "They say they look fo seven."

"Seven what?"

"Sto-weetellas."

"Are you a Storyteller? Is that why you can hear them?"

He looked at me as if I had just asked the most asinine question ever. "No, no, no." He giggled a little. "I'm the janito."

"Why do they want these Storytellers?"

"To finish the sto-wee." He gave me the same perplexed look. I could see the wheels turning in his head. He was trying to assess exactly how stupid I was.

A thunderous crash came from outside the chapel. I jumped to my feet. Valerie and Tyrone stood behind me. Stevie ducked under the pew and curled up in the fetal position.

"They don't want me to say anymo'," he said. "They don't want me to say anymo'." He repeated it over and over again until it became a fast rhythmic chant.

I had both hands on J.J. Tyrone, Valerie, and I were backing away, scanning every inch of the chapel, looking for the Takers to materialize out of thin air. Kimball paced excitedly in the back of the room.

"No!" Stevie screamed. "Don't make me do it!"

"Stevie, calm down," I said. "Don't let them get in your head."

"They want me to say they name," he said.

"Don't do it, Stevie. Don't do it."

He stood. His face was red. I could see his temples pulsing. His hands were covering his ears. Tears streamed down his cheek. "Beway," he gurgled. His tongue was turning purple. He was fighting it, but he was losing. "Beway..."

I took Valerie's hand. "Tyrone grab on to Valerie." He did as requested. I pulled them around the side of the pews to the back of the chapel. We raced for the door.

"Beway the Takas!" Stevie shouted.

With that his body relaxed, and his shoulders slumped. He turned to us, sopping wet from his battle. "Won," he said.

"Won?" I said. "You won?"

He shook his head and screamed, "Won!"

"Run." Tyrone pulled on my hand. "He said, run."

The words barely had time to leave Tyrone's mouth when the door to the chapel came flying open, hitting Kimball and knocking him across the room. A Taker entered, its teeth chattering. This one was bigger than the ones we had encountered in the Kroger's. It stooped over to avoid hitting the ceiling. It let out a roar that shook the building. The Taker stomped toward Stevie.

"Won! Save the sto-weetellas!" Stevie picked up a hymnal from the pew and threw it at the Taker. The monster caught the fat book in its mouth and thrashed its head back and forth.

I slid against the back wall with Tyrone and Valerie in tow. The Taker was fixated on Stevie. The door had been knocked from its bottom hinge. It hung precariously from the top hinge. I pushed it easily and peered up and down the hallway. It was clear. I pulled Tyrone and Valerie in front of me and sent them into the hallway. "Kimball," I said. I had not noticed until that moment that he had not moved since he was hit by the door and sent flying across the room.

I handed J.J. to Tyrone "Go down to the wagon and tell Lou to get out of here."

"But what about you?" he asked.

"I'll catch up. Just go. Get Valerie down to the wagon and get out of here."

He brandished the heavy sword with some difficulty and ran towards the exit with Valerie.

I stepped away from the battered doorway and made my way toward Kimball. The Taker was nearly on top of Stevie. Stevie was screaming and throwing every hymnal and Bible he could get his hands on as he backed away from the creature. I bent to the ground and scooped Kimball up in my arms. He had regained some of his weight since I first saw him a few days ago, so the task of carrying him took every bit of strength I had. I stood and heard the horrible gurgled scream of Stevie. The Taker had him half way in his mouth. Stevie's legs kicked and flailed about as the monster began to swallow him whole.

My mind raced. I had to do something to help him. I put Kimball down and quickly pulled a lighter and M-98 firecracker out of my pocket. I fumbled with the lighter. I flicked the lighter over and over again unable to get it lit. Finally, as my thumb throbbed from my unsuccessful attempts, the flame appeared. With a shaky right hand, I lit the firecracker and prepared to throw it at the Taker, but much to my dismay, Stevie was gone and the creature had turned his focus on me. He stepped toward me, and I could see his overstuffed stomach involuntarily expand and contract. Stevie was still alive. He was fighting the Taker from within.

I threw the firecracker. It exploded near the creature's shoulder. It stopped momentarily. An open wound smoked on the Taker's shoulder. The monster shrugged it off and continued its pursuit of me. I lit a second firecracker and tossed it in the

Taker's mouth. The M-98 exploded. Two teeth shot out of the monster's mouth, but it still pressed forward. I tossed a third and fourth firecracker, each time striking a direct hit on the creature and slowing its advance. But I could not stop it. I had a fifth M-98 lit when its huge hands wrapped around my neck. It lifted me off the ground with its mouth open and its remaining teeth folded in. It was going to swallow me. Its slimy tongue licked my face. I took the lit firecracker and stuffed it down its throat, and then grabbed the Taker's snout and tried with all my might to push myself away from its mouth. I heard a muffled pop. The monster dropped me. It grasped its throat with both hands.

The Taker stumbled back and fell over a row of pews. I took the opportunity to pick up Kimball and run to the door. Before I exited, I looked back at the fallen creature. It was still alive, but in pain. It rolled over on its hands and knees, coughing and wheezing. I wanted to go back and see if I could help Stevie, but I convinced myself that he was dead now, churning in the monster's stomach. I leapt through the broken door and headed towards the exit with Kimball who was now beginning to stir.

I threw my shoulder into the stairwell door and was surprised to see Ajax and Lou standing on the other side. "What are you doing here?" I asked short of breath.

"We came to help."

The Taker stumbled out of the chapel. It was still grasping its throat with one hand. It spotted me by the stairwell exit and headed towards me.

"Well you can start by getting out of the way!"

Lou saw the creature and quickly complied. We reached the third floor before we heard the fifth floor stairwell door crash open. The Taker was slowing. We heard it let out a strained roar. It sounded as if it were dying. I had mortally wounded it.

When we reached the first floor, the Taker was finished. The unmistakable sounds of it tumbling down a flight of steps echoed through the stairwell.

Kimball groaned and lifted his head. He began to squirm making it impossible for me to continue to hold onto him. I set him down and he stood on wobbly legs. Ajax gently patted his old pal on the back and hooted.

We opened the door to the hallway and stepped out into the corridor. I collapsed to the floor. The slime from the Taker's hand was still on my neck. I frantically tried to wipe it off.

"You all right?" Lou asked.

"No," I said. "Didn't Tyrone tell you to leave?"

"Yep," she said.

"So, why didn't you?"

"I don't know how to drive that stupid wagon," she said. "Besides I couldn't just leave you."

"Yeah, well next time do what I say." I stood. The emergency room sign caught my eye.

"You're not the boss of me," Lou said.

I ignored her and headed for the emergency room.

"Where are you going?" She asked.

I didn't answer. I continued down the hallway.

"We should get back to the wagon," she said. "I left the baby with Tyrone and Valerie."

"Go ahead. I'll be out in a second." I opened the emergency room door and disappeared inside. All that I could think about was seeing the Taker swallow Stevie whole. The poor guy was eaten alive. I wondered to myself if there was a chance, however small, that he was still alive in that creature's belly. I stepped behind a curtained partition and saw a silver tray of instruments, just what I was looking for. I grabbed the scalpel and turned to see Lou staring at me dumbfounded.

"What are you going to do with that?" she asked.

"I thought you were going out to the wagon."

"I sent Ajax and Kimball. What are you going to do?"

I held the scalpel up. "I don't know if you want to see this."

***

Thankfully the Taker had fallen on its back. Its extended belly was easily accessible.

"This one is bigger than the other two," Lou said.

"You don't have to tell me," I said kneeling down beside it. I placed the scalpel on the monster's stomach and hesitated. "You might want to look the other way," I warned. Lou didn't respond. She stared tight-lipped at the monster. She was determined to watch me cut it open. I silently counted to three and then lightly moved the blade across the Taker's stomach. Blood oozed along the expanding slit. A rush of hot steamy air rose out of the opening that carried with it the foul odor of spoiled milk. When I had made about a two-foot cut, I put the scalpel down. I rubbed my hands together, said a quick prayer and then pulled back the thick leathery skin. A layer of fat obstructed my view so I cut it away. Once I sliced past the fat, I stared at the insides of the creature in amazement. There was nothing there, no Stevie, no stomach, no bones, nothing. It was literally a black hole.

"What do you make of that?" Lou said sounding a little relieved not to find the partially digested body of Stevie Spangler inside.

"I don't know." I stuck my hand inside. I slowly pushed it past the fat and into the black hole. I was in it up to my wrist and then my elbow and then my shoulder.

"Gross," Lou finally said.

I pulled my arm out, and except for a little bit of slime from the layers of fat, it was clean. "There's nothing there I said."

"Isn't that a good thing?" she asked.

"Where'd Stevie go?"

***

We were in Dalton, Georgia when it started to rain again. The closest shelter we could find was a carpet outlet warehouse. The loading dock was open and I was able to drive the wagon up the ramp and inside the enormous building. Gigantic rolls of carpet stacked ten feet high were placed throughout the entire building. Dozens of carpet manufacturers' signs hung from the ceiling. It was a carpet lover's paradise.

We all found a spot and attempted to relax. The morning at the hospital left us all a little worse for the wear. We were battle fatigued. Kimball was doing better, but he was still a little woozy. Ajax tried to coax him into a rough-and-tumble play session, but Kimball snapped at him and lay down on a stack of throw rugs.

I sat propped up against a roll of green carpet and flipped through Dr. Fine's book. My conversation with Ajax the day before kept replaying in my head. He had said something about "Gorilla's always know," and "Old future." And there was something nonsensical he said about "Sentence tell." I flipped through the pages of the book and stopped when I saw a series of photos of Ajax's artwork. Most of it was just handprints and paint splatters, but some of it could pass for real art, I suppose. A lot of it looked pretty dreary. He painted a few that looked like flames. But there was one in particular that drew my attention, hidden in globs of black and gray paint, I could almost detect glowing red eyes peering out. I was stunned when I read the caption, "Ajax calls this one 'Old Future,' though no one on the staff can ascertain what he means." I flipped the page. There was a picture of Dr. Fine sitting on the floor with Ajax. He looks to be making the sign for sentence. The caption read, "Ajax worries about the storytellers again." Storytellers! I felt as if I would explode with anticipation. Ajax wasn't signing, "Sentence tell." He was signing "Storyteller." More specifically he was saying, "Baby Storyteller."

On the next page of the book, there was a brief explanation of Ajax's obsession with the storytellers. Dr. Fine wrote:

"To those disbelievers who think gorillas aren't capable of cognitive thought, that they lack imagination or the ability to invent fantasy for the sake of entertainment, I direct you to Ajax's Storytellers. On most nights, Ajax will regale visitors with fantastic stories of the end of the world. He tells vivid tales of grotesque creatures from what he calls 'Imagined Lands,' that seek out eight storytellers that will give them 'Permanent Blood.' He speaks of warrior heroes that sacrifice their lives to protect the storytellers. It is a classic tale of good versus evil that only lacks an ending."

I read the passage several times. Is it possible that a gorilla knew that the end of the world was coming? That he knew about the Takers and their origins? "Possible," I thought. I had just seen a man swallowed by a creature that did not exist in the known world, and I was asking if something was possible. It was obvious that anything was possible. It was apparent that what he meant by "All gorillas know," and "Old future," was that what was happening to the world right now with the

Takers and the Storytellers is old gorilla folklore. That it is a precognitive story of the world shared by all gorillas. "Old future." They've always known this would happen.

I called out to Ajax. He knuckle-walked his way over to me and sat down. "Tell me about the old future," I said.

He signed, "Old future now."

"Who are the storytellers?"

"Eight," he signed.

I told him Stevie Spangler had said there were seven.

"Seven now," he signed.

Seven now? I thought about his answer. The comic book. Stevie Dayton was one of the Storytellers, but now he was dead. Eight had become seven. I asked Ajax if this is what happened.

He nodded and signed, "seven now," again.

"Where are the other Storytellers?"

He signed, "All world," and "baby Storyteller."

"Baby Storyteller?" I looked at Lou who was feeding Nate. I turned back to Ajax. "Our baby is a Storyteller?"

He grinned and nodded. "Protect baby," he signed.

I remembered Stevie Spangler yelling "Save the Sto-weetellas," as he was backing away from the Taker. It was all too big a responsibility for me to bear. I was just a kid. We were all just kids. How could we be expected to protect Nate from the Takers? We were outmatched in every way.

He pointed to me and made the signs for "war" and "man".

"War man?" I asked.

He repeated the sign, and pointed to Lou and then Kimball. "War man."

I flipped through the book to see if I could find a reference for this. I did. It was a phrase he used frequently. To Ajax "War man," meant "warrior."

He continued. "War man find keep. Protect baby."

I tried to tell him I wasn't a warrior, but he responded that I had always been a warrior. "I'm just a dumb kid," I said. "I've never been in a fight in my life."

He huffed and repeated, "War man find keep." He was getting frustrated with me.

"What's a keep," I asked.

"Keep," he signed emphatically. "Keep protect Storytellers. Keep help remove take. Keep good."

He was getting more and more frustrated with me and as a result his signing was getting sloppy and his phrasing was off. I tried to calm him by assuring him that I understood, but he knew I was lying. He let out a pained groan and lurched away. All the while I'm sure he was thinking to himself that I was possibly the dumbest human he had ever encountered.

I leaned back against the roll of carpet and closed my eyes. I was angry. Not at Ajax, but at the situation. I didn't want to be a warrior. I wanted to be a kid. I wanted to go to Titans games. I wanted to spend my time coming up with creative excuses for not raking the yard.

Nate started to get restless and cried out. Lou quickly tended to him. He's not my responsibility I told myself. I don't care what Mrs. Chalmers said. If the Takers wanted him, they could have him. I wasn't going to risk my life for something that does nothing more than poop, sleep, and vomit. I had had it.

I opened my eyes to find Lou standing over me with Nate. "What?" I said unintentionally sharp.

"I have to..." she hesitated.

"You have to what?"

"I have to... You know?" She was shifting from one leg to the other.

"No, I don't know," I said, not really in the mood to play a guessing game.

"Go to the bathroom," she whispered.

"Oh," I said trying not to smile. "So."

"So, can you watch Nate?"

I looked at the wriggling little baby in her arms. "Get Tyrone and Valerie to do it."

She turned and watched the two little kids chasing each other around the warehouse. They looked as if they were playing tag. "They're not old enough to watch a baby."

"I'm busy," I said.

"Doing what?"

"None of your business."

She bent down and put Nate on my lap. "You're watching him," she said. "And that's that." She stood and sped away before I could protest.

"Hey," I shouted. But she never looked back. I looked down at Nate. His eyes were open wider now than when I first saw him on the floor of the attic in his house. He seemed to be more aware. I looked at his belly and the little brown crusty knob had disappeared. He had a normal pink belly button. His tiny hand reached out for me and grabbed my Titans sweatshirt. "You like the Titans?" I asked, not expecting an answer. "Of course you do, we're from the same neighborhood." I looked at his ears. "You know, your ears do look kind of funny, but I wouldn't let that get you down, kid." I looked around to see if anybody could hear me talking to the baby. I didn't want to look foolish. I was in the clear so I continued my conversation. "I don't think it's fair, Nate. I'm only 13. I can't protect you. Have you seen those things that are after you? They're huge and ugly and... hungry. What's a kid like me supposed to do against something like that?" Nate looked up at me and smiled. "Hey, that's the first time I've seen you smile." I reached in my back pocket and pulled out the picture of Nate with his parents. I looked at it and then showed it to the baby. "I wonder if they knew what you were." I laughed. "Listen to me, I'm starting to buy into this whole nonsense." I looked at the picture again. "They sure did love you, kid."

Lou suddenly appeared in front of me. "I'll take him back."

"Hmm? Oh, okay," I said. I lifted the baby up to her and she took him. She bounced him up and down as she walked away. I stared at the picture of the Chalmers. "We all have our cross to bear," I said to myself. "I guess it's time to bear mine."

***

That night we ate well. I pulled out the propane grill, a pot, and some instant Ramen noodles. Not a gourmet meal by any stretch of the imagination, but it was our first hot meal since the corn-on-the-cob. Kimball enjoyed a double helping of dog food and Ajax feasted on a bucket of fruits and vegetables.

The conversation never veered toward the horror we witnessed at the hospital. We talked about our lives before the end of the world. Tyrone had eight brothers and sisters. He was the youngest. Valerie was an only child being raised by a single mother. Lou was home schooled. We all had different backgrounds and now we were all headed for the same future.

We relaxed by playing a game of hide and seek. I wasn't too keen on the idea at first, but I agreed hoping to give Tyrone and Valerie a sense of normalcy. I have to admit I had a pretty good time. Even Ajax got in on the game, although there weren't many places for a 400-pound gorilla to hide.

By nine o'clock that night, I encouraged everyone to get some sleep because we had something important to do the next day. I didn't tell them what, because I wanted them all to get a good night's rest. They protested at first, but eventually they gave in and settled down for the night.

I laid in my sleeping bag next to the wagon. Lou and Nate were close by. The baby was being unusually quiet. As I lay there staring at the ceiling of the warehouse, I asked Lou, "I wonder why he liked me?"

"Who?"

"Stevie Dayton. I mean I was a real jerk to him."

"Maybe he saw the magic in you," she said.

I turned to her. "You better get some sleep. We've got a big day tomorrow."

"You might as well tell me what you've got planned. I'm going to know soon enough anyway."

I smiled and closed my eyes. "You'll see." I didn't know how to tell her tomorrow was the day we would read the comic book.

SIX

I woke up the next morning trying to convince myself I was a warrior, but it never really sunk in. Warriors were big muscled grown men who could defeat entire armies with nothing more than their fists. I was a puny kid who had trouble making a fist let alone defeating an army with one.

I woke everybody up and treated them all to a hearty breakfast of honey and chunky peanut butter sandwiches. Ajax ate three and got peanut butter all over his face.

After they were well fed, I sat them in a circle and began my speech. "I know this is kind of sudden, but we have to do something that's not going to be too pleasant today. If you don't want to do it, I'll understand."

"We're going to do it, aren't we?" Lou said with excitement in her voice.

"Do what?" Tyrone asked.

"It's time," I said. "We're going to war today."

"War?" Valerie said apprehensively.

"We're going to read the comic book." Lou stood and started for the wagon.

"Hold on," I said. "We've got to get prepared first."

"What comic book?" Tyrone asked.

"The one that brings the Greasywhoppers," Lou said.

Tyrone and Valerie looked at each other. They were certain we had lost our minds.

"Why would we want to do that?" Valerie asked.

"We don't want to," I said. "We have to." I looked at Ajax. "We're warriors." He stood and pounded his chest. Valerie and Tyrone were unsure. I could imagine they were now sorry they had left the bicycle bandits to join us. "You don't have to be part of this," I said.

"What choice to do we have?" Tyrone asked.

"I'll hitch the horses to the wagon," I said. "You can take off."

"We'll stay," Valerie said.

"We will?" Tyrone didn't look too thrilled.

"We're warriors," she said putting her arm around him.

He looked at me and said, "Better than being a bandit, I guess."

Our first order of business was to load up on weapons of some kind. We had plenty of fireworks and J.J., but beyond that we weren't prepared for a battle. I exited the front of the warehouse and scanned the street to see if there was a store that might have what we needed. To the left, beyond the interstate overpass, was a series of shopping centers. I called for Tyrone to bring Ryder around, and I mounted the gentle old mare.

"Get all the candles together," I told Tyrone. "And start unloading the fireworks. I'll be back." He smiled and saluted me like he was a soldier taking orders. I gave Ryder's ribs a tap with my heels and he trotted off towards the shopping centers.

There were plenty of fast food places and clothing stores among the shopping centers, but nothing that could help us in our impending battle. I was just about to give up when I spotted what looked like a giant pair of deer antlers poking up over the hill beyond the last shopping center. I guided Ryder in that direction. When we reached the peak of the hill, I saw the giant antlers were part of a sign that stood above Rankin's

Outdoor Outfitters. Their slogan bragged that they were the outdoorsman's best friend. I hoped they were the warrior's best friend, too.

The store was locked so I threw a heavy rock through the glass front door. The inside was in pristine condition. It was wall-to-wall camouflage. They had every outdoor item known to man. I made a mental note to bring the wagon by the store before we left Dalton to restock on some survival essentials. I briefly thought of the possibility that we may not be leaving Dalton depending on how our face-off with the Takers went.

The place was replete with guns and ammo, but they didn't do me any good. Past the row of guns, I saw something that caught my eye. It was a crossbow. It was a thing of beauty. I moved around the counter and took it from the wall. Like virtually everything else in the store, it was decorated in camouflage. It had what looked to be a highly complicated pulley system and strong, durable cable. It was even fashioned with a scope that placed a red dot on your target. I held it to my shoulder. It weighed about nine pounds. It felt surprisingly natural in my hands. The price tag said $1,000. I smiled like a kid waking up on Christmas morning. I had to have it. In fact, I had to have four.

I found a large canvas bag and filled it with four crossbows, as many arrows as I could find, a half dozen quivers that could hold up to ten arrows, a variety of hunting knives, a dozen lighters called pocket blow torches, and some hunting vests with pockets everywhere.

Mounting Ryder with such a heavy load wasn't easy. I set the bag on the roof of a nearby car and jumped on Ryder's back. From there it was just a matter of leaning over and snatching the bag of goodies from the car roof.

I was back at the warehouse in less than fifteen minutes,

anxious to show off my new toys. Tyrone was as enthusiastic as I was, but Lou and Valerie were a little reticent. Realistically they knew that it would come to this, that we would have to arm ourselves in order to successfully fend off the Takers. But seeing the crossbows with their almost sadistic looking arrows was another thing all together. It brought the point home to them that this was for real. We would have to kill in order to avoid being killed. They didn't like the idea even though all we'd be killing were uncaring monsters that saw us as food.

Reluctantly they joined Tyrone and me in a crossbow shooting practice session behind the outlet warehouse. We took turns cranking the cocking mechanism and firing out arrows at a basketball backboard the outlet employees must have made full use of during lunch. Tyrone, Lou, and I got fairly efficient, but Valerie never quite got the hang of it.

We continued preparations for the battle inside the warehouse. I gave the others the pocket blowtorches. They lit with an easy push of a lever, and the flame was big. It was perfect for lighting a firecracker and throwing it at an assailant quickly. As a backup, I lit all the candles Tyrone had placed throughout the warehouse. If we got in a spot and our pocket blowtorches wouldn't work, we wouldn't be far from a lit candle.

I hitched up the horses, loaded the wagon with all our supplies, and moved it outdoors. "Valerie," I said, "You stay with the horses and Nate." I pulled a bottle rocket from my pocket and showed it to her. "You see this? It shoots off red and blue sparkles." She nodded. "I'll shoot this off for only one reason."

"What?" she asked.

"To tell you to get out of here. If you see red and blue sparkles, you slap Phil and Ryder with the reins as hard as you can and go. Don't look back just keep going until you get to Atlanta. You understand?"

"But I want to help," she protested.

"You are." I took Nate who was lying in his sling around my neck and placed him across Valerie's shoulder. "You're making sure the monsters don't get Nate. We can't let them get him."

She reluctantly agreed.

I reached in the back of the wagon and pulled out the rolled up comic book. I gave one last reassuring look to Valerie and went into the warehouse.

Lou and Tyrone were nervously standing by. We were all armed with our crossbows and wearing two quivers filled with ten arrows each. Our first shot was cocked and ready to go. In addition, we all had on hunting vests with each pocket filled with firecrackers. We had knives strapped to our waists. We were armed to the teeth.

I handed Lou the comic book. "You read," I said, "How many pages do you think you can get through before they show up?"

"Five, maybe six," she said.

"Make it four and then hide it in that roll of carpet." I pointed to a large roll of carpet to my right. "There's answers in that comic book. Things those Greasywhoppers don't want us to know. If they get their hands on it, we may never know what we need to know."

"What do we need to know?" She looked at me hoping I had some clue.

"I don't know," I said.

"What do you want me to do?" Tyrone asked.

"You and I are going to keep a close eye out. We have no idea which direction these things are going to come from.

Aim for the chest. Give yourself a big target." He looked at me nervously. "You up for this?"

"I guess so."

"Yeah, me too," I said. I turned to Ajax. "You ready, warrior." He grunted. I didn't have to ask Kimball. He was already pacing pack and forth ready for action.

"Lou," I said. "You're the only one who's going to know what you read."

"So?"

"So, you have to survive. If we lose you, this whole thing will have been for nothing."

She smiled anxiously, and sat down in a folding chair we placed in the middle of the warehouse. Tyrone and I put our backs to her and stood three feet away. We both readied our crossbows and kept a guarded eye out for any signs of the creatures. Kimball and Ajax took positions close by.

"Ready?" I said.

"Ready," Tyrone answered.

"Okay, Lou, do your stuff," I said.

I heard her take a deep breath and then I heard her open the comic book. It was eerily quiet as she read. We were too scared to even breathe. Lou flipped a page and then another. She was reading fast.

"Lou, what are you doing?"

"This is stuff that already happened," she said. "South Pittsburg, the rest area, Chattanooga, he wrote about it all."

"Get to the part we don't know about."

"I'm trying."

A noise came from the far corner of the warehouse. Tyrone and I both turned towards it, our crossbows ready to fire. "Time's up, Lou."

"I just need a few more minutes."

A roll of carpet tumbled to the floor from the same direction the noise had come from. "Time's up, now!" I tried to shout like a commander, but it came out as a plea.

Tyrone slowly started moving toward the noise. "Stay put, Tyrone," I said. He hesitated, but then continued to move forward. "Tyrone!"

"I need to get closer to get a better shot," he said.

"Trust me, it will come to us."

He stopped. "Yeah, I guess you're right." He was now standing at the end of the largest roll of carpet in the entire building.

I turned to Lou, "I said that's enough." She didn't respond. "Lou..."

Suddenly she stood and shouted, "Tyrone get away from there!"

Stunned by Lou's tone, Tyrone was about to comply when he was jerked to the ground. I could see a Taker's hand wrap around his ankle and pull him behind the roll of carpet. Kimball was the first to run to Tyrone's aid. I followed. Ajax grabbed Lou and pulled her to the other end of the warehouse.

By the time I reached the other side of the roll of carpet, Tyrone was gone. Kimball was growling and barking down a large hole in the concrete floor. I could hear Tyrone screaming, "Help!" from below the floor.

From the other end of the warehouse where we first heard the noise, two more Takers appeared, their teeth chattering, their claws extended. They were fifteen footers easy. Ajax raced past us and barreled towards the two monsters. Kimball charged after him.

"Oz!" I heard a screech rise up from the hole.

Lou ran towards me. She fired her crossbow at one of the Takers pursued by Kimball and Ajax, and hit it between the eyes. It wobbled to its knees, and placed both hands around the arrow jetting out from its forehead. Kimball leapt on it and sunk his teeth into its neck. "Go!" she said. "We can take care of these two."

I did not immediately jump into the hole. I thought about it first, which was a big mistake. Fear grabbed hold of me. I wrestled with myself, fighting to work up the courage to jump in the hole and save Tyrone. I looked to see Lou turning the crank on her crossbow to cock it and insert another arrow in the barrel. Ajax was tormenting the Taker. He had hold of its leg and was trying to pull it off its feet, but the monster swung wildly and caught Ajax on the head, sending him tumbling to the ground. Ajax quickly recovered.

"Oz!" Tyrone cried. His voice was distant and muffled. I couldn't wait any longer. I jumped into the hole.

It was pitch black. I couldn't see three feet in front of me. I searched through my pockets and pulled out a small penlight I had picked up at the outdoor shop. I turned the head of the light and it came on. I was astonished to see the Takers had dug a large tunnel that ended at the hole in the warehouse. I shined my light down the tunnel. The walls were dripping with the ooze from the Greasywhoppers. I walked forward, increasing my pace with each step. "Tyrone!" I called out.

"Oz!"

He was alive and just ahead. My beam of light caught some movement. I slowed my pace. It was the back of the Taker. In its left hand it held tightly to Tyrone, while it dug its way through the earth with the right. It was removing huge chunks as it frantically clawed at the rock and dirt in front of it.

I shot my crossbow and hit it in the shoulder. The creature stopped digging. It seemed to be unfazed by the arrow sticking out of its back. It turned slowly, its teeth chattering. I dropped the light and furiously turned the crank on the crossbow to cock it. The bottom half of the Taker was the only thing illuminated now. I could see Tyrone struggling to free himself from the monster's grasp. The crossbow cocked, I reached back and pulled an arrow out of one of my quivers and loaded it in the barrel, but I couldn't fire without the light. I saw the monster take a step toward me. As I bent down to pick up the flashlight, it went dark. I ran my hand across the muddy tunnel floor, but I couldn't find it in the darkness. I stood and searched my pockets again, this time looking for my pocket blowtorch. I couldn't remember which pocket I put it in. I searched them all and didn't locate it. I could hear Tyrone whimpering. The Taker was dragging him along the ground as it walked toward me. I searched my pockets again. This time I found it on the first try. I pushed the lever and lost all feeling in my body when the light from the pocket torch flame revealed the creature's slimy snout just inches from my face. I screamed and my finger involuntarily twitched, pulling the trigger on the crossbow and striking it in the chest. The monster flinched, but that was it. It almost seemed to smile at me. Looking down I could see Tyrone's knife sticking out of the Taker's leg. Tyrone was wriggling like a worm on the end of the hook trying to break free from the creature's grip.

"Do something," Tyrone ordered.

I dropped the crossbow, reached in my pocket, pulled out an M-98 and lit it with the pocket torch. The Taker slapped the firecracker out of my hand and sent it flying behind me. It exploded, kicking up rocks and mud.

The Taker opened its oversized mouth and its teeth bent down. Looking inside the mucus-covered cavern, I couldn't help but think I had been in this situation before. It was going to swallow me. I reached down and pulled the knife from my waist and thrust it up into the Taker's chin. It reeled back and let go of Tyrone.

"Go, go, go," I said to Tyrone as I helped him to his feet. We ran toward the opening. The Taker screamed in agony.

When we got to the opening, we realized it was too high for us to reach. I lifted Tyrone up as high as I could, but that wasn't very high. A long hairy arm dropped down from the opening. It was Ajax. I lifted Tyrone up and he reached for Ajax. The gorilla grasped Tyrone by the wrist and pulled him up to safety. Ajax dropped his arm down the hole again to pull me up. I jumped and missed his hand. I jumped again. As I felt the leathery grip of Ajax latch on to my hand, I also felt the monstrous grip of the Taker grab me by the waist. Ajax roared trying to lift me against the strength of the Taker, but he couldn't do it.

The monster yanked me down to the ground. I scrambled back on the muddy surface. The Taker was on all fours. It snapped its mighty jaw as it lurched towards me. It suddenly lunged backwards and howled. Ajax was on its back, pounding it with his enormous gorilla fists. Kimball stuck his head down the hole. He barked, desperately wanting to jump down and help his friend, but it was too far down.

The Taker slammed backwards into the wall. Ajax bellowed in pain, but he fought on. I darted in and pulled the knife out of the monster's leg. The Taker swung its clawed hand at me, but missed when Ajax jerked it to the ground. It flailed on its back. It was now or never. I jumped up on its chest and with both hands around the knife's handle, I plunged it into the Taker's neck. It jerked and flopped, sending me flying against the tunnel wall. In a matter of minutes, it made one last spasm and then stopped moving.

Ajax was wounded. Blood was coming from his chest.

The Taker had sliced him with its claws. I crawled to his side. He moaned and cupped his huge hand around my head. His breathing was uneven. "Hey," I said. "C'mon, now, they can't hurt you. You're a warrior."

He roared in pain.

I ran to the opening. "We got to get Ajax out of here. He's hurt."

"Now, how do you propose we get a 400-pound go-rilla out of that hole?" A familiar voice answered back.

"Wes?" I said.

Wes peered down the whole. "The one and only. Sorry I missed all the fun." He smiled. "Hold on to your britches. We'll get a ladder down to you."

"How did you..."

"I told you I was working on something. As soon as we get you and that ugly go-rilla out of there, I'll show you."

Ajax roared in protest at being called ugly. I sat next to him and waited for our old friend, Wes, to pull us out of the hole.

***

Topside, we tended to Ajax's wounds. He had two deep gashes that ran about four inches across his chest. They were deep cuts, but Valerie and Lou did a good job of patching him up.

I was anxious to talk to Wes, but I needed a moment to gather myself. I found a secluded spot in the manager's office in front of the warehouse and dropped to my knees. I was angry, happy, terrified, and emboldened all at once. My entire body was trembling. We had voluntarily engaged the Takers in battle, and we had won, but I didn't know if I had the courage to do it again. I allowed myself only a few moments of reflection before I returned to the others.

Wes took me outside and showed me what he had been working on. It was a 1972 VW bus. The short, green and yellow van glistened in the October sun.

"But the gas?" I said.

Wes smiled. "Converted it to run on propane.

"Propane?"

"Didn't think this old redneck could do much more than fart and cook on the grill, did ya'?" He walked over to the German-made vehicle and ran his hand across the driver's side door.

"You're a genius," I said.

"Nah, I ain't no genius. Just an old grease monkey who reads Popular Mechanics."

I walked over and looked inside the van. He had it half loaded with supplies, mostly food. Wes leaned against the VW and soaked in my admiration.

"I see you picked up a couple of strays," he said, motioning with his head toward Valerie and Tyrone standing inside the warehouse.

"Yeah." I leaned on the van next to him. "Picked them up outside of Chattanooga." I looked at Tyrone and could scarcely believe what he and I had just gone through in the tunnel. "How'd you find us anyway?"

"Seen the horses and wagon from the interstate." He pointed over his shoulder with his thumb. "You kids is playing with fire," he said. "Conjuring them things up will only lead to trouble."

I thought about how to respond. I couldn't tell him that, like Lou, I believed we were on a mission. It sounded too corny, and he would just think it was nonsense.

"We were prepared."

He was about to give me a lecture on the fallacy of that

statement when we heard some whining and yelping from inside the van. His eyes opened wide. "Hell, I almost forgot." He ran around the other side of the van and opened the door. "Got me some future Greasywhopper killers."

I walked up as he was pulling out a box full of puppies from the van. There were eight. They were all, different variations of the colors black, tan, and white. They looked to be about six weeks old.

"Found 'em out back of my garage the other day. Don't know what happened to the mother. I waited for her to come around, but she never did, so I figured I had to bring 'em with me. Didn't feel right just leavin' them there."

I picked one up. Its little tail was wagging uncontrollably. It started licking my face. "It'll be a while before these things can take on a Greasywhopper."

"Old Kimball will give them all the training they need." We started to walk back to the warehouse. He carried the box with the remaining seven puppies, and I carried the other tightly to my chest. "You don't mind if this old redneck tags along with ya', do ya'?"

"Mind? I'd be mad if you didn't."

Predictably, Tyrone and Valerie were elated to see the box of puppies. They greeted us as we entered the warehouse and started plucking puppies from the box before Wes could set it down. I carried my puppy over to Ajax, who was resting comfortably on a stack of throw rugs, and placed the puppy next to him. His eyes lit up. I patted him on the shoulder as he gently picked up the puppy and began tickling its belly. Kimball watched the exchange with just a hint of jealousy.

I motioned for Lou to follow me to the manager's office, and invited Wes to look over our new weapons cache, asking him to come up with a list of things we would need from the outdoor shop. In truth it was just busy work so Lou and I could speak in private.

When Lou and I entered the manager's office, I turned to her and said, "What did the book say?"

"I didn't get that far ahead."

"You knew what was going to happen to Tyrone?"

She nodded. "It was in the book. I knew you were supposed to go in the tunnel after him."

"What happens next?"

"All I know is our next stop is the Atlanta Zoo."

"The Atlanta Zoo?"

"That's where I stopped reading."

I sat on the manager's desk and rubbed my eyes. "How many more pages do you have left?

"Twenty, maybe."

"Twenty?" I sighed deeply. "We'll never be able to pull this off."

"We have to." She looked at me, determined.

I nodded. "Agreed."

She smiled and started to walk away.

"But," I said.

She stopped and turned to me.

I hesitated and then said what had to be said. "We're not all going to make it. I just wanted you to know that."

She processed the information and nodded. "Understood." She exited the manager's office.

***

That night, after returning from the outdoor store with replenished supplies, we sat down to a meal prepared by Valerie. It was a decent assortment of raw vegetables and some powdered milk. In my life before the Takers, I would have barfed at the mere thought of such a meal, but our present situation changed my expectations and severely altered my tastes. I ate it as gratefully as I would have eaten a super-sized meal from McDonald's just weeks before.

"Something's been bothering me," Wes said after chomping a handful of carrots.

"What?" I said.

"No cars." He phrased it simply and offered no further explanation.

I turned and looked out the warehouse door to the interstate. I wasn't sure what he was talking about. "No cars?"

"Yeah. I ain't seen one car since I took off from Manchester yesterday."

Lou and I looked at each other. Of course he hasn't seen any cars. There's nobody left to drive them. "You do know what's going on out here, don't you?" I said.

"Of course I do," he said. "I ain't expectin' to see nobody drivin' around, but how come there ain't no cars on the sides of the highway or in the middle of the road for that matter?"

"What do you mean?" Lou asked.

"I mean them Greasywhoppers snatched people from their cars. You look off on any side road and you'll see all kinds of abandoned cars. Some wrecked in piles. But not on the interstates. Not on 24 and not on 75. Hell, not this exit either."

I thought about it. He was right. We hadn't come across one car that was abandoned or wrecked on our entire journey. Not even the little side trips we took. I hadn't thought about it until now, but he was right. The Takers came suddenly and quickly. Surely people were driving when the Takers yanked them up.

"It's almost like somebody's give us a clear path." He said. "There's really only one question."

"What?" I asked.

"Is that a good thing or a bad thing?"

I looked at Lou and the others. They had all stopped mid-chew thinking about Wes's question. I felt obligated to say something inspirational, but nothing particularly awe-inspiring came to mind. "It's good," I said with no explanation to back up my claim.

The others didn't buy my assertion, but they didn't offer any arguments either. They were all tired of talking about our current situation and what had to be done. They just wanted to relax and prepare for another day of travel.

***

We all awoke in the middle of the night to the sound of what we thought was thunder. Initially we didn't pay much attention, but as I lay there and listened to the rumbling of the thunder dissipate, I noticed that it actually wasn't dissipating. It was growing louder and more intense. It sounded as if it was building to a crescendo, that at any second, we would hear another roaring boom.

I turned on my side to look out the loading dock door and was surprised to see Ajax sitting in the open doorway, his silver back to us as he watched the night sky. I stood and joined him.

"Something wrong?" I asked.

Without acknowledging me he signed "Warrior," and then he made the sign of a 'V' with one hand and ran it across the palm of this other until it went over the edge of his fingertips. Before I could get up and get Dr. Fine's book, Lou was standing next to me with the book in her hand.

"It means fail," she said. "He's been sitting here for the last fifteen minutes signing 'Warriors fail' over and over again."

"Warriors fail?" I put my hand on his shoulder. "Did we fail, Ajax?"

He made the sign language symbol for the letter 'A' and first pointed in one direction and then another. Lou flipped through the book.

"Other," she said.

"Other warriors fail?" I said. The phrase shook me. Not only because the implications of it were horrifying, but also because it was the first time Ajax gave any indication that there were other warriors out there. "There are more like us?"

He grunted and nodded.

"And they failed, meaning the Takers got one of the Storytellers?

He signed, "Six now."

"How do you know?"

He pointed to the sky. I looked and saw a fat purple crack etching itself across the blackened horizon. "What is that?" It was sickening. There was no other way to describe it. It looked as if our world was being ripped apart.

"Day long here," Ajax signed.

"What's a day long?" Lou asked.

Ajax put both hands to his head, placed his thumbs to his forehead, held up two fingers on each hand and wiggled them up and down. I turned to Lou. She frantically flipped through the pages of the book. Her face turned ghost white when she found the description.

"What?" I asked.

She could not say it out loud so she held up the book. I shared her fear when I saw the meaning. I took the book from her and sat back down next to Ajax.

"Are you sure?" I asked him.

He nodded.

Wes had snuck up behind us. He had been standing there long enough to hear most of the conversation. "What's it mean?" he asked.

A little startled by his voice, I turned to him. I cleared my throat and said, "Demon."

SEVEN

I think it's time you come clean with me," Wes said. He was bent next to his propane-converted '72 VW bus checking the air pressure in the front passenger side tire. The sun was stretching above the horizon. The purple crack was ever present. "You kids seem to be messin' around with something you shouldn't be messin' around with."

I squatted next to him. "I don't know exactly what to tell you. I'm not really all that clear on everything."

"Why don't you tell me what you know then?" He sat down on the ground and leaned against the van.

I placed my hands on the paved surface and stretched my legs out. We looked deceptively relaxed, but we were far from it. The purple crack above us rattled both our nerves. "Well, come to find out we're warriors."

He raised an eyebrow. "What do you mean 'warriors'?"

"We have to protect Nate." I tried to make the conversation as matter a fact as possible.

"From what?"

"The Greasywhoppers."

He wiped his dirty hands on the front of his shirt, although I suspected they picked up more dirt from his shirt than they left behind. "What in Hades do them ugly buggers want with Nate?"

"He's a Storyteller." I said it, but didn't know how to explain it.

"Storyteller? The little guy can't even hold his head up. How you figure he's a storyteller?" Wes snickered at the idea.

"Because Ajax said..."

"Hold on, now," he interrupted. "You mean to tell me you're listening to the go-rilla?"

"He knows things," I said.

"He barely knows how to peel a banana."

"He says we're warriors. He says we have to protect Nate, to get him to something called the Keep."

"It's not the Keep," Lou said. She appeared from the back of the VW bus. "It's the Keepers."

"How do you know?" I asked.

She produced Dr. Fine's book from behind her back and pointed to a picture of one of Ajax's paintings. It was a simple, yet crude bright yellow circle. The caption read, "Ajax's Keepers."

"Don't you see?" she said. "If we get Nate to the Keepers, the Greasywhoppers will never be able to get to him."

"I still don't know what them things want with a little baby," Wes said.

"He's only a baby now. He'll grow up to be a Storyteller." She pointed to the purple crack in the sky. "See, the Greasywhoppers already got one of the Storytellers last night. What did Ajax say? Day long demons? That's what happens. They get the Storytellers and the others can cross over."

"What others?" I asked.

"The others," she said as if it were an unnecessary question on my part. "The other monsters that live in the minds of the Storytellers."

Something that Ajax had said a couple days earlier came to me. "Baby have army. That's what he meant."

Wes was still skeptical of the entire conversation. "You kids have gone plum crazy."

"Ajax said, 'Baby have army.' The Storytellers have the armies. The Greasywhoppers are building an army. They need the Storytellers to increase their numbers."

Wes let out a raspberry. "Look around ya', Oz. The Greasywhoppers don't need an army. They done destroyed and conquered. There's nobody left to fight."

Lou stood straight and proud. "There's us and the others that are out there."

Wes shook his head. "No offense, but it sure won't take a whole army to beat the likes of us."

"You're wrong," I said standing. "We're warriors."

***

We started out for Atlanta an hour later. Wes took Tyrone, Valerie, Ajax (who was still convalescing), and the puppies in his bus. They moved faster than us so they took point. They were miles ahead of us within just a few minutes. We kept in touch through a pair of high-powered two-way radios we'd picked up at Rankin's Outdoor Outfitters.

It was risky to split up like that, but Wes could not contain himself when he got behind the wheel of his VW bus. He had to drive as fast he could, which by his standards wasn't as fast as he was used to driving, but he still could out pace our horses and wagon by a good bit.

Lou and I didn't talk much. I think we had said all we could stand to say. We just sat and lost ourselves in the rhythmic clop-clop-clop of the horses' hooves on the pavement as we methodically made our way south.

The purple crack in the sky remained stamped on the horizon. It taunted us, letting us know that the Takers were not our only foes now. There were new creatures we had to deal with, and we knew nothing about them. Ajax had called them the Day Longs, although we couldn't be sure if that is what he really meant or if they were just the closest words in his vocabulary. We looked through Dr. Fine's book, but there were no references to these new monsters, or demons as Ajax called them. We had no idea what they looked like, or if they followed the same rules as the Takers. The comic book may have had some answers, but we could not chance another reading until we were all rested and healthy.

We got a call from Wes on the two-way that he was stopping at the Calhoun exit to wait for us to catch up. I could hear Valerie and Tyrone laughing through the static-filled airwaves of the radio. It made me smile. They were good kids who deserved a little bit of happiness. Unfortunately, that's about all the happiness you could find on this side of our planet's history, a little bit.

As soon as I put the radio down, I got the funny feeling we were being watched. I couldn't pinpoint from where, but I definitely could feel the eyes on me. I didn't tell Lou because I didn't want to ruin her moment of relative peace. I gave Phil and Ryder a light tap with the reins and urged them to pick up the pace.

As we went under an overpass, I got my first look of what or who had been watching us. I saw a shadowy figure on a horse. I got just a glimpse, but I could see that whoever it was, was not a master horseman. I watched the chubby figure in the saddle sway from side to side trying to get the horse to move behind an abandoned semi truck off the exit. The horse kicked up its back legs and whinnied. Lou was now aware of our visitor.

"Somebody's following us," she said.

"I know." I looked to my left and saw another amateur horseman skulking his horse behind a row of trees in the median. "I've seen two so far."

With Nate around her shoulder she carefully stepped to the back of the wagon and retrieved a crossbow. "There's a third one behind us," she said.

I turned to see a long slender figure riding a white and black spotted Tiger horse. I couldn't make out her face, but I could tell by her stance in the saddle, it was Reya. Another horse and rider joined her from the median, the kid who had no name. That meant Devlin and Miles were the ones to our sides. I pulled the wagon to a stop. Kimball barked. We both jumped off.

"What are you doing?" Lou asked.

"Stopping," I said.

"But why?"

"Because we need them."

"What for?"

"Even a warrior needs some friends to help him win his battles."

She shook her head. "These guys are losers. I don't trust them."

"We've got no choice." Kimball and I stood in the middle of the interstate behind the wagon. Reya and the other kid trotted up to me.

"Where's your monkey, horse-boy?" she said, trying to get the horse to stop. Instead of pulling back on the reins, she leaned back in the saddle and nearly fell over the mare's rear.

I tried not to laugh. "Gorilla. He's up ahead of us in Calhoun."

The other kid rode up and grabbed Reya's reins and stopped her horse. "I told you, you gotta pull back on the reins."

"I am," she snapped. She spotted Lou holding the crossbow to her side. "Your girlfriend going to shoot us?"

I turned to Lou and motioned for her to put the crossbow

down. She refused. "She's not my girlfriend." Kimball started to growl. I placed my hand on his head and tried to sooth him. "Doesn't look like you're too popular around here," I said to Reya.

"What of it?" she said. She peered into the back of our wagon. "What you got in there that we might want?"

"A lot," I said, "but you can't have any of it."

"You best look at Devlin and Miles. They got something to say about that."

I looked at her two minions. They were pointing what looked like two nine-millimeter guns at us. I chuckled. "I guess you didn't get the memo. Guns don't work any more."

"The kinds that fire bullets don't," she said smugly. "But these kind shoot darts. They're air pistols."

I pointed to Lou. "In case you aren't of aware of it, arrows do a lot more damage than darts."

She looked confused. She searched and searched for a reasonable retort to my logic, but she couldn't come up with any.

The other kid climbed off his horse, "Reya will you stop trying to bully the kid."

"Shut up, Roy. I'm in charge." She shot him an evil look.

"Hell of a lot of good it's done us. We're about to starve to death." Roy walked toward me. "Look, just ignore my sister," he said. "All we really want to know is if you'll share some of your food with us."

"Sure," I said, "but why don't you just go to a grocery store and take what you need."

He looked embarrassed. "Ask her." He shot a thumb toward Reya.

"Because we're bandits," she said proudly. "We don't shop in grocery stores. We take from unsuspecting travelers."

He turned to her. "Look around, Reya. There aren't that many travelers to take from."

"What are you doing, Roy?" She hopped off her horse. "You shouldn't be undermining my authority." Devlin and Miles still had their air guns trained on us, but they were more than mildly amused by the fight between the brother and sister.

"You're a real idiot, you know that?" Roy said. "You're too busy playing bandits to know that me, Devlin, and Miles are about to fall over from hunger."

"Guys," I said, but they didn't hear me. They continued their argument.

"I suppose you think it's easy being the leader," Reya said.

"You're not the leader," Roy shouted.

I went to the wagon and pulled out a box of granola bars. I walked over and handed bars to Devlin, Miles, and Roy. All the while, Reya and Roy were arguing over her role in their troupe. I tried to hand a granola bar to Reya, but she slapped it away.

"What are you doing?" she asked.

"I'm sharing our food with you," I said.

"You are not sharing your food with us." She looked at the others in her gang. "Put those granola bars down." Devlin was just about to raise the bar to his mouth when she gave the order. He wanted to disobey, but he thought better of it. Miles followed Devlin and dropped the granola bar.

Roy looked at her defiantly. He ripped open the granola bar.

"Stop that," she said.

Roy smiled and took a bite.

"That's it. You're out of the gang."

"Fine," Roy said with his mouth full of granola. "I'd much rather ride with..." He turned to me. "What was your name?"

"Oz."

He turned back to Reya. "I'd much rather ride with Oz, anyway. At least they eat."

She let out a low frustrated scream and headed back to her mount when Devlin's horse suddenly reared. The jolt almost threw him from the saddle. He reached to grab hold of the horse's neck and inadvertently pulled the trigger on his air gun. Reya yelped and put both hands on her backside. Devlin had shot her in the right butt cheek.

Lou and I struggled not to laugh. Roy did not show the same restraint. He bent over in spasms of laughter as he watched his sister hop around the interstate trying to pull the dart from her butt.

I looked at Lou. "You better help her." Lou jumped from the wagon and handed me Nate in his sling before she walked over to Reya.

Reya was dancing in little circles now. "Get it out! Get it out!"

Lou reached her and calmly stopped Reya. The injured bandit was a full foot taller than the little warrior. "Breathe deep," Lou said holding Reya's arms and looking up at her. Reya did as requested. Lou reached around and pulled the dart from her rear end. It had penetrated fairly deep. "C'mon," Lou said, "we've got a first aid kit in the wagon."

Reya looked at Lou suspiciously. She thought about declining her offer, but realized that, given the location of her wound, riding a horse was probably next to impossible. She grudgingly limped to the wagon following Lou.

Devlin and Miles immediately jumped from their horses and picked up their granola bars. They frantically tore off the wrappers and started chomping away.

"We've got somebody waiting for us in Calhoun," I said to Roy. "You want to come along?"

He smiled and said, "Absolutely."

***

When we reached the Calhoun exit, Valerie and Tyrone were justifiably unhappy at the presence of Miles, Devlin, Roy, and Reya. Reya had ridden in our wagon on her belly the whole way, her horse tied to the back. She moaned and complained the entire way. She mostly wanted us to be aware that just because we were helping her didn't mean that she was beholden to us in any way. I assured her that we expected nothing in return.

Wes had gorged himself on three cans of chicken, and he was napping on the side of the road when we arrived. The puppies were climbing all over him licking chicken grease from his shirt.

Ajax gave our old adversaries a curious glance from the VW bus and then returned to resting comfortably. He looked terribly depressed. Valerie said she could not get him to eat. I invited Roy and the others to help themselves to any food we had. Lou was more than a little upset that I was being so nice to these self-described bandits, but I had a reason. We needed more allies. I had a feeling things were about to get a lot stickier for us.

I climbed in the back of the bus with Ajax. He had his back to me. His blanket and doll were uncharacteristically out of his reach. I grabbed them and crawled to him. I attempted to hand him the blanket and doll, but he shooed them away. "You all right, big guy?" I asked.

He huffed.

"What can we do for you to make you feel better?" It

was a question my Mom had always asked me when I was feeling under the weather. Somehow it seemed to help me. I was hoping it would do the same for Ajax.

He rolled over on his back and signed, "Bring baby to Keepers."

"We will," I said. "You should get some rest. We need you at full strength." I turned to leave, but he grabbed my arm.

"Warrior friend," he signed. He cupped his huge hand and pulled me to his side. I tried to pull away, but he didn't want to let me go. After a few seconds of struggling, I gave up and lay next to him.

Minutes passed and Wes stuck his head inside the bus. "What's with these stragglers you picked up?"

I slid from a now groggy Ajax's grasp and quietly exited the VW bus. "They were hungry."

"They're bad seeds, Oz." He guided me to the back of the van. "The girl is full of piss and vinegar and the little fat one has already gone through a row of Oreos."

"We've got enough to go around."

"That ain't the point. We don't know nothing about these people..."

"Yes, we do," I said. "They've tried to rob me three times. They're bandits."

"Rob you?" He was incredulous. "What in the name of Knotty Pines are you doing letting a bunch of bandits eat our food?"

"They're not very good bandits." I laughed, but he didn't get the joke. "Look, we need all the reinforcements we can get..."

"Reinforcements?" He threw his hands up in the air. "You're letting this warrior stuff go to your head. We're one old fat redneck mechanic and a bunch of kids. We ain't warriors.

Now, I think this trip to Charleston is just a fool's errand, but you had your heart set on it, so I figured I'd come along, but this warrior talk and fightin' them Greasywhoppers is just plain dumb. There ain't no way around it. You're going to get yourself and all the others killed."

"Wes," I said as emphatically as I could without sounding angry. "This is something we have to do. I didn't want to believe it at first, but..."

"But what?" he asked.

"If we can get Nate to the Keepers, I think we can find a way to get everything back." I had tried to keep myself from believing it, but as the days went by, I was starting to convince myself that our mission wasn't just to save the Storytellers, but to restore our old world, to bring back our parents, and Wes's sister and everything else as it was before the Takers came. I had nothing more than a gut feeling, but it was a feeling I couldn't shake.

"You're nuts, boy," Wes said as he chortled at my expense. "You're just out and out nuts." He put his hands on his hips and dropped his chin to his chest. "But seeing how you're about the closest thing to a friend I got in what's left of this upside down world, I'm willing to lend you my support."

I smiled.

"That don't mean I believe a lick of this nonsense, but I got to admit, I've seen some pretty crazy things in the last couple of weeks." He massaged the back of his neck. "I guess your theory ain't any crazier."

I extended my hand and he shook it enthusiastically. We both smiled and turned to see the group of newcomers rifling through our supplies in the wagon. "You sure about these bandits of yours?" he asked.

"I'm not sure of anything," I said walking towards the wagon.

Kimball was sitting on the road watching the bandits with a distrusting glare. His ears were upright and he sniffed the air. The eight puppies had gathered around him and were playing in his shadow.

I stepped up on the wagon and perched myself on the side. "You all getting everything you need?"

Devlin and Miles didn't bother to answer. Their mouths were full with an assortment of food. Reya stood gingerly, trying to pretend she wasn't enjoying the feast she had finally agreed to take part in.

Roy smiled with peanut butter on the corners of his mouth. "This sure is appreciated," he said.

"No problem." I waved his gratitude off. "Look, what are you all planning to do?"

"What do you mean?" Reya said, bitter and insolent.

"I mean do you plan on going with this bandit thing forever or do you see yourselves doing something else?" I treaded very carefully because I knew how intensely committed Reya was to her moniker of bandit.

Devlin raised his head from his frosted apple pie pocket, "What else is there?" Particles of food shot from his mouth as he spoke.

"There is nothing else," Reya snapped.

"I was thinking you might join us," I said.

"To do what?" Miles said after a long sustained belch.

"We're going to Atlanta," I said. I was beginning to get sick watching Miles and Devlin eat. They ended up wearing most of the food.

"Why Atlanta?" Roy asked.

"We don't care where you're going," Reya interrupted. "We're headed someplace else."

Miles stopped eating at hearing this news. He turned to

his leader and wiped the slop from his face with his shirtsleeve. "Where we going?"

"Wherever I say," Reya said, her voice shrill yet commanding.

Roy ignored his sister's announcement. "What's in Atlanta?"

I didn't know exactly how to answer. I mapped my argument out in my head before I spoke. "We're on a mission," I said trying to sound as confident as I could. "We're going to fight the Greasywhoppers."

"What's a Greasywhopper?" Devlin asked.

"The monsters," I said.

Everyone stopped eating. They all looked at each other and then me. Roy spoke. "The things? The people-eaters?"

I nodded.

Miles slowly chewed his food. "Why would you want to do that?"

"We don't want to," I assured him. "But it's the only way we can get Nate to the Keepers."

Reya tried to remain indifferent to my story, but she couldn't contain her increasing interest any longer. "Who's Nate?

I pointed to Lou who was changing Nate's diaper. "That's Nate."

Reya laughed. "The baby?" She felt a twinge of pain coming from her dart wound. She flinched and gently rubbed her butt cheek. "We'll just go our own way. You kids go off and get your baby to your Keepers and leave us out of it."

"I'll go with you," Roy said.

Reya was enraged. "No you won't."

"Those things ate Mom and Dad, Reya. You saw them. I'm going to make them pay." The hatred was bubbling up inside of him as he spoke.

"Yeah, I saw them," she said. "There's no way we can beat them. They'll eat us, too."

"We've already beat them three times," I said.

She looked at me. "You lie."

"It's the truth," Lou said, standing with Nate in her arms.

"I don't believe it," Reya said. Her dart wound still burning. "They're too strong and too fast. I've seen them with my own eyes."

I remained as level-headed as I could. "But they only know how to do one thing, eat. We've killed four of them."

"And how many have you lost by fighting?" Reya asked, stern and unwavering in her opposition to joining us in our mission.

I thought about Stevie Spangler and his horrible muffled screams as the Taker swallowed him. "One."

"That's one too many," she said. "We'll do just fine by not fighting."

"That's not true," I said. This time I raised my voice and stood. "They brought the fight to us. They started this. Just because you don't want to fight them doesn't mean they're not going to get you. It's not a matter of 'if.' It's a matter of 'when.' We have a better chance of beating them if we take the fight to them, on our terms, than if we just sit and hope that they won't ever find us. Cowards hide, and they devour cowards."

"He's right," Roy said. "We have to stand up to them."

Reya's lower lip began to tremble. She crossed her arms in front of her and tried not to cry, but the tears slowly formed in the corners of her eyes. "They'll kill us."

"Maybe," I said. "But maybe we'll kill them."

She bowed her head. "I'm scared. I don't want to die."

Miles and Devlin were shocked by Reya's sudden

admission. They had never seen her this way before. They saw her as tough and hard-nosed, but there she was, tears falling freely now, hands shaking. She was just a teenager who was running from the horrors she had seen.

Roy approached her and put his arm around her shoulder. "We have to do this for Mom and Dad."

She looked up at him. She wanted to protest. She wanted to get her roughrider persona back, but it was gone. She was shaken to her core. She nodded and laid her head on her brother's shoulder.

I refrained from pumping my fist in the air. I didn't think it was appropriate. I looked at Devlin and Miles. They looked at each other. Eventually they shrugged their shoulders and returned to gulping down their food.

I walked over and shook Roy's hand. "Glad to have you aboard."

He only half-heartedly smiled. "Can't say I'm glad to be aboard, but if there's one thing I've been wanting to do, it's making those ugly monsters pay for what they did to my parents."

I squeezed his hand to let him know I meant what I was about to say, "We will," I said. "We will."

***

We were a caravan now, a 1972 VW bus, two Belgian horses pulling a wagon full of passengers and supplies, and four spotted Tiger horses with young unskilled riders (me included) of different degrees on their backs. Wes held back on his NASCAR driver instincts and drove at a pace we could match. Lou drove the wagon, while I took over Reya's mount, who Devlin for some reason called Chubby even though he was no bigger than the other Tiger horses. Chubby was a bit sprier than Phil and Ryder. He had the urge to run, and I had the fear that he would take off at any moment. I was a more confident rider than I was when Wes first introduced me to the horses in Manchester, but I had not experienced a horse at a spirited gallop yet, much less a full out run. I wasn't all together sure I could handle it. I gripped the reins tightly and tried to fight the run out of him, but he was raring to go.

"Might as well let him get it out of his system," Roy said. He had been shaking his head for the past fifteen minutes watching me fighting the inevitable.

I tried to think of an excuse why the horse should not run, but I could not think of anything. Finally, I just blurted out the truth. "I can't ride that well. I don't know if I can handle a run."

He guided his horse next to mine. "There's only one way to find out." He slapped Chubby on his hindquarters and whistled loudly.

The horse reared slightly and then bolted down the interstate. I spread my arms out and held loosely to the reins. The rest of my body flopped uncontrollably. We quickly passed the VW bus.

"Squeeze your legs to his body," Roy shouted. "Move with him, not against him!"

I was too panicked to listen to his instructions at first, but as the horse grew faster and faster I implemented his advice. Before long, it felt as if I were riding the horse instead of just sitting on him, my fate at the mercy of his whims. I brought my hands in and tightened my grip on Chubby's reins. It was an incredible feeling of power. I could feel the horse's muscles restrict and contract as it moved its hooves across the paved terrain. I steered the mare toward the median to get him off the pavement. Once he touched grass, he dug his hooves in and picked up the pace. We were flying and I involuntarily hooted.

I looked behind me. Roy had his horse, Mr. Mobley, running at full speed. Roy was dipped down in the saddle, almost hugging the animal's neck. They were gaining on us. I kicked Chubby in the ribs and prayed I wasn't pushing my luck. The horse snorted and puffed. I could feel him trying to pick up the pace, but he couldn't go any faster. I looked back again. Roy and Mr. Mobley were even closer now. They would overtake us at any minute. I looked beyond him, and was amazed how far behind the others were now. We had covered an incredible distance in a short period of time.

Roy pulled up beside me. "Looks like you can handle it," he said, his voice raised to be heard over the pounding hooves of our horses.

"Yeah," I said, "but I'm not sure I can get him to stop."

"Just ease back on the reins. Not too hard." He showed me. His horse slowed to a gallop and then stopped.

I followed his example. Chubby slowed to a fast walk. He was out of breath from the exercise. I was out of breath from the excitement.

Roy and Mr. Mobley rode up beside us. "That was fun."

"That was incredible," I said, my voice exuding excitement. I heard a click and a hiss come from the two-way on my belt. I looked back and the caravan was about a mile behind us. The click and hiss came again. I unclipped the radio and pushed the talk button. "This is Oz, go ahead." There was no response. I tried again. "This is Oz."

A voice I didn't recognize answered back. "Hello, Oz." The tone was low and brooding. The words crackled from the radio, cold and piercing.

"Who is this?" I asked the question even though I really

didn't want to know the answer. Roy appeared drained and pale. I imagine I looked the same way.

A throaty laugh crept out of the two-way's tiny speaker. "We're coming."

Mr. Mobley and Chubby came to a complete stop. I wanted to drop the radio and have my sturdy Tiger horse crush it with one of its hooves, but I knew I couldn't do it. "Who's coming?" We peered up in the sky, and watched in amazement as the clouds spelled out the word, "Délons."

The laugh shot out of the two-way again, and then in a sing-songy voice the answer came over the radio, "The Délons are coming, the Délons are coming."

I looked at Roy. He was white as a sheet. "What are Délons?"

"Day longs," I said. I turned Chubby around. "C'mon, we have to get back." I nudged the steed in the ribs and bounded toward our caravan.

"What are Day longs, then?" Roy and Mr. Mobley were running neck and neck with us.

"Don't know," I said, "but they're not the welcome wagon, that's for sure."

We rode back to the caravan at an even greater speed than we left. Lou did not recognize the alarm in our expressions when we pulled to a stop next to the wagon. She rolled her eyes at what she perceived as boys-will-be-boys antics on horseback. "You two having a good time?"

I climbed down from Chubby. "Stop!" I yelled.

Wes looked out of the van's window. "What for?"

"Just stop," I said, sounding more demanding than I had intended.

The bus and the others came to a stop. Everybody eyed Roy and me curiously. "We've got visitors. Who's got the two-way?"

Wes disappeared back into the VW bus and then returned to the window holding the two-way radio. "It's right here."

"Did you just hear... something?" I asked.

"On the radio?" He looked perplexed. "No. Did you try to call?"

I shook my head. "Okay we need to be alert. Wes, Roy, Lou, and Reya, grab the crossbows and quivers. Everybody else grab the hunting vests and load the pockets with firecrackers. Make sure to get a pocket blowtorch." I jumped up in the wagon and searched through my stuff until I found what I was looking for, J.J.

Wes stepped out of the bus. "What's going on?"

"Day longs," I said. "Make sure Ajax stays put. He's in no condition to fight." I climbed back on top of Chubby.

"Where are they?" Lou asked.

"Don't know," I said. I watched as the others scrambled to get ready for a fight.

"They called us on the radio," Roy said.

"What's a day long?" Reya asked.

"Délon," Roy said, pronouncing it like the sound of a single horse gallop. He looked at me. "At least I think that's what he said."

"Whatever," Reya snapped. "What is it?"

Lou pointed to the purple crack in the sky. "It made that."

Devlin pulled out his air pistol.

"Don't think that will do much good," I said.

"Damned if it won't," Miles said, holding his air pistol. "We shoot the suckers in the eyes, you can bet it will do some good."

"Are you that good of a shot?" I asked, not really hiding the doubt in my tone.

"Heck, yeah." Devlin smiled.

"You better be," I said.

Everybody armed themselves. They all stood around waiting for my next set of orders. It was only then I realized that I had taken charge of our defense. It was not a conscious choice on my part. I was simply reacting to what I thought was an impending attack. I struggled to find the right words to say to them. I wasn't the oldest. I wasn't the strongest. I wasn't the most experienced combatant. But there I was with a group of fighters waiting for instructions from me. Finally I spoke. "We should keep moving. I saw a sign for an Alltoona Lake not too far ahead. We'll need somebody to ride point to scout it out."

Roy cleared his throat. "I'll do it."

I considered his offer. I felt like I should do it, but I didn't want to put that much separation between Nate and me. After all, I was ultimately responsible for him. "Fine." I threw him my two-way. "Take this."

"Why does he have to go?" Reya was fuming. She didn't like her brother being sent on such a dangerous mission.

"Because I volunteered, Reya." Roy was coarse with his sister.

Reya stomped over to me. She looked up at me sitting on Chubby's back. "Send somebody with him."

"I can't," I said. "We have to protect our cargo." I motioned toward Lou and Nate.

"I'll go with him," Reya said.

"No you won't." Roy turned Mr. Mobley south. "If we're going to survive this thing, we stick together and do as Oz says." He kicked Mr. Mobley and darted down the interstate.

Reya pursed her lips together and sighed deeply. "Who made you boss?" she asked.

It was a question I couldn't answer so I ignored her. "Everybody load up, and keep your eyes peeled."

Reya thought about asking the question again. She wanted to defy me so badly I could see it in her face, but she didn't. I don't know why exactly, but I'm guessing her concern for her brother began to take over her every thought. She turned and climbed back on the wagon.

Our caravan moved slowly. The sound of a small VW engine and bounding horse hooves echoed across the empty interstate. We all kept a wary eye on every inch of road, countryside, and sky. We didn't speak. We were all afraid that any distraction would be a costly one. I rode in front of Wes's tiny bus. Devlin and Miles brought up the rear. We looked like we were from an old western movie I had seen with Pop, a group of marshals giving a Wells Fargo stagecoach an escort to Dodge city.

Some 45 minutes later, we got our first call from Roy. He had found a campground off I-75. He would wait for us at exit 290.

"I didn't see any signs of trouble," he said. "You can breathe easy."

"Not likely," I said. I turned Chubby around to inform everybody that Roy was safe, and he had found a place for us to bed down for the night. Best of all, he reported that we had a safe passage. I was hoping that it would put the others more at ease than it did me.

As I made my way to the wagon, I gave Wes the news, and he informed his passengers, Tyrone and Valerie. Chubby moved past the van and we approached the wagon. I was about to give the others the news when I saw something on the horizon behind us that gave me pause. Then again I couldn't be sure if I saw anything. Though the temperature was in the fifties and the pavement below me wasn't conducting any heat, I was hoping I was seeing a heat-induced mirage. Far off in the distance, I saw what looked like an army marching our way. It stretched across both sides of the interstate, and the soldiers were the size of specks, thousands of them, all dressed in black. I blinked my eyes to try and push them out of my vision but they were still there.

Miles saw my awed expression. "What's up, boss?" He turned to look over his shoulder to try and see what had me so spooked. He had no reaction.

My gaze went from the approaching horde to Miles and back to the advancing throng. They were gone. Miles clearly had not seen them. "Nothing," I said not sounding very convincing. I turned Chubby around next to the wagon and we trotted along side the others. My head was turned to the rear. I looked for the marching people to reappear.

"Did Roy call?" Reya asked. I didn't immediately answer. My eyes were fixed on the real estate behind us. "Captain Kid," Reya said, her voice impatient and terse.

I snapped out of my fixation. "What?"

"Roy – did he call?"

"Yeah, yeah, he called. Everything is fine. He found a campground for us." I tapped Chubby on his ribs with my heels. "Let's pick up the pace." I ran up to tell Wes the same thing. I was filled with a sudden sense of urgency.

***

As promised, Roy was waiting for us at exit 290. He escorted us to McKaskey Creek Campground. The mixture of the evergreens and turning fall colors made it a picturesque spot for traveling campers or, in our case, traveling warriors. A slight wind blew in from the east and turned the lake into a churning pale green pool. Had I not been worried about the mission we were on, the impending next meeting with the

Takers, the eerie call from the Délons, and the either imagined or real marching army to our rear, I would have found the atmosphere very relaxing. As it was, I was a bubbling caldron of trepidation and fear. I could not escape my inner feeling of doom. I scanned our ragtag group, and cursed myself for getting them involved in this. I should have walked out of the Kroger's grocery store the first night I met Wes and Lou, and I should have kept on going until I reached the interstate. Then none of them would be here. I sat on a picnic table away from the others, kicking myself for even leaving my parents' closet.

Wes and Roy approached me with some fishing poles. "Where'd you get those?" I asked.

Roy smiled. "There's a bait and tackle shop up the road. I got one for everybody." He handed me a rod and reel. "Got a tackle box full of spinners and lures."

"I'm the king of fishing," Wes said, his voice almost giddy. "Alltoona's known for its stripers and rock fish. Bet you I hook the biggest."

I looked at the rod and reel and tried to make myself seem excited. I couldn't pull it off, and Wes noticed.

"C'mon, Oz," he said. "Kick back a little. Relax. There's enough trouble ahead to keep us occupied for the next hundred years or so. Might as well enjoy the simple things when you can."

I smiled out of courtesy more than sincerity. "What's the winner get?"

"What?" he asked.

"Your bet. What's the winner get?"

"Oh, well the joy of watching all the losers clean and cook up the day's catch."

I smiled, this time sincerely. I had been so down in the dumps it had not occurred to me that fishing would not only provide us with some much needed distraction from our current situation, but it would also provide us with a hot, freshly cooked meal. Somehow adding that little practical matter to the task made it even more enjoyable. When you do something out of necessity, it always feels more rewarding. I jumped off the table, and we all headed for the rocky shore.

I cocked back the open face reel and tossed my spinner into the murky lake water. It was as if I were instantly bathed in an invisible shield of relaxation. The sound of the clicking gears, the gentle splash of the water, the breeze blowing through the colored leaves, it was so calming that I forgot all about Takers, and crossbows, and firecrackers, and battle plans. It poured out of my mind like water pours through a break in a damn. I looked up and down the shore and was happy to see everybody in our group was fishing. Ajax and Kimball even sat with Tyrone and Valerie, patiently waiting for them to untangle their lines and make their first cast.

Wes was true to his proclamation. He was the king of fishing. He not only caught the biggest, he caught the most. There was a mixture of striper, largemouth bass, and perch. The biggest was a striper that Wes bragged weighed at least 15 pounds. The losers of the bet pitched in and cleaned the bounty under Wes's very close and often irritating supervision.

We cooked the fish over an open fire and ate what was by far my most hearty and delicious meal since I woke up from my fever-induced slumber. I was not a big fan of fish, but at the moment, I would have told you my favorite food of all time was anything with gills and a dorsal fin.

Ajax and Kimball were the only ones who did not eat the fish. I was afraid Kimball would choke on the bones so I fed him his normal diet of Alpo. Ajax wasn't a meat eater by nature, so he stuck to a small portion of apples and berries. His appetite wasn't quite back to normal, but I could tell from his eyes that he was getting back to his old self.

We ate all the while knowing that just a few short hours ago, we were preparing to do battle with the Délons. Had Roy not been witness to the voice on the radio, I'm sure the others would have believed I was just being overly paranoid. Where did they go? I didn't tell anybody about my sighting back on the interstate. I couldn't be sure it was real since Miles had not seen anything at all. There was a possibility that the stress of the situation had played tricks on my mind. Perhaps I did see a mirage. The conditions weren't perfect for it, but it was possible.

We hadn't given up on the idea the Délons would make an appearance, but as time passed we were becoming less and less apprehensive about it. We gathered around the campfire and talked about better days. Roy spoke about his parents. Reya still remained aloof and didn't participate much in our conversation, but she smiled as her brother talked about their mom and dad. Their father was a truck driver, and their mother was a special education teacher. They were hard working people who were strict but loving parents. Miles lived with his mom and saw his dad on weekends. Truth be known, he didn't really like going to his dad's house. Miles didn't get along with his dad's ever-changing lineup of girlfriends. He spent most of his time playing Play Station 2. He was a Madden freak just like me. Devlin lived with his grandparents. His dad ditched him when he was three and his mom died in a car crash a year later. He never really felt loved by his grandparents. They cared for him the best they knew how, but they were cordial and off-putting when they interacted with him. He sometimes thought that, given the opportunity, his grandparents would have gladly turned him over to the state and washed their hands of him.

As the fire crackled and popped into the evening, Reya finally asked the question she had wanted to ask for some time. "Why don't we just give them the baby?"

There was a thick, unsettling silence that hung in the air after she spoke. I could tell some of the others had been wondering the same thing. The baby after all was a Storyteller, and it was a Storyteller that was responsible for bringing the Takers into our world.

"We have to get him to the Keepers," I said, trying to sound assured that was the best thing to do.

"Besides," Lou said looking up at the purple crack in the sky, "you see what happens when they get their hands on a Storyteller."

"So let's kill it." Reya said so directly and coldly that it chilled me.

"What did you say?" I was daring her to say it again.

"Reya!" Roy wanted to pounce on her for saying such a stupid thing.

"I'm serious. He ain't nothing but a baby now. He ain't no Storyteller yet. We should kill him before he causes more pain and suffering in this world." There was a certain unassailable logic to her statement. If we kill Nate, then he can never grow up to be a Storyteller. The Takers can't use him to bring forth their army.

Ajax was showing more signs of his old self now. The more Reya talked, the more agitated he became. He hollered as she continued to make her case.

"All I'm saying is, we should think about it. The Greasywhoppers might go away if the baby is dead." She avoided looking anyone in the eyes.

"There's nothing to think about," I said, the anger dominating my tone. "We have to get Nate to the Keepers. If the Greasywhoppers want him because he can help them, then that means he can hurt them, too."

"A whole lot of trouble over a little retard," Reya snapped.

My heart stopped when I heard her use that word. I stood, my hands balled in a fist. "What did you say?"

She stood and towered over me. "He's a retard. He's got Down syndrome. Believe me, I know. My mother taught those little short bus freaks."

I looked at Nate who was in Lou's arms. "How do you know?"

She smiled smugly. "My momma worked with retards of all ages. She looked after babies, too. Look at Nate's ears, they're what's called dysplastic, all tiny and funny shaped. You see his fifth finger is dysplastic too." None of us knew what she meant. "There's only one joint." We all looked at Nate and then each other. "He's got the retard eyes, too..."

"Stop saying that word," I said. I was more than a little angry. I could have beaten the living crap out of her, but I controlled myself. "If you ever harm a hair on that kid's head or even so much as talk about it again, I'll feed you to a Greasywhopper myself."

Her mouth dropped. She was sizing me up to see if I could back up my threat. I could see that she was torn. Finally she turned to her brother. "Are you going to let him talk to me that way?"

"Hell, Reya, I was just about to shake his hand. You just don't know when to shut up." Roy stood and walked away.

Reya stomped a foot and groaned angrily. She hated me now more than ever because her brother had taken my side one too many times. I could see her plotting her revenge in her mind even as she sat back down and returned her steely gaze to the flames of the campfire.

I grabbed Nate from Lou and headed toward a nearby picnic table. Wes followed after me.

"You gotta do something about her," he said.

"We need her," I said, not knowing if I believed that any more.

"We need her like we need a thorn in our keisters," he said as I sat down.

Roy approached. "I can handle her."

"I don't think you can." Wes was insistent.

I raised my hand. "She stays," I said unapologetically. "Roy you're in charge of her. If she gets out of hand, you're going to have to make a choice."

Roy nodded. "I've already made my choice. I'm a warrior. I'll keep her under control."

"And if you can't?" Wes asked.

"I'll personally toss her out on her rear," Roy said unequivocally.

Wes looked at Reya sitting next the fire. "You may have to do more than that."

"Meaning?" Roy said.

"Meaning she's a hothead that won't go quietly." He turned back to Roy. "You prepared to do whatever's necessary?"

Roy swallowed hard. "Yeah."

I rocked Nate in my arms. "She'll come around," I said. "It won't come to that."

When Wes and Roy left, I focused my attention on Nate. Was Reya right about him? Did he have Down syndrome? If so, that would make him like both Stevies. One was a Storyteller and the other who could hear the Takers in his head. I thought about how I treated Stevie Dayton and was racked with guilt. I was the one who put the monsters in his head. I made him feel so useless and unwanted that he created the Takers. Stevie

Dayton wasn't responsible for the end of the world. I was. I held Nate close and vowed to myself that no one would ever treat him like I treated Stevie Dayton.

***

We posted sentries in shifts until morning. Six of us paired off in groups of two. Each pair took a three-hour shift. I'm not sure how necessary the guards were because none of us really slept more than a couple of hours. And, when we did sleep it was a restless unsatisfying respite from the insanity that came with being awake. The craziness waited for us in our dreams, too.

I took second shift with Wes. We kept each other awake reliving Titans football games. He was almost as big a fan as I was. Turns out he was there for the Music City Miracle, too. We both agreed it was the greatest play in the history of professional football.

It wasn't until late in our shift that we turned to more serious matters. After some talk about how the game of football related to war and battle strategies, Wes leaned in and said, "You know you're a born leader, kid."

I felt embarrassed and unworthy. "Nah, I'm just trying to get by."

He snickered. "Yeah, right. I've seen you in action, Oz. You answered the call, my friend. Not everybody does."

"You did," I said.

"Please, if you hadn't have come along, I'd still be sitting in that mattress store in Manchester. Everybody in this campsite tonight is here because of you." He yawned, and then continued. "Well, maybe not Reya, but she's a different story all together."

I caught his yawn and shook my head to fight off fatigue.

I surveyed the sleeping bodies in our camp. "I don't know if we can do it." I looked at Wes. "Win, I mean."

"Your job isn't to win," he said scratching his belly. "Your job is to lead. The winnin' will take care of itself." He could tell by my expression that I was confused. "The greatest army in the world with the greatest equipment and the perfect battle strategy can't win without a good leader." He motioned to the campground with his head. "That scraggly bunch of misfits don't care about the fight. They care about the man leadin' them into the fight. You understand?"

I tried to look like I did, but I wasn't sure. I had never been called a man before. I was waiting for him to correct himself and change it to boy, but he never did.

"Look," he said. "If you sacrifice yourself for them, they will die for you."

I nodded. "Some of us will die, won't we?" I had told Lou as much earlier, but now hearing somebody else say it, it really sunk in.

He ran his thumbnail across his lips and gave me a compassionate gaze. "Yeah, Oz, some of us will."

I smiled. "How do you know so much anyway?"

He laced his fingers behind his head and leaned back, his elbows out like chicken wings. "Because I'm an old fart."

***

When our shift ended I woke up Roy and Reya to relieve us. Reya was unhappy about the arrangement, but after some prodding by her brother she reluctantly agreed. I imagine they kept each other awake by arguing until morning.

Before lying down by the waning fire, I walked to the edge of the campground to pee. Before I could get my pants unzipped, I heard jumbled almost unintelligible voices from the trees above me.

"Look, everybody, it's Oz." Hundreds of voices giggled and hissed in response.

I froze. "Who-who's there?"

"Who-who?" A raspy voice called out. "Who-who?"

"The Délons are coming. The Délons are coming." The same sing-songy voice from the two-way belted out.

I looked around and wondered why no one else in the camp was reacting to the deafening babbling from the trees. Roy and Reya were in a heated argument, and the others were lying in the same position they were in before. I was the only one who could hear the voices in the trees.

"The Délons are coming," the voice said again.

"So, come on already." It was a foolish use of bravado considering that it was obvious they outnumbered us a hundred-fold.

"It's not your time, warrior," a voice to my left said.

"It's not your time," a voice to my right said.

"It's not your time," a voice whispered in my ear. I could feel its lifeless and stale breath on my neck. I backed away.

"You're not really here, are you?" I said.

"Wish you were here," a Délon giggled.

"We've so many warriors to fight," another moaned.

"The Délons are coming," the sing-songy voice said. The voice suddenly turned grave. "The Storyteller is ours." With that, the prattling stopped. They left as suddenly as they came. I scanned the tree line. Nothing. My ears ached from listening to the incessant mumbling. I stumbled backwards and struggled to get solid footing. Still in a state of semi-shock, I rejoined my sleeping comrades and sat next to the fire. The urge to pee had been scared out of me. I sat and stared into the hot embers of the fire. I looked up at the purple crack in the sky. A warrior was fighting the Délons tonight, of that I was sure. I pulled my knees to my chin and wrapped my arms tightly around my legs. I closed my eyes and tried to wish our fellow fighters to victory.

EIGHT

Atlanta, home of the NFL's Falcons. We arrived in the southern metropolis around mid-morning. The highway system was a twisted mass of concrete and steel spaghetti. On the side roads and looping bypasses, there were thousands of abandoned vehicles, but there were none on I-75. Wes was right. Somebody was giving us a clear path. I thought about his question. Was it a good thing or a bad thing? Something or somebody could be leading us into a trap. I shrugged the thought off. Even if they were, it didn't really matter. Our goal was to find the Keepers. If that meant fighting our way out of a trap, then so be it.

We stopped at a convenience store and picked up a city map. We were all a little surprised to see the store had been looted. About the only thing that remained were maps. It had been savagely stripped bare of everything else.

"Who do you suppose did this?" Miles asked.

"Survivors," Wes said.

"Survivors?" Devlin was picking through the wreckage looking for any morsel of candy. "Like us?"

I made my way across the broken glass and fractured display shelves to the counter and snatched a folded city map from a wire rack on what was left of the wall. I scanned the wreckage. "I wouldn't say they're exactly like us."

"Yeah," Wes said. "They don't appear to be as friendly as us." He looked at Reya and corrected himself. "Most of us, anyway."

She smirked at him as he exited the store.

"We should go," I said. Ajax stood on all fours in the doorway. He was feeling a hundred percent, and he was anxious to face the Takers again. He knew it was the only way to the Keepers. "We have to get to the zoo."

"Cool, the zoo," Devlin said.

"Alright," Miles gave his fat friend a high-five. "The zoo rocks!"

"You idiots," Reya said. "We ain't going there to sightsee." She flashed me an evil eye. "We're going there to die."

I started toward her. "Wrong." I stopped when we were side-by-side; shoulder to shoulder, her facing one way, me the other. Without looking at her I said, "We're going there to fight." I walked out of the store.

We had left the wagon and VW bus parked on the side of the interstate due to the congestion of abandoned cars on the on-ramp. Roy, Kimball, and Lou stayed behind to guard our supplies and Nate. Wes sat on Mr. Mobley and waited at the edge of the convenience store parking lot for the rest of us. I climbed aboard Chubby and stuck my hand out to help Miles aboard. Ajax started down the grassy slope to our awaiting caravan. After giving up on finding anything edible in the convenience store, Devlin exited and mounted his horse. Reya followed. We weaved our way through the maze of cars, some in pristine condition, some torn apart at the metal frame.

Miles was the first to spot the strangers approaching from the east side of the overpass. There were a couple dozen men on horseback headed our way. They were all dressed in military uniforms, but they were unkempt and none of them exuded the discipline and pride of an average soldier.

"What do you make of that?" Wes asked.

I shrugged my shoulders. "Our survivors?" I turned to

Reya and Devlin. "Get down to the wagon and bus. Tell Roy to drive the VW. Keep heading south."

"What are you going to do?" Reya asked.

"We won't be far behind," I said.

She watched as the band of horsemen inched their way closer.

"Do you need me, boss?" Miles asked. I could tell that he wanted to go with Devlin and Reya.

"No, we can handle it."

Miles quickly dismounted Chubby and climbed aboard Devlin's steed. Together with Reya, they headed down the on-ramp to the caravan.

Wes and I rode slowly toward the horsemen. They moved methodically around the abandoned vehicles. The rider in the middle turned to the others and said something. Two riders suddenly broke away from the pack and headed down the off-ramp on the other side of the overpass. The rider who had spoken galloped toward us with three other riders. The others stayed behind.

As they got closer, I recognized the one in the middle. He was a large man with a thick neck and a muscular build. His name was Pepper Sands, a linebacker for the Atlanta Falcons. I knew him because I saw him get three sacks against my Titans just last month. My Pop had cursed his name every time he broke through the offensive line and crushed our quarterback. I'd studied his resume later that night on the internet.

We met in the middle of the overpass. I was star struck. The man was a professional athlete that could bench press a Buick. Now, here we were face-to-face, both designated leaders. In a sense, we were equals. The idea blew my mind.

"You fellas passing through or looking for a place to hang your hat?" Pepper asked.

I couldn't bring myself to answer. I was mesmerized by his celebrity.

"Passing through," Wes said.

Pepper pointed to our caravan. "How'd you get the van to work?"

"Runs on propane." Wes wasn't as impressed by the great Pepper Sands as I was.

Pepper turned to his men and laughed. "Damn, boys, it runs on propane." His men laughed with him. He turned back to us. "There's a passing through tax." He sat up straight in his saddle and involuntarily flexed his forearm.

"A passing though tax?" Wes was incensed.

"That's right," Pepper said.

"Says who?" Wes asked. His voice was a little too sharp for Pepper's liking.

"Says me." Pepper moved his horse closer. He was headed for Wes when he stopped at the sound of my voice.

"What's the price?" I asked.

Pepper smiled. "Now the kid's got brains." He looked at his cronies. "The children are the future, boys." They laughed. "How many in your party?" he asked me.

"Does it matter?" The star worship was starting to wear off. This time I sat up in my saddle and flexed what little muscle I had in my forearms.

"Don't get smart, kid." He looked at our caravan. "The VW bus will do."

I followed his gaze and spotted the two horsemen who had broken off earlier riding toward our group. "No," I said. "You can't have the van. We've got food and weapons. You can take your choice."

Pepper circled me on his horse. "I said we'll take the van." I could see he was wearing a small tank on his back. Tubing and a metal nozzle were stuffed in the back of his pants. It was a small flame-thrower.

"And I said no."

He didn't know what to make of me. I was thirteen, all of 100 pounds soaking wet, yet I was standing my ground like I was the giant and he was the puny one. "Kid, do you know who I am?"

"Pepper Sands," I said. "You had twelve and a half sacks last year. You played college ball at Michigan. You still hold the record for tackles in a season there."

"Good, then you know my nickname ain't Pepper Grinder for nothing." He had an insufferable swagger that pissed me off. "I used to pulverize punks bigger than you for a living."

"You were a great football player," I said.

"You're damn right I was..."

I interrupted him. "But in case you haven't noticed, football season's over."

"What the hell..."

I raised my hand to shush him. "Like I said, I won't give you the van, but maybe we can work something out."

He studied me carefully. He had not expected my defiance, and he didn't know quite how to handle it. "What do you have in mind?"

I pointed to Wes. "That's Wes. He converted the VW bus to run on propane."

"You giving us your mechanic?" Pepper smiled.

"What are you doing, Oz?" Wes was a little peeved that I would trade him for safe passage.

"I won't give you my mechanic, but I'll give you his knowledge."

Pepper thought about the offer. He examined his crew. He finally gave his decision. "Deal".

"Not quite," I said.

Pepper wanted to leap out of his saddle and throttle me, but he showed remarkable restraint for a man who used to crush people for a living. "What do you mean, not quite?"

"I mean, what Wes knows could change your whole way of life. I need a little more than safe passage in exchange."

"You're pushing your luck, kid." He considered my statement. "What did you have in mind?"

I turned to Wes and smiled. "I need an army." Wes smiled back. For the first time, he knew where I was going.

***

"You're crazy, kid." Pepper Sands leaned forward in a leather recliner on the fifty-yard line in the Georgia Dome. His feet rested on the Falcon's logo. His men sat in recliners (all considerably less nice than Pepper's) behind him. They had made the Georgia Dome their home. The emergency lighting worked due to an industrial-sized solar powered generator. It was a 75,000 seat indoor stadium that made me feel even smaller than I already was. Even with it empty, I got the tiniest sense of the kind of thrill Pepper and his teammates must have felt on Sundays.

Wes, Roy, and I sat in folding chairs across from Pepper. The others in our party remained with our supplies in the underground loading dock area of the dome.

Pepper reclined in his chair. "You're asking too high a price."

"That's the offer," I said. "Take it or leave it."

He smiled. "You're a hard-nosed little snot, aren't you?" He snapped his fingers. A smallish mousy man stood up quickly and ran to Pepper's chair. "I'll give you Donny here." Donny's eyes opened wide. He had the look of a man who'd just been told he would volunteer to stand in front of a firing squad.

Wes snorted. "You gotta be kidding. He looks like a strong wind would break him in two. No offense, Donny."

Donny nodded and shrugged his shoulders as if he agreed with Wes's assessment of him.

"You're one to talk." Pepper pointed at me. "Your little general here hasn't hit puberty yet." He rubbed his hands together and cracked his knuckles. The popping bones made an echo in the cavernous dome. "I'll give you three men."

"All or nothing," I said.

"Kid, you're not really in any position to negotiate. I'm not about to send every man I've got to die just because you're on some silly mission."

"Fine," I said standing. I turned to Wes and Roy. "We're leaving."

Pepper bristled. "Hey, nobody told you that you could leave."

Wes and Roy slowed down, but I told them to keep walking. This enraged Pepper even more. I had my back to him, but I could feel him getting out of his chair.

"I said you can't leave!" He shouted. His voice bounced around the arena.

We kept walking.

"You can't beat them," he said. He had lost the command in his voice. He was scared.

I stopped and told Wes and Roy to do the same. I turned to Pepper. "Yes we can."

He tried to laugh and make it sound menacing, but it came out weak and unsteady. "What makes you so sure?"

"Because," I said, "we have to." Wes, Roy, and I continued to walk towards our party.

"Okay," Pepper said, sounding almost embarrassed that he

had been out negotiated by a kid. "We'll help, but not tonight and not without a game plan."

I stopped and turned with a smile on my face. "Deal."

***

Wes spent a good portion of the day showing the most mechanically inclined members of Pepper's group how to convert a gas-guzzling vehicle to one that runs on propane. Wes erupted into fits of frustration many times during the impromptu workshop, but eventually they came around and grasped the concepts Wes was trying to teach them.

I introduced Pepper to Ajax, while Lou sat nearby with Nate and Dr. Fine's book. Roy and the others in our group gathered around to listen to the next day's plans. Pepper invited only two of his men, Hollis and Shaw. The others milled around the south end zone. Hollis was tall and lean, if not a little on the lanky side. He did not speak unless spoken to, but he had the chiseled look of intelligence that did all his speaking for him. Shaw was the opposite of Hollis in almost every way. He was a rotund little man who swayed nervously as he flanked Pepper to his left. His left eye twitched distractingly and his belly rumbled almost continuously.

"You're trying to tell me this gorilla can talk?" Pepper said.

Ajax signed, "Gorilla think man dumb."

Lou giggled after she interpreted what Ajax had said.

"How do you like that?" Pepper said to Shaw. "A gorilla just called me dumb." The round man heckled more than laughed.

Ajax signed, "Go zoo now."

"He wants to go to the zoo now," Lou said. She was consulting the book less frequently than she had before. I realized she must have been studying Ajax's sign language on her own.

"Tomorrow," I said.

He signed, "Why?"

"We have to make a plan." I pointed to Pepper. "We have new warriors."

Ajax signed, "More warriors at zoo."

"Yes," I said. "More warriors for the zoo."

He grunted and hooted. He was clearly irritated. He signed, "More warriors at zoo."

"I think he literally means there are more warriors at the zoo," Lou said.

This surprised me. "What warriors?"

"Gorilla warriors," Ajax signed.

Pepper crossed his arms and raised an eyebrow. "Is he saying what I think he's saying?"

"Of course," I said. "Gorillas always know," I signed. "They've been waiting for this, preparing for this for generations."

"You expect us to fight along side a bunch of monkeys?" Pepper shook his head.

Shaw's stomach roared before he spoke. "If I want a bunch of bananas et, I'll call me some monkeys, but I got no use for 'em in a fight." He waited for his fearless leader to laugh, but Pepper ignored him.

"Apes," Devlin said.

I smiled. "That's right, apes."

"I don't give a damn if they're super-apes, I'm not asking my men to put their trust into a bunch of dumb animals."

"The Greasywhoppers can't see them," Lou said. She was more than a little offended that Pepper had insulted Ajax. "Besides I'd bet money this dumb animal is smarter than half the men in your group."

Shaw squinted one eye and looked her way. He was trying to determine if she was referring to him.

Kimball barked.

"Kimball, too," Lou added.

"Look," I said, "Ajax knows these things better than any of us. All the gorillas do. It's part of their folklore."

"You expect me to believe gorillas have a folklore." Pepper elbowed Hollis. "How do you like that, Hollis? These rubes think this gorilla is some kind of ape historian..."

"Historian? That's a good one, Pep," Shaw said trying to win favor with his boss.

Hollis cleared his throat. "I've seen a lot of weird things the last couple of weeks, Pepper. Once you've seen a monster eat your family, you'll believe just about anything. What they're saying doesn't sound all that crazy to me."

Pepper looked at his soldier. It was obvious Hollis had not questioned him before. He didn't quite know how to react.

Ajax started signing frantically.

Lou had trouble interpreting. "Day soon... He's going too fast." She gently reached out and grabbed his hands. "Slow down, Ajax. I can't understand you." He huffed and repeated his signs, this time slower and more pronounced. "Day longs come soon. Doctor knows. Must go zoo now," Lou said. "The Délons."

"What does he mean, 'doctor knows'?" I asked.

"What are the Délons?" Pepper asked.

"Monsters," Roy said.

"Wait a minute." Pepper twisted in his chair. "I thought you called them Greasywhoppers."

"The Délons are... different," I said. "We don't know much about them."

"Now hold on, we didn't sign up for this. We said we'd

help you with these Greasywhoppers at the zoo, but nobody said anything about these Dalungs, or whatever you call them."

Ajax signed, "Doctor knows," again.

"What doctor?" I asked.

Ajax huffed and motioned his head toward Hollis.

Hollis's expression changed. He tilted his head and studied the ape. "I think he means me."

"You?" I said.

He became even more reflective. "Interesting," he said after a long pause.

Pepper looked at his second. "What's interesting, Doc?"

"Doc?" I said.

"He was the team shrink." Pepper smiled. "He kept all us savages out of the loony bin and on the playing field."

"I'm a psychologist. I specialize in sports psychology." He spoke about his credentials unremorsefully in the present tense. "In particular, I train athletes in the art of mental imagery or visualization as it's most commonly called."

"He's a genius. My sack total went up thirty percent after he started working with me," Pepper proclaimed happily, as if it were still a relevant achievement.

"The key is to get athletes to visualize each play before it happens. In doing so, you increase motivation, focus, and endurance. The brain can duplicate physical energy without the actual physical activity. In effect, the brain tricks the body into thinking the outcome has already taken place. In a properly trained athlete, the actual event becomes a reflexive formality. In some cases, the lines between reality and imagination can become very blurred."

"What does this have to do with the Délons?" Roy asked.

"A colleague, Dr. Bashir, in Buffalo was working with

a group of patients that had underdeveloped brain functions for various reasons." In the telling of his past, Hollis had transformed himself from Pepper's number one, to proud psychologist before our very eyes. "Traditionally, society has taken the path of least resistance when treating such patients. The goal is to teach them to cope in society, but not to excel. Dr. Bashir had a different approach. He felt that through intensive mental imagery, these patients could do more than cope, they could thrive."

"This is all very interesting, Doc, but..."

Hollis cut Pepper off. "Let me finish."

Pepper gritted his teeth. He didn't like being cut off by his underling.

Oblivious to Pepper's frustrations, Hollis carried on. "It worked more successfully with some than it did with others, but what he found with his patients who suffered from Down syndrome was they possessed a keen talent for the mental imagery exercises."

There were those words again, Down syndrome. They'd haunted me since the day I walked into Stevie Dayton's house. It was absolute torture every time I heard them.

"In fact," Hollis said, "he found that with some of these patients the lines between reality and imagination not only became blurred, they were obliterated. Particularly in one case. He had one patient who developed what Dr. Bashir called Hyper Mental Imagery, or HMI. That is to say, this patient not only visualized prior events in his mind, he created events in the physical world; a snowy day in May, a particular food on the hospital menu every day, small things that he would image onto the physical world. Understand that these findings were largely discredited by mainstream scientists, but still they offer some fascinating possibilities."

"Doc, the Délons?" I said.

"Oh yes, of course." He put his hands behind his back and rose up on his toes. "This particular patient took to drawing what he wanted to image. They were quite spectacular drawings. In one noteworthy drawing he imaged a race of strange creatures that he called Délons. Anatomically they didn't make much sense. They were part man and virtually part everything else, thousands of tentacles that looked like spider legs on top of its head and outlining its corpse-like face, a set of insect mandibles for teeth, milky white protruding eyes, horrible, horrible looking creatures. "

"Why would he want to image something like that?" Pepper asked.

Hollis considered the question. "I don't know exactly, but it's likely he created the Délons to punish those who made fun of him. According to Dr. Bashir, he suffered enormous humiliation at the hands of his classmates."

Lou looked at me. I knew what she was thinking.

"Enough of this," I said. "We need to come up with a battle plan." I was harsh, and I didn't care. I wanted to get off the topic of HMI and retarded kids abused by their classmates. I had lived it. I didn't need to hear about it again.

"We still haven't settled on this Délon business," Pepper said.

I snapped. "We fight who we have to fight!" My voice carried throughout the entire dome. Pepper's men all turned my way. "Be a man, Sands!" I couldn't stop myself. I don't know if the pressure had finally gotten to me or the guilt for Stevie's death had been rekindled because of Hollis's little lecture on HMIs, but I was on the edge, and I brought Pepper with me.

Shaw snickered a hideous, insufferable laugh.

Sweat formed on Pepper's brow and his eyes turned blood

red. The veins on his neck started to convulse. He wanted to kill me, and I didn't blame him. I had challenged his manhood in his house in front of his men. If he was any kind of leader, he would have to make me pay. The only thing I had going for me was I that I was only 13 years old.

Roy pulled me aside. "What are you doing?"

"We don't have time for this, Roy. We need to be talking battle strategy..."

"Listen to me," he said. "You can't force this guy to help us. All you're going to do is piss him off."

I looked at the now enraged Pepper Sands and turned back to Roy. "Too late, I already did."

Unbeknownst to us, while we discussed a way to get Pepper back on our side, Shaw approached Lou and the baby. Kimball growled as the fat man waddled closer. Ajax stepped in front of Lou and Nate. Shaw's stomach gurgled loud enough to shift Roy's and my attention to the increasingly tense scene.

"I just want to say hello to the baby," Shaw said pleading his case to Ajax and Kimball.

They would have none of it. Ajax gave a short roar and tried to shoo Shaw away. Kimball was stooping lower and lower to the ground. He looked as if he were about to pounce at any moment.

Pepper stood. "Call off your pets, kid! In fact, pack up your stuff and get out of my house! Our deal's off!"

Shaw tried to move in closer to see the baby. Kimball snapped at his leg. "Hey, that ain't nice," he said, backing away.

"Kimball, back!" I yelled.

Wes approached. His puppies were on his heels. "What's going on?" The eight little junior Taker slayers saw Kimball and clumsily bounded towards him. Their demeanor became as vicious as Kimball's when they got closer to Shaw.

"Would you look at that," Wes said. "I ain't never seen them react to somebody like that before."

"Yeah," I said. I caught a quick glimpse of Shaw's face. His eyes started to tremble, and for a fleeting second they seemed to bug out from their sockets and turn a milky white, but it was for the briefest of seconds. I wondered if my mind was playing tricks on me again. I moved in and grabbed Kimball by the scruff of the neck and pulled him away. The puppies yapped and growled as menacingly as they could at Shaw, but they couldn't quite pull it off. As I was dragging Kimball away, I saw Ajax signing something.

Lou swallowed hard. "Day long here."

Ajax erupted and flung himself on top of Shaw.

"Get him off!" Pepper shouted. "Get him off!"

The man we thought was Shaw was pinned beneath Ajax's massive 400-pound frame, and began to morph before our eyes. His round shape shifted into a long slender build. Thin, hairy tentacles sprouted from his face and head. His eyes bulged and turned milky white. He opened his mouth and two vertical pinchers shot out and snapped at Ajax. The military uniform was replaced by a black tattered uniform that left some of the creature's purple skin exposed. It began to squawk like a bird. The sound suddenly started to come at us from all sides. Looking around the arena, we saw half of Pepper's men undergo the same change as Shaw. They pounced on their former comrades. The thrashing tentacles held tight to the victims' faces while the pinchers cut through to their brains.

Pepper didn't know what to do. He watched in horror as his men were ambushed and destroyed.

I turned to Roy while I held Kimball back. "Weapons! Now!" Roy raced to our supplies.

To Tyrone and Valerie, "Get Lou and Nate to the wagon."

To Devlin, "Go with them."

That left Reya, Miles, Wes, and me waiting in a defensive posture against the Délons. Hollis approached Ajax and the Délon who was once Shaw. The grotesque creature struggled against the great ape's weight, but to no avail. It looked up at Hollis and hissed.

"Interesting." The psychologist dropped to one knee and examined the Délon like it was a science experiment. "It matches the drawing perfectly."

The Délon squirmed and manically tried to work its arms free, but he was no match for Ajax's strength. "Come a little closer, Doc." The Délon spoke. "I'll show you something really interesting."

Hollis was floored. "It talks!"

Pepper backed his way to us. "Looks like the deal's back on, kid. Got any ideas?"

"Fight," I said. I let Kimball go and he bolted toward Ajax and the Délon.

Four Délons released the lifeless bodies of Pepper's men from their tentacles and focused their attention on us. The bodies flopped and twitched until they too morphed into Délons.

"That's not good," Wes said.

Roy galloped into the arena on Mr. Mobley's back carrying a sack and holding a loaded crossbow. He fired an arrow at one of the advancing Délons, striking it in the mouth. It continued toward us undaunted. Roy dropped the sack to the ground and our weapons spilled out. Wes, Miles, and Pepper grabbed the crossbows. I picked up J.J. and ran to Ajax's side. With a quick, unthinking thrust, I drove the sword through the Délon's head.

The creature flailed about and a putrid gas emanated from the open wound. Ajax rolled off the Délon.

Hollis looked up at me. "Interesting."

"You said that already." I pulled the sword out of the Délon's head and wielded it in front of me. The four Délons advancing toward us had become eight.

Wes, Miles, and Pepper readied their crossbows. They fired in unison. The arrows flew true and struck three of the Délons, but they had no effect. Reya gathered all the arrows and waited to hand them out as needed.

"Fall back," I said. "We have to get to the zoo."

I turned to Hollis. "C'mon, Doc. Time to go."

He stood and for the first time showed some concern, when he took in the carnage on the field behind him. "Oh my."

Wes, Miles, Reya, and Pepper wasted no time in falling back. They quickly backed toward the loading dock, their weapons loaded and ready to fire. Pepper made a small detour to retrieve his mini flamethrower and then fell back in line.

"Go with them," I said to Hollis. I turned to Kimball. "Kimball, wagon." He started for the loading dock, but stopped. He barked once. The puppies yelped and chased after him.

Roy fired another arrow from horseback, but something spooked Mr. Mobley, and the arrow flew far off target. The Tiger horse reared and bounded toward the scene of the massacre.

"Roy!" I shouted.

He had no control over Mr. Mobley. The horse approached the virtual sea of Délons with Roy frantically trying to reload his crossbow.

"Roy," Reya yelled. I turned to see Pepper and Miles dragging her to the loading dock.

I stepped forward. I had to help him. I had to. The fire was in my gut to race after him, but... I hesitated because helping him meant most certainly that I would die, and that terrified me.

The first Délon seized upon Mr. Mobley and drove him to the ground. Roy tumbled to the artificial turf, still holding tightly to his crossbow. With cat-like reflexes, he jumped to his feet and fired an arrow into another approaching Délon. The creature went down, but another one emerged and leapt for Roy. He dropped the crossbow and pulled an arrow from his quiver. The Délon grabbed his arm. Roy stabbed the creature in its dead eye with the arrow, and then reached for his knife, but before he could pull it free another Délon was on top of him.

"Roy!" I shouted again. Finally, I shook the paralyzing fear and headed for him, but Ajax stepped in front of me.

He pushed me back. "Go zoo now," he signed.

I tried to run around him, but he pushed me to the ground. "Get out of my way! Roy's in trouble!" I didn't shout. I screamed.

"Go zoo now," he signed. The hair on his shoulders and back flared. He meant business.

Roy shouted. "C'mon you ugly mothers! C'mon." He had broken away from the two that had hold of him and was holding his knife.

"Yes," I said standing, relieved.

He hooted and raised the knife in victory. Another Délon blindsided him from behind and shoved him to the ground. "Roy!" This time I was determined to get to him. Ajax had other plans. He roared and displayed his fangs. The eight Délons were just ten yards away. I felt a hand on my shoulder. Startled I turned to see Wes staring at me.

"There's nothin' we can do. Let's go."

I didn't want to believe it. I could do something. I could

save him. I was the leader. It was my job. Without being aware of it, I started to cry. I'd failed. I let Roy down when he needed me. I let my cowardice prevent me from sacrificing myself for him. I was no warrior. I was a scared little kid who had no business on the battlefield.

Ajax pushed me back again. I looked at him with all the hate I could muster, and he understood. He knew exactly how I felt.

Wes yanked me back. "Now!" He was as steadfast as Ajax.

I surrendered and followed Ajax and Wes to the loading dock, listening to Roy's pleas for help as we went.

NINE

It was a solemn trip to the zoo. I sat in the back of the wagon trying to come to grips with what I had done, or not done as the case may be. I didn't want to talk to anyone. I wanted to stew in self-pity and crawl under a rock.

Reya rode atop Chubby next to the wagon. She alternated between fits of blinding tears and looks of rage directed at me. She had witnessed the whole thing, and she knew I was a fraud. No words were spoken between us, but we shared an understanding that she would not let my cowardice go unpunished. Someday, somehow, she would pay me back, and I couldn't blame her.

For some reason, the Délons did not follow us out of the arena. I'm not sure if they could have overtaken us, but they didn't even try. It was as if they understood we had a rendezvous with the Takers, and they didn't want to interfere. It was even more of a reason to think we were being set up, but we were in too deep to turn back now. We had to follow through.

We had sent Pepper and Miles to scout out the road ahead. They came back and reported it was clear sailing. Pepper saw me sulking and maneuvered his mount next to the wagon on the opposite side of Reya.

He showed all the tact of a man who hurt other people for a living, "Get over it, kid. I lost a lot of men back there and you don't see me crying about it."

Reya fumed. "That was my brother."

Pepper stuttered. "Oh, well... Sorry..."

"This little twerp just let him die." I didn't look at her, but I knew she was referring to me. She kicked her horse and road ahead of the caravan.

Pepper waited until she was out of earshot. "Don't let her get to you, kid. She'll calm down after some time has passed."

"She's right." There was no other way I could've said it. "I let him die."

Pepper shifted in his saddle. He looked at me with a genuine look of compassion that I did not think he was capable of. "Show me a hero, and I will write you a tragedy." He winked at me. "F. Scott Fitzgerald wrote that." I gave him a strange look. "What'd you think, I was some dumb jock who never went to my English Lit class?"

"I'm no hero," I said.

"An old coach once told me that brave men overcome fear while fear overcomes cowards, and no man always overcomes." He smiled. "Fear has to win out every now and then, kid. It's how the world works." He leaned forward in his saddle. "It's even beaten me a few times." He looked at his watch. "Now, take the next five minutes or so to feel sorry for yourself and then snap out of it because things aren't going to get any easier." He moved his horse to the front of the caravan.

He was right. I couldn't afford to go into the zoo feeling the way I did. It wouldn't do me, and more importantly, any of the others any good. I closed my eyes tight and buried my morose feelings deep inside. I stood and took the horses' reins from Lou. She smiled, relieved that I was back, for the time being anyway.

We pulled up in front of the zoo's entrance. Ajax was eager to enter, but I urged more vigilance. Remembering my conversation with Wes about what had become of the zoo animals, we had no idea what was waiting for us on the other side of the gates. An abundance of caution was called for. Everyone armed themselves, and formed a tight-knit group. We all entered the zoo with Ajax and Kimball leading the way.

Some of us were more surprised than others when we were greeted by a large African elephant on the other side of the entrance in the Flamingo Plaza. It plodded toward us with a strange curiosity, glaring at us, inspecting us. Ajax approached it and to my amazement began signing to the hulking gray beast. He was trying to talk to the elephant. What's more amazing is that the elephant understood what Ajax was saying. It nodded its massive head, raised its trunk, bellowed a trumpet-like blast, and stepped back to let us pass.

The pink flamingos bobbed their heads from their habitat and watched us with a great deal of interest as we journeyed farther in. Unlike every other town and community we had traveled through over the last couple of days, the zoo was alive. The animals had not only survived, they had thrived. There was no explaining it. They had no food, no caretakers, but they were definitely flourishing within the confines of the zoo. Some of the animals had escaped their habitats and were roaming about the grounds with little or no fear of us as we traversed from one exhibit to the other. A male lion crossed our path outside the Masai Mara habitat, but he only gave us a passing glance before moving toward a grazing zebra. Once he was in striking distance of the black and white feast, he simply lay down and yawned. He had no interest in eating the zebra. It was a little disconcerting to see such peace among species that did not usually live in harmony with each other.

Ajax led us through the zoo like he had lived there his entire life. He knew exactly where he was going. I even thought

I detected looks from the other animals that suggested they had been expecting the great ape. A black rhino nodded in recognition at our presence, a giraffe seemed to point us out to another giraffe as we approached. They both bowed their heads as we passed. It was as if they had been waiting for us.

Outside the Ford African Rain Forest, gathered around a massive bronze statue of Willie B., the late legendary silverback of Zoo Atlanta, were 23 gorillas of various sizes and ages. Ajax loomed toward them stoically. We stood back and watched as a larger, more powerfully built silverback than Ajax met him in front of the group of apes. The two circled each other. The other gorillas screamed and hooted. It looked as if the two silverbacks would tear into each other at any moment. Instead, they stopped, grunted, and embraced each other in a bear hug that few bears could survive. In an extraordinary scene of joy, the other apes converged on the two silverbacks and emitted deafening sounds of happiness. It was a reunion unlike any I had every seen. Yet, could it have been a reunion? Ajax had been in Dr. Fine's care since he was an infant. How could it be that these gorillas knew him?

Just when I thought I could not be more confused by the gorillas' behavior, something even more astonishing happened. The silverback that first greeted Ajax began to sign to him. Ajax signed back. They were having a conversation. Some of the other gorillas signed, as well and joined in on the conversation. A group of gorillas with no known exposure to American Sign Language were using it like they had been using it their whole lives.

Lou put her hand on my shoulder. "Are you seeing what I'm seeing?"

I nodded.

"What's going on?" Pepper asked.

"I have no idea," I said.

"What are they saying?" Hollis stepped up to the front.

Lou scanned the group. "I don't know exactly. They're all signing at once. Something about a theater."

Over to our left was the Elder's Tree Theater. "They must mean that one," I said. I broke from the group with Pepper and Miles in tow. We advanced on the small open-air theater with caution. Once we reached the perimeter, we could see a group of orangutans sitting on the stage surrounding a massive white-haired animal with its back to us. It wasn't until it turned that I realized what it was. It was a Taker.

"What the hell?" Pepper said.

Furious, I ran back to the others. "C'mon, we're leaving." Lou, Wes, and the others gave me a look like I had lost my mind. "Ajax sold us out."

"What are you talking about?" Lou asked.

I grabbed her by the arm and dragged her to the theater. "See."

The Taker was chattering its teeth now. The sound sent a chill down my spine. Lou's chin dropped. She became visibly shaken. "What..."

"Looks like our gorilla friend was in charge of dinner," I said.

I felt a hot rush of wind on my back. I turned to find Ajax and the other silverback looking back at me. Wes and the others kept their distance.

Ajax started to sign. Lou interpreted. "Not take. Keep."

"What?" The white Taker stood and circled the stage. It sniffed the air. It was becoming more and more excited with each passing moment.

Lou said with a thinly veiled sense of horror, "That's a Keeper?"

The orangutans began to scream and dart back and forth as the white monster's unrest grew.

I looked at Ajax. "What are we supposed to do?"

"Keeper protect baby," Lou said as Ajax signed. "Keeper save Storyteller."

Pepper chimed in. "Something don't smell right. I wouldn't trust that thing with the baby."

The other silverback rushed Pepper and roared. Pepper cowered back.

I studied Ajax. He had saved my life. He knew more about what was going on than the rest of us. It seemed to be absolute folly not to trust him now, but hearing that familiar chatter coming from the Keeper, I could not help but have reservations. My mind flashed back to Mrs. Chalmers walking down the stairs of the attic, giving her baby one last look before she entered the hallway and gave herself to the Takers. "He's your responsibility now," she said. I thought about Stevie Spangler's thrashing legs dangling from the Taker's mouth. The monster had consumed him in front of my eyes, swallowing him whole. The Keeper on the stage matched that Taker in size and ferocity. The only difference was the coloring.

I took a deep breath. "Stay here," I said to Lou. Before she could ask where I was going, I entered the theater. I slowly walked up the outer aisle. I hung on loosely to J.J. My legs ached. My chest hurt from the pounding of my heart. The Keeper locked me in an eye-to-eye stare as I approached. Its short fleshy snout raised, its massive nostrils flaring, it sniffed the air getting a bead on my scent. The orangutans moved to the front of the stage. They bounced and wailed, trying to discourage me from coming any closer. Ajax knuckle-walked down the middle aisle with the other silverback behind him. They both hoot-growled, and the orangutans calmed in response. They moved to the rear of the stage.

I stood at the base of the stage and looked up at the massive creature. It did not have the greasy coating the Takers had. Its hair looked soft and silky. Ajax moved beside me and signed something to the Keeper. It breathed in deeply through its nose and let out a short guttural chuckle.

"The warrior?" it said.

Its thick throaty voice startled me. The tone of it rattled from its vocal cords and vibrated through the air like the sound of a horrible crash.

"He's too small." The Keeper reached down and pulled me up on the stage by the scruff of my shirt.

"Hey," I heard Wes shout. The other gorillas held everyone back at the perimeter of the theater. Wes tried to break through, but he could not get by the powerful apes.

"This is a boy," the Keeper tossed me about as it examined me.

Ajax continued to sign, and the Keeper continued to treat me as if I were a rag doll. He held me by my feet and lifted me above his head.

"This one saved the Storyteller?"

"Put me down," I said.

"Shut up!" The Keeper growled. "I should eat you and wait for a real warrior."

I swung J.J. at its hand, striking it on one of its huge knuckles, but it only flinched the tiniest bit as if it were just struck by a gnat.

Nate began to yowl from his sling around Lou's neck. The Keeper directed his interest on the pained cry. "Bring him to me," the Keeper demanded.

A female gorilla reached for the sling, but Lou slapped her hand away. The gorilla protested with a high-pitched screech. Another gorilla grabbed Lou by the hair. Wes punched it on the nose, causing a chain reaction that resulted in a melee between the apes and humans. Ajax stood and pounded his chest. The apes took heed and backed off. They clearly had the advantage and could have disposed of their human counterparts with ease, but at the behest of Ajax they showed restraint and retreated into the theater. Kimball had stayed out of the fray. He was unusually tranquil.

The Keeper held me upside down to his eyelevel. "I want the Storyteller."

"No," I said.

"The gorillas promised this to me..."

"It was not their promise to make," I said. "He's my responsibility."

The Keeper gnashed its teeth and tossed me to the back of the stage. I landed with a thud on top of three agitated orangutans. Had it not been for Ajax running immediately to my rescue, the three gangly-armed orange apes would surely have torn me apart.

The Keeper leapt off the stage and stormed towards Lou and the others. He was determined to get his hands on Nate.

"Stop!" I yelled, battered and bruised from the fall.

Amused, the Keeper turned to me. "Such a loud voice for such a little boy..."

"We came here to finish the book."

"What book?" With his hands curled under his wrists, the monster stomped toward me with an ominous glare.

"Stevie Dayton's book."

Fear smothered his menacing expression. He had not expected this. "You have the book?"

Ajax signed, "Read book now!" He pointed to the purple crack in the sky.

The Keeper peered upward. "That is why the Délons do

not come." The white creature began to pace. "They are waiting for you to read the book."

"I don't understand," I said.

Ajax signed again, "Read book now."

The Keeper barked, "We cannot!"

"What's going on?" I asked Ajax.

"The Délons need us to read the book," the Keeper answered. "They are in allegiance with the ones like me."

"The ones like you? You mean the Take... the Greasywhoppers?"

He smiled at this name. "The Greasywhoppers? Ahhh, yes, you cannot speak their true name. We are a brother race, not of this realm. They are here to conquer your world. We are here to restore it."

"You can restore our world?" This heartened me.

He looked toward Lou and the others. "We cannot do it without the Storytellers." He looked back at me. "Nor can we do it without the warriors."

"Why did this happen?" It was hard to hide the immaturity in my voice. I wanted to sound authoritative and commanding, but instead I sounded like a little kid asking his mommy if Santa really existed.

"Because he was afraid."

"Stevie?" I asked, hoping against hope that the Keeper meant somebody else.

He nodded. "Your kind always seeks solace inward. Most of the time you find peace there. The one called Stevie did not. He found bitterness and fear. He became so afraid that he could not hold back his inner world any longer, and the Takers escaped his mind. They are here to find others like Stevie, Storytellers to bring forth legions of dark warlords. To rule the outer world as ruthlessly as they rule the inner world of those like Stevie."

"It was because of me," I whispered.

"Yes," the Keeper said, simply, unapologetically. "This is your burden to bear." He smiled. "And your wrong to set right." He looked at Ajax. "There is no turning back if the book is read."

Ajax signed, "Gorillas always know. Read book now."

The Keeper turned back to me. "I'm afraid Ajax may be right. You have to understand by reading the book you are opening the gate between the two worlds. The Takers will enter freely, as will the Délons. Their numbers reinforced, they will seek out the other Storytellers with little resistance and a renewed vigor."

Hollis interjected. "It sounds like the prudent thing to do is not read the book."

The Keeper huffed. "In order to vanquish the inner world, you must face it." He scanned our group and the apes. "The book will show you the way, but understand, you may not like where it takes you. You must trust that the journey is a small price to pay for the destination."

I could see my troops giving the Keeper's remarks deep consideration. We all had survived the end of the world. Nothing seemed so awful to us to keep us from bringing it back.

Wes stepped forward. "Let's stop this yapping and get on with it."

Pepper raised his fist and let out an ear piercing war cry. The others, including the apes, followed suit.

***

Lou sat in the middle of the stage surrounded by the gorillas and orangutans. She needed all the protection she could get. There was little to no chance the Takers could get to her. The book was face down on her lap. She sat anxiously, waiting for the defining moment.

Ajax paced in front of his band of simian brothers. He was as majestic and noble as any general I had ever seen in history books or on television surveying his troops. The apes were his to send into battle. They fought at his command. It was really a spectacular sight to see.

The rest of us huddled together on the opposite end of the theater. We were all well armed. Nate was in his sling around my shoulder. The Keeper approached.

"It is time you entrust the Storyteller to me," he said.

I hesitated.

"The Takers will come en masse this time. If they find the Storyteller, they will open a new gate and others will come, a different race, more brutal than you have ever seen."

I nodded. Opening the sling, I fought back tears. "Okay, little guy, we'll see you when this thing's all over with." Nate's eyes squinted in the late afternoon sun. He stuck his tongue out and cooed. I handed him to the Keeper before I began to bawl like a baby.

The white giant cupped Nate in his enormous left hand, and trudged to the entrance of the theater.

Pepper called out. "Hey, big guy, where you going? We could use your help."

The Keeper paused. "This is not my war. I cannot help. I can only protect the Storyteller."

He was about to exit when I shouted, "What's your name?"

He stopped, and his eyes brightened. "I am Tarak, son of Zareh."

"Well, Tarek, son of Zareh, if they harm one hair on that kid's head, I'm holding you personally responsible." I puffed out my chest in an effort to intimidate. It was a comical attempt.

The Keeper bowed its head and exited the theater.

Devlin cleared his throat. "You sure about this, Oz?"

"No," I said. "But what choice do we have?" Valerie and Tyrone were visibly shaken. Even though they wanted no part of the coming battle, they stood by us valiantly. I knelt down beside them. "I've got a special mission for you guys." They looked at me nervously. "I want you two to protect the elephant."

"But I want to stay here and fight," Tyrone said.

"Me, too." Valerie tried to stand tall and look brave.

"I know," I said, "but the elephant is very important to us. We can't afford to lose him. Do you understand?"

They both reluctantly nodded their heads.

"Good, now go back to the entrance and wait there until somebody comes and gets you."

They started to run out of the theater.

"Be sure to find a place to hide," I said standing.

When they were gone, Devlin asked, "What's so important about the elephant?"

Miles snickered. "Nothing, dufus. He's trying to get the kids out of the way for their own safety." Miles stuck out his hand. "You're alright, boss."

I shook his hand and nodded without comment.

"He's a coward," Reya said.

Wes peered at her. "This ain't the time. If we don't fight as one, we all die."

She glowered at Wes. "Unlike him, you can count on me."

"Enough," Pepper shouted. "Let's get this thing started."

Reya and I exchanged an awkward gaze. I turned to Lou and yelled. "It's time."

She closed her eyes, breathed deeply and turned the book

over. Quickly she flipped through the pages to where she last left off. The apes' posture stiffened. Kimball began to pace in front of the stage. They were bracing for action.

We stood in a circle, our backs to each other. I held J.J. with both hands. Wes gripped his knife tightly. Pepper, Reya, Miles, and Devlin readied their crossbows. Each wore quivers filled with arrows. Hollis clumsily held onto the nozzle of the flamethrower. The small tank was strapped to his back. We had all stuffed our pockets with firecrackers.

A wind blew through the open-air auditorium. Thunder rolled and shook the ground. Lou read. She flipped through the pages. She was racing to the end, one page, two, three, four... The wind suddenly stopped. The air stood still as though we were in a vacuum.

Miles stepped out of the circle. "They chickened out."

With that, the theater bleachers to our left exploded into the air. A single Taker crawled out of the ground. Chattering, it grabbed Miles by his throat. I lunged at it with J.J. striking it on the arm. It screamed and dropped Miles. A second taker crawled out of the ground and then a third. Four more popped up in front of the stage. They came in bunches, dozens of them. The apes furiously assailed the Takers that advanced on Lou with little trouble.

Pepper, Reya, Miles, and Devlin fired their crossbows. Three hit their targets, one did not. They quickly reloaded. Wes rushed an oncoming Taker. The monster backhanded him and sent him crashing into the broken bleachers. Another Taker sprung on top of him. I hurried toward him, but a Taker behind me took hold of my shirt and yanked me backwards. It grinned, flashing its pointy teeth. I thrust J.J. into its chest and watched with euphoria as it dropped to the ground. I turned back to Wes and was pleased to now see him standing on top of the Taker, pulling his knife from its throat.

"These suckers ain't so tough," he screamed. He hooted and jumped on the back of another Taker. He frantically stabbed it in the head.

Pepper pulled another arrow from his quiver. Before he could load it, a Taker leapt from twenty feet away and landed on top of the former linebacker. Its claws ripped across his chest, and Pepper screamed in pain. He squirmed from under the Taker and rammed his thick muscled shoulder into the monster's knee, knocking it to the ground. He quickly raised the arrow and drove it into the Taker's chest.

A Taker stalked after Hollis. The sports psychologist hunched over and with shaky hands repeatedly tried to ignite the flamethrower. He could not get it to work. The Taker backed Hollis to the exit. The doctor gave one last useless try at the flamethrower, and then turned and ran out of the theater. Before the Taker could pursue him, Kimball tore into the Greasywhopper. The monster screeched in pain as the canine warrior ripped it apart.

Miles and Devlin were teaming up on a Taker near the theater entrance. They fired their crossbows simultaneously, hitting the creature in the eyes. It reeled backwards, screeching, groping at the arrows' shafts.

I turned to strike at the nearest Taker and was surprised at the sight of an arrow pointing at my chest. Reya stood, hate in her eyes, finger on the trigger of her crossbow.

"Reya..."

"You killed my brother," she said, applying pressure to the trigger. As she fired, she was jerked backwards by a nearby Taker. The arrow sailed over my head and struck a Taker sneaking up behind me. The creature fell to its knees, pulling the arrow from his temple. It struggled to stand and then collapsed lifelessly to the ground.

The Taker that had grabbed Reya held her up by her throat and opened its mouth. Its teeth folded down. I ran as fast as I could and plunged J.J. into its groin. It wailed in pain and dropped Reya. I quickly helped her to her feet. Furious, she ripped her arm from my grasp and ran to the theater entrance.

Waiting for her there, I could see a single Délon. It held on to the reins of a familiar horse, Mr. Mobley. The Délon was Roy. It looked nothing like Roy, but by the way Reya greeted it warmly, with a familial fervor, I knew it was him. They hugged. The tentacles on the Délon's face began to pulse and thrash. They clasped onto the back of Reya's head. The pinchers shot out of the Délon's mouth and clamped down on her face.

I ran to the exit, but my legs were swept out from underneath me half way there. J.J. flew out of my hands. A battered Taker lifted me in the air, its mouth open and its teeth folded in. I squirmed and jerked about trying to release myself. Its grip was too tight. I dug through my pocket and pulled out an M-98. I pulled a pocket torch from my other pocket and frantically tried to light the firecracker. My hands were too shaky. Without warning, the Taker doubled over and dropped me. I fell hard to the ground.

Wes yelled in victory and pulled his knife out of the Taker's chest. "That's the way you do it, boy! That's the way you gut a Greasywhopper...

He went down with a crash. A Taker pulled its massive fist back and sent it down on Wes again. I scrambled to get up and find J.J. The Taker hit Wes once more, knocking him unconscious. The evil monster smiled and held the inert Wes above its head. It opened its huge mouth.

"No!" I screamed. My foot kicked something across

the ground. It was J.J. I picked the sword up and ran at the Taker.

Before I could take two steps in its direction, it swallowed Wes.

"Ahhhhh," I screamed, furious, inconsolable. I lifted J.J. above my head and wildly swung the sword at the huge beast. I brought the sharp blade down on the monster over and over again, until it dropped to the ground. Then I jumped on its back and repeatedly stabbed it in the neck. I shouted, "Wes!"

Pepper saw me, and rushed to my side. "Kid."

I didn't answer. I continued to pound the Taker with J.J.

"Kid!" Pepper repeated. He grabbed my wrist in mid swing. "He's gone."

I was starting to hyperventilate. "No, he's not." I bent down and tried to push the Taker over.

"What are you doing?" Pepper stood over me.

"Help me turn it over," I said.

"Why?"

"Just help me!"

He bent down and helped me turn the slain Taker over. Another Taker rushed us. Pepper fired an arrow and hit it in the head. He reloaded. "We ain't got time for this," he said.

I ran J.J. across the dead Taker's belly and sliced it open. Quickly, I pulled back the flaps of skin and stuck my arm in the open wound. Reaching past the thick layers of fat, I felt a hand. It grabbed onto my wrist. I pulled with all my might. I strained and grunted. Little by little I made progress. I stood and pulled harder. Eventually my hand emerged with Wes's hand tightly gripping mine.

Pepper fired another arrow and then turned his attention back on me. "Good God almighty!" He ran to help. He grabbed hold of Wes's now visible forearm and pulled.

We were doing it. We were pulling Wes out of the belly of the beast. His shoulder came through and then his head. He gasped and struggled to breathe.

"Get me out of this thing," he said, coughing and hacking. "It smells like rotten feet."

Pepper and I stopped only for the briefest moment to gather our strength when Wes was yanked back inside the Taker. He could no longer hold tightly to my wrist. I slipped and tumbled backwards. Wes disappeared into the Taker's belly. Pepper was pulled along with him. He was inside the monster's stomach shoulder deep before he too lost his grip on Wes. He slowly pulled his arm free.

I didn't have time to mourn the loss of Wes for very long. The sound of Devlin screaming caught our attention. I stood to see the stocky warrior pulling on Miles's foot. The rest of Miles was inside a Taker's mouth.

Pepper and I raced to their location. Three Takers greeted us as we approached. Kimball leapt over some dislodged bleachers and stood between the Takers and us. He growled and snapped at the towering beasts. They backed away, clearing a path for us to Devlin and Miles.

When we reached them, Devlin was still holding tight to his friend's foot. He was losing the battle. Pepper fired an arrow into the Taker's thigh, and I swung at the back of its knees. The monster dropped with a thud. Pepper grabbed Miles's other leg and pulled him from the Taker's mouth.

Miles struggled to breathe. He was covered in a thick pink mucus. He rested on his knees, spitting and coughing. "That was fun," he said sarcastically.

I turned to the stage. The apes had disposed of a dozen or so Takers. Ajax beat his chest as he rushed another monster.

Lou continued to read. She showed incredible focus.

She was in the middle of the battle. Death and destruction happening all around her, but she kept her head down and read.

More Takers emerged from the ground. Pepper grabbed me by the shoulder. "We gotta do something about that hole kid. They just keep on coming."

I reached in my pocket and pulled out a handful of firecrackers. "This might slow them down." I ran to the hole, swinging J.J. at Takers as I passed. I stopped at the hole and started dropping lit firecrackers down it. A chorus of pops went off, and smoke rose from the ground. But still they came. I swung J.J. at an emerging Taker and struck it on the neck. The monster stopped and thrashed about, plugging up the hole. I lit a string of poppers and wedged them past the Taker's backside. A cacophony of explosions went off and the monster thrashed about even more. The onslaught of new Takers was stopped for the moment.

"Oz," I heard above the near deafening pop-pop-pop of the firecrackers. Lou stood from her chair. "The Queen..."

The Taker lodged in the hole let out a high-pitched scream, drowning out Lou's voice.

"What!"

"The Queen," she shouted. "You have to kill the Queen."

"The Queen?"

"The Taker Queen." She stepped outside of her protective circle of apes. "I know how to get everybody back. You have to kill the Queen."

I moved towards her. The battle raged on all around us. The influx of Takers had stopped. The apes were easily defeating the greasy monsters with little trouble. Miles, Devlin, and Pepper were holding their own with the help of Kimball. It appeared we would win this encounter with only two casualties. It was two too many.

"How do I kill the Queen?"

"Find the Keeper..." A Taker's huge hand swept her off of her feet. The monster held her like a banana.

"Lou!" I ran toward the Taker.

"The Keeper," she shouted. "Find the Keeper."

With that the Taker stuffed Lou in its mouth and swallowed her.

My heart felt as though it exploded in my chest. I felt a rage I had never felt before. I gritted my teeth and raised J.J. above my head. The Taker roared and swung its massive fist. The wind from it knocked me off my feet. My head slammed into a bleacher. Woozy, I sat up on my elbows. My vision was blurred. My head throbbed. I tried to stand but couldn't. The Taker hovered over me. It raised its snout and bellowed wildly. It took great pride in what it was about to do to me, and I didn't care. I wanted it to eat me. I had failed my friends. They were dead because of me. I deserved to die. I lay back down on the ground and waited to be eaten.

Through my blurred vision, I saw three apes leap through the air and land on the Taker's back. Ajax's leathery hand wrapped around my wrist, and he dragged me across the ground. I lost consciousness shortly thereafter.

TEN

It was several hours later before I came to. The sun had long since disappeared over the horizon. I lay in a mental haze for a long time. Parts of the battle replayed in my mind. I saw Wes raise his fist in victory. I saw him come to my rescue. I saw him fall prey to one of the Takers. I saw Reya locked in the clutches of the Délon that was once her brother. Finally, I saw Lou snatched up by a Taker and swallowed.

I shot up when the last image played through my mind. My head felt like a lead weight. A sharp pain throbbed at the back of my skull. I leaned to my left and vomited. After resting a few more moments I tried to stand.

"You should stay down."

I turned to the voice. The blurred face of Hollis looked back at me. "She didn't scream." In my mind my voice sounded clear and decisive, but Hollis cocked his head and shrugged his shoulders.

"What?"

"Lou..."

Hollis looked over his shoulder. "He's mumbling something about Lou."

Pepper's face came into view. "You took a good wallop on the head, kid. Probably got a concussion. You shouldn't try to move."

"Lou," I said. I wasn't asking for her. I knew she was gone, but I thought somehow if I said her name out loud, it would erase the past, and she would reappear out of thin air.

"He's out of it," Pepper said. "The girl's gone."

"Listen to me, Oz, you suffered a pretty severe blow to the head. You should really stay still." Hollis placed his hands on my shoulders.

"She didn't scream." My voice was clearer now. They could understand me.

Pepper's face turned sullen. "No, Kid, she didn't. She was brave until the end."

"Don't you understand?" The world around me began to spin. My stomach rolled. The urge to vomit hit me again suddenly. I worked myself up on my hands and knees, fighting my need to purge. I was shaky and weak.

"Kid..."

"She knew it was coming," I said. I could hold it no longer. I vomited violently, my body convulsing.

"Son," Hollis said, "lay back down."

"No," I said in between dry heaves. "We don't have time..." I breathed deeply to gather myself.

"We won," Pepper said. "They're gone. Listen." He stood, threw back his massive chest and yelled, "Come and get us, you friggin' ugly Takers! You mutant freaks, c'mon!"

We waited. They would come soon. He had spoken their name. They craved to be noticed. They yearned to be feared. Terror was the air they breathed. The seconds turned into minutes. I stood on wobbly legs. I was sure they would come, but they didn't.

Pepper smiled. "You see, nothing."

"But they..." I lost my balance. Hollis caught me.

"I really think you should lay down..."

"Where's Nate? Where's the Keeper?"

"Gorilla habitat number three," Pepper said.

"They're alive? They weren't taken?"

"No," Hollis said. "Why?"

"It doesn't make sense." I moved toward the habitat area, but had to quickly stop when I became nauseous.

"What doesn't make sense?" Pepper asked.

"The Takers. They came for Nate... the Storyteller. If they didn't get him, why don't they come?"

Hollis and Pepper had no answer.

With my head pounding and my stomach turning, I headed toward the gorilla habitats.

***

The Keeper was sitting on a boulder in the middle of gorilla habitat number three. His back was to the Willie B. Gorilla Conservation Center. Unable to shake the effects of the blow to my head, I approached gingerly.

"They wanted Lou," I said. It was the only explanation I could come up with for the Takers sudden lack of interest in the rest of us.

The Keeper did not acknowledge me. He was hunched over, cradling Nate in his huge hand.

"Hey, Tarek, I'm talking to you. The Takers wanted Lou."

"What they want doesn't matter."

"It does to me."

"You have done your part. You have delivered the Storyteller to me."

The angrier I got the more my head hurt. I desperately tried to keep calm to save myself the agony. "Why do they want Lou?"

"It doesn't matter."

"It does!" My head felt as if it would explode.

"Because they want you."

I held my hand to my temple and tried to rub the pain away. I tried to process his answer. "Me?"

"And the Storyteller." Tarek looked at me for the first time. "They know you will come for her. But you must let it end here."

"Come for her?" I couldn't believe what I was hearing. I recalled the memory of trying to pull Wes from one of the Takers. "That means Wes... Everybody... They don't eat people..."

"They transport people."

"Where?"

He looked away from me.

"Where, Tarek?"

"To their Queen," He stood.

"Everybody's alive..." I tried to let the information soak through my throbbing skull. "Lou said to kill the Queen... That's how I get everybody back, isn't it? If I kill the Queen, everything will be back to normal..."

"It's not that simple," Tarek said. "The Délons are here now. Things won't be the same. They benefit if you kill the Taker Queen."

"Why?"

"Because it makes them stronger." The hulking Keeper circled me as he spoke. Nate lay content in his hand. "The Takers hold one Storyteller, the Délon creator. His capture brought the Délons into this world. Because of this, the Délons are subservient to the Takers. If you kill the Taker Queen, the Délons will rule. They will continue their hunt of the other Storytellers with the intent to hold dominion over all other races."

"Then we'll defeat the Délons just like we defeated the Takers," I said it with a dangerous naiveté. It was fool's logic.

Just because we defeated the Takers didn't mean we could defeat the Délons. I knew that deep down inside, but my desire to see Lou and Wes and my parents again made me more than willing to take my chances with the Délons.

"They are more cunning. More than you can imagine…"

"How do I find the Queen?" My adrenaline began to build. My head hurt less and less as I thought about the mission now clearly laid out for me.

"Let it end here," Tarek said.

"I can't," my voice cracked as I felt urgency run through my veins. "I want my parents back. Now, how do I find the…"

"Don't ask me again." Tarek looked panicked.

"Why?"

Ajax appeared from the back of the habitat and stood on top of the nearby boulder. The moon hovered above his pointy head. He peered down at me and spoke. Not with his hands, but with a booming voice that shook the ground. "Because he must show you the way."

"You can talk?" My mouth was agape. My eyes felt as though they would pop from their sockets. "How?"

"Only because the one you call Stevie Dayton has made it so. This is still his story. It is not over." He held up his hand and tossed something to me. It was the comic book. "The Keeper must show you the way to the Taker Queen. As it is written."

I flipped through the book. Our entire journey was cataloged on the pages before we even took it. I reached the part about our final battle. I saw Wes slipping back into the Taker's belly. I saw the Taker's huge hand swoop down and pick up Lou, a strange look of contentment on her face. The words "Kill the Queen," were written above her head. I turned the page and saw myself coming to, Pepper and Hollis trying to convince me to stay down. On the next page were Tarek and me having the conversation we just had. It was all so strange. Stevie had written what we said word for word.

The next page showed Ajax talking for the first time, and me reading the comic book as I was doing at that very moment. It was like looking into some strange comic book mirror.

I hesitated before turning the next page. Instead of rehashing the journey behind me, I was about to see the journey ahead. I considered the possibility that perhaps Stevie had not written a happy ending. Maybe this whole mess was his way of paying me back for the torment I had put him through.

I turned the page and read. The way to the Queen was not easy. I read the page over and over again making sure I was reading it right. This was Stevie's payback. He had planned to torment me. I did not know if I could do what was asked of me.

"This is the only way?" I asked Ajax.

"As it is written." He said.

My head began to ache again. It was too much. How could I possibly work up the courage to do what was written? I turned the page and was horrified to find the words "End of Book One," written in big bold letters.

"Wait a minute... Wait a minute, this doesn't tell me if I kill the Queen or not."

Tarek smiled. "The outcome is uncertain. You must not pursue it. Let it end here."

"The outcome has never been certain," Ajax said. "Only predicted."

I looked up at Ajax still perched on top of the boulder. "Why do they want me?"

Tarek chimed in before Ajax could answer. "You can destroy them."

"Me? I'm just a kid."

"The one called Stevie Dayton has written it this way," Ajax said. "You are the warrior. The one they fear. The Storytellers can give them life, but you can take it away."

"I don't understand why he wrote it this way," I said in frustration. "I was mean to him. I made fun of him... made him do things..."

"He saw the magic in you," Tarek said.

The words hung in the air. It was what Lou had said her grandmother used to say. Look for the magic in people. As long as I knew Stevie, I always thought he was dumb, that I was better than he was because I had a superior command of the English language, or because I was more athletic, or because I looked normal and he didn't. But the truth is, I didn't look hard enough at Stevie. I didn't try to see what he was really all about. He was a sweet kid that loved to tell stories about fantastic worlds where the good guys always won. I didn't look for the magic in him.

I looked at Tarek. "Show me the way to the Taker Queen."

***

Everyone who was left had gathered around gorilla habitat number three. They assumed we had come together for a celebration. We had beaten the Takers. We deserved a little slap on the back, but I had really brought them together to say goodbye.

I stood in silence in front of them with Nate's sling around my shoulder. They were all truly heroic, but I couldn't think of the proper words to convey my real feelings. I had no idea what waited for me when Tarek showed me the way to the Taker Queen. The chances were that I wouldn't succeed. The Takers were waiting for me after all. And if I did succeed, Tarek may be right; the Délons would become a bigger problem. I sighed and spoke very softly. "Nobody will ever know what we did here today. Nobody's going to give us medals. They aren't going to throw us a parade. Nobody will ever read about this in the history books. You didn't fight for the glory. You fought because it was the right thing to do..."

"No, we didn't, kid," Pepper said. "We fought for you."

I looked at him stunned by his assertion. The others nodded.

"Warriors win battles. Leaders win wars. We won this battle so you could win the war." He stepped forward and shook my hand. "It ain't over yet. We all know that. You do what you have to do. We're your army. We wait for your command."

I swallowed hard and looked past him into the faces of all the others. They smiled and nodded in agreement. "I might be doing the wrong thing," I said.

"Yeah," Pepper said. "But you might be doing the right thing, too."

I stepped back, gave them all one last smile and turned to Tarek. "I'm ready."

"I don't want to do this," Tarek said.

"I asked. It is written you must show me the way."

"Very well," he said annoyed. "But it will not be a pleasant journey."

"I know." I stepped toward him, but stopped when I heard a high-pitched whine to my left. I turned to see Kimball, ears down, paw up. I knelt down beside him and rubbed his head. "You can't go, boy." He whined louder. "I wish you could. You've been with me the whole way." He licked my face. "You've got a bunch of puppies to take care of, and I've got to get Mom and Pop back." I stood and looked at Tarek. "Ready."

With that, Tarek picked me up in his gigantic hand and lifted me to his mouth. His jaws unhinged as he shoved me past his slimy tongue and down his throat. I started to suffocate as I was pushed through his narrow gullet. I couldn't breathe. I was caked in mucus. I gasped for air, but there was none to be had. I started to kick and flay about. I had made a mistake. I was dying. The Keeper wasn't transporting me, he was eating me. This was Stevie's revenge. I would rot in the belly of a monster he created.

As I struggled one last time, I felt the constricted passageway expand. I felt a breeze. Air! I breathed in, choking on mucus, but still feeling the sensation of breathing again. There was darkness all around me as I felt the sensation of falling. I landed with a thud on a brittle, charred surface. I lay on the ground, coughing and spitting up fluid from my lungs.

I rolled over on my hands and knees. My lungs cleared, I breathed deeply and attempted to take in my surroundings. My eyes slowly began to adjust, and the darkness gave way to an increasing influx of light. I stood, Nate's sling still around my shoulder.

Shapes started to form in front of me. Hundreds... thousands of trees surrounded me. More light. They weren't trees. They were Takers. They were lined up as far as the eye could see, all of them peering at me, slobbering, seething. They wanted to tear me apart, but they didn't. They kept their distance, laying out a path for me to follow.

I slowly walked along the twisting lane, my eyes shifting from the pathway to the Takers that outlined it. They breathed heavily and flashed their teeth as I passed. They wanted to smash me, but something held them back. It was clear to me now. I was about to die.

Ahead, the path widened. The Takers diverted their gaze from me to the direction in which I was walking. I rounded a sharp corner and caught a glimpse at what held their interest. Sitting on a mound of burnt dirt was the biggest Taker I had ever seen. If it were standing, it would probably be thirty feet high, and it looked to be as big around as it was tall. Chubby legs gushed out from under its oversized belly. It was the Queen.

I held tight to Nate's sling. The Takers sniffed the air as I passed. The scent of a Storyteller was nearby. It was giving them fits.

Ten yards from the Taker Queen, I saw Lou standing by the massive creature's side. "Lou."

"Oz," she smiled. "I knew you'd come."

I looked at the Queen. "Where's Wes?"

The Taker Queen groaned and motioned to a Taker to my left. The Taker stepped forward. I backed away, guarded and unsure. The creature's teeth began to chatter. It convulsed wildly and fell to its hands and knees. Its mouth opened and its entire body began to contract and expand. I watched in horror as it regurgitated a large slimy pink mass. A hand extended out of the blob. It was Wes. I ran over and pulled him free of the plump ball of goo.

Wes spat and snorted. "Good goose crap almighty. That is 'bout the foulest experience of my whole life." He stood and wiped the pink slime from his face. He froze when he saw the legion of Takers. "What in tarnation? Where are we?"

"Almost home," I said. I turned to the Taker Queen. "Now what?"

"You have to give huh the sto-weetella."

Stepping out from behind a group of Takers to my right was Stevie Spangler.

"Stevie?"

"She can't take it."

"You know this guy?" Wes asked.

"Yeah, I do." I walked over to Stevie. "What are you doing here?"

"They need me to talk," Stevie said. "I'm da only one who undastands."

I nodded. "What do you mean by 'she can't take it'?"

"She can't take it. It has to be given to huh." He leaned in close. "I want to go home."

"So do I," I said. "So do I." I turned to the Queen. "You can have him."

Lou stomped her feet. "Oz, what are you doing?"

The massive beast reached for Nate's sling. I backed away. The Taker Queen roared her displeasure.

"Not so fast," I said. "Send my friends back."

"Don't do it, Oz," Wes said. "You can't let them have Nate."

"I got it under control, Wes." I looked up at the Taker Queen. "Wes, Lou, and Stevie back to my world, now!"

The Queen nodded. Three Takers broke from the group and rounded up Wes, Lou, and Stevie. Lou kicked her Taker. Wes struggled briefly but quickly gave in. Stevie went willingly. They began to march back up the path.

"Wait a minute," I said.

They stopped.

"Lou, what's your real name?"

She turned to me, tears in her eyes. "Emily," she said. "Emily Bristol."

"We'll see you around, Emily Bristol."

The Takers continued to escort them up the path. I turned back to the Queen. "How will I know you've really taken them back?"

The Taker Queen picked me up. Her hand covered me from neck to toe. She held me to her eye. The image of the zoo appeared in her black eyes. I saw Ajax sitting with Pepper and Hollis. They were a somber bunch. Suddenly their mood brightened. Wes, Lou, and Stevie walked into the scene. There were hugs all around. The Taker Queen held me out and reached over with its other hand. She was asking for me to give her Nate.

I shook my head. "He's not going alone. Take both of us."

The Taker Queen groaned and roared. She did not like this arrangement. She tried to coax Nate from me again, but I refused again. The greasy monster opened its mouth and shoved me inside with Nate's sling around my neck. I had a sudden sense of dèjà vu.

I quickly moved into action once I was inside the monster's mouth. I didn't think I would be able to do what needed to be done once the Taker Queen started to swallow me. I flopped onto my back on the beast's slippery tongue and pulled Pepper's homemade flamethrower from it. It was wrapped in baby's clothes to make it smell like Nate. I fumbled with the lighting mechanism and tried to activate it once, twice, and a third time. It wouldn't work. As the monster's mouth closed, I tried it a fourth time and was almost giddy when I saw a small blue flame pop out from the end of the nozzle. I felt the sensation of being forced into the Taker Queen's throat. I pulled the trigger on the flamethrower's nozzle. Flames filled the beast's gullet. She lifted her head and thrashed it back and forth. I bounced about like a rubber ball in a small room. I pulled the trigger again and aimed it down the Taker Queen's craw. I reached back in Nate's sling and pulled out a hunting knife. As I shot flames to and fro, I jammed the knife into the

212

roof of the monster's mouth. This time she let out a blood-curdling scream that caused her to open her mouth. As her head whipped about, I could see the Takers on the ground below in a panic over their Queen's distress. This emboldened me. I jammed the knife upward again, driving it into the roof of the mouth and making a deep hole. I rammed the nozzle of the flamethrower into the oozing hole and pulled the trigger.

The Taker Queen screeched. She tried to stand on her chubby legs, but her weight was too much for the underused appendages to take. She tumbled over and fell face first into the blackened soil. I crawled from her mouth, knife in one hand, the flamethrower in the other. The other Takers converged on me. I held them at bay with the flamethrower. I had to deliver the fatal blow to the Queen. If I didn't she would survive and continue her hunt for Nate and the other Storytellers. She was wounded, but not fatally. She screamed again. The other Takers hesitated at the sound of their Queen in pain. I took the opportunity to quickly climb on top of the Queen's head. I had one last surprise in Nate's sling, a string of M-98s.

Below the monster's ear, I rammed the knife deeply. The mighty beast twitched and struggled to push herself up, but her great weight kept her immobilized.

I grabbed the M-98s and shoved them into the hole. It was gushing a greasy deposit. With the flamethrower, I lit the single fuse and jumped from the monster's head. I heard them go off. Bang! Bang! Bang! I put my hands over my head, closed my eyes tightly, and waited for the other Takers to pounce on me and tear me apart. I waited, and I waited, and I waited.

I opened my eyes and lifted my head. A bright light blinded me. I shielded my eyes from the intensity of it. I rolled on my back. The hard ground had turned soft.

"Osmond, what are you doing?"

The voice. I couldn't believe my ears. The light began to dim. I wasn't on the charred ground of the Taker's lair. I was in my room in Tullahoma.

"Osmond, get out of bed."

I sat up. I was in my pajamas lying in my bed. "Mom?"

ELEVEN

The figure of my mother stepped into view. She was beautiful, more beautiful than I remember ever seeing her. Her short red hair was held back with a black hair clip. Her face was perfectly pale and Irish. It was really my mother. I sprung from my bed and ran to her as fast as I could.

"Mom!" I wrapped my arms around her and squeezed her tight.

"What has gotten into you, Osmond Franklin Griffin?"

I started crying. I couldn't help myself. I was back home. I was in my bedroom. I was hugging my mom. This was the greatest day in the history of the planet.

She bent down and lifted my chin up with her finger. "Hey, hey, hey, what's this?"

"You're alive." It's all I could manage to say before I choked on a gush of emotion.

She hugged me. "Of course, I am, sweetie. What's wrong with you? Did you have a bad dream?"

I sniffed and pulled myself away. I was beginning to feel embarrassed. I didn't know what was going on. Maybe it all was just a dream. I nodded not knowing what else to do.

"Well, don't you worry about it. Everything's going to be all right. Except that you're late for school..."

"School? But I can't go to school, I'm sick."

"Sick?" She felt my forehead. "Honey, don't you feel well?"

"Mom, I've got mono, remember?"

"Mono?" She raised an eyebrow. "Oz, what are you talking about?"

I stood there dumbfounded. Had I dreamt of having mono, too? "Nothing."

She lightly slapped me on the butt as she stood. "Good, now get dressed. If you're sick and can't make it to school today, I'm afraid you won't be able to make it to the Titans game this weekend."

My ears perked up. "The Titans?"

"Yep, your Pop got tickets last night."

"Alright!" I shouted.

"The games at 1:00." She moved to the door to my room and smiled. "In Délon City." With that she walked out of the room and pulled the door shut behind her.

My mouth went dry. "Délon City?"

The End
of
Book One

15069437R00133

Printed in Great Britain
by Amazon.co.uk, Ltd.,
Marston Gate.

F
CALLED TO THE
STREETS

To everyone who has made the move
and is living the life. . .

Eden:
Called to the
Streets

MATT WILSON

survivor

Unless otherwise indicated, biblical quotations are from
the New International Version © 1973, 1978, 1984
by the International Bible Society.
NLT = New Living Translation copyright © 1996 by Tyndale
Charitable Trust.
Used by permission of Tyndale House Publishers, Wheaton,
Illinois, USA.

Some names have been changed to protect identities.

ISBN 1 84291 219 4

2 3 4 5 6 7 8/10 09 08 07 06

Survivor is an imprint of
KINGSWAY COMMUNICATIONS LTD
Lottbridge Drove, Eastbourne BN23 6NT, England.
Email: books@kingsway.co.uk

Printed in the USA

Contents

Foreword

Warning! Don't start reading this book unless you can drop whatever else you are doing for the next few hours. And definitely don't make a start after 8 p.m. unless you are prepared for an all-nighter. Some books you grind through. This one you fly through. It's a 'page-turner', as the whodunnit advertisers say.

The style makes for an easy read with its lively, breezy text. But don't let that fool you. The text never resorts to hype. It is honest and earthy. It provides encouragement, but does not conceal the pain. The underlying message is the need for gutsy persistence. *It is the most challenging and inspiring book I have read in many a day.*

Don't let the catchy turn of phrase fool you. This is a book that not only tells a story, and tells it well, it also takes us behind the scenes and digs deep to expose the foundations. Here is great missionary theology – incarnational stuff, but not the usual esoteric, academic treatments I have to plough through. It is all there in plain language and short words: captivating words, yet at times jolting, stinging words.

Matt helps us see that incarnation means more than identification. What may seem to us like identification all too often appears as patronising imitation to the folks on the receiving end. No, incarnation means immersion without submersion. It means boarding up any bolt hole when the going gets tough. It means being not just a presence, but a transformative influence. In terms of the long haul of urban mission these are still early days. Winter conditions still prevail, but spring is on the way.

This could have been a very long introduction, because there is so much I like about the book. But you haven't bought this book to read the ramblings of an old guy. So without more ado, let's hit the street, with Matt and the Eden team members as our streetwise guides.

Eddie Gibbs
Professor of Church Growth at the School of World Mission,
Fuller Theological Seminary, California

P.S. Before you get to the end you need to check your messages to see if there is a call from God awaiting your reply. Jesus may be inviting you to join with him to get personally involved – especially you guys!

1

A Place Called Eden

They will say, 'This land that was laid waste has become like the garden of Eden; the cities that were lying in ruins, desolate and destroyed, are now fortified and inhabited.'

Ezekiel 36:35

Extraordinary grace

1   teaspoon
1   knife
1   mug
1   plate
1   kettle
1   loaf of bread
1   jar of peanut butter
1   jar of coffee
1   bag of sugar
4   pints of milk
1   huge fridge freezer*
1   fold-out 5 ft camp bed**

1   pillow
1   duvet
1   radio alarm clock
1   wooden fold-up chair

*   Empty apart from the milk
**   Dave is 6'2"

Dave Nuttall has a memory for details and, not surprisingly, some fairly vivid memories of when, on 9th October 1996, he became the first person to move into an 'Eden project'. The notorious Benchill area of Wythenshawe, officially the most deprived ward in the whole of the UK, had been highlighted as the place where this altogether different approach to Christian mission would be piloted. The list above doesn't describe Dave's intention to enhance his first week in the house with a sort of ascetic twist. And he wasn't travelling light just in case he had to beat a hasty retreat back to Cheadle Hulme either. No, about two months prior to the moving in date Dave's mum had bought a new lawnmower. It had arrived in a huge, shiny, sturdy cardboard box. And day by day Dave had been neatly packing all his worldly goods into that box, all the personal things that defined him, his favourite books and videos, his treasured Beatles albums, all safely stacked in the lawnmower box.

Not having his own car, Dave had arranged a bit of help to get him and his lawnmower box the five miles down the road to Wythenshawe. Just as the sky was turning to dusk he heard the gentle pip of the horn and knew it was time to make his move. Bending his knees and wrapping his arms around the box 'bear hug' style, he counted down to the clean and jerk … 3 … 2 … 1 … LIFT! And then time froze as the box, with no respect for time or occasion, emptied its precious contents all over Dave's feet like a tourist with a nasty case of Delhi belly. Deflated, frustrated and feeling the pressure of needing to arrive and unload before dark, he now only had time for a quick whizz round the house. In true Matthew 10 style,[1] Dave would be travelling light.

Moving into Benchill and becoming founder member of the new Eden team there was not entirely a leap into the unknown for Dave. For over a year his fiancée Colette Vickers, a trainee physiotherapist and dancer with The World Wide Message Tribe, had sensed God speaking to her about his desire to make himself known there. Every day the bus she caught to her placement at Wythenshawe Hospital would drive right through the estate. Often she would feel the Holy Spirit stirring compassion in her heart for the area's young people, so many of them growing up in those streets without love and without hope.

Dave and Colette's decision was that they would get married on 19th October and together move into Benchill, trusting that the rest of the team would gradually begin to fit together around them. Another family from the local church backing the project, Nick and Yvonne Carrington and their two young kids Alex and Jenny, had already moved into the area about six months earlier and had established good relationships within the community, particularly with the local housing office. Their good standing, encouragement and support were tremendously valuable, not only to Dave and Colette but to the dozens of other Eden volunteers who would follow them in the next couple of years. It was in the middle of a meal round at Nick's and Yvonne's the week before moving into the area that Dave got to take a viewing of his new house. A bit of a commotion coming from the back yard got everyone's attention. Opening the door, they saw several shifty teenage lads legging it out of the empty house next door and disappearing into the wildly overgrown privet hedge at the bottom of the garden. It seemed like a great opportunity for Dave to take a look around his new house as the lads had very thoughtfully prized open the steel security shutter and the back door. Looking around, Dave was annoyed to find that they'd been trying to strip the house of its copper during the raid – worth a few quid at the scrap metal yard. It would be a lot of hassle repairing the boiler and fixing the central heating system which the lads wrecked that night. Cold showers and extra jumpers are not always recommended as an introduction to married life, but that's how it was.

Dave and Colette's story is just one of about 300 different journeys of extraordinary grace. Individuals, couples and families have chosen to follow the voice of their Saviour leading them into some of the toughest neighbourhoods in Manchester. The book you have in your hands provides an opportunity for some of those stories to come to light. And they need to come to light. Not for the fame or glory of those who feature in them, but because of the hope they offer to everyone who yearns to live out an authentic Jesus life in this multi-mart world of so many thin veneers. You'll discover in these pages that the people who have joined Eden teams in the last few years aren't some kind of elite Christian SAS, door-knocking Britain's equivalent of Baghdad in knee-high Doc Martens with boot polish smeared on their cheeks. They're actually just ordinary people, reaching out to ordinary people. The only thing that's unusual really is that the places where they've chosen to live aren't the places where Christians usually choose to live. And the people they choose to share their lives with are not the people Christians usually choose to share their lives with either.

In case you're wondering, Dave and Colette are doing great. Since the day in 1996 when they took possession of the keys to their council house, they have devoted themselves to the redemption of their community. They're still going for it, along with their little boy, Joseph, who'll be starting at the local primary school pretty soon.

Urban landscape

So what fills your mind when you hear the phrase 'inner city'? Foreboding concrete tower blocks? Layer after layer of graffiti? Burnt-out cars? Menacing gangs peering through their hoods? Or how about an old geezer wobbling on a ladder to water his hanging basket? Or a group of young mums sat around a corral of buggies in the brightly painted park? Or a young dad splashing his son as they wash the car together?

Of course the inner city, and the city's outer estates, like Wythenshawe, can be all these things all at the same time, and a million and one other things as well. In fact, even using a million and one different personal brush-strokes of city life, the landscape produced would be more impressionist than photo-realist. Britain is just so densely populated. The latest government figures show that 90% of its population live in urban areas. Four of those areas together account for more than a quarter of the total UK population.[2] The Greater London metropolis is home to a population of 8.3 million; the West Midlands industrial heartland encompassing Birmingham, Wolverhampton, Dudley and Walsall has 2.3 million; the Greater Manchester urban sprawl which swallows up huge northern towns like Bolton, Oldham and Stockport houses 2.2 million and the tightly packed towns and cities of West Yorkshire such as Leeds, Bradford, Huddersfield and Wakefield contain a total of 1.5 million lives. Of Greater Manchester's 2.2 million residents, half a million are under the age of 18.

Most of these children and young people live in the post-war council estates – vast mazes of anonymous streets. Wythen-

13

shawe is the biggest of these, covering an area of about 15 square miles and at its peak home to around 100,000 souls. For many years it held the title of 'largest council estate in Europe', but in recent years it's been shrinking as its tower blocks have been reduced to rubble and its edges have been eaten away by the growth of the Barratt Belt. In other quarters of the city you'll find young people trying to get to grips with life in row upon row and alley after alley of ancient back-to-back 'Coronation Street' housing. This image, more than any other, probably explains why so often Manchester is used as representative of UK urban dereliction and depression. Looking for a story about high crime, poor health, shoddy housing, educational underachievement, unemployment, lack of opportunity? You won't have to look far in Manchester. If you've got the bottle to take a little detour away from the slick tarmac of the main arterial routes in and out of the city you'll soon come across some neglected no-go neighbourhood, once tightly knit, now falling apart like a worn-out garment. And these are the places where Eden is, where the people of God are reweaving with threads of grace.

REALITY BITES

Steven has been an Eden volunteer for a few years now. He describes in his own words his impressions of the neighbourhood he relocated to.

I was only living about a mile from Longsight when I first moved to Manchester but the difference between living in Studentville, Victoria Park and living in Longsight proper was huge. When I made the move in June 2002 my first impression was simply the sense of hopelessness that hung over the place. The poverty, the run-down properties, the negativity and just sheer loveless-

Godly obsession

Eden is part of a family of pioneering youth ministries operated by The Message Trust, a Christian charity based in Manchester. The Message is passionate about young people, believing that whatever their circumstances, they shouldn't be excluded from an opportunity to hear about Jesus. Somebody needs to give them a chance to respond to his amazing love. But there's more. Our years of urban ministry have proved that just hearing and responding doesn't bring lasting change. So, over the years we have designed projects which help young people move from decision-making to discipleship. Our dream for them is that they will develop into 'somebodies' not 'nobodies'. We long to see them expressing the full potential God has given them. And after years of hard graft it seems to be working! All over the patch of earth God has called us to reach – Greater Manchester – young people are discovering destinies they never knew they had. The buzz is growing and spreading, people are talking, and this book will no doubt fuel that conversation. Within these pages you'll soon learn that we're really

---

-ness of the relationships between most of the people I saw and met.

After two years I think a bit differently about the place. It has been regenerated physically, with house prices up and crime rates down. The people seem slightly softer and less suspicious of the Bible-bashers that had moved into their neighbourhood.

The area still has big challenges of course, but I guess you could say that there is a sense of a hope and a future where perhaps there wasn't before. The truth is that after much prayer and presence, it seems like God's light is slowly rising over the area, and in fact the whole of Manchester.

serious about this vision, perhaps to the point of obsession. It's true: we'll do anything to see young people reached for Jesus. Ideas which to others might seem outrageous, dangerous or just plain ridiculous make perfect sense when you're driven by a godly obsession.

Take The World Wide Message Tribe (WWMT), for example. Which sane denomination, at their annual missions conference, would suggest hiring a 30-year-old elastic-braces manufacturer to shout bizarre religious rhymes into a microphone whilst jumping around on a stage in an ostentatious costume to the sound of frantic synthesisers and heavy drumbeats? Nobody would come up with that in a million years. But fortunately that elastic-braces manufacturer had a finger on the pulse of youth culture and sensed an imminent 'kairos' moment – a time of dangerous opportunity when the gospel advances at incredible pace. With a team of passionate dancers, Andy Hawthorne (the elastic-braces man) and his musical mate Mark Pennells took their high-energy gospel show to schools in Manchester, meeting thousands of young people riding high on a wave of 'rave'. All the sweaty nightclubs, all the pirate radio stations, all the Ford Escort XR3is were pumping out this music 24/7. The Message and The Medium found a perfect synergy.

The growth of this fledgling evangelistic ministry was explosive. Hundreds and hundreds of teenagers were committing their lives to Christ. Week after week, The World Wide Message Tribe would move from school to school making the most almighty commotion for the Kingdom. The volume of the opportunities meant hiring more team members to cope with the demanding schedule of assemblies, RE lessons and after-school concerts. For about three or four years the whole thing was a blur – time just flew by. However, a pattern was beginning to emerge, very subtly at first. Andy and the team would take a booking with any school anywhere in Greater Manchester.

The call would generally come from a local church contact in the area who had a link in the school, or who would be prepared to 'try the door' of the RE department, or the head teacher. Typically the churches where such links existed were in the leafy suburbs. Here, well organised youth workers did their stuff, employed by the well resourced churches who could make a generous donation at the end of the mission to WWMT's ongoing work. A ministry which had its original divine spark in Longsight, right in the heart of the inner city, was gradually being suburbanised. Yes, of course the middle-class kids needed the gospel too, but once again the youth of the ghettos were getting overlooked.

Painful birth

One place that was still on the list was Wythenshawe, which had four state high schools at the time. Over a fortnight WWMT visited the toughest two and then brought them together for a massive evangelistic gig at the local Civic Forum, a concrete leviathan with a 1,000-seater auditorium. This crumbling sixties venue rose like a grounded oil tanker out of the barren grey-ness of Leningrad Square, a Manchester City Council monu-ment to tenuous Soviet comradeship. On the positive side the Forum was well known and nowhere else for miles around had a capacity nearly as big, which was just as well, because on the night of the concert the place was absolutely packed out. WWMT were on top form and Andy preached his heart out, describing with great insight the pain and the power of the cross. Around a hundred of Wythenshawe's young people responded to the message – including some real live-wires. In the cramped and chaotic counselling room Andy prayed with

17

them all and then, as was the tradition, invited them along to church on Sunday. And that's when things started to get interesting.

King's Church, a small fellowship meeting every Sunday in an anteroom at the Forum Centre, had happily agreed to partner with The Message for the good of the young people of Wythenshawe. They'd supported in every way they could, a few members of the congregation had donned the obligatory yellow jackets and stewarded the event, many more had joined in praying for a breakthrough, but nobody quite expected what happened next. It was Sunday evening and a few church members were busily setting up the PA system and organising the chairs for the special 'youth-friendly' follow-up event. Amazingly, young people started turning up – but not in ones and twos. They came in great mobs, well up for the new experience of finding out what church was all about. In total about a hundred of them showed up, bringing with them their 'interesting' language, 'interesting' smoking habits and 'interesting' personal hygiene. The challenge for this little church was massive. How would they ever cope? How could they possibly begin to disciple these wild young people? Unsurprisingly, over the next few weeks these young people just disappeared. A small handful made meaningful connections and began to grow in God, but the vast majority simply evaporated like yesterday's puddles on a sunny morning.

The genuine pain of seeing young people slide away so fast was too much for King's Church and The Tribe to take. The agony of the experience caused a fundamental shift of mindset for all involved. Young people in the city were desperate to know God, but the existing church was not fit to take them on, not on the scale required, with such heavy baggage. A revolution was needed, and how strangely appropriate that it should rise from the cracks in the paving slabs of Leningrad Square.

Welcome to Eden

The personality profiles of the guys and girls who've joined Eden represent infinite variation, but certain demographic trends are quite apparent and Lisa Deirmendjian probably represents a large segment of those recruited over the last few years. She grew up in the outskirts of London and thanks to her local Anglican church, a strong youth group and a great Christian mum, she'd become a fairly solid Christian. Life had not exactly been a breeze – her parents' separation had taken some getting over – but by her late teens she was in a good place with God. And so, when at the age of 23 she began to sense a dissatisfaction in her heart, she wisely concluded that maybe God was challenging her. The textbook London life, the daily commute, the promising career, the social life and the designer wardrobe … was Jesus at the heart of it all? Maybe she should call that number, the organisation in Manchester, just to have a little peek at something different.

The Golden Lion pub on Rochdale Road in North Manchester certainly is different when you're used to the shiny bars of Holborn and Covent Garden. The interior design can't be far from the sort of look Jack Duckworth might create by bringing his pigeon shed into the lounge while Vera's away for the weekend, with all the associated smells too. And of course Saturday night is karaoke. The whole experience is quite an irony for the Cosmo girl in the corner who, while exiting an Eden seminar at Soul Survivor a couple of years earlier, had thought to herself, 'I'm not funky – I can't sing, I can't dance, what have I got to give?' Even as that thought hangs like the smoke in the air a commotion erupts from near the bar: shrieks, screams and obscenities from the dark side of the U-bend ... a young woman is slugging it out with another woman old enough to be her mother. Apparently it's a dispute over the prestigious karaoke pecking order, all clumsily choreographed to the tempo of the old fella crooning 'I love you baby'. Welcome to Harpurhey.

Besides the comedy catfight at the Golden Lion, three other impressions linger in Lisa's memory from that first ever visit to the area:

Number 1 is the great relief and reassurance she felt when introduced to the members of the team, that they were all normal people. Yes, maybe one or two were modelling dubious baggy jeanswear, but there were no superheroes from the Planet Incarnation anywhere in sight.

Number 2 is the great provocation of the young people she encountered. Wild kids, loads of them, everywhere, totally misbehaving and out of control, respecting no rules or boundaries, but clamouring for attention and affirmation.

REALITY BITES

Jordan (19), on growing up in Harpurhey, an area of narrow streets and tightly packed estates two miles north-east of Manchester city centre.

There's robberies, people mugging old ladies – and that's a fact, it's disgusting. In the past two or three years there have been murders – like three or four just in the Harpurhey area. It could be a friendly community, but there's always something that gives it a bad name. There's always some group of people that want

---

Number 3 is the pleasant surprise of the partner church, Christ Church Harpurhey, 'a proper Anglican church' led by 'a real vicar', built of sandstone with a tall spire and pews with colourful knitted prayer cushions, no doubt the work of the faithful contingent of saintly old ladies.

Moving into the area presented a severe challenge of comfort for Lisa. Housing wasn't immediately available so a temporary arrangement was hooked up with a couple of girls in the team who shared a two-bedroom 'Coronation Street' terrace. For a whole month Lisa's bed was the blue Ikea futon in the front room. The street was a dead end and passers-by few and far between. Late at night every noise sounded like an attempt to break into her car. The local gang of a dozen or so teenage lads did show an awful lot of interest in it, leaning against it to smoke a cig or sitting on the bonnet to drink a can of Coke.

Communicating with these lads was probably the number one challenge Lisa faced. They were from a completely different universe and it took her months to get to grips with their thick northern accents. Their street uniform consisted of head-

---

to go and hurt someone and that's just how it is round our way – it's unpredictable. It's a horrible area to grow up in. I moved away for nine months when I was 11 and that's the longest I've been away from Harpurhey, I've not lived anywhere else in Manchester. It's a kind of slum area, it's where bad dirty deals go on, and if I could change that – I'd do it today.

Since the Eden workers have come in they've got the kids active and doing things and it relates to God. It's making the kids realise Harpurhey doesn't have to be like this for ever.

to-toe Nike. Every scalp was shaved beneath the two-tone baseball caps. None of the lads seemed to understand the function of the pockets in their trackie bottoms, preferring to keep their hands tucked down the front instead. The general tone of the group was smut and bravado. If ever a lost tribe needed the gospel translating into their language, it was these guys. And Lisa and her friends have managed to do that over the last few years. The initial proposition to the lads was a straightforward frontier exchange: 'You can knock on the door for a cup of tea and a chat, but there's one rule: please keep your hands out of your pants!' From that starting point all sorts of spin-offs have developed, including a regular Tuesday night lads club where the gospel can be explored. For Lisa, after three years this Eden thing is still quite unpredictable, but some things are certain:

Living there = the most amazing welcoming committee will be waiting on the pavement every night after work.

Living there = being ready to help the teenager kicked out of home in the middle of the night.

Living there = being the one who will care for the kiddies who are wandering the streets looking for their parents who've been arrested.

Living there = togging up for a snowball fight when the winter clouds empty to show how clean the streets could be.

Tipping points

World-renowned architect Sir Richard Rogers, in his clever little book *Cities for a Small Planet*, describes how he sees the health of the city directly related to the health of the world:

Cities have never contained so many, nor so large a proportion of the human race. Between 1950 and 1990 the population of the world's cities increased ten-fold, soaring from 200 million to more than 2 billion. The future of civilisation will be determined by its cities and in its cities.[3]

To those of us who look on the world through the lens of Christian mission, this kind of statement leads to a very simple conclusion. God has a passion for people, and lots of them are living in cities. So the most important thing we can do is focus our attention onto cities, and get on with the job of reaching the people in them. Ah, if only it were that simple; if only there weren't so many good reasons to keep 'hands off'. For example, you've probably heard the little story often used by Christian leaders to describe the current crisis facing twenty-first-century evangelists in the UK. It involves a vivid description of a burning building and a solitary person with a single bucket of water frantically wondering what to do with it. Why the indecision? Well, behind this person is a fire engine whose crew is fast asleep. What should the would-be hero do? Of course we are led to the logical conclusion that it would be entirely sensible to throw the bucket of water over the sleeping fire crew to wake them up. Then they can get back to their job of saving lives and putting out the fire. Sounds like a rational thing to do, doesn't it? Sounds quite smart, actually. But how does that person feel when the bucket has been emptied over the sleeping fire crew, and they're still asleep? They just spluttered a bit, looked like they might do something, then rolled over and carried on snoring.

That little parable of the church and the world has kept many would-be heroes from people-saving missions and redirected them towards waking-up duty. The drama of Eden offers no such smoke-free solace. You see, that little story is entirely flawed. Its weakness is its logic, because being a hero has never been a logical pursuit. In this world real heroes – the Jackie Pullingers and Heidi Bakers – do exist, they aren't just the stuff of myth and legend. They aren't extraordinary in and of themselves, but they do share our world, living lives that fly in the face of logic, testament to the fact that a single person can make a difference. Where will you find them? The best place to start looking

---

REALITY BITES

Stacy (15) tells her story.

Before I met the Eden team I was quiet. It's hard to believe but it's true! I never really went out because I was scared of where I lived. So I preferred to be indoors and not mix with troublemakers. I didn't like school whatsoever because I was the quiet, geeky kid who constantly got bullied. I never really had proper friends. I first met the Eden team when one of the girls off the team, Laura, who lived on my street, knocked on my door and asked me whether I wanted to come to a group at her house. I was unsure at first but I decided to go along. The club was great. I got to know Laura and another Eden worker called Sarah. Some other girls got invited too and I got to know them and we got on really well. At the club we watched films, played games and sometimes went out to places like the cinema. After a little while the team started to talk about God. When this happened some of the girls stopped coming to the group but I stayed. I thought the God stuff was very interesting. I finally became a Christian because to me it all made sense, that God loved me. Laura gave me a Bible and explained things and gave me a 'God book' to write prayers and notes of verses. This is my way of communicating with God.

---

is at the centre of a Tipping Point.[4] One of the best summaries of the stunning Tipping Point phenomenon has been made by missions boffin Dr Martin Robinson:

> It is an observable reality that the world is constantly changed by committed minorities and not by apathetic majorities.[5]

Malcolm Gladwell, the guy ultimately responsible for bringing the Tipping Point phenomenon to the attention of the world,

---

Laura invited me to Roots, a Christian festival, and I decided to go. It was an amazing experience. During Roots I felt loads closer to God and I understood more about him. Also I met some new friends who were Christians and they were from Openshaw, where there is another Eden project. I have visited them since then. Since Roots I have tried to live my life to the fullest as God would have intended me to. I have made a few slip-ups but now I am well and truly back on track. Now that I am a Christian my life has changed so much. I have more confidence and am not so quiet any more. I have more friends and when I get problems at school I have learned to ignore it. I can also proudly tell people I am a Christian.

Eden Harpurhey have been such an inspiration to me because they introduced me to church and fellowship. I still go to Girls Club but I am involved in more clubs now, such as TNT (Thursday Night Teaching). Since this has started I have got to know God much better and have a better relationship with him. I also get asked to sing in the worship band sometimes. As a close, I think that God has changed my life and he is AMAZING. Also I hope I learn more about God in the future.

Thank you for reading.

Stacy x

---

includes a study in the introduction to his book that bears uncanny relevance as we set off on our journey into Eden:

> A sociologist at the University of Illinois has looked at the effect the number of role models in a community – the professionals, managers, teachers whom the census bureau has defined as 'high status' – has on the lives of teenagers in the same neighbourhood. He found little difference in pregnancy rates or school drop-out rates in neighbourhoods of between 40 and 5 percent of high-status workers. But when the number of professionals dropped below 5 percent the problems exploded. For black schoolchildren, for example, as the percentage of high-status workers falls just 2.2 percentage points – from 5.6 percent to 3.4 percent – drop-out rates more than double. We assume, intuitively, that neighbourhoods and social problems decline in some kind of steady progression. But sometimes they may not decline steadily at all; at the Tipping Point, schools can lose control of their students, and family life can disintegrate all at once.[6]

Isn't that fascinating? It cuts right across our natural instincts and assumptions about the dynamics of community life. Martin Robinson has done his own research into remarkable transformations that have taken place in society, looking at the efforts of small groups of envisioned Christians like the Clapham Sect. He adds even more substance to this case by collating evidence of the mechanics of social change and offers the following statistics:

- To break through and see a real transformation brought to the collective mind and behaviour of their culture a group of activists must achieve a Tipping Point (critical mass) of 15% of the population of that group.

26

So by that rationale, totally transforming a whole generation of young people in a city the size of Manchester would require the mobilisation of 37,500 teenagers. We've still got a long way to go! However:

- To see a tangible difference in the prevailing atmosphere of an identified culture or subculture those activists need only achieve a Tipping Point of 2% of the population of that group.

If this is correct, a team of 30 people can make a significant impact on a population of 1,500. Those numbers are actually tremendously encouraging as they practically mirror the ratio created by the Eden model as teams of fired-up Christians have been placed right at the heart of inner-city communities. Andy Hawthorne, Founding Director of The Message, often quotes Acts 5:28 to motivate the guys and girls on the ground: *'… you have filled Jerusalem with your teaching …'* This accusation from the Sanhedrin to Peter and John, who were described as *'unschooled, ordinary men'*,[7] finds instant application with the Eden teams as they daily saturate the networks of their neighbourhoods with the news of Jesus. Their effectiveness in doing this could be measured in various ways. We could use the academic systems that Gladwell and Robinson might employ, or we could just listen to the history-makers themselves. It probably won't surprise you to hear that this book will be taking the second of those approaches.

---

1   Matthew 10:9–10: 'Do not take along any gold or silver or copper in your belts; take no bag for the journey, or extra tunic, or sandals or a staff …'
2   Office of National Statistics, 2001 Census.
3   Richard Rogers, *Cities for a Small Planet*, Faber & Faber, 1997.
4   Malcolm Gladwell, *The Tipping Point*, Abacus Books, 2000.
5   Martin Robinson and Dwight Smith, *Invading Secular Space*, Monarch 2003.
6   Malcolm Gladwell, *The Tipping Point*, Abacus Books, 2000.
7   Acts 4:13.

2
Calling All the Heroes

Remember, dear brothers and sisters, that few of you were wise in the world's eyes, or powerful, or wealthy when God called you. Instead, God deliberately chose things the world considers foolish in order to shame those who think they are wise. And he chose those who are powerless to shame those who are powerful.

1 Corinthians 1:26–27 (NLT)

Fingerprints of God

'Calling' is possibly one of the most overused words in the charismatic lexicon – apart from 'anointed'. But when a pastor or team leader is in the process of forming a new team to move into an inner-city estate it's a concept that comes in pretty handy. Try putting yourself in their shoes for a minute …

You strongly sense within your heart that the time is right to be true to the word of God and commence a significant long-term effort to see an urban area transformed by the power of God. You are convinced that this change won't be achieved by a few organised prayer walks and a fun day on the rec. You're going for the ever so slightly bonkers model of moving people in. You're not daft, it's going to be costly, your money, your time, your energy, your relationships are all going to be drained … and this gangly 20-year-old sat before you, who speaks with a bit of a lisp, who only finishes uni in the summer, who probably lives off Pot Noodles, who doesn't appear to own a washing machine and doesn't really know how he's going to earn a living, wants to be on the team!

The words constructing the scripted questions on your Eden interview sheet begin to perform a mad dance around the page as your mind scrolls through a thousand fragments of dusty Bible verses searching for something, anything, to anchor the situation, then <click>. You begin to think about Timothy, a bit weedy, a bit of a mummy's boy, but chosen by the apostle Paul and shaped into an awesome church-planter. Your glazed eyes blink into focus again just as the candidate begins to say, '… so I was up all night praying about it, and I just couldn't get this verse out of my head, from 1 Timothy 4:12, *"Don't let anyone look down on you because you are young, but set an example for the believers in speech, in life, in love, in faith and in purity."* I just, well, it's like, God is really calling me to do this, to get out of my comfort zone and to be part of a community, to start really making a difference. I'm not the finished article by any means but I'm ready to make a jump to something new. I believe I can really go the distance. I'm up for it, whatever, yeah?'

The muscles in your back begin to relax as $1 + 1 = 2$ again. This is a God thing; he's up to something here. You look again at this young man and see him as God sees him: a hope-bringer, a grace-giver, an overcomer, a champion, a warrior, an encourager, a father, a comforter. The regiment is taking shape right before your eyes. Who's next?

Common people?

Call it what you will – , 'calling', 'destiny', 'purpose', 'vision' – there is something incredibly exciting about discovering the fingerprints of God on the affairs of someone's life. Whether the call has come like a lightning bolt or a dripping tap, the evidence of divine involvement – the sense that *'Right here, right now, this is exactly what I am supposed to be doing with my life'* – is really what sets apart those who join the Eden teams from those who simply volunteer to help out a bit with our inner-city youth ministries. Eden 'workers' (staff or volunteers) are part of what we believe to be a twenty-first-century urban missionary movement. Eden is not a year-out or short-term missions programme. It's not a high-impact hit-and-run event; neither is it run for the benefit and qualification of the workers. In fact, although Eden may often be described with the word 'project', it's actually so much more. Each Eden is born out of and functions through relationship – a partnership commitment. For those choosing to live in the targeted Eden communities it's a deliberate way of life. It's a high-commitment, incarnational, Christ-commissioned lifestyle that's not for the fainthearted or the restless. It's about throwing away your armchair, taking up your cross, and living for something far greater than the world around you. Eden workers choose to exchange their own ambitions and agendas for promises of 'streams in the waste-land'.[1]

In the first seven years about 300 people have come from all over the UK, the largest contingent, maybe up to 50%, from the south-east, their accents being a source of constant amuse-ment for the local kids. The rest represent the breadth of Britain's cities, towns and villages and even other nations of the world including parts of Europe, America, Africa and Australia. The minimum age for an Eden worker is 18, although it's unusual for team leaders to accept anyone that young unless they really do have a level of maturity and a quality of life experience which is well beyond the average. There's no upper age limit and so long as an applicant can show an ability to relate to youth, grey hairs (or baldness) won't be a problem. Many people have been massively encouraged by Liza, who in 2002 became Eden's first granny recruit – at the age of 73. Every shade of the social spectrum is represented, from self-described 'chavs' and 'trailer trash' through to Oxbridge grads and even the heir of an ancient Scottish estate complete with 52-bedroom mansion, riding stables, botanical gardens and swimming pool! Where else but in the Kingdom of God could all these people enjoy the buzz of serving shoulder to shoulder? The key element everyone shares is an ownership of Eden's core value: making a redemptive home right in the heart of a difficult community. To this they are totally devoted, deliberately choosing to live an alternative lifestyle in the face of some of the highest crime, deprivation, drug, alcohol, teen-pregnancy and unemployment rates in the country. From the base of their

---

REALITY BITES

Claire, in Swinton Valley, a council estate in Salford.

I first considered Eden about six years ago. I was at Soul Survivor and The Message were talking about their vision for reaching out to young hurting people in Manchester's roughest places. It just grabbed my heart and I wondered whether God might be calling me to this. However, as I was at school I filed the feeling. God continued to catch my attention about what The Message were doing through prayer mailings and at Soul Survivor. I went

home they reach out to the youth of their area, which may require taking time with the entire family to bring lasting change. Deep in the psyche of every team is faith that through such efforts their neighbourhoods will see transformation as God's love thaws people's hearts.

Call me!

Far from being the 'Christian textbook' or 'life manual' it is often described as, the Bible basically gathers and arranges extracts from the minds and experiences of loads and loads of people God interacted with. Some bits of it make sense immediately; other bits only reveal their layers of meaning through deeper study and cross-referencing. Indeed, a powerful argument for its authenticity is its warts'n'all personal portraits and its unequalled multi-dimensional mega-plot. As the beats mix from the Old Testament to the New the atmosphere changes tangibly. It's as if someone opened the fire exit and let a huge gust of fresh air into the party. In fact the change is even more radical

---

along to the big mission event 'The Message 2000' where I led a team and enjoyed the experience. I prayed for confirmation of my calling as I led a team three years later at Festival: Manchester. It was a fantastic week. I talked to lots of Eden workers who were very encouraging. I particularly liked the way the church was so involved in the community and felt God really was calling me to join Eden, which I found very daunting. It would involve a big change in focus and lifestyle. I sensed God reassuring me, though, reminding me of the way he'd prepared me for this, and so I took a deep breath and decided to trust God and go for it!

than that – more like the whole club's been turfed out and a brand-new crowd let loose. There are some lessons waiting for us as we start meeting the new crew.

Peter and Andrew are amongst the first people we meet. Noticeably, they aren't standing in a queue under a sign saying 'STAND HERE FOR EXTREME LIFE-CHANGE'. We watch as Jesus just turns up, interrupts their work and says, ' *"Come, follow me ... and I will make you fishers of men." At once they left their nets and followed him.'* [2]

REALITY BITES

Jane, on waiting for the right time to join.

I grew up in Radcliffe, north Manchester, and thought I knew from a pretty early age what I wanted to do in life. By the time I went to high school I was already aiming to be an engineer and ranting to all who would listen about the joys of community and the importance of being a Christian where the people are – at school, home and work. I first heard about Eden in about 1998. My youth leader at the time mentioned what was just starting in Wythenshawe and I felt my heart jolt (I'm pretty sure I heard a clunk as well). I knew there and then that I would join Eden. I also knew I had to train first – and at some point would have to leave Manchester to do that. Throughout my time at sixth-form college in Bury and four years down south at university I held Manchester and Eden very close to my heart – and talked about them incessantly. Being part of the crowd at Oxford Uni was fantastic and I know that God used that time and the church I joined down there to train me for work and Eden.

Their mates James and John had it coming too. *'Going on from there, he saw two other brothers, James son of Zebedee and his brother John. They were in a boat with their father Zebedee, preparing their nets. Jesus called them, and immediately they left the boat and their father and followed him.'*[3] Jesus pulled the same stunt on them, but they had the added problem of having to make their decision right in front of their dad. Their personal loyalties and priorities were challenged by Jesus from day one.

In 2001, during a summer mission in Salford, I desperately wanted to sign up – just to express how I felt really – but I felt God put his hand over those thoughts and say, 'Wait – you're not yet in the position to do that.' Eventually, just before my finals, I felt God say that the time was right, so I applied for Eden and engineering jobs in Manchester ... it was time to come home. God was so faithful. Praying about where in Manchester to move to, he reminded me of things he'd put on my heart and mind when working at a kids' club in Oxford – to encourage kids who saw themselves as 'failures' with a godly confidence that brings 'worth' – so 'Fails-worth' it was! This strange way of selecting a project was confirmed when my dad, who I'd asked to pray over a map of the projects, returned with the same answer. God also provided a job that I love – honestly far more than I could ever expect or imagine! I've been living in Failsworth as part of Eden, the local church and community for a year or so now. I pray for and believe in the kids here – that they will grow to love our town and community, that they will serve and enjoy being in this community for God's glory.

Levi (Matthew) was having another good day, surrounded by all his cash, raking it in with the help of the Romans. Was he scanning the *Jerusalem Evening News* every Thursday night for the latest vacancies? Not likely, he was on a right cushy number. *'Jesus went out and saw a tax collector by the name of Levi sitting at his tax booth. "Follow me," Jesus said to him, and Levi got up, left everything and followed him.'* [4]

Philip and Nathanael were a different kettle of fish. Phil was keen as mustard, but not someone you'd put in charge of your PR department. He didn't really home in on Jesus' USP[5] when describing the Messiah to his brother:

Philip found Nathanael and told him, 'We have found the one Moses wrote about in the Law, and about whom the prophets also wrote – Jesus of Nazareth, the son of Joseph.'

'Nazareth! Can anything good come from there?' Nathanael asked.

'Come and see,' said Philip.

When Jesus saw Nathanael approaching, he said of him, 'Here is a true Israelite, in whom there is nothing false.'

'How do you know me?' Nathanael asked.

Jesus answered, 'I saw you while you were still under the fig-tree before Philip called you.' [6]

Here we see Jesus beginning to break his established recruitment and selection policy. Up until this point it seemed like Jesus preferred head-hunting his staff to picking them up from the job centre. Peter, Andrew, James, John, Levi, Philip – all busy guys, all with great enthusiasm, great work ethics. Jesus doesn't appear at all keen on calling people who are sitting around doing nothing, until Nathanael. Here we witness Jesus calling a cynical, sceptical, confrontational layabout. And what's more, he's the one who gets a personal promise thrown in with the deal: *'I tell you the truth, you shall see heaven open, and the angels of God ascending and descending on the Son of Man.'* [7] Nathanael is the example to us of God's ability to find potential in the most unlikely places. No one is too busy or too lazy for Jesus to call.

McChristianity

These aren't the only lessons in the Gospels on the subject of calling. There are umpteen more. At least two of them need singling out in this context for special attention. First, there's the whole issue of personal baggage, the stuff of life which restricts our agility and leaves us unable to cope with any terrain beyond the broad, flat path. The rocky heights of Christian mission dictate travelling light as the only way up and over. We read about one young guy who found this out in Matthew 19:16–30.

> *Now a man came up to Jesus and asked, 'Teacher, what good thing must I do to get eternal life?'*
>
> *… Jesus replied, '… If you want to enter life, obey the commandments.'*
>
> *'Which ones?' the man enquired.*
>
> *Jesus replied, ' "Do not murder, do not commit adultery, do not steal, do not give false testimony, honour your father and mother," and "love your neighbour as yourself." '*
>
> *'All these I have kept,' the young man said. 'What do I still lack?'*
>
> *Jesus answered, 'If you want to be perfect, go, sell your possessions and give to the poor, and you will have treasure in heaven. Then come, follow me.'*
>
> *When the young man heard this, he went away sad, because he had great wealth.*
>
> *… Jesus said to them, '… everyone who has left houses or brothers or sisters or father or mother or children or fields for my sake will*

receive a hundred times as much and will inherit eternal life. But many who are first will be last, and many who are last will be first.'

This is a massive challenge to our twenty-first-century McChristianity. Our wealth, meaning the way we all define and identify ourselves by certain products and lifestyle choices, is almost always, upon examination, a direct contradiction to the message Jesus walked and talked. This is where our second example comes in, the challenge to be a cross-carrier.

- *'Anyone who does not take his cross and follow me is not worthy of me.'* [8]

- *Jesus said to his disciples, 'If anyone would come after me, he must deny himself and take up his cross and follow me.'* [9]

REALITY BITES

Anna, coming to a realisation, coming to Harpurhey.

I remember hearing about this thing called Eden at places like Soul Survivor and thought that it looked great. However, I didn't have any desire to be in the inner city at all and thought that it was somewhere that God would never want me to be.

Some people I knew left my home church to go and do something a bit unusual – to lead one of these projects. I remember them showing a video in church and I was really excited by what I saw. I found myself thinking that I would love to do something about that. It all seemed a little bit too extreme for me, though, and I didn't think that I had much to offer. My life hadn't been exactly hard!

I was engrossed in my teaching job, activities in my local church and generally enjoying being in my early twenties. Life

---

- *Then he called the crowd to him along with his disciples and said: 'If anyone would come after me, he must deny himself and take up his cross and follow me.'* [10]

- *Then he said to them all: 'If anyone would come after me, he must deny himself and take up his cross daily and follow me.'* [11]

- *'And anyone who does not carry his cross and follow me cannot be my disciple.'* [12]

The image Jesus uses is deliberately provocative and completely unambiguous. The smell of death is all around as he beckons us closer. 'You know that "follow me" stuff I said, that you said you were so up for? Well, there's something else I need to tell you ...'

---

then hit an extremely bumpy road and for a long time nothing went right. I never knew that things could be quite so 'grrrrr' as they were. I was ready to turn my back on God, on everything, but some really remarkable things happened within the space of a week.

In that week I came to visit Manchester; I just had to go and see and get it out of my mind once and for all! There was no bolt of lightning, no loud voice from God telling me what I should do, but there was a realisation inside me. I realised that I had loads to offer, I could show love and acceptance to the kids, the families, the people I would come into contact with. That was something I could do. I knew that things had to change. I had seen another side to life and was so frustrated. I couldn't continue with things the way they were. I had to do more. By the end of that week I had made some big decisions! I decided that God really is who he claims to be (how gracious of me to realise it!) and I decided that I'd apply to Eden. It certainly was a week I'd never forget.

The sky over this sunny discipleship adventure has suddenly got dark, the path has suddenly got very steep and the temperature has suddenly dropped about 20 degrees.

'Er, where are you taking us, Jesus?'

To preach good news to the poor. To bind up the broken-hearted. To proclaim freedom for the captives and release from darkness for the prisoners. To proclaim the year of the LORD's favour and the day of vengeance of our God. To comfort all who mourn, and provide for those who grieve in Zion. To bestow on them a crown of beauty instead of ashes, the oil of gladness instead of mourning, and a garment of praise instead of a spirit of despair. To become oaks of righteousness, a planting of the LORD for the display of his splendour. To rebuild the ancient ruins and restore the places long devastated. To renew the ruined cities that have been devastated for generations.[13]

Quality and quantity

We've already mentioned the idea of Tipping Points – that when a critical mass of people commit themselves to an objective amazing things can happen. Eden has always aimed to create these significant clusters of people, between 20 and 30 living in quite a small area. It's hardly surprising that each of these Eden teams comprises a range of passions, experiences and abilities. It's also evident that God looks after the big picture of bringing together these individual personalities to complement each other and enable a wide variety of activities to be undertaken. However, moving missionaries into the inner city is about a whole lot more than kidnapping some gullible graduates from the nearest summer conference. Before they even make it to a team, some essential qualities must be recognised.

40

- Workers must understand the sense of lostness felt outside the grace of God. At the core of every team is a passion to see broken hearts healed and lives restored through Jesus.
- Workers must have a desire to grow up in God. There are hard lessons to be learned through Eden and no worker arrives as a finished product with all the answers.
- Workers must be willing to follow the leadership of the church leader and team leader with an openness to be stretched, challenged and to try new things.
- Workers need to see where their contribution is located against the backdrop of the local host church and the horizon of God's big plan for the city.

It's amazing really, considering the lengthy application and screening process, that any of the teams ever formed at all.

Then consider the general church climate. In recent years, evangelical Christians have tended to stay away from the inner city. 'In Manchester around 75% of the population live in the urban areas of the city, but 75% of the Christian population live in the suburban areas. This means most of the salt and light is spread among a minority of the people.'[14]

Eden has chosen to work actively against this statistic by arranging the relocation of all sorts of people from the relative safety of the suburbs to the volatile streets of the inner city. The recruitment job is a really tricky one. How can you raid friendly, warm-hearted churches of their best people without putting everyone else in the congregation on a downer or a guilt trip? This is where the urban missionaries concept comes in. If the whole church took the great commission to 'go' in its rawest form very seriously, we'd all pack our bags tomorrow, about a million of us, and change the nation overnight. The whole social, political and economical structure of the nation would be completely overturned in one fell swoop. More revolutionary readers will probably read that and think, 'Cool – let's do it!' However, as we touched on in chapter 1, big numbers are not the be-all and end-all when it comes to community transformation. Just the right people in just the right ratios are what's needed. Sending out and supporting missionaries is something which many churches have become accustomed to, and in some cases even good at. This existing frame of reference now forms a doorway through which a new generation of people-reachers can be directed. As Rick Warren notes, 'A church's health is measured by its sending capacity, not its seating capacity.'[15]

South to north

A definite trend in the recruitment of Eden missionaries has been the gravitational pull from the south to the north. Take Brighton, for example – that's about as far south as you'll get before you fall into the sea. Since the early nineties Gary Bishop had been employed by the Salvation Army to develop the youth work from their lively Brighton Congress Hall. As a host church it was well established, Gary's ideas were well resourced and the prevailing atmosphere was sunny and optimistic. Understandably Gary was not immediately turned on by his friend's suggestion that he should take a look at a new opportunity appearing on the horizon in Manchester. Was he guilty of some gross heresy? So why should he be condemned to this youth work gulag? But being open to the often mysterious will of God, Gary agreed to visit the Salvation Army's Manchester HQ and meet the officers responsible for developing a new Eden project in east Manchester.

Returning from this first ever trip to Manchester, Gary was met at Watford Junction train station by his girlfriend Hannah. In the passenger seat of her clapped-out blue Metro he confided, 'I don't care if I never go there again!' What a classic invitation for God to shift into calling overdrive. Meanwhile, oblivious to Gary's private assessment of the situation, the senior guys responsible for making the big decisions about this new Eden offered the following 'generous' ultimatum: 'Gary, we like you a lot, we really sense that you're God's man for this pioneering task and we'd like to offer you the job. Could you let us know if you'll be taking it by this time next week?' With all the grace he could muster at the time, Gary resisted the temptation to commit GBH over the phone and politely requested a bit more time to think and pray about it. 'Give me a month. This is a big deal.'

That month Gary began engaging God in dialogue, and it wasn't fluffy pillow talk either. During a training conference at which he'd been invited to speak Gary got down to brass tacks. 'God, I'm supposed to have free will, yeah? So why do I feel so pressurised? What happened to my right to choose?' And immediately the response came, forming in his mind with matter-of-fact tenor: 'You do have a choice — obedience or disobedience — and there's the door.' That very instant Gary blinked and found himself looking up and across the grand hall to the massive oak-framed exit. The clarity of the word and the added drama of the setting were far too powerful to deny.

But there was another complication: his relationship with Hannah, the soulmate he was sure his destiny was entwined with. They'd not been going out all that long, but all the signs were good for their future. What would she make of it all? Surely it was all going to end in tears. To Gary's great relief Hannah was into the idea of paying a visit to Manchester to help in the process of decision-making. They'd go and meet some of the guys from Eden projects already started in other parts

43

of the city and try to get a perspective on what sort of challenge really lay ahead. Stuck in an M6 traffic jam caused by heavy November rain and thick fog, Gary made Hannah an offer. 'I tell you what, if the sun shines tomorrow in Openshaw we'll say yes!' Ladbrokes would have given nice long odds on that one. But it's funny, isn't it, how God listens and responds, even to our sarcasm. The very next day Gary was buying Hannah an ice-cream as they enjoyed a freak afternoon of blazing Manchester sunshine together. 'I could see us making a home here,' said Hannah. And right there a whole month of pressure just melted away. God smiled, and there was nothing more to decide.

REALITY BITES

Serena, reflecting on four years in Wythenshawe.

It is early spring 2001 and I have just unpacked my final box of things, having moved to St Louis, Missouri. That seems more than a million miles away from Wythenshawe but really it isn't. This move is just an extension of the principles I learned from four years as an Eden worker. This is highlighted to me even more when I discover in the last box I unpack a Soul Survivor ministry tape from August 1997 – Andy Hawthorne speaking from Romans 12. He gives such a powerful and challenging message on those verses about living life as a sacrifice before God that even as I listen I am again moved to tears. Then I remember that the previous evening at Soul Survivor I had

---

Foreigners will shepherd your flocks

People in Kenya understand the concept of missionaries; they've had missionaries living among them for well over 100 years. Cyprian Yobera has got it; his own Christian faith was founded in that heritage, after an English missionary travelled the globe to bring the gospel to his village, in the region of Busia at the back end of the nineteenth century. At the turn of the millennium Cyprian and his lovely wife Jayne were living in the capital city of Nairobi. They'd been blessed with two gorgeous kids and both found fulfilling jobs. Jayne was working as a teacher and Cyprian was working as part of the team at the huge All Saints Cathedral, the centre of the Anglican church in

---

nervously introduced myself to Andy knowing that God had spoken to me about moving to Wythenshawe. The next morning during Andy's oration it was as if God took out his permanent marker and wrote this value on my heart. I realised that I, Serena McCarthy, living my life as an offering before God was the only sacrifice that could be a spiritual act of worship.

This was such a foundational part of the lessons we lived out on our estate in Manchester that now it's become part of my everyday life. I can't escape the power of it. Emotional to the extreme at the end of the tape I got on my knees and worshipped. Eden is all about ordinary people living ordinary lives in worship of an extraordinary God. Now, 6,000 miles away and seven years later I am still using the gifts God has given to me as a sacrifice to him and that will continue for a lifetime. For me Eden was a time of understanding foundational things about God in a practical environment in a real way; no lights, no glory, just worship.

Kenya. From time to time, crinkly copies of the *Church of England Newspaper* would turn up in the offices and he'd flick through them. Perhaps because of his sensitivity to the origins of his own faith, Cyprian felt concerned whenever he heard on this extended grapevine about problems facing the church back in Britain. As youth was his area of responsibility, that was the area he yearned most passionately for and felt most disturbed about whilst reading. Having a modest youth group of about 1,000 teenagers, he felt the difference was like night and day – and knew his calling was to be a light in the darkness, not in a place already gloriously bright.

REALITY BITES

Sharon and family, on starting a new team in Hattersley.

In 2000 our family came to Manchester to take part in Message 2000. My husband John stayed at his mum's house in Hattersley and my teenage daughter Marie and I camped at Heaton Park. Marie was a delegate and I was part of the Welfare Team. John and the rest of the family came to the MEN Arena in the evenings. Whilst we were in Manchester God spoke to John and me but we didn't tell each other until we were on the drive home. We both felt God had called us to Manchester, which was surprising because I was an out-and-out Essex girl and John had no desire to move anywhere. The one stipulation that John put on this calling was, 'Lord, not Eden and definitely not Hattersley.' John didn't want to live in Hattersley because he'd lived there as a child and left when he was 18. But God had different plans.

On our subsequent visit to The Message to pursue this call we were met with the words, 'We've been praying for you and wonder what you think about living on an Eden project in Hattersley.' John said at that point he felt the conviction of the

One of these old newspapers contained a job advertisement and with a little encouragement from some close friends he applied for the job. Of course, by the time his application reached the address in England it was hopelessly late – but as it sat there on an anonymous desk it caught someone's eye. Out of the blue he received a call from his Archbishop telling him, 'The Church Missionary Society in England want to talk to you about a job opportunity.' The job was with a church in Manchester which was about to embark on a radical new youth project called Eden. What made this project different from all the other jobs advertised was that it was in the community, in

---

Holy Spirit that this was the will of God. We went home and took some wise counsel. All said they agreed it was the call of God on our lives. We asked our children aged 4–14 to pray and ask God what he was saying and one by one they came back to us saying yes, they felt it was right. There were so many different confirmations, including a really weird one: I was visiting the local garden centre and looking at the menu in the tearoom. The menu was on a wooden stand and engraved on the top of the stand was the word 'Hattersley'. Hattersley was 250 miles away and yet here was the name on a menu stand!

We drew up a list of the things we needed in a house – a large kitchen for our large family, an extra bathroom, and for me a view that I would enjoy looking at. As far as we knew there were no such houses in Hattersley. We started praying. Six weeks before we were due to move to Hattersley we still had nowhere to live, but we still trusted that we had heard from God clearly. We found a house advertised on the Internet and came up to view it. As we walked in we knew it was the answer to our prayers. It had a large kitchen, an extra bathroom and a view of woodland. We were able to move in six weeks later.

partnership with the church, not inside the walls of the church. To Cyprian this made perfect sense. In no time at all two tickets arrived for Cyprian and Jayne to come and take a look. They had many questions and so decided that the only way to get the answers was to go and see.

Whilst looking around the church with the vicar, Cyprian heard the story of a local lad messed up with drugs and all sorts of other issues, who would mess about on the church property. Members of the church had tried to get alongside him in different ways, but tragically the boy had committed suicide on the church grounds, while a service was taking place inside the building. It was all Cyprian needed to hear. There was no way he could stay in Kenya while young people died just a stone's throw from the altar. Cyprian is now having an amazing impact in the Harpurhey area as Eden's youth and families worker. Whole families including extended relatives have been reached through his adaptations of the Alpha course and a home-grown 'Church on the Streets' programme.

A planting of the Lord

The way that God has selected his dream team for each of the Edens that have been pioneered is truly amazing. But Christ didn't actually say, 'I will build my team.' He said, 'I will build my church.' When it came to planting a team into Swinton Valley, 'church' was the missing link. That's why Howard Kellett was about to have his life divinely interrupted. As we close this section we must recognise that it's not just the team members who need to be called – the leaders of the churches through which Eden expresses its ministry also need to 'know in their knower' that Eden is a God-thing.

Howard was doing pretty well on the staff of a church in Lewisham when a sudden course of events made it evident to him and those close to him that his future would be elsewhere. He found himself for the first time driving to the annual Stoneleigh Event in 2000 knowing that he was on his network's 'transfer list'. The whole place was buzzing with talk of mission, and lots of that buzz was related to things happening in the churches dotted around the Manchester area. Behind the scenes the Newfrontiers leadership team were talking about laying down Europe's largest Christian festival in favour of just getting out there and doing the stuff in Britain's towns and cities. One of these senior guys took Howard on one side to show him a piece written in the *Daily Telegraph* about Eden, under the intriguing headline, 'Could these people raise your house price?' Howard was slightly baffled by what he was reading. All he knew about Eden was that it was somehow connected to those people in the shiny tracksuits who would jump around making a din on the stage in the Revive youth venue. What was going on?

Standing out from this general backdrop of faith for a future in which evangelism was back at the top of the network's agenda, news was spreading around the site about something going on just two hours up the M6 in Manchester. Overlapping Stoneleigh in the summer's event diary, Soul Survivor and The Message had recruited 10,000 young people to bring the life and love of God to people in the city's toughest communities. One of those communities was the Valley Estate in Swinton, where crime had dropped to zero, feuding neighbours were being reconciled and hardened criminals were weeping tears of joy in the street.[16] Newfrontiers had been asked by Andy Hawthorne to help follow up by planting a church and in no time at all Howard found himself framed as the man for the job. Within a week Howard was in Manchester meeting with Andy and Newfrontiers' 'man in the north' Colin Baron, flicking through a folder stuffed with newspaper cuttings about 'The Week That Crime Stood Still On The Valley Estate'. He'd already predetermined in personal time with God that 'I'll only plant if you'll give me a team – I'm not doing it on my own!' Andy and Colin explained the Eden model: a team moves in, led by a gifted team leader accountable to the local pastor. In this case the team leader had already been found – a guy called Hayden Brophy.

'Hang about, I know Hayden. We've worked together at Revive – he's a top bloke ...' Any convenient excuses Howard had were evaporating fast. This thing had momentum. It was all happening really fast and the ball was now in his court.

Still, Howard didn't have a problem playing it down to his wife when he got back to London. 'I don't know, I'm just not sure.'

'Well, it sounds to me like God's in it!' his wife replied, and within a few weeks Howard accepted the invitation.

---

1   Isaiah 43:20.
2   Matthew 4:19–20.
3   Matthew 4:21–22.
4   Luke 5:27–29.
5   Unique Selling Point, for those of you who didn't pay attention during GCSE Business Studies!
6   John 1:45–50.
7   John 1:51.
8   Matthew 10:38.
9   Matthew 16:24.
10   Mark 8:34.
11   Luke 9:23.
12   Luke 14:27.
13   See Isaiah 61:1–4.
14   Stats taken from www.urbanpresence.org.uk. Urban Presence is a Christian charity seeking to resource Christians, churches and organisations living and working in inner-city Manchester.
15   Rick Warren, *The Purpose Driven Church*, Zondervan, 1995.
16   For more on these amazing events read *Diary of a Dangerous Vision* by Andy Hawthorne, published by Survivor Books, 2004.

3

Coming – Ready or Not!

By faith Abraham, when called to go to a place he would
later receive as his inheritance, obeyed and went, even
though he did not know where he was going. By faith he
made his home in the promised land like a stranger in a
foreign country.

Hebrews 11:8–9

Laws of attraction

Tracing the history of the first Eden initiative, in Wythenshawe, a
definite momentum was building for a couple of years before
anything dramatic happened. King's Church, which consisted of
about 25 people meeting every Sunday in the community
centre, was undergoing the most major restructuring of its
10-year history. Leader Adrian Nottingham had begun to relate
to the elders of a much larger charismatic church based in
Manchester city centre, called Covenant Community Church.
King's Church as a whole felt strongly that joining themselves
with CCC was God's will for them as a congregation. They took
the step, sacrificing their independence and autonomy but
gaining a whole layer of leadership and a new extended family

of relationships. Through the efforts of key workers and short-term missions teams sent from CCC a new perspective on the issues and struggles of life on the local estate was gained. King's Church found that calling on the Lord for real people you've met and begun to get to know is a very different dynamic from praying over a generic A–Z map of a city. A big shift was going on in the hearts of those involved.

The sequence of extended events unfolding through the work of The World Wide Message Tribe described in chapter 1 formed a parallel track to this revolutionising of King's Church Wythenshawe. Just as a church was being 'rewired' for the future, a breakthrough of power was happening right on its doorstep. As any half-decent chaos theorist would tell you, moments of crisis (like 100 crazy young people turning up) during conditions of disturbed equilibrium (like adjusting to a whole new style of leadership) are exactly when you would expect something radically new to emerge.[1] However, any clued-up geneticist will tell you how immensely difficult it is to reproduce in the lab what nature does without even thinking. So what were the conditions like in the other places where Eden now exists? Are they all clones of Wythenshawe? Have the 10 current expressions of Eden followed the birthing process of build-up before breakthrough? Fasten your seatbelt for a whistle-stop tour of Eden right across Greater Manchester …

Feeling the He@t in Salford (1999)

Salford is a city within a city. It sits right next to Manchester's flashy city centre on the opposite side of the River Irwell and stretches out west from there along the route of the historic ship canal. Salfordians take great pride in their heritage, but their beloved city has been unfairly labelled by the media as the 'crime capital of England'. The city itself is a patchwork quilt of tight-knit communities, each with very defined boundaries. This territorialism means that young people from certain areas won't cross from one side of an invisible boundary to the other without a good reason.

Growing up in the middle of all this was the youth group of Mount Chapel Church. Fired up by powerful experiences of the Holy Spirit during the years of the 'Toronto Blessing', they'd often left the Sunday night church meetings and passionately prayer-walked through the dodgy local streets around Mount Chapel's building. In time they launched their own monthly youth event called 'He@t', which attracted youth groups from far and wide to worship and intercede. Lots of directional input was coming their way so the job of sifting 'the word of the Lord' from 'people getting excited' was a challenge for the young leaders. Visits from Soul Survivor's Mike Pilavachi and 24–7's Pete Greig are remembered as being especially helpful at this time. Chris Lane, who headed up this group, was having his eyes opened to God's great purposes and it was all getting a bit overwhelming. One night at He@t he saw a vision from God in his mind's eye – aeroplanes were flying over the neighbour-hood they'd prayer-walked, and they were dropping curious bombs. Wherever the bomb landed an orb of light would ignite, illuminating the surrounding darkness. From a vantage point high above, Chris could see these lights having a transforma-tional effect on the prevailing blackness. The interpretation formed very simply in his soul: these lights are Christians moving in.

This was taking place at about the same time that the Wythenshawe Eden was just kicking off. It was a time when, by tradition, The Message would hold a monthly prayer meeting in a local church, moving around the city from place to place. On the invitation of Andy Hawthorne, He@t had become the resident band. As they spent so much time together, conversations inevitably happened about the viability of Eden – which was only really designed as a response to Wythenshawe's problems – travelling to Salford too. The team of elders at Mount Chapel needed to be consulted, as their ability to host the team would be critical to any project launch. The necessary meetings were arranged and they expressed their desire to get behind the idea. Eden number 2 was off.

The identified project area of Langworthy consists of endless rows of Victorian two-up two-down terraced housing complete with narrow alleys ideal for backstreet shenanigans. There was nothing for young people to do, the typical invitation for a host of social problems such as vandalism, violence, alcohol and drug abuse. The neighbourhood had endured these issues bravely, but with zero investment void properties became endemic, negative equity ruled. In a full-page article the *Guardian* reported, 'Not long ago, houses round here were changing hands in pubs … People were saying, "Here are the keys – give me a couple of thousand pounds." '[2] At least that meant team members coming into the area could do so with a short-term loan rather than a mortgage. The move-in dates of the team coincided with this part of Salford being named as a Regeneration Zone through the government's SRB programme. The area was recognised as being high need and through the scheme £25 million was allocated to be pumped into the area. Team members joined long-term residents on consultative panels organised by the agencies involved in the regeneration of the area. The timing of the whole thing seemed to have a divine perfection. If Eden Salford had arrived after all the regeneration work had been done, credibility would have been much harder to come by. As it stands, Eden workers are amongst the longest serving members of many local action groups.

From day one the Salford team put loads of effort into the local high schools. One school suffering acutely from truancy and bad behaviour welcomed the new team with open arms. He@t and The Tribe performed a gig there which will go down in history as one of the most raucous nights ever! Working in the school was massively helpful in illuminating the particular issues faced by young people in the local area. The team blended this approach with a busy programme of detached street work. Walking in small groups around the eerie streets at night also proved to be a great team-building exercise! During the first year of the project the team were out four or five nights a week meeting local youth who were hanging around. The team were making themselves visible and beginning to 'own' the streets. However, it did become clear that a base was needed for these young people. The potential for really meaningful work on the street was limited. Having somewhere the young people could come to chill out, learn some skills and engage in issue-based workshops would really help.

The Message commenced talks with Open Hands International and the Shaftesbury Society, who began a feasibility study into where to put a youth centre in the area, what it might look like and what it would offer. To the delight of the local youth, LifeCentre Salford was launched during all the buzz of The Message 2000 event. The location was perfect: a converted shop right on the local high street, Langworthy Road. The interior was kitted out as a state-of-the-art youth base. It has computer games systems, a café area, a kitchen, an IT suite, a DJ workshop, an arts and crafts room and offices. A fair old wedge of the funding came from the SRB budget – at the time it was quite unheard of for a rather wacky faith group to be trusted with so much dosh!

Longsight, where it all began (2000)

The Manchester district of Longsight is where the vision of The Message began, where Andy Hawthorne and his brother Simon first began to sense the call to the wild young people of Manchester's inner-city estates. Their little fashion enterprise was enjoying bumper orders in the late eighties on the back of the Princess Diana fuelled craze for elastic braces worn over a crisp white blouse. Operators for the production line at their factory premises in Longsight had to be found as quickly as possible, and the qualifications for such a job were zero. The police would often need to raid the homes of the kleptomaniac youth they employed to reclaim endless yards of multi-coloured elastic the lads had smuggled out in their jackets at the end of the shift. Eventually the Hawthorne boys moved the business out of the area and in the years that followed Longsight challenged Moss Side for the dubious honour of being Manchester's drug capital, with all the associated gang activity.

The Message had for some time felt a heart resonance with South Manchester Family Church, which had an involvement in the area – although its meeting venue and offices were based a few miles away. Their pioneering leader Colin Baron had a proven track record of being able to crank the handle of mission within his network, which was definitely felt to be an advantage if a team was to be established in this challenging context. Also on the scene and up for it were a fantastic couple, Dan and Kit Leaver, who knew the area well and had an obvious gifting for the type of work that would be going on. They agreed with Andy and Colin that taking responsibility for the new Eden team was exactly what God had been preparing them for.

Like every new Eden, loads of strategic planning was required, which in this case involved getting the geography just right. Longsight is a fairly big area, split into chunks by busy arterial roads leading in and out of Manchester. Each patch has a distinct identity, and some were being reached by local churches, while others weren't faring so well. Positioning for maximum impact and minimum duplication was key at this stage. A remnant of dingy terraced streets that had miraculously survived the Christmas blitz in 1940 was decided on as the target area. A plus for the project was the nearby park, which would prove really useful in later years for the development of sports programmes and community events. The project was launched during The Message 2000 for the sake of posterity.

A notable feature of the Longsight team is the way that Eden has acted as a catalyst within the larger body of their host church, which is several hundred strong. Inspired by the sacrificial lifestyle the team has demonstrated, about a dozen members of the congregation have also decided to join them living in the Longsight area. They haven't taken on the title of Eden team members, but have joined the community to support, encourage, pray, and reach out to kids, families, the elderly and others outside Eden's primary focus group. A structure of cell groups ties them all in together. In 2004 the church elders, recognising the significance and maturity of this Christian community, 'promoted' the team leader to a position of responsibility for this whole zone of church life and ministry.

New possibilities in Openshaw (2000)

Throughout the nineties Phil Wall and his Salvation Army Missions Department had gained the respect of their peers from other networks across the nation as they journeyed back to their roots – the essence of what old Boothy had been on about all those years ago. They had rediscovered their great movement's raw passion for saving broken people through the love of Christ, and they were beginning to re-imagine the future. For them the stuff of dreams was entering the realm of possibilities. The dream was of new, vibrant expressions of urban church, and the possibility was Openshaw, situated in east Manchester, about three miles from the city centre. It's one of the many small townships that grew up around the collieries, eventually expanding out to merge into one another and form the solid mass of Manchester as we now know it.

Phil has been good mates with Andy Hawthorne for a long time, and they share intense 'Type A' personalities. Just a few minutes in a room together would be likely to lead to a

---

REALITY BITES

Paul and Nicky, squeezing into Salford.

We had a big house, so we knew the move would be a downsizing exercise. But we had a fantastic plan ... we were aware that lots of other people were moving onto the Salford team at the same time as us, and many of them would be young singles coming straight from their parents, without any of the grown-up clutter that we'd had a chance to accumulate. The idea was to bless the rest of the team on our arrival by passing on lots of this extra stuff. 'Still sleeping on a mattress on the floor? Have a bed!' 'Hanging your clothes on a curtain rail? Have a wardrobe!' It would be great!

So we hired a 7.5 ton removal lorry and headed up north. We'd never actually seen the house we were moving into and on the way up we pondered over how a terraced house acquires the

---

three-phase revival plan for the whole Milky Way. And the Openshaw idea came about in that sort of way. Although Eden projects were rolling out faster than the recruitment machine could cope with, it was felt that the expansive Salvation Army family was an 'unfished pond' and so finding the right people wouldn't be a problem. A clapped-out old citadel at a busy set of traffic lights just off the high street provided a useful locus for the project hub and the promising young leader, Gary, was on the scene. Right around this time Openshaw was awarded SRB status as part of the extensive east Manchester regeneration masterplan – a surprise to all involved in the project's planning, as nobody involved with Eden was particularly clued up about the regional regeneration agenda back in those days.

number 11a – isn't it a bit difficult to squeeze in another house once the row is built? But 11a did exist and we were bowled over by the amazing welcome we received, with Carl, the team leader, gathering most of the other new team members who'd recently arrived to help us unload.

You've never seen anything so comical. Every single bit of available space in the house was filled up. There was even a wardrobe in the lounge, which meant that the sofas were pushed so close together your knees would touch the knees of the person sitting opposite. The only real advantage was that with so much stuff it was hard to notice that the house actually had no carpets. There's probably a good reason why Jesus told his disciples to travel light!

A small area within Openshaw of about 600 houses known as the Toxteth St Estate, made up of rotting red-brick terraces from the 1900s, was selected as the residential focus for the team. The young team was immediately faced with the depressing effects of decades of decline, including the now familiar Eden landscape of violence, crime, unemployment, youth nuisance and drug abuse. The local MP was overheard saying, 'Moss Side and Hulme are bad, but the toughest bit of my constituency is Openshaw.' Sixteen 20-somethings joined the team from August 2000 to November 2000. During that time they focused on team-building and vision, creating a fabric of interpersonal relationships. This was really important as Openshaw would be the first Eden church plant. The team also gave a lot of intentional time to getting to know their neighbours and going out on detached street work to meet people. They were very aware that with no established congregation behind them, if they didn't go out and see lives changed, there would be no church. This proved to be a great motivation and gave the team a tremendous sense of purpose. It was the right thing to do; in less than four years their Sunday morning church gatherings were pushing the walls of the 100-seater hall.

A golden opportunity in Swinton (2001)

Eden Swinton is focused on a small pocket of deprivation in a fairly average town, in the area known locally as 'the Valley'. It's a 1930s council estate and has had one of the worst reputations in Salford for being a hive of criminal activity and drug dealing. The Valley is a warren of about 450 houses, but has had problems way out of proportion to its population. The Valley estate became a big story during The Message 2000. Holy pandemonium broke out as 1,000 young Christians descended on the estate to clean up the streets, gardens and community centre while they talked to the local residents about Jesus. During the ten days of the project there was miraculously no crime on the estate as the entire community got in on the action. Neighbours and families were reunited; streets at war got on peacefully together, and butch policemen cried as they saw things they could not have dreamed of!

During M2K it was clear that an Eden team would be needed in the Valley immediately to continue the work that had started. However, a by-product of The Message 2000 was that all the void properties on the estate were quickly assigned tenants. Nobody expected that the houses which had been impossible for the council to rent would suddenly develop a waiting list! Consequently it became impossible for team members to make their homes in the community. It took about six months before the team leader was able to move onto the estate, then six more to recruit and move in another half-dozen team members. Initially life was difficult for the team because some of the local residents felt disappointed by the abrupt end of M2K and the failure to complete a number of tasks which had been promised. They were still angry and had become cold to God and church. Nevertheless, the team focused on youth work, using the facilities on board the new double-decker Eden bus to get things going again. For a long time the team felt they were making little headway on the estate, but they persevered, holding on to the promise that the work started in 2000 would come through to completion.

Howard Kellett found a local primary school willing to rent out their hall for Sunday meetings. On the first Sunday in October 2001, a group of about 30 people, including Leon and Hayden, plus other girls and guys who were totally sold out to the vision, began to demonstrate what a thriving, vibrant, worshipping community of believers looks like. The church, known as 'The

Hope', has grown to the point that it's outgrown the primary school and desperately needs to find another local venue. The church has reached local people, integrated youth and families, and developed gifted leaders. God has used the church to bring transformation to the lives of many people. A thriving youth group exists, consisting mainly of 'unchurched' children and teenagers from the Valley Estate and other parts of Salford too.

Fresh streams in Harpurhey (2001)

Eden Harpurhey is hosted by Christ Church, an Anglican parish church which is a well established part of the community. Some of the church members have been prayer-walking the area and

---

REALITY BITES

Leon, part of the M2K action in Swinton Valley.

I came from Runcorn, as a student, to Salford Uni in 1995. Bizarrely, I *knew* God wanted me to be in Salford. It just so happened that there was a course I quite wanted to do there as well. In 1997 I saw a TV programme about The World Wide Message Tribe winning awards and doing schools evangelism stuff. Tacked onto the end of it was a short section about some Wythenshawe youth work thing with the radical notion of living in the area where the kids lived! It caught my heart and I knew God was right behind it.

The problem was, due to two years' praying, I knew that I was meant to be in Salford. If you look at the area of Greater Manchester like a clock face, Wythenshawe is at 6 o'clock and Salford is at 9, and never the twain shall meet. Bum. Anyway,

---

calling on God for revival for decades! In 1996, in partnership with another local church, they surveyed the local community knocking on every door and getting over 400 responses. The biggest thing that was identified, to no great surprise, was the lack of facilities or opportunities for youth. The community literally said, 'We want the church to do more work with youth.' A bit of youth work did exist in Harpurhey – there was an 'Urban Action' project, and a contemporary youth event called 'Alive' was hosted at Christ Church once a month. It was late one night, after preaching at this event, that Andy Hawthorne sat in a chilly little vestry with Rev. Mark Ashcroft and his youth worker Chris Clark discussing the possibility of using the Eden model as a way of tackling the town's major youth issues.

God's big, I thought, I'll wait. If there's one in Salford I'll join that. By the end of the year there was one announced to start in Salford. Cool! No. Because by the time I'd sorted my application form and references and was in a position to have an interview I'd already joined a small Newfrontiers church plant in Salford. I knew that was where God wanted me and joining Eden would mean leaving the plant. I was in a really tight spot because deep down I sensed that the church plant and Eden were both God's will for me, which left me divided and confused.

Angry at the seeming nonsense of it all, I turned down Eden Salford to continue with the church plant, saying, 'Frankly, if God really wants me to do Eden he's going to have to start another Salford Eden and attach it to this church plant!' And there it lay for a couple of years. Our little church just hovered at around eight people – it felt like the doldrums. One of the

---

Bringing this proposal to the church was rather daunting for Mark. Eden had developed a reputation around Manchester for seriously shaking up the churches who chose to go for it – and not always in ways the church wanted to be shaken. However, a member of the PCC suddenly came over all prophetic and announced, 'This will be like a fire for us. It's dangerous and it could burn us up, or it could set the community ablaze for Christ.' The risk was agreed to be worthwhile and the light changed from amber to green.

In many ways, being in an established church has been great for the team. However, some of the team, especially those from charismatic backgrounds, have struggled to relate to more traditional aspects of church life, especially the style of services and structures such as the PCC. Equally it's been hard for the

---

senior leaders in our network, Colin, suggested we should shift our geographic focus a few miles up the road to Swinton. We had two people living there but it felt a bit out of the way, so we filed the idea 'Under Consideration'.

Around this time a big city-wide outreach event was being organised called 'Soul Survivor – The Message 2000'. Keen to be part of the action, I sent my booking form in. Shortly after that I remember an announcement at a prayer meeting, that a massive project would happen on the Valley Estate. It sounded like my kind of madness, but where was the Valley Estate? I couldn't find it on a map, nobody I knew had heard of it, although it was apparently somewhere in Salford. And anyhow, my team assignment had arrived in the post and I'd be spending the week in Oldham. Buttocks!

The Message 2000 started and on the first day I dutifully went to Oldham to hand out leaflets. And then the God stuff

---

long-term church members to adapt to the cultural change the Eden team has brought in such a short space of time. While the congregation are fully behind Eden and its vision, some members are literally afraid to attend church because of the types of youngsters the team attracts. These issues are par for the course in the 'grafted' Eden model where a team is attached to an existing, established church. On the plus side, Eden Harpurhey has demonstrated a rapid development curve: it has reached young people much quicker than teams that have gone into an area 'cold'.

Eden Harpurhey's team leader, a dynamic evangelist called Ian, opted for a 'streamed' youth work approach. Young people would go to different groups and activities according to their age, gender, relationship to the team and level of interest in God. This

---

started happening ... The second day started with a surprise meeting with Andy Hawthorne, who was gibbering at high speed. I picked out the words 'Valley Estate', 'go' and 'bus' from the rest of the verbal blur. Andy finished with, 'Do you want to do it?' I skipped trying to process the information entering my ears and simply answered, 'Yes.'

It turned out that I had volunteered to help run a bus for the people on the Valley Estate, which was in Swinton, a town in Salford. It was a massive success but required some serious follow-up which would include planting a church. So our little plant decided to listen to that word we'd filed about Swinton and jumped in with both feet. A top-quality church leader and a top-quality youth leader decided to relocate from the other end of the country to get things moving. Eden Swinton was launched. One year on, I was living on the Valley Estate and the church had exploded with life. Come on!

idea had double-edged genius. Not only did it do away with the chaos and carnage of the 'open youth club' concept, it also enabled workers to focus on what they specifically had a heart for. Great strides have been made this way as team members have built quality relationships with young people. Teenagers from the area can attend a group that is specific for them and everyone receives lots of personal attention. Of course they needed a team large enough to facilitate this, at least two dozen, many of whom Ian personally challenged to relocate and get involved. It has proved to be a great way of doing youth work and evangelism safely and effectively with over 150 young people every week.

REALITY BITES

Nathan, Failsworth's team leader.

Wow! Over the last year here in Failsworth God has been doing some outstanding things. We have seen growth in every area of our ministry. Young people have been giving their lives to God and getting discipled. God has blessed our relationships with local authorities, especially the police, whose partnership has been very beneficial to our project.

Our performing arts school has grown significantly and we now have 45 young people attending regularly and 10 dedicated leaders working hard at making it the best performing arts project in Oldham. Create is now mentioned alongside Oldham Theatre Workshop as a quality youth service in the Oldham borough! We are so excited at the future of Create and how God is going to use it to transform Oldham. Every young person

---

Planting people in Hattersley (2002)

Hattersley sits on the eastern fringe of Greater Manchester, almost in the Peak District. It was created in the sixties as an overspill estate from Manchester – an extremely unwelcome addition to the landscape from the perspective of the wealthier neighbours in Mottram and Longendale. Hattersley is in effect an island of council housing that is cut off from everything around it. Few community facilities were created and the area very quickly developed a bad reputation. Hattersley was the home of the infamous 'Moors murderers' and the associated stigma has played a big part in shaping the identity of the community. There is a high unemployment rate which aggra-

---

knows exactly what the Create leaders are all about and what they believe. This personal witness has led to a growth of interest in God and the establishing of lads' and girls' groups. These are basically cell groups, but because of the demand and numbers we have to hold them in the church building, rather than in someone's house. We have 20 girls attending the girls' group. A dozen of them have made a commitment and it is really encouraging to see them growing in their faith. Six of these girls are regular attenders at both our Sunday services and have started helping out at our Kidz Club. The girls often share what God is doing in their lives in church and they have even preached as well! It's fantastic seeing a new generation growing up in God and affecting their peers.

The lads' group has 10 attending regularly and we are starting to see them wanting to know more about God and they have been attending church as well. Only last Sunday one of the lads

---

67

vates crime, drugs and a whole host of related problems, including widespread depression. To make a bad situation worse, many of the people in the area lost relatives at the hands of local GP Harold Shipman. The area is in the lowest 3% of academic attainment statistics in the UK and many of the families in the area are the fourth generation to live in Hattersley, making the problems deeply rooted in a generational cycle.

Just up the road in the village of Mottram a vibrant Christian community has existed for a good number of years. Mottram Evangelical Church grew out from an existing Congregational church in the seventies and since then has felt challenged in somehow sharing the gospel in Hattersley. Over those years various zealots have crossed the social and cultural divide to

---

walked two miles to get to church so that he could pray with someone. We are seeing some great things in these groups and we believe God has got some amazing plans for these young people!

We run a weekly Kidz Club every Tuesday night for 6 to 11-year-olds and we have grown from 8 to 50 children in the last year. The night is activity-based and then we finish with a 30-minute ministry time when the children learn all about God, the Bible, church and stuff. These times are very interactive and we also invite the parents to sit in as well and they really get into it! There is an atmosphere and attitude within the club now that it is 'cool' to talk about God and that is one of our key aims. From Kidz Club we encourage the children to attend Sunday School and Children's Church, which run during our morning and evening services, and we have seen attendances grow in those areas as well.

---

reach out to their neighbours, with varying rates of success. Never had there been any conversation about an incarnational approach to the challenge, until Eden appeared on the radar. The catalyst for the emerging discussion was the arrival of a new pastor at Mottram Evangelical – Gareth Lloyd-Jones, a proper northerner from the not too distant climes of Rochdale. Gareth had felt strongly led to quit his successful career as a sales manager in the steel industry to serve God full time as a church leader, and Mottram was clearly the place God had prepared for him. Here were a bunch of people who loved God and were ready to receive his leadership, a mandate for mission in the power of the Spirit.

Gareth was introduced to Andy Hawthorne within weeks of taking up his new post in July of 1999. Andy and Gareth had a

---

We bring the Eden bus into the area every week, which is a great opportunity to build relationships and encourage the young people in the neighbourhood. They line up on the street at least an hour before the bus arrives so they can get on and spend time with the leaders on the bus. The bus has had a positive impact on the whole area and it is well supported by the police and local authorities.

The host church has grown over the last year through this work and other initiatives for adults. We've just changed our name to 'thefaithworks', which has raised a few eyebrows. At our launch service 100 people turned up, including lots of people from the local area. Four local residents got up to share about the church and how it helped them and their families – and they aren't even Christians yet! These are just some of the amazing things God is doing in Failsworth. We still have lots more to do, but we are expecting some amazing transformation in our area! *Come on...*

---

number of open and honest conversations about partnership during which the Eden 'package' was discussed. Typically The Message would provide a deluge of workers and the church would provide a pastor and some finance. However, Mottram Evangelical were not in a position to supply a pastor for the potential church plant, The Message was running short on Eden workers to share around the growing number of projects, and neither had any money! Out of the discussions around these challenges a friendship began to grow and realistic goals were set. The key guy in Eden at that time, Wythenshawe's team leader Mark Smethurst, was given the task of working out the detail of the planning and implementation process, and he got straight to work. By October 2000 the leaders at Mottram Evangelical and the management at The Message, having worked through their hopes and fears together, felt that it was time for decision. In the preceding weeks the congregation had heard the city-wide Eden vision from Andy, and they'd heard the Wythenshawe story directly from Mark and King's Church pastor Adrian Nottingham. Everyone now knew that an Eden project was not only desperately needed in Hattersley, it was also viable financially and managerially. A pragmatic solution had been proposed to the church-planting question – it could go ahead, under Gareth's leadership stretching out from Mottram. When the critical midweek members' meeting was called at Mottram Evangelical there was a real sense of anticipation. The agenda was short and sweet, consisting of one question: 'What is God saying to us as a congregation?' The answer came back unanimously: 'Go for it!'

Friendship in Failsworth (2002)

Back in 1988, when a sprightly young Andy Hawthorne was racing around Manchester trying to rev up support for an ambitious youth event at the city's biggest rock venue, the inertia of the church was palpable. But a stream of encouragement was flowing from the office of a small Assemblies of God church tucked away down a narrow street in the north of the city. An entrepreneurial young leader called Paul Gibbs had caught the vision and accepted the challenge of making sure that anyone in his area who had so much as a cobweb of a connection to a local church got behind the idea. In the years to come Andy was to be even more impressed by Paul's ability to recruit, train and commission dozens of teams of workers to spread the gospel throughout the region's schools. This initiative, called the PAIS Project, has now become one of the nation's most popular gap-year programmes, attracting hundreds of young evangelists, and is now even spreading internationally.

Flowing out of this mutual respect and affection, it was perfectly natural for Andy to accept Paul's invitation to come and have a look around a church building he'd been offered as a base for the expanding ministry of PAIS early in 2001. As part of the deal Paul had agreed to 'reboot' the congregation, a small group of people struggling to recover from a split several years previously. Paul could see, and Andy agreed, that the only future for the church was a complete reinvention of its identity and mission. Taking a tour of the local area on foot, Andy saw numerous similarities to the communities in which Eden was making such a positive impact. All the symptoms of inner-city deprivation were there: the unsightly rash of graffiti, vandalism, dereliction and grime. It was also very clear that the Hope-O-meter for local youth had been stuck at zero for a long, long time. 'I think this would be the ideal spot for an Eden project, mate. Would you be up for it?' asked Andy.

REALITY BITES

Amy (and Ben), on starting out in Old Trafford.

We'd been living in our house for about two months and from day one had been building up a brilliant friendship with our neighbours. They were really friendly from the first day we moved onto the estate. We easily got to know the whole family in various ways, shopping together, having tea at each other's house, having a party for Donna's birthday (the mum), as well as being invited to go and watch TV, videos and generally just be friends. However, what happened one Tuesday night solidified the friendship through an event that could never be reconstructed again. We were sat upstairs watching a bit of quality Tuesday night TV when something caught the corner of Ben's eye. To his amazement a little mouse shot across the room into a well-covered corner. After a couple of phone calls to the council's emergency repair helpline and to Amy's mum it was suggested we went next door to ask if we could borrow their cat! Donna wasn't sure if Buttons (the cat) was around, but Marice (Donna's daughter) promptly informed us that Buttons was sat on the landing and she would go and fetch him. Donna was unsure if Buttons would be happy to help out, but was willing to give it a try. So with Donna, Marice and Buttons in tow we set out on a mouse hunt. Within minutes we were joined by Donna's other kids, Marcus (aged 15) and Devonte (aged 2).

For the first five minutes Donna, with my husband Ben, Marcus and Buttons searched the room to see where the mouse was hiding, whilst Marice, Devonte and I listened with much amusement to the laughter and noise that came from inside

As with so many of the Edens that have been established over the years, the relational foundation between the key

---

the room. Phrases were heard such as, 'There it is behind that box!' Donna's reply being, 'No, Marcus, that's a plug!' Soon Marice gave in to the excitement that was coming from inside the room and decided to join the mouse hunt. I kept well away, trying to entertain Devonte and stopping him from opening the door and letting the mouse out. Ben and Marcus now had the job of taking turns to take one box each out of the suspected corner whilst Donna stood perched on the sofa and Marice was wobbling around on a coffee table. It came to the last box and Ben was nominated to make the final move. Silence fell as Ben approached the box. No sooner had Ben's slightly sweaty hand touched the box than the mouse shot out and hid under the sofa. There was screaming, shouting, laughing and jumping around – it was bedlam!

This went on about half an hour. We don't know what the neighbours on the other side thought was going on that night, because to the outside world it probably sounded like a slightly weird and drunken version of musical chairs. Alongside the commotion Buttons spent the whole time chilling out underneath the sofa. Eventually, after the mouse had jumped from the table to the floor and tried to climb up the curtains, Buttons grabbed the mouse and, well, basically killed it. So it had finished. About 40 minutes of brilliant chaos to catch one poor little mouse. Everyone felt like they had just done a full workout and Marice claimed she had wet herself (but only slightly) from laughing! Once the poor rodent had been disposed of we all felt a bit bad, but at least we'd sleep that night. I don't think we ever thought having a mouse in the house could be such a bridge-building blessing!

partners can't be overstated. In this case there was an extended family that proved very helpful as well. As an AOG minister and a director of the national Youth Alive network, Paul had access to great strategic brains, a bit of seed money, and a well stocked pool in which to fish for volunteers. These factors helped to accelerate the lead time needed to get the project off the ground. However, beyond these visible elements there was, and still is, a powerful wind of the Spirit. Eden Failsworth is moving forward quickly and confidently. The future's bright.

Fitton Hill, a unanimous agreement (2003)

With the Openshaw Eden project maturing into a vibrant inner-city church, the Salvation Army's divisional leadership were understandably excited and wondering if the whole thing was just a fluke or whether it could be repeated. The quality of the people was such that perhaps one or two could be sent out without the thing falling apart. As it happened, Chris Neilson, one of the full-time team with extensive urban mission experience, not just in Manchester but also in southern Russia, was up for a new challenge. Chris was engaged to a great youth worker called Laura from the Harpurhey team and both were feeling good about starting their married life in a new place with a new vision. The Salvation Army has bases all around the Manchester area, many of which would have qualified as candidates for a new Eden project, so would it be a case of reverting to the Acts 1 model and drawing lots?

Back in 2000, just before The Message 2000 event, Andy Hawthorne had been introduced to a philanthropic Jewish businessman who was very keen on giving his money away to youth projects. He'd written out a fairly large cheque to help meet some of the financial needs which The Message had around that time. Handing over the gift, he'd expressed to Andy his particular heart for the town of Oldham, at the time simmering with racial tension which was soon to break out into riots. 'If you ever think about doing one of these Eden things in Oldham,' he said, 'give me a call.' Of course it was only a matter of time before that call was to be made.

In spite of its many social problems, Oldham does have a strong sense of identity. Its local churches have worked hard at presenting a consistent positive witness through unified prayer and outreach initiatives. In the run-up to 2003's Festival: Manchester event church leaders began to meet together to discuss strategy. How could this short-term mission initiative be used to lasting effect in their borough? Three years previously churches had engaged with M2K and welcomed evangelistic teams every afternoon, even in the far-flung foothills of the Pennines. However, this time the church leaders sensed that the Spirit seemed to be humming a rather different tune. At a prayer and strategy meeting organised by legendary local youth worker Dave Saville, a suggestion was put forward that had an uncanny Kingdom naivety about it. 'Why don't we all forget about what would be good for our little "patch" and all get behind whatever the Spirit is saying?' When church leaders start talking like that it must be the Lord!

Local Salvation Army officer Alec Still was at the meeting and took advantage of the pause in proceedings to explain a bit about an estate called Fitton Hill. This was one of the areas the Salvation Army and The Message had on their shortlist of potential locations for their next joint Eden venture. Of course everyone present knew Fitton Hill. Its notoriety had even been the subject of a glossy in-depth *Sunday Times* supplement feature, reminding the home counties just how grim it is up north:

Oldham is not like London, a vibrant melting pot with interior designers scouring Southall for saris, barristers buying mangoes from Brixton, and kids drawn to the bright lights of clubland. The young people here stay put, nervous even of Manchester city centre; the normal dreams of exotic long-haul exploration are blighted by association with the impoverished 'foreigners' down the road. The apathy is infectious. Though 50% of local-authority housing on Fitton Hill is in disrepair, only 14% of residents declare themselves unhappy about it. Most have come to see themselves as worth no more.[3]

The leaders present were very keen that Festival: Manchester should prepare the way for a long-term strategy – and if the chosen strategy was to be Eden, even better; they'd all heard the exciting stories of transformation. Alec's busy Salvation Army citadel just over a mile away could provide some ongoing help after the event, but Eden would require a new expression of church to emerge from the heart of the estate. That's where Chris and Laura would come in. Festival co-ordinator Ian Rowbottom was present at the meeting with Citywide prayer co-ordinator Debra Green. They'd heard some pretty good ideas in the run-up to the Festival, but this was like God stepping in and saying, 'Let me show you what my ideas really look like.' The two of them came rushing back to The Message HQ gushing with this breaking news. From there on in the course was set. Fitton Hill would be Eden number 9.

Grafting in Old Trafford (2005)

Year after year St Bride's Church has proven a solid commitment to reaching out to the community on its doorstep. With a building located at the apex of black, white and Asian micro-communities, embracing cross-cultural ministry has been a necessity not an option. The congregation meeting at the parish

76

worship centre has worked hard to embrace the diversity of its surroundings and the services are full of life, colour and lots of different languages. St Bride's is a church that understands and models what it means to be incarnational.

Local rector Phil Rawlings has been a great encouragement to The Message over the years and talk of a partnership for the benefit of Old Trafford's youth has ebbed and flowed. However, by the time these partnership conversations began getting serious the model of 'grafting' Eden projects into existing congregations was meeting increasing scepticism at the Eden Steering Group. Painful issues had begun to emerge in the earlier partnerships and some wondered whether it was curtains for Eden altogether. Certainly planting brand-new Eden churches was being touted as the only future framework for Eden, so how on earth would Old Trafford ever get off the ground?

Central to these regular debates were the ideas of integration and 'fit'. Precisely what issues could be expected to emerge if 20 or more young adults with a strong bent towards youth work suddenly arrived? And therein was the answer. Who said that they needed to 'suddenly arrive'? Yes, other teams had come together relatively quickly, but why was that assumed to be the only way that Eden could work? Maybe Old Trafford was presenting an opportunity to prove that grafting is possible and doesn't need to be painful – if it's done gently and skilfully. The church would need to be led through a period of consultation and preparation, with lots of honesty and space for questions. The Message would need to be patient and flexible, taking more seriously than ever before the issues of project sustainability. But Eden Old Trafford would go ahead, because God was clearly up to something that neither party could deny.

[1]   See *Surfing the Edge of Chaos* by Pascale, Millemann and Gioja, Three Rivers Press, 2000, for a great study of the effects of chaos in organisations.

[2]   *Guardian*, Wednesday 20th October 2004, p. 10.

[3]   Article by Lesley White, in *Sunday Times* magazine, 13th January 2002.

4
Be the Message

... being in very nature God ... but made himself nothing, taking the very nature of a servant, being made in human likeness ... being found in appearance as a man, he humbled himself and became obedient to death — even death on a cross! Therefore God exalted him to the highest place and gave him the name that is above every name ...

Philippians 2:6–9

No 'Tally Ho!'

After the hectic pace of dashing here and there throughout the last chapter you probably need a bit of time to chill. Let's kick back and muse for a little while on why on earth we're doing this moving in thing anyway. Why is it so important? We didn't set out saying, 'Tally Ho! Here we go to do some Incarnational Evangelism!' None of us had even heard the terminology, let alone understood the theology. In fact, most of our revelation came from pretty flaky exegesis of the Pentateuch – a whole lot of Joshua and Caleb and talk of 'taking the land'. It was only later on that friendly Christian boffins pointed at what we were doing and said, 'Look, they're doing Incarnational Evangelism, jolly good!' And indeed it was only later, when truly facing up to the long-term challenge of redeeming totally messed-up lives, that we began to realise that stories of armies and battles and blowing trumpets weren't going to be much help. Does anyone expect to really identify someone's features from his shadow? So how could we gain a vision of action and interaction with the people we're reaching out to from those Jewish history books alone? Perhaps God in his wisdom might have included a better image in his word for us to take a look at? To really understand the true face of ministry there was only one place we could go: we needed to flick forward to the Gospels and gaze in wonder at Jesus.

There's a lot of material out there on the shelves of the Christian bookstores, and there are a lot of people travelling around with the latest Big Idea. Although at first glance it may all look very similar, there's a pretty significant difference between the worldly wisdom which is propped up by a few nifty Bible verses and the godly wisdom which points out where divine truths may be found in everyday life. The apostle Paul, for instance, was clearly a master of the latter with little tolerance for the former.[1] In amongst all this we now find Eden. Fortunately it's far too ridiculous an idea ever to be accused of being a human endeavour dressed up in spiritual clothes – it's at the opposite pole, it's wisdom of the 1 Corinthians 1:25 variety, 'for the foolishness of God is wiser than man's wisdom'.

This chapter isn't about backing up Eden with enough scriptural references to assure readers of its evangelical legitimacy. It's simply going to be a sketch of the features of the face of Christ[2] which the Holy Spirit has revealed to us in the word of God and to which we try to remain true.

In the beginning …

One of the bizarre things about the way the Bible is structured
is the order of the four Gospels. Which one of the early church
fathers actually won over the distinguished guys assembled at
the Third Council of Carthage in AD 397 with the ridiculous
suggestion, 'OK fellas, this new book, this "New Testament",
let's open it up with Matthew's Gospel. People in the future are
just gonna love finding out that Abraham begat Isaac; and Isaac
begat Jacob; and Jacob begat Judas and his brethren! And isn't
it particularly fascinating that Azor begat Sadoc; and Sadoc
begat Achim; and Achim begat Eliud?' Slap that patriarch! Isn't
it blatantly obvious that John was supposed to be the first
Gospel? Look:

Genesis 1	John 1
1 In the beginning God created the heavens and the earth. 2 Now the earth was formless and empty, darkness was over the surface of the deep, and the Spirit of God was hovering over the waters. 3 And God said, 'Let there be light,' and there was light. 4 God saw that the light was good, and he separated the light from the darkness.	1 In the beginning was the Word, and the Word was with God, and the Word was God. 2 He was with God in the beginning. 3 Through him all things were made; without him nothing was made that has been made. 4 In him was life, and that life was the light of men. 5 The light shines in the darkness, but the darkness has not understood it.

Okay, now before you tear up the book as complete heresy for
even suggesting that the holy canon might have gone a bit
skew-whiff, this isn't the start of a campaign to have the job
repaginated. It's just a little illustration to highlight the vital
importance of these verses John presents us with as the
foundations of our understanding of the incarnation. If we skim
ahead to verse 14, the fulcrum of history is unveiled: 'The Word

became flesh and made his dwelling among us.' Or, as that Canadian chap Eugene Peterson puts it, 'The Word became flesh and blood, and moved into the neighbourhood.'[3] Quite apt as an image, isn't it – considering this book's subject matter.

When God the Son left the glory of heaven to come to earth, this time it wasn't just an excursion. This was no Old Testament theophany – the day-tripping was over. Listen to the way Luke tells the story in the opening of his first New Testament book:

> *... God sent the angel Gabriel to Nazareth, a town in Galilee, to a virgin pledged to be married to a man named Joseph, a descendant of David. The virgin's name was Mary. The angel went to her and said, 'Greetings, you who are highly favoured! The Lord is with you.'*
>
> *Mary was greatly troubled at his words and wondered what kind of greeting this might be. But the angel said to her, 'Do not be afraid, Mary, you have found favour with God. You will be with child and give birth to a son, and you are to give him the name Jesus. He will be great and will be called the Son of the Most High. The Lord God will give him the throne of his father David, and he will reign over the house of Jacob for ever; his kingdom will never end.'*
>
> *'How will this be,' Mary asked the angel, 'since I am a virgin?'*
>
> *The angel answered, 'The Holy Spirit will come upon you, and the power of the Most High will overshadow you. So the holy one to be born will be called the Son of God. Even Elizabeth your relative is going to have a child in her old age, and she who was said to be barren is in her sixth month. For nothing is impossible with God.'*
>
> *'I am the Lord's servant,' Mary answered. 'May it be to me as you have said.'*
>
> *Then the angel left her.*[4]

Doesn't it sound like something pretty significant was going on there? Through the miracle of this immaculate conception the whole economy of God's dealing with his creation was about to change, eternally and irreversibly. Over 100 Old Testament prophecies were to find their fulfilment in the course of this incredible life. The time had come for God to make his move – the Son, the Living Word, was willing to leave the glory of heaven, the worship of the angels, and join our struggle for survival on this spinning lump of rock. Throughout the ages God had generally entrusted the major developments in his world rescue plan to big strapping bearded blokes, but this highest of honours was given to a teenage girl. In just the same way that your whole town would feel honoured if the Queen came to stay at your house, so the whole human race was dignified in a new dimension when the one who is the image of the invisible God, the firstborn over all creation,[5] was knitted together[6] by the agency of the Holy Spirit in a teenage virgin's womb to become the Last Adam,[7] an entirely new category of being, a 'God-Man'.

Tongue of the universe

Probably the most illuminated mind on this matter belonged to an old Egyptian guy called Athanasius. He just missed out on the meeting where they decided the order of the books in the New Testament – he died 23 years too early. Shame, really, as he'd definitely have voted for John first! Athanasius described in amazing, lucid terms how it was so correct for a core member of the Omnipresent Godhead to emerge into our time and space in the way he did.

> A man's personality actuates and quickens his whole body. If anyone said it was unsuitable for the man's power to be in the toe, he would be thought silly. Similarly … He has willed to reveal Himself through men … there can be nothing ridiculous in His using a human body to manifest the truth and knowledge of the Father. Does not the mind of a man pervade his entire being, and yet find expression through his tongue? Does anybody say on that account

83

that Mind has degraded itself? Of course not. Very well, then, no more is it degrading for the Word, Who pervades all things, to have appeared in a human body.[8]

What our ancient friend says there could be expanded a bit like this. Imagine you're a stalker. You follow the object of your obsession around everywhere. It doesn't take you long to become familiar with the general pattern of his life – out at 8.30, back again between 5.30 and 6.00. Likes to shop at Tesco, hangs around with mates in the Hogshead on Saturday night. Then you get really clever and fix secret cameras in his house. You start to get to know all the little habits: singing into the mirror, pigging out on chocolate ice cream late at night. In your freaky stalker way you really feel like you know this person now, you are friends … *No you aren't, you creep!* How could you possibly claim to *know* this person just based on these external observations? Getting to know someone involves personal exchange. Only when someone chooses to begin sharing with you their hopes and fears, memories and dreams, can you claim to be getting to know that person, the real 'who' living inside the 'what'. This is what Athanasius is leading us to, with heavy echoes from Romans 1: *'For since the creation of the world God's invisible qualities – his eternal power and divine nature – have been clearly seen, being understood from what has been made, so that men are without excuse.'*[9]

If we reflect on this metaphor, the whole universe as the body of God, we can easily form some opinions and assumptions about him. He must be creative, powerful, and infinitely wise. But what's in his mind, and what moves his heart? How can we possibly lay any claim to knowing him merely by the movement and pattern of the things we see? If only you would speak to us, God! And of course as Christians we believe he has: he's spoken to us in the most universal way, he's spoken in body language. '... in these last days he has spoken to us by his Son, whom he appointed heir of all things, and through whom he made the universe. The Son is the radiance of God's glory and the exact representation of his being ...'[10] The incarnation of Jesus was so much more than the clichéd 'baby born to die' we've reduced it to – it was literally an explosion of personal expression straight from the Godhead. Every second of that unique life was a syllable in an unparalleled divine conversation that opened our understanding to the true character of the Creator behind the creation.

The price

Now, before you get too worried, this is not some kind of build-up to a flaky new doctrine whereby we announce that Eden has become a new manifestation of God in the world. Far from it. All this waxing eloquent is in honour of the uniqueness of Christ, the Apostle of our faith, the one who commissioned us with these words: '... go and make disciples of all nations ...'[11]

Don't you get really, really annoyed when someone asks you to do something that you know full well they aren't prepared to do themselves? But there's no way anyone can lay that sort of criticism on Jesus. His parting shot wasn't just 'See ya then, lads – it's been great knowing you. Keep it real, eh?' Jesus could lay down what's actually quite a heavy commission and expect total obedience because he'd been commissioned with the toughest job ever imagined and had totally fulfilled the brief. 'As the Father has sent me, I am sending you.'[12] And think what fulfilling that brief involved for Jesus. Giving up the glory of heaven's throne room with the constant worship of a million angels. Being born in a shed converted for animals to make their noise and smells in. Spending childhood either running from the law or struggling to shake off the rumours of a 'bastard' label in the first place you can really call home. Then, when you should be getting to grips with running the family business, you're coming to terms with a cat-o'-nine-tails. Finally, allowing

---

REALITY BITES

Jim and Gemma, on the sacrifice of Eden.

In November 1999 God excited us at the prospect of getting involved with Eden. At the time my wife Gemma and I were living and working in Chad, Africa, but were intending to return to England. We settled back in Reading and I started a job working for the Environment Agency. During the two years in Reading we wondered whether God wanted us to move to Manchester. Our questions were answered when we went to Spring Harvest 2002 and heard Andy Hawthorne speak, and we knew for certain that God wanted us in Manchester. A couple of months later we visited two Eden projects and came back knowing that we were to move to Hattersley. Shortly afterwards I went to my boss and told him that God wanted us to move to Manchester and so I was handing in my resignation. My boss slapped his hands over his eyes, shook his head and said nothing. He was obviously impressed! I tried all I could to get a job transfer up to the north-west, but nothing materialised. In the end I took three months' unpaid leave so that I could move and still be eligible as an internal candidate for jobs.

During these three months we struggled financially, especially as we needed money to decorate the fairly grotty council house we'd moved into. As the months passed I prayed more and more about finding a job, but nothing came. It was January 2003, my three months were up and I had no job. I was now officially unemployed. I was forced to swallow my pride and join the ranks

---

the very flesh that cost so much to wear to be torn apart at the sharp end of three Roman nails. Whatever we give up to 'move into the neighbourhood', and whatever price we are asked to pay when we get there, it's nothing compared to what he

---

queuing up to sign on. During this time our overdraft grew and grew. This was hard, as we 'lived by faith' in Africa and had seen God provide for our needs. But now for some reason God was not providing. We kept praying and trusting that God would provide me with a job. It looked like my prayers had been answered when I was offered a job with the Environment Agency in Leeds. However, I didn't have any peace about the job and I wondered what the Lord was saying. It became more and more clear that God wanted me to sacrifice my career to him. Not knowing what I was going to do for a job, I called the Environment Agency and declined their offer. I also e-mailed my old boss to tell him to stop looking for jobs for me, as I was no longer interested. I'd taken a step of obedience to God, but still I had no job.

In March 2003 we were given some money to go on holiday, where we spent a lot of time seeking God's guidance. One day shortly after returning from holiday, God woke our pastor up at 6 a.m. and told him to contact us. He came round that morning and asked us what God had been saying to us. We explained that during our holiday God had told us to be willing to lay our lives down for Hattersley in prayer, availability and service. Three days later I was offered a full-time job as youth worker in our partner church just up the road. I knew then what all the waiting had been about! Our first six months in Hattersley had been hard and our overdraft had grown considerably, yet I'm glad that we'd answered God's call and joined Eden. God had used our obedience to change the direction of our lives and to force us to focus and rely more upon him.

---

gave up to make his dwelling with us 2,000 years ago. And that's what we really mean when we use the term 'incarnational'. We don't treat mission like a day-trip. We pack our bags for the long haul and fight the tendency to make our home a mini 'missionary compound'. We are deliberately setting out to 'make contact', to commence a redemptive conversation, and our moving in is the loudest and most consistent statement we will ever make. The strategy is what Steve Sjogren would describe as 'High Risk – High Grace',[13] where he defines Risk as, 'What is the cost emotionally, spiritually, relationally, financially?' and Grace as, 'How much of God's presence is necessary for this outreach to be a success?'

Hi-viz

Another idea related to incarnation can be borrowed from the police, who have a tactic they refer to as 'hi-viz policing'. If you've ever been to a football match you'll be familiar with the approach: lots and lots of those luminous yellow jackets dotted around the ground. This policing style has become a remarkable deterrent to misbehaviour and is being rolled out all over the UK as part of a programme known as 'Operation Reassurance'. Residents of communities comment that they feel safer when there is a regular and noticeable police presence around. In a similar way Eden is a sort of 'hi-viz' Christianity – which doesn't mean the teams wear bright yellow jackets. Hi-viz Christianity means that the church of Jesus has deliberately and noticeably repositioned itself back into those places from which it had withdrawn.

After about five years doing the stuff in Openshaw, which is wedged right in the middle of the multi-million-pound east Manchester regeneration zone, Gary Bishop has seen a lot of people in suits around. There's always an initiative going on, there are always people trying to make things happen. But there's something very obvious to Gary and the rest of the community about the way the people in the suits do their work. They turn up in the neighbourhood at 9 o'clock in the morning and they ship back out as soon as the clock hits 5 in the afternoon. Their work is often good quality and of value, but their lives are elsewhere, somewhere quite separate. Their approach is never going to earn the description 'incarnational'. Conversely, Eden's staff and volunteers must live in the area. It's one of the firmly established cornerstones without which Eden would not be Eden.

Living in the area affords the teams a perspective that no external agency will ever gain: a 360-degree insight, because making your bed in the city's toughest streets is the equivalent of jacking right into the matrix. The street's problems become your problems. Sitting in a meeting about which houses are going to be knocked down is important when you and your neighbour both have a red 'X' on the new masterplan. Making a statement to the police about the joyriders who keep everyone awake at night is way beyond advocacy, because this is your issue too. You discover the hidden things and the dark secrets you would never see just by passing through – the drug abuse, the alcoholism, the domestic violence, the shameful neglect of the young and the exploitation of the vulnerable. It was a year and a half before Gary first met a drug addict in his community. Once that door was ajar, however, it was only weeks before his eyes were opened to the chronic nature of the problem right on his doorstep.

Keeping it real

With this unique perspective comes a unique set of conceptual challenges for the incarnational evangelist. One frequently nagging question is, 'Am I being truly incarnational?' The other residents of the neighbourhood generally aren't there by choice. They don't have a parachute option, the ability to jump in the car or on a train and head off back down south to Mummy if it all gets too tough: 'Sorry it didn't work out, dear. What do you want for tea?' But the flip side of this incarnational coin is that Jesus' ministry never cut him off from the Father or from the great inheritance that was rightly his. And so the internal argument turns full circle.

These conundrums are constant background noise for Eden workers, whose lives blur into many grey areas of ministry. There's no textbook for incarnational life, the goalposts are always moving and there are no clear lines. To expect to put in two hours a week at the youth club and another two doing detached work and then to clock off is just not an option. The lives of the young people and their family affairs spill out onto the street, often even messier than the back alleys where the stray dogs roam. It's not unusual for teams to find themselves doing the jobs of overworked or undermotivated social workers. There are high-level intervention issues to deal with, when acting in the interests of the child becomes a matter of urgency. The risks associated with this sort of involvement are multiplied when you're well known in the community. Being labelled a grass is very scary when either you, or your partner, or your car, or your house might be targeted in anger. It's been known for the head of Social Services to advise a team leader and his wife, 'You really ought to think about moving out of the area for your own safety.' But it's very hard to uproot a planting of the Lord.[14]

90

Currency of the Kingdom

We've spent a long time looking at the way Eden is influenced by the physical revelation of who God is, represented in the arrival of Jesus in human history. It's also right for us to offer ourselves to be shaped by what Jesus said in his brief time here. We'll skim through the pages of red letters and home in on a few short verses where he's speaking to those around him in the picture language that he was so fond of.

> You are the salt of the earth. But if the salt loses its saltiness, how can it be made salty again? It is no longer good for anything, except to be thrown out and trampled by men. You are the light of the world. A city on a hill cannot be hidden. Neither do people light a lamp and put it under a bowl. Instead they put it on its stand, and it gives light to everyone in the house. In the same way, let your light shine before men, that they may see your good deeds and praise your Father in heaven.[15]

Hold those images in your mind for a moment, and compare them to these:

> Then Jesus asked, 'What is the kingdom of God like? What shall I compare it to? It is like a mustard seed, which a man took and planted in his garden. It grew and became a tree, and the birds of the air perched in its branches.'
>
> Again he asked, 'What shall I compare the kingdom of God to? It is like yeast that a woman took and mixed into a large amount of flour until it worked all through the dough.'[16]

Talking on two separate occasions and using five different images, Jesus expresses the in-built paradox of his Kingdom currency. On one side of the coin Jesus carves a picture of our presence in the world as being like the working of an invisible agent of change: salt or yeast. There's no way in which we should ever expect to be noticed as 'the key ingredient'. Our job is not to be singled out in and of ourselves, but to affect the taste and the shape of the world around us, for the better. But the other side of the Kingdom coin is this: his Kingdom has a 'wow' factor! There is something spectacular and breathtaking about the people of God expressing the life of God. It's attractive and on display like the bright lights of a city at night or the illuminating glow of a lamp on a stand. It's prominent and obvious like a great tree in the middle of a garden. This isn't a case of either/or; Jesus gives us a mandate to be both/and. Eden seeks to be nothing more than an invisible agent of change and nothing less than a 'wow' window on all God's goodness and grace.

Jesus-style ministry

Along with who Jesus was and what he said, we should really take a little peek at what he did. Is there any sense in which we

---

REALITY BITES

Jen in Harpurhey, on the privilege of prayer.

One night, I remember opening my front door expecting to see the usual faces of young people, but I was greeted instead by two policemen. Our neighbour, and father to some of the young people we work with, had just been stabbed in our alleyway and the police were going door to door asking questions. Most of the Eden team were round my house for a birthday party at the time, so after the police left we gathered and prayed. Later that night I went over to the neighbours' house to see if we could do anything to help. The man's wife answered the door and instantly broke down in tears. She said that her husband had only been gone for a few minutes to get a kebab and had been attacked on the way back, only a stone's throw from their

---

can aim or claim to have a 'Jesus-style ministry'? Notably Jesus didn't have a lot of time – 33 years of earthly life, 90% of that in preparation for ministry – so how strange that the Gospels don't ever give us the impression that he was really in a bit of a rush. The simple answer would be, because he wasn't! His interactions with the people he met could be quite brief, but they were always meaningful. Clearly there were some people who were radically affected by hanging around him day after day, week after week, month after month; others only got one chance to meet him, but once was enough. Let's look closer …

John 5 opens with a description of Jerusalem's mysterious lido, the open-air pool known in Aramaic as 'Bethesda'. Just a few narrow streets to the north of the great temple and in the shadow of the five elegant colonnades, people suffering with all sorts of infirmities and disabilities would sit or lie. They were waiting for the occasional angelic visitor who would turn up

---

front door. She then asked if I'd come in and pray for the family as they were all so scared and worried.

Once inside, she started to move all the furniture in her front room to the side so we could all kneel down and pray – she just thought that's what you had to do! I knelt down on the carpet and we all held hands. Then I prayed with her and the two younger children that Dad would recover really quickly and that the peace of God would rest in their own hearts. It was an incredible privilege. In the following few days, I was able to drive the family to the hospital and amazingly, three days later, Dad was back home. Mum joined an Alpha course run by our host church where she was able to meet some other Christians and ask all her questions. The family's still around and as a team we still have a unique relationship with them because of what took place that night.

---

unannounced to stir the water with a healing hand. On the angel's departure the first spectator to get wet would receive this physical blessing and become whole. Into this morbid scene comes Jesus, surveying the heaving weekend crowd.

One who was there had been an invalid for thirty-eight years. When Jesus saw him lying there and learned that he had been in this condition for a long time, he asked him, 'Do you want to get well?'

'Sir,' the invalid replied, 'I have no one to help me into the pool when the water is stirred. While I am trying to get in, someone else goes down ahead of me.'

Then Jesus said to him, 'Get up! Pick up your mat and walk.' At once the man was cured; he picked up his mat and walked.[17]

Accounts like this are tremendously difficult for our rational minds to process. Thoughts flash in our heads like those annoying pop-up security messages when you're browsing the Internet. Surely it's not fair of Jesus, surrounded by all sorts of needs, to focus on just one man? Can we really assume that every other cripple lying by the pool would immediately praise the Lord for their brother's healing – or might they feel a tad ripped off?

The way Jesus lived his life, the things he did, and the things he left undone, can teach us so much about God's priorities. We're given situational models which help us weigh what is right against what is fair. Daily we have to make God-choices in a world which may not recognise '... right and wrong. Just fair and unfair.'[18] Surrounded by needy people, Eden teams need to develop great discernment if they're to resist the urge to try to meet every need, all the time – that's the road to burnout-land. They need to ask the Holy Spirit, 'What are you doing?', 'Where are you working?', 'How do you want me to do this?' Try thinking of it like a scene in an operating theatre: the great surgeon is performing open heart surgery and periodically calls on the theatre nurses for assistance. 'Scalpel.' 'Swab.' 'Oxygen.' We follow the Holy Spirit's orders, not quite understanding exactly how our little bit contributes to the fixing up of this life – we just do what he asks.

Jesus' priorities

In chapter 9 of Mark's Gospel, just minutes after the mind-boggling scenes of the transfiguration, Jesus has to step in to straighten out an argument which the inept disciples have allowed to brew to boiling point. Quickly Jesus finds out what it's all about and ushers the central character, a Jewish father, away from the noisy crowd for a bit of a man-to-man chat. The guy's son is in trouble, and it's a bit more serious than forgetting his homework. The kid's being bullied by an angry demon that won't leave him alone. It has so much power over the boy that it won't let him speak; it's even tried to throw him into fires to really hurt him. When Jesus finds out that his disciples haven't dealt with it, he starts to lose his rag and demands that the lad is brought to him. Right on cue, the demon throws the boy into a full-blown epileptic fit complete with flailing limbs and foaming gums. What Jesus does next is fascinating. Instead of switching to action-combat mode and getting stuck into the cocky demon, he switches into mild-mannered GP mode.

> Jesus asked the boy's father, 'How long has he been like this?'
> 'From childhood,' he answered. ' … if you can do anything, take pity on us and help us.'[19]

You need to picture this. Imagine you're there while this little chat is taking place, and the boy is still violently thrashing around on the ground, kicking up a great cloud of dust …

' "If you can"?' said Jesus. 'Everything is possible for him who believes.'

Immediately the boy's father exclaimed, 'I do believe; help me overcome my unbelief!' [20]

Jesus seems to think that it's perfectly appropriate at a time like this to get involved in a bit of dialogue with the dad about his own dubious spiritual journey. In fact you get the feeling that Jesus probably had a lot more to say on the matter, but:

When Jesus saw that a crowd was running to the scene, he rebuked the evil spirit. 'You deaf and mute spirit,' he said, 'I command you, come out of him and never enter him again.'

The spirit shrieked, convulsed him violently and came out. The boy looked so much like a corpse that many said, 'He's dead.' But Jesus took him by the hand and lifted him to his feet, and he stood up. [21]

How did Jesus remain so completely composed and unfazed during that whole freaky drama? Why did he treat the demon as a secondary issue and spend his time challenging the father instead? What kind of priorities did Jesus have that we can learn from as his twenty-first-century agents in the world? We know that when he ascended to heaven he didn't leave Israel 100% healed, 100% free or 100% convinced, but he had declared, '*It is finished.*'[22] The conclusion would appear to be that God gives every life a purpose. And every day we give to that purpose will be filled with opportunities somehow curiously staged for our involvement.[23] Eden is much more than a bunch of do-gooders with a box of sticking-plasters trying to heal the wounds of the world. Eden is people united by a determination to become everything God made them to be and to do everything he's designed them to do – people determined to 'Live Full and Die Empty', as popular preacher Paul Scanlon puts it.

There will always be need all around us, but we must be careful, because the need is not the call.

1 1 Corinthians 2:6–7.
2 2 Corinthians 4.
3 Eugene Peterson, *The Message*, NavPress, 1993.
4 Luke 1:26–38.
5 Colossians 1:15.
6 Psalm 139:15.
7 1 Corinthians 15:45.
8 St Athanasius, *On the Incarnation*, circa AD 373, available from SVS Press.
9 Romans 1:20.
10 Hebrews 1:2–3.
11 Matthew 28:19.
12 John 20:21.
13 Steve Sjogren, *Conspiracy of Kindness*, Vine Books, 1993.
14 Isaiah 61:3.
15 Matthew 5:13–16.
16 Luke 13:18–21.
17 John 5:5–9.
18 Jackie Pullinger, *Chasing the Dragon*, Hodder & Stoughton, 1980.
19 Mark 9:21–22.
20 Mark 9:23–24.
21 Mark 9:25–27.
22 John 19:30.
23 Ephesians 2:10.

5
The Power of Partnership

The God who made the world and everything in it is the
Lord of heaven and earth and does not live in temples
built by hands.

Acts 17:24

DNA of unity

Manchester has been really blessed in the last 10 years to have
seen an amazing heart for unity develop amongst the leaders
of its many and diverse church denominations and streams.[1] In
fact, without this pervading atmosphere of co-operation, Eden
would probably now just be an idea that never happened,
gradually turning yellow in a dusty filing cabinet somewhere.
Consider this:

A pair of hot-headed brothers not accustomed to ministerial
manners and etiquette manage to corral the leaders of Manchester's most significant churches – the ones with a bit of clout
when you count bums on seats and money in the bank.[2] They
explain their heartache, their first-hand witness from the front
line of hundreds and thousands of teenagers enduring a hellish

existence in parts of the city that the church appears to have forgotten. They describe in detail the particular needs of the Wythenshawe area, where they'd like to try out 'a new thing',[3] a new idea called 'Eden', in partnership with King's Church, which at the time was not everyone's favourite fellowship! They calculate that the endeavour will require about 30 switched-on 20-somethings and about £60,000 a year. And they'd like those gathered to chip in, with people and pounds. In the next 12 months the leaders gathered on that day gave both generously. But, more importantly, on that day something of the unique DNA of unity was formed in the Eden embryo.

We're going to spend time talking about church in this chapter, so our starting co-ordinates need to be stated. The Eden vision has not found its form from any single tradition, theology or emphasis. It is born from, and returns affection to, the whole of the body of Christ. Even though on the ground Eden is about as 'local' as you can get, its DNA is more complex than 'local church'. Genes are present in Eden's double-helix that have long since been bred out of that institution. It's true that in many parts of England, as well as in some further flung corners of the British Isles, the church seems to be wriggling its way out of the final buckles of its 'Sunday morning, sit and face the front' straitjacket. But, like watching an embarrassing esca-pologist, it seems to be taking far too long for those who are desperately waiting to cheer a fresh moment of freedom. To what extent is Eden still buckled to limiting traditions? Has Eden learned any lessons in 'escape technique' that it can share? Let's explore.

Grafts and plants

Borrowing terminology from Romans 11, the idea of launching an Eden project from within an existing local church congregation has become known as a 'graft'. Three of the first four projects, Wythenshawe, Salford and Longsight, were all partnerships of this form, although they differed widely in other respects. Wythenshawe's host congregation was fairly small, met in a hired hall and connected relationally with a much larger outfit. Salford's was much larger and better established, having a membership of well over a hundred and its own property too. Eden Longsight was simply a geographic focus for a several-hundred-strong 'translocal' church also covering the whole south Manchester area. Wythenshawe and Longsight recognised apostolic oversight from charismatic networks[4] which had emerged from the house church movement; Salford was Renewed Brethren and as such had greater independence.

Openshaw, launched at the same time as Longsight, was the first Eden 'plant', under a totally new church on a blank canvas, albeit in an old Salvation Army building and under their divisional governance. Next came Swinton, another plant but different from Openshaw because the Eden team formed only part of the planting group. This new church, led by Howard Kellett, was related apostolically to the Longsight church, sharing the translocal vision of being a resource to numerous local neighbourhoods, of which the Valley was one. Harpurhey later in 2001 was a classic graft, although for the first time within the ancient parochial structures of the Anglican Church. Hattersley a year later was planting time again, this time from a fairly well resourced evangelical church nearby which would undertake the vital leadership function.

Eden Failsworth's host church, an Assemblies of God fellowship now known as 'thefaithworks', is perhaps the only anomaly so far, being not quite a graft and not quite a plant either. It's what some church growth commentators might term a 'reboot', or perhaps 'replanting' to keep up the gardening metaphors.

Most recently the Fitton Hill project launched in 2003 has been a plant, drawing extensively from the key learnings of the Openshaw team. Old Trafford, a traditional parish, has followed the Harpurhey model, learning from both its strengths and its weaknesses. These last two have both taken a deliberately extended lead time over their project development plan for two good reasons: (a) to aid integration with the local community, and (b) to aid the development of team relationships within the church.

Partnership with a capital P

Early in 2004 The Message Trust's management produced an internal report reflecting on the experiences of the first six years or so of Eden. The study included a section examining and summarising the most basic questions which need to be answered before a new project can be commenced. Four important criteria were identified:

1. Is there a clearly identified need for youth provision in the area?
2. Is there a partner who will own the project at a local level?
3. Are there financial resources available to undertake the project?
4. Is there agreement that to proceed is really God's will?

Questions 2 and 4 are always the most difficult to answer as they're the ones containing all the 'soft' factors like people, values, vision and expectations. Since day one, every Eden partnership has been a partnership of The Message and a host church. We've already seen that these host churches can be from any denomination or none, they may be an existing local church, a brand-new plant or a 'reboot'. The mutual understanding of partnership has grown and been tested over time.

Various forums for enhancing the quality and effectiveness of the partnerships have been tried out – pastors' committees, steering groups, team leaders' meetings and think-tanks. There have been moments of real revelation and seasons of great momentum, but there have also been issues of major contention and plenty of hot-potato controversies. Rather like the way we're left wondering exactly what it was Barnabas noticed on his first sniff around Antioch when he 'saw evidence of the grace of God',[5] so the Eden partnerships seem to bless anyone who comes to Manchester to take a look. Things have been far from perfect, however. Researchers from the Shaftesbury Society noted a tug of war that seemed to be happening in the Wythenshawe project only a couple of years after it had been launched. Intrepid Church Army investigator George Lings, looking particularly at the early stages of the Swinton project, noted, 'What I met was the evidence of a normal process. Pioneering ventures take time to mature. At the start, vision, passion and fire predominate ... Structures are minimal with the emphasis on the relational, functional and flexible ... The culture is "go for it" not "weigh it up".' He also mentions 'the inescapability of learning some things the hard way'.[6]

God never said partnership in the gospel was going to be a sunlit stroll down Lovers' Lane. Take a look at the relationship between the first apostles and the churches they planted, especially Paul's – his letters are not quite in the same genre as Song of Songs, are they? A little-known maxim within the Billy Graham organisation is, 'We will never do alone what we can do in partnership.' The Message feels exactly the same way, even if it means the job takes twice as long and is three times as hard (which it usually is). You see, The Message continues to resist the label of 'parachurch', which is generally used by those self-appointed judges of who is or isn't allowed to use the label 'church'. As theologian Jim Thwaites has been known to say with a tinge of sarcasm, 'Whoever gets the name "Church", wins.' But The Message wouldn't ever refer to itself as 'church'. Even if it could get away with it, God has already given us a word with which to define our identity, and that is 'evangelist'. We belong to, and work in, through, for and from the many local expressions of the body of Christ in the city of Manchester. The Message stimulates prayer for the soul of the city, tells the good news of Jesus to its residents, and equips the saints to do the same. Eden is really just an expression of the evangelist's threefold calling to prayer, proclamation and presence – having first a Christology, then a missiology, and waiting to see what kind of ecclesiology is produced in the wake.

Double vision?

Eden's present steering group consists of senior management from The Message, the host church leaders and a couple of the more experienced team leaders. It meets monthly at The Message HQ. Hardly a month has gone by in the last seven years without the need for discussion and decisions relating to a whole host of complex issues to do with ownership and sharing of vision. Random snippets from the folders of monthly minutes reveal discussions covering the level of volunteer commitments, evangelism methodology, equal opportunities policy, responding to crime and violence, partnership with other agencies, and a whole load more. In 2003 during discussions on strategic direction a simple graphic device was developed, with good old-fashioned 'back of a napkin' finesse, to guide the development of any future partnerships. If a potential local church partner, or a potential planting partner, could articulate and prove the way that the Eden vision would fit into and remain within the orb of its wider vision of ministry, progress could probably be made. However, if it became apparent that the vision of that potential partner was distinctly different from that of Eden, negotiations would draw to an end with everybody still being friends.

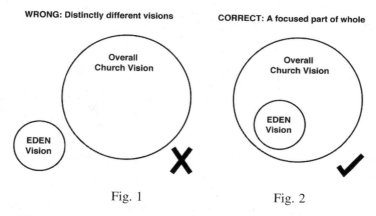

WRONG: Distinctly different visions

CORRECT: A focused part of whole

Fig. 1   Fig. 2

There is, of course, a third scenario, which is where the two visions overlap. This scenario is perhaps the most difficult of all to work out, because of the temptation on both sides to begin to compromise their vision under the allure of exciting possibilities. It wouldn't be unfair to reflect back on the complications of the first three Eden partnerships and conclude that they all fell into this third category. God clearly knew what he was doing when he instructed the angels in his grace factory to package it in just the one size – lavish![7]

Outreach or in-drag?

Eden workers are expected to be actively involved in their host church. They attend the main weekly gathering, generally on a Sunday, so not so radical there, plus a midweek home/cell group. It's quite normal for them to have an involvement in, or possibly lead, any aspect of church life, be it the Sunday

TRICKY: An overlapping vision

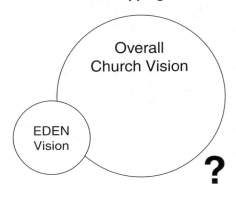

Fig. 3

school, the worship team, the Alpha course, the early morning prayer meeting. Nobody would really ever expect this to cause problems, and yet they do come along, with regularity. A big challenge wherever Eden has been undertaken, especially in the grafts rather than the plants, is the uncomfortable co-existence within a church congregation of two different seismic plates. You can build a house in San Francisco, you can even build a skyscraper, but you do so on the understanding that the San Andreas fault is beneath you, so you'll need to build very carefully, and not get too precious about what you've built if the plates start to move! What are these plates? They are paradigms described by Australian missiologists Frost and Hirsch as the 'attractional' mindset and the 'incarnational' mindset. We've spent a whole chapter trying to understand what incarnation's all about, so what's this other great force?

... the traditional Christendom mode of church and the world around it can be described as being fundamentally *attractional*. The

106

church bids people to *come and hear* the gospel in the holy confines of the church and its community ... If our actions imply that God is really only present in official church activities – worship, Bible studies, Christian youth meetings, ladies fellowships – then it follows that mission and evangelism simply involve inviting people to church-related meetings ... Evangelism therefore is primarily about mobilizing church members to attract unbelievers into church where they can experience God. Rather than being genuine 'outreach,' it effectively becomes more like an 'in-drag' ... The only means to evangelize people becomes organizing little 'patrols' to go into the world and rescue them and bring them back into the safety of 'church'.[8]

Michael Frost goes on to describe in lucid terms the limitations of a church operating an attractional mindset:

... I was watching my daughter play soccer in a local park. Next to the field was an asphalted area where a group of model-car enthusiasts had set up a track and were using remote controls to race their cars against one another's. The constant buzz of the miniature motors caught our attention and we wandered over to see what they were doing. We soon realized that we had encountered a lost suburban tribe. Everyone looked the same. They all wore tight black jeans and checkered flannel shirts. They wore baseball caps with car manufacturers' logos on them. They had parked their cars – virtually all drove pickups – beside the tracks, and their wives or girlfriends sat in one of the truckbeds talking and laughing loudly. It was a tribe in every sense of the word – dress code, language, culture and customs. We learned that once a month on a Sunday morning they met to race each other, to discuss the latest designs in model cars, and to drink and laugh and build community. If the nearby church decided that this suburban tribe needed to hear about the saving work of Christ, how would they reach them? The attractional church would hold special services for model-car racers. It would design an excellent flyer explaining that Jesus loves model-car enthusiasts, and they would place one under the wind-shield wipers of each pickup. It would try to find a recently converted model-car enthusiast and have him share his testimony on a Sunday morning. The attractional church would seek to do anything it could to draw the car racing fraternity into its church building.[9]

Control v. freedom

It may not be the case that the existing church has intentionally chosen the attractional model or is even aware that it is operating an attractional model, but all the same the mindset may be present and prevailing. Introduce into that context a whole bunch of people who *do* know that they have *deliberately* chosen to be incarnational, and before long the friction may produce smoke. It needn't do – after all, people do live enjoyable lives on either side of the San Andreas fault – but certain other factors may bring the differences into relief sooner rather than later. The single biggest factor is that of leadership style and how it's expressed in processes of decision-making. Contemporary management theorists, particularly those who study the effectiveness of organisations and teams, would call this the control/freedom dynamic, a sliding scale principle from authoritarian to democratic. Take a look at the diagram, and this should all start making sense.

REALITY BITES

Caroline, in Harpurhey, talking about Christchurch.

It's a blessing to have a strong team of people who are just there to support you and help you. To be part of that is really cool.

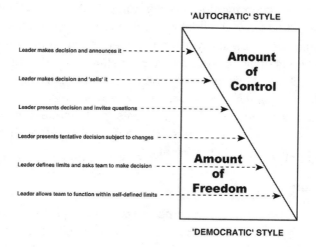

Fig. 4 [10]

Given the kind of free-thinking, risk-taking personalities that are often drawn to join an initiative like Eden, it would clearly be a disaster waiting to happen to link in with a church showing signs of an autocratic leadership. However, this assumes that all autocratic leadership is as obvious as walking around in a special khaki uniform bearing a rather unique little moustache. In reality the power and politics of church life may be more awkward to discern from the outside in. The bottom line is, Eden teams need a lot of space. They need freedom to chart new landscapes, permission to experiment, to try, and to fail.

I know Christian friends at uni have had to spend time in building up a strong group of Christian friends – yet mine was there instantly!

The issues team members come up against in their 24/7/365 ministry may leave them feeling a huge need for pastoral care but suffering a low tolerance for formal church commitments. That uneasy balance should cause leaders considering Eden to reflect on Paul's words, *'When I planned this, did I do it lightly? Or do I make my plans in a worldly manner ...?'*[11] Graft or plant, the challenge Eden presents to church leadership is enormous. And as with most challenges of Christian leadership, the glory is invisible. What a job!

Partners in sending

It's probably worth giving some attention to the forces working on the hearts and minds of would-be Eden missionaries as they make deliberate steps away from what they know and into what they don't. It's fair to say that they're not always encouraged – not everyone they ask for advice really gets the idea. Yes, it is the case that even in the church of Jesus there can be a risk-averse culture which resists the kind of mission that Stephen or Philip would have recognised. The suggestion of becoming 'downwardly mobile' – giving up the rat race and moving into a council house – may not immediately solicit excited bouts of backslapping. Andy Dorton, a guy living incarnationally with his wife and kids on an estate in Hull, thinks he knows why: 'Because people have swallowed the Thatcher line: council estate tenant, second-class citizen; owner occupier, better-class citizen. And Blair has done nothing to reverse this ...'[12]

It's sad but true that one Eden volunteer's sister pointed out with vitriol, 'You must admit that it's not intrinsically nice living with pikeys.' Mercifully nobody in the Bible had a calling of 'sensibleness' on their life, and neither is 'caution' a fruit of the Spirit. So our guys and girls press on to obey God regardless of the mind games. They're in good company, anyway. Remember what Peter had to say about Jesus' future plans?

> 'Never, Lord!' he said. 'This shall never happen to you!'
>
> Jesus turned and said to Peter, 'Get behind me, Satan! You are a stumbling-block to me; you do not have in mind the things of God, but the things of men.'[13]

And how did Luke feel about Paul's big idea of travelling back to Israel's cosmopolitan capital after prophetic mime artist Agabus had thrown in his twopenn'orth?

> . . . we and the people there pleaded with Paul not to go up to Jerusalem. Then Paul answered, 'Why are you weeping and breaking my heart? I am ready not only to be bound, but also to die in Jerusalem for the name of the Lord Jesus.' When he would not be dissuaded, we gave up and said, 'The Lord's will be done.'[14]

Whilst it's probably quite unlikely that at an Eden volunteer's 'sending service' someone from the congregation will attempt to remove their funky snakebelt and tie them up with it, more subtle forms of disapproval may be employed. But thankfully it's not all bad news ... hopefully for every horror story there are half a dozen stories of real blessing. From all corners of the nation people continue to feel called and those who love them continue to send them out.

NEO (New Expressions Of church)

The Openshaw partnership is one of four so far that have used Eden as either part of, or the whole of, an urban church-planting strategy. The first church gathering was in the front room of a terraced house in the middle of the estate. The six founder members of the team were there, plus Major Chick

Yuill, the dynamic commander of the Salvation Army in the region, bringing encouraging prophetic insight from the book of Daniel mixed with raw Scottish humour quick enough to lift any sense of trepidation about the future. Things moved fast: within a week the team were trying out their building for size, a run-down old Sally Army hall that had not seen any action for many, many years. Those first Sunday gatherings were essentially a private affair, a chance for the team to hang out with God together and form a corporate identity together, to work out how their styles and preferences could complement to bless the heart of God.

Fairly early on, curiosity got the better of passers-by who heard the sound of music and singing. A young mum might pop in with a pram, or a few of the local youth might create 10

REALITY BITES

Mark, on making a home in Wythenshawe.

I am one of those privileged people whose dad and mum are Christians. I thank God that they brought me up teaching me the Bible and training me to live for God. And as they did that, I'm sure they knew that one day it would all come back their way, when I would tell them that God had put some wacky and scary call on my life. They had always taught me to ask God what to do with my life, and one day God did tell me what to do – move to Wythenshawe.

I can remember talking to my dad and mum and describing what God was calling me to do, and I can remember the conversation when I tried to paint a picture for them of what Wythenshawe was like. As I was telling them all about it I could sense that they were concerned about what I was getting myself into. Not Eden – they were convinced immediately that it was a fantastic initiative –

minutes of havoc before making a bolt for the door. Christians from other churches passed through but rarely came back. The team began inviting neighbours and people in the community they were getting to know to an Alpha course, with a little uptake. They also found a few people who were pleased to return prayer cards dropped through doors that they then brought into their first 24/7 prayer room.

A big struggle in becoming recognised locally as a bona-fide outfit was relating to other churches in the vicinity. Dotted around the place are a number of small denominational churches which the team sought to gain some conversation with. The process was a deliberate one of trying to find common ground, to express a broad churchmanship and not throw into relief the liberal-evangelical divide. With no existing contacts in

---

but concerned about the area I would be living in. After talking through with them the risks that I was taking, their statement was amazing: 'Well Mark, if this is what you believe God is asking you to do, then we support you. We are concerned for your safety, but we will pray for you, and trust that God will keep you safe.' I'm so glad they're Christians – because they understood that someone greater than them would be watching out for me – and if God was watching over me, they could be at peace.

A few months later, after I had been accepted onto the team in Wythenshawe, I took them to see my new house on Haveley Road in Benchill. At this time Benchill was renowned for crime, and as you walked or drove into the area you could feel the oppression of life hit you like a punch in the gut. Showing my parents my new house was an interesting experience – the council hadn't finished repairing it yet for us to move in, and all of the windows had steel sheets on them to try to keep the house secure. These steel sheets had small holes in them so that if you

---

the area, it was a case of cold-calling, literally opening the phone book and ringing anyone who might be vaguely Christian. They tried to be up front with the other leaders, most of whom were two or three times their age and tended to be Dr This and Dr That, the chair of umpteen local committees. One particular church leader, after weeks of unanswered calls, came out with this: 'Yes, I know who you are, I know what you're doing, I don't agree with it and I'm not going to meet you.' What a classic! Ironically, God's blessing has been so amazing on everything the Eden team have put their hand to that the same guy has now invited them to develop an approach for the young people hanging out on his church doorstep.

After about three years of Eden Openshaw, Gary began to

---

pressed close up to them you could see inside. As my mum walked up to the house she began to cry. She looked through the steel shutters one by one, continuing to cry. When she had finished looking she walked back to the car, still crying. I was gutted – the move that I was making was obviously bigger for my dad and mum than I could comprehend; at the time I didn't have children of my own. I was 19, full of excitement for what God had for me to do, and I can honestly say that I really wasn't worried about any danger in Wythenshawe. My zeal was so great it had blocked the risks out of my mind. But for my parents, they saw the risks. All my mum could voice through the tears when I got into the car was, 'Well son, we're going to have to pray hard for you, for God to protect you here.'

There was a particularly unhelpful old lady in my dad's and mum's church who insisted on keeping them updated with the latest bit of crime that she had heard on the news had happened

notice a tilting of the scales taking place. The early years of the planting were a time when 'church was something Eden did'. Now, though, he was asking big questions about the expression of the church he was leading. Visiting speakers might well compliment the resounding New Testament authenticity, but was it full-blown church according to the Scriptures? Very gradually, but inexorably, an internal transition was taking place. The result was predictable and essential: a more mature congregation and focus of ministry in which 'Eden is something church does'. With the right order understood, and of course with trademark youthful winsomeness, Openshaw Community Church has taken its rightful place in the local landscape. Now, building on lessons learned in those first few years, Gary is

---

in Wythenshawe. She would say, 'I hear there's been another-shooting in Wythenshawe this week,' or, 'Did you hear that someone was stabbed in Wythenshawe last week?' In the words of my mum, 'All we could do was just keep committing you and your safety to God, and praise God, he did keep you safe.'

As I look back now I realise that I wasn't the only one who paid a price when I moved to Wythenshawe. My dad and mum paid a price too. Having a son of my own now and understanding the feelings which go along with that, I can now see why they were so concerned. In some ways, though, I'm glad they were concerned for me, because that concern made them pray, and I'm sure it was their prayers, along with others, that kept me safe. But I have learnt a lesson: for every person who does something dangerous for God, there are people behind them who love them so much, paying a different price from them, but paying a price all the same. I thank my dad and mum for paying that price so that I could do what God wanted me to do.

networking nationally with other friends from the Salvation Army to enable other young leaders to create their own New Expression Of church in the inner city.

REALITY BITES

Mike and Dani's pastor talks about sending them to Hattersley.

After nearly 14 years in Jersey I hopped over to Guernsey to embark on full-time pastoral ministry at Vazon in January 2003. My wife and I were delighted to get reacquainted with Mike Ozanne and his family, whom we'd met previously when they'd visited Jersey on short-term mission. Mike was now sharing in leadership as part of the worship group, along with his dad. Another brother was regularly on the drums, while the third oversaw PA and the older youth! The whole family clearly loved the Lord, and were using their talents in his service. Along with his musical gifting and talent as a mime artist, Mike also led a thriving children's club. I have to say that they were, indeed still are, the best behaved children I have ever seen! The club seemed to have hit the correct balance of fun and games, cooking and craft, and what some would call the 'God Spot', the last always supervised by Mike, and never out of hand or disrespectful.

There is always the desire for a pastor to keep talented, godly people close by him, to work in the local church. However, my wife and I prayed years ago that the church in which I then served as an elder would be a sending church. We had grown from nothing to over 200, but nobody had been sent to full-time service away from the local fellowship. Well, as we might have

Partnership with other agencies

This whole issue of partnership wouldn't be complete if we just discussed our buddies in the church. Working in neighbour-

---

expected, we were among the first to go, along with another elder! Consequently, we were not surprised when Mike announced his intention to leave Guernsey with his wife Dani and daughter Destiny, to serve the Lord as part of Eden in Manchester.

We already knew that Mike had spent some time with the project, and that his heart was clearly in returning to it. For someone brought up in a compact and safe environment such as Guernsey, with beautiful surroundings and a high standard of living, life on an estate on the outskirts of a city with an area far bigger than his native island must have been something of a culture shock. We are full of admiration for Mike and Dani, and thankful that, despite many difficulties, they know that they are where the Lord wants them to be. We cannot deny that there is a certain emptiness where Mike used to be, but despite that everything carries on. Among the young people in the church, he was the real motivator. Nevertheless, we are happy to still be a sending church, with 'missionaries' to support in prayer and in other ways. We are thrilled to hear of the things that the Lord is accomplishing through Eden, and that Mike and Dani are themselves overjoyed to be part of this unique ministry. We love them and we are proud of this couple.

Pastor Paul Drury
(Vazon Elim Pentecostal Church, Guernsey)

---

hoods in the throes of various secular regeneration and renewal initiatives begs the question: how do we relate to the other organisations and agencies operating and overlapping in our areas? Do we collide or collude?[15] Or is there a third way?

The day Gareth Lloyd-Jones first tried to strike up a partnership with the other agencies working on the Hattersley estate is permanently etched on his mind as The Worst Meeting In The History Of The Universe Ever! A bad atmosphere already existed in the area following the collapse of a promising housing stock transfer which could have brought with it a significant amount of fresh investment. The last-minute cancellations of the three previously arranged meetings also contributed to Gareth's and Mark's general feelings of uneasiness. Mark conveyed to Gareth his experience from such meetings in Wythenshawe: 'Look, however we approach this, three things are going to happen in this meeting: (a) we will be accused of being arrogant; (b) we will be accused of being a cult; (c) we will be told we are making promises we can't deliver.' And so the two pioneers tentatively entered the conference room and looked around at the 15 stony faces of their potential New Best Friends. Mark opened by telling the Wythenshawe story, all the genuinely good stuff that was really hard to argue with. He stated that Eden was seeking to co-operate with the efforts of the other agencies for the good of the young people of Hattersley, and Gareth backed him up with nods, smiles and comforting, affirming Mmmm's.

The first member of the group spoke, and laid into the guys for being 'non-communicative'. Why weren't they consulted about this at an earlier stage? (Doh, you've cancelled on us for three months on the trot!) The next member of the group took objection to the suggestion that they actually needed any help in Hattersley: 'The greatest problem Hattersley has is that people perceive it to be a problem when it's not!' Another member then suggested that the group formally pass a motion that 'The Hattersley Development Trust officially stands opposed to you and all you stand for – and I'll be warning my kids to stay away!' Fortunately the guys were spared being burnt at the stake by the local councillor, who did seem to have some limited grasp of the point of local democracy: 'As a faith group these people don't need our permission to work on the estate; they are only seeking to communicate their intentions to us.' And with that veiled compliment ringing in their ears they were shown the door. That meeting was held in July 2001. Below are a few snippets from letters on file received from those same agencies three years on in the life of the project.

> Please pass on my thanks to your colleagues and the young people you worked with on this. Like yourself they deserve great credit as they really did Hattersley proud.
>
> *Neighbourhood Manager*

> Eden is a very professional and hard working group of committed people who have extensive knowledge of most issues concerning young people on Hattersley ... I would recommend anyone to either work with or request advice in relation to young people from this organisation.
>
> *Police Youth Liaison Officer*

> The Eden team ... have consistent and regular access to the youth on the estate, often those most hard to reach. Eden run various projects to support and encourage the youth in healthy lifestyles etc. They are experienced and keep very high standards on issues like child protection and confidentiality.
>
> *Local NHS Trust Health Visitor*

Doesn't God have an amazing knack of turning things around?

---

[1] For more on the recent history of church unity in Manchester, read *City-Changing Prayer* by Debra and Frank Green, Survivor Books, 2005.

[2] For more of this, read chapter 7 of *Diary of a Dangerous Vision* by Andy Hawthorne, Survivor Books, 2004.

[3] Isaiah 43:19.

4   CMI and NFI (nothing to do with furniture).
5   Acts 11:23.
6   George Lings, *Encounters on the Edge No. 14 – The Eden Puzzle*, The Church Army, 2002.
7   Ephesians 1:8.
8   Michael Frost and Alan Hirsch, *The Shaping of Things to Come*, Hendrickson, 2003.
9   Ibid.
10   Adapted from the work of management theorists Tannenbaum & Schmidt.
11   2 Corinthians 1:17.
12   Andy Dorton, 'On the Estate', in *Urban Church*, edited by Michael Eastman and Steve Latham, SPCK, 2004.
13   Matthew 16:22–23.
14   Acts 21:12–14.
15   A phrase used by the researchers at the William Temple Foundation.

6

Jackals and Owls?

The LORD will surely comfort Zion and will look with compassion on all her ruins; he will make her deserts like Eden, her wastelands like the garden of the LORD. Joy and gladness will be found in her, thanksgiving and the sound of singing.

Isaiah 51:3

Words and pictures

When you're living in a 100-year-old terraced house, in a crumbling inner-city street and either side of you are empty properties shielded from junkies and vandals by clumsy steel shutters, certain passages in the Bible come to light in glorious technicolour. Take Isaiah 58:12, for example: '... *you will be called Repairer of Broken Walls, Restorer of Streets with Dwellings'*. That's really going to hit the spot. Unfortunately not every page of the Bible is quite that easy to contextualise. The Holy Spirit may choose to highlight a flowery poetic scripture, or a line of Levitical law, or a shard of apocalyptic vision. These special words and promises can take on tremendous significance to those they are delivered to, bringing encouragement in a lonely moment, becoming an anchor during a sudden storm.

Andy Hawthorne has established the thriving youth ministry of The Message on God's promises revealed in the Bible. He frequently returns to touchstone scriptures the Holy Spirit has brought to his attention.

The *logos*

Divine 'communications', which every team member will receive in their spirit, often quite regularly, tend to be clumped

---

REALITY BITES

Andy Hawthorne, Founding Director of The Message.

There are probably two Bible passages that we have quoted more than any others as we have pushed on with our dream of seeing a whole area soaked with the love of Jesus.

The first passage came to have special meaning to us way back in 1987 when my brother Simon and I first had the wacky idea to step out in faith and write to every church in Manchester challenging them to get involved in mission to young people. We'd booked what was then the biggest rock venue in town for a week of funky evangelistic gigs. It was going to cost a fortune, but despite that fact we really felt we were on a roll with the idea.

I can't deny panicking a bit inside. I remember saying, 'Pleee-ase God, if this is right will you speak to me from your word, this week?' I wish I'd had the bottle to ask him to speak to me right there and then, but God knew what he was doing. I was reading

---

together under the generic heading 'Prophecy'. But the minute that rather grand title is attached, the words heard almost take on a new aura in the minds of those trying to unpack them. Is there any helpful way to discern what is relevant personally or corporately? What needs to be shared right now and what should be held in the heart until the right time?

Ask any member of an Eden team about this stuff, about the way they've been shaped by words from God, and you're going to find the vast majority, if not all, referring to times when the only thing keeping them rooted has been the promise God has given them. They'll also bear witness to times of apparent conflict between what God appears to be saying and the evidence of the situations they are facing on a day-to-day basis.

---

through the Bible from cover to cover at the time and happened to be up to Isaiah 43. The words I read, particularly verses 18–21, left me completely stunned:

See, I am doing a new thing! Now it springs up; do you not perceive it? I am making a way in the desert and streams in the wasteland. The wild animals honour me, the jackals and the owls, because I provide water in the desert and streams in the wasteland, to give drink to my people, my chosen, the people I formed for myself that they may proclaim my praise.

I put my Bible down convinced that God had spoken to me and that we were going to see rivers flowing in this desert city called Manchester. We put those verses on the bottom of our first newsletter and still have them boldly displayed in our offices almost 20 years later. To be honest, what we've seen so far seems more like a trickle or perhaps a stream, but I am absolutely convinced the river is coming.

Each one is likely to have been drawn at different times to opposite poles, at one end the temptation to overspiritualise stuff and at the other end wondering if those promises which once seemed so imminent were actually from God at all. Team leaders who have a responsibility to model spiritual leadership will often create space in the diary for the discipline of a 24/7 prayer week or the special dynamic of team worship time to keep the team's holy fire burning.

In chapter 4 we tried to enter into the mystery of God and his Word become flesh. We established a critical relationship and it was a bit philosophical. We reflected on Genesis, the pattern-making book:

The second scripture came to us in an even more amazing way. In 1996 we received the most 'God idea' we'd ever been given: the idea we started calling 'Eden'. We knew it wouldn't work without the total support of Manchester's church leaders. Simon and I met with as many of them as we could muster and asked them if they would give some of their best people to be missionaries to Wythenshawe. On top of that we asked them if they would pray for us and even give us some cash to make it all happen. To our delight they said they would and since then they have been as good as their word.

Straight after the meeting, Simon and I were sitting in his car in a car park in Manchester city centre when a complete stranger came and knocked on the window. He said that he didn't know if we were Christians, but as he'd been sitting nearby eating his butties, he had felt compelled to read us some verses he had just been reading from the Bible. We invited him into the back of the car and once again God gave us the perfect verses for that time. The guy read out Psalm 37:5–11:

124

... the earth was formless and empty, darkness was over the surface of the deep, and the Spirit of God was hovering over the waters.

And God said, 'Let there be light,' and there was light.[1]

Notice, '*And God said ...*' How many more times did God speak in Genesis 1? Another eight times, all in the first chapter of the Bible. No rambling introductions in this book – we're introduced to God in full flow: a God of speech, a God of action, a God of creativity, a God of order, a God whose word has power! We contrasted this account of the creation with the introduction to John's Gospel:

In the beginning was the Word, and the Word was with God, and the Word was God.[2]

> *Commit your way to the LORD; trust in him and he will do this: He will make your righteousness shine like the dawn, the justice of your cause like the noonday sun. Be still before the LORD and wait patiently for him; do not fret when men succeed in their ways, when they carry out their wicked schemes. Refrain from anger and turn from wrath; do not fret – it leads only to evil. For evil men will be cut off, but those who hope in the LORD will inherit the land. A little while, and the wicked will be no more; though you look for them, they will not be found. But the meek will inherit the land and enjoy great peace.*

What a promise – a whole area inherited for Jesus! Once again I was sure that Almighty God had spoken to us and had promised that through all the challenges, we'd see some amazing fruit. I'm now trusting to see the full measure of these fantastic promises right across the work of The Message.

John does something here in language which we must recognise as we go deeper into this matter of hearing what God's saying. When John refers to Christ as 'the Word' he uses the Greek noun *logos*. A legendary Bible scholar called Merrill Unger, who wrote classic stuff on interpreting the Bible, explains:

> Words are the vehicle for the revelation of the thoughts and intents of the mind to others. In the person of the divine Logos, God made himself fully knowable to man … Christ as the Word constitutes the complete and ultimate divine revelation.[3]

As we grasp more fully this unity of God with his word, so its power is unlocked to us. Hearing the word of God is so much

---

REALITY BITES

Ruth, with a vision for the Valley.

I found myself at The Message 2000 event totally by accident – my mates dragged me along literally on the day, I hadn't even booked! I was put onto the Valley project. I will never forget the things I saw that week. I've often heard 'big name speakers' exaggerating stories of revival and God moving, but when it comes to what actually happened on the Valley I've only ever heard it played down. Policemen were literally crying in the streets at the sight of hundreds of scallies running round singing 'We wanna see Jesus lifted high'!

Families, streets and neighbours were reunited, prejudice dissolved and every single person worked together with the Christians to feed everyone and clean the streets and gardens. The hardest of people laid down years of pain and hurt as they accepted Jesus as Saviour and wept in the street before their neighbours at his amazing grace.

As I watched in amazement, I saw a vision of God's love

---

more than studying a collection of chapters and verses. It starts with an encounter with Jesus Christ, the living Word. Within the orbit of that mysterious relationship of God and man, pure communication can begin to flow like deep calling to deep.[4] From that position you will find illumination of the great scriptural themes of God's intentional self-revelation, because:

> *The Son is the radiance of God's glory and the exact representation of his being, sustaining all things by his powerful word.*[5]

It's so important that there's no divorce of the Word of God from the God of the Word. All who come to God for direction have to get to grips with this deep down or else risk quoting this and

---

flowing like a river down every street, in every house. The river was seen through spiritual eyes, but the effect it had as it washed over every person was physical. I asked God what would happen the following week, when the mission was over. Would the river still flow? Who would teach these people? He simply told me that I would. As I stood there, God said it would take a lot of work and time, even years, but this was a foretaste of what was to come. The river would flow again, but not just for 10 days – it would flow all day, every day.

As clearly as I was called, I refused. I had no intention of living on a council estate and definitely not in Manchester and definitely not the Valley! Apparently, when it comes to things like that, God doesn't make jokes. He was serious. I gave in.

The estate went back to normal. Most of it still is. The residents still get a faraway glazed 'good old days' look whenever The Message 2000 is mentioned. When times get tough I know that I have that promise to fall back on. Sometimes I forget, but that promise is in me and I'm holding God to it! The river will flow again, and that's why I'm still here.

---

that and spouting off to absolutely no effect. Essentially, use of Scripture and concept of God should be entwined. Our concepts of God (who is Spirit) are defined by study of Scripture. Our study of Scripture is illuminated by the Spirit (who is God). The combination of Word and Spirit is the most powerful force in the universe. No, really, that's not just hype. How did God activate creation back in Genesis 1:2–3? By the Spirit and the Word!

The *rhema*

Setting apart the divine Logos we've recognised as Christ, the use of *logos* (lower case l) has long been understood as the accepted written revelation of God – the Bible, Scripture. But in

---

REALITY BITES

Claire. Maybe God's saying something about Salford?

I was clear about one thing while I was away at uni – I wasn't going back anywhere near Manchester when I'd finished. But when I was at Soul Survivor in 1997, just when the first few Wythenshawe lot were moving in, it became clear that I was meant to do Eden. I was in one of the main meetings at SS and in the middle of the worship I remember turning round to my friend and saying, 'Erm, I've just had this great big long bit of Isaiah going round my head.' I didn't know that bit of the Bible in detail, but fortunately my friend was a bit more on the ball, so we looked it up and sure enough there was the stuff that had been in my head, all that '… Spirit of the Lord God is upon me … bind up the broken hearted …' So I thought to myself, 'Mmm, maybe God's trying to tell me something,' but I didn't quite know what.

Literally the next minute, Matt Redman started up the song, 'The Spirit of the Lord God is surely upon me', so that got my

---

Ephesians 6:17, and loads of other places too, *logos* is not used. A different Greek word, *rhema*, is used instead, and through this word a new concept is introduced. Another great Bible translator called William Vine explains:

> [Rhema] is exemplified in the injunction to 'take the sword of the Spirit, which is the word of God' ... here the reference is not to the whole bible as such but to the individual scripture which the Spirit brings to our remembrance for us to use in time of need.[6]

So it is the case, and we know it from our experiences too, that the Holy Spirit really does take the word and ignite it in our hearts and minds. And in fact, even though the phrase 'God's given me a word for you' drips with Christian cliché, it is

---

attention. But I still had no idea what it was all about. The time of worship ended and Andy Hawthorne got up and started speaking and read out the same bit, Isaiah 61, from the Bible ... and then started to talk about Eden. I kinda got the message! I took up his invitation to find out more at an afternoon seminar where I saw some film of Eden Wythenshawe. At that point something inside me just clicked.

So I went back to uni, finished my final year and applied to Wythenshawe. During my final year I felt I really needed to do a discipleship programme called 'Soul Time' at Soul Survivor Watford, so I contacted someone at Wythenshawe and told them that was what I was up to. They said, 'You know a project in Salford is about to start? You're from Salford, aren't you?' Well, I was, and so I knew – I was not going back there!

Off I trotted to Soul Time, and during those five months I realised it had to be the Salford project. Five years later, I'm still in Salford and I'm still living on the estate in a house I bought two years ago.

technically correct. That phrase is in fact communicating that 'God has given me a *rhema* for you'. He has taken a word from the Bible, or given a pictorial snapshot, made it ignite in the heart and then inspired the mind with the appropriate application for the context, whether that's outreach or prayer ministry or a friendship or whatever. These '*rhema* words' are the ones which sit uncomfortably under that 'Prophetic' heading. That term, especially used with its capital P, should be reserved for words which have been weighed up by witnesses and agreed on as a true revelation of the will and purpose of God. A '*rhema* word' may simply be an encouragement, or a timely reminder, or an expression of God's care, or a nudge back in the right direction for those who are getting distracted. Personally receiving the word of God is the bread and water of the soul for those involved in Eden. It has nothing to do with human physique or technique. Rather, it's a faith exercise, rooted in knowledge of Christ and in close partnership with the Spirit. In this world and the world beyond its effect is mighty.

Images that inspire

The briefest glance at the Bible's prophetic books would show quite clearly that God is fairly partial to appropriating the material contents of the world around us and imbuing them with holy meaning. Jeremiah's opening visions involve an almond tree and a boiling pot. Amongst the many images of Amos are a swarm of locusts, a builder's plumb-line and a basket of ripe fruit. Zechariah starts off fairly straightforwardly seeing a bloke on a horse, but things get increasingly bizarre until he is confronted by a flying scroll, 30 feet long and 15 feet wide! Poor Ezekiel can't even retell the things he saw, he can only resort to feeble descriptions: '*...what looked like ...*', '*... what looked* *like ...'* and *'... what looked like ...'.* Is there any reason why we shouldn't expect God to speak to us like this now?

One guy moved into an Eden council house and would get up early every morning to pray. His regular routine was to go into the lounge, turn the gas fire on full and kneel in front of it in a foetal position letting the heat waft over his head and back. One morning, feeling concerned about the huge commitment he'd made and not knowing what the future held, he asked God for reassurance. Right at that moment the gas boiler, which was fitted into the chimney alcove behind the fire, let out an almighty 'whoosh'! The central heating thermostat had kicked in to warm the house before the others got out of bed. In that split second of ignition God had answered the prayer with a physical sign saying, 'I won't let your heart grow cold. I've fitted you with a thermostat and I'm setting the level. When you begin to sense a chill in your soul my Holy Spirit is going to kick in and you'll feel the fire.'

Many workers would relate similar experiences and events. Some would speak of dreams in the night, others of visions in the day. One guy on the Wythenshawe team was strolling through the neighbourhood at about 8 p.m. He was prayer-walking with members of his home group, enjoying a bit of time with God. Passing one of his friends' houses, he looked up into the darkness and was suddenly stunned to see a huge bright angel – wings, sword, the works – sitting up on the apex of the roof and looking around as if on guard duty. As he looked ahead up the street to his left and right he could see the houses occupied by other Eden workers. Every single house had an angel, just one, sitting on its roof. All the angels were similar, and yet had slightly different personal features. All seemed to be charged with the same task – ensuring the protection of the servants of God. Of all the guys on the team this guy certainly didn't have the reputation of being the 'out there wacky prophetic one' – quite the opposite, really. And that's maybe why God chose on that particular evening to peel back the supernatural veil to provide this glimpse into what's really going on in the overlapping dimension.

Easily led

It's not just the prophetic books that God uses to bring us revelation. Every single verse from every single genre in the Bible could become a signpost on our journey (although Ezra 1:10 is an unlikely candidate). The epistles of Paul speak

---

REALITY BITES

Andy, on hearing God in Harpurhey.

It seems an unattainable thing to hear the voice of God. Often things we read in Scripture appear to be more than a stone's throw from the reality of our everyday situations. On Eden we've been taken on some mad journeys – seeing God radically turning lives around – and loads of these journeys begin with a revelation from God's word. Paul, in the beginning of Romans 12, says that to know the will of God, you need to be made like Jesus and have a change of mind. He tells us this begins by offering ourselves as a living sacrifice of worship, which is a response of gratitude to the massive mercy he has shown us. We have found that the first thing to do is to value spending time in the presence of God, giving space for him to reveal stuff to us. A load of us, from all the different teams, got together over a weekend to do exactly that.

---

amazingly well into pioneering situations like Eden, bringing great wisdom to the team dynamic. His encouragements to maintain unity, guard personal holiness and not get swayed by smart-sounding teaching are dietary essentials for any project hoping to make it to the five-year mark in one piece. When he affirms the foolishness of the gospel and notes the believers' lack of worldly clout, he's speaking straight to us.[7] When he takes time to contrast our clay pot lives with God's infinite abilities, we can nod along and agree, 'That's exactly how it is.'[8] When he goes on to describe our ambassadorial role with its associated personal cost, we just know we're in esteemed company and everything's gonna be OK.[9]

On this weekend together, something we do every year, during a time of worship, one of the Eden team leaders felt that God was speaking through Ezekiel 37, 'the valley of the dry bones'. In that chapter Ezekiel is told by God to tell a huge pile of bones to rise up, so that's what he does – and up they get. Ezekiel is amazed as God works this bizarre miracle of re-animation, causing sinews, flesh and skin to form on the bones. Then he was told to 'prophesy to the breath' as the bodies had no life in them. He obeyed and witnessed a further miracle as God's breath filled the bodies and they came to life, standing up together and forming a massive army. From my perspective as an Eden worker, I had arrived on Eden thinking I would change the world. I'd been working for the last three years trying to convince some really rough lads on my estate that Jesus was worth following, but not seeing much happen. On this weekend away we felt challenged by the Holy Spirit to apply Ezekiel's vision to our situation. It seemed that we took on

---

Paul's short pastoral dispatches to the younger guys he's been investing in become like a familiar duvet for an urban missionary's personal devotions. The warnings about who is worthy of trust, and how to tell, offer a step to maturity for the naive. The insistence on being a fighter and being the one who sets the example counters the subtle onset of apathy. His choice words on financial management are a great affirmation of our counter-cultural calling – and a cautionary reminder when the regeneration effort starts kicking in and your £20,000 home is suddenly worth £100,000. Ultimately, the companion-ship of such an awesome brother-in-arms, if only through the distant echoes of his letters, is a massive comfort that can't be underestimated. The attitude he displays in the closing words of

---

Ezekiel's role of prophesying to the breath, knowing it's God that breathes the life, not us. About a hundred of us, from all over the city, called out and prophesied life into the lost young people back home. We had faith that they would be the ones to see real change, not just a few imported Eden workers on their own. This word raised my perspective, because now my eyes were on God, waiting for the opportunities he was providing. I was fired up and envisioned for what he could do through these young people.

Just a week later, two lads we'd known for more than three years asked to watch the film *The Passion of the Christ*, as it had just come out on DVD. As we watched this retelling of the death and resurrection of Christ, round at my house, both of them were blown away and decided to follow Jesus because of all he'd done for them. While praying together, one of them said to me, 'Don't take this the wrong way, but

---

his final letter to Timothy is dripping with poignancy, as no matter how tight the team, everybody has certain things they can only walk through one to one with God. In many ways his remarkably upbeat statement, *'The Lord will rescue me from every evil attack and will bring me safely to his heavenly kingdom',*[10] is an echo of the great 'hang in there' passages of the Old Testament:

> *But I said, 'I have laboured to no purpose; I have spent my strength in vain and for nothing. Yet what is due to me is in the LORD's hand, and my reward is with my God.'*[11]

Though the fig-tree does not bud and there are no grapes on the vines, though the olive crop fails and the fields produce no food though there are no sheep in the pen and no cattle in the stalls, yet

---

I think God's saying that it's going to be us that see the big stuff, not you …' I explained to him what we had heard from Ezekiel 37 about an army coming together from a pile of scattered bones. Right there and then, the Holy Spirit filled him in a pretty dramatic way. But that wasn't the end of it. In no time at all these lads were asking to get baptised in water too. We'd arranged to take them away for a weekend and thought it would be a good idea to do the baptism the week after. Our vicar gave the 'OK' to the idea and then proceeded to tell us that he was preparing to speak on Ezekiel 37 for that service. Coincidence, or God at work?

None of this would have happened if we hadn't got into that place where God could raise our perspective with a revelation from his word. We're now walking the journey of a good work that God has started and one that he has promised to bring through to completion.

I will rejoice in the LORD, I will be joyful in God my Saviour. The Sovereign LORD is my strength; he makes my feet like the feet of a deer, he enables me to go on the heights.[12]

What was it Jesus quoted to the devil when he was being tempted; something about our lives needing more than just bread for survival? We live on *'every word that comes from the mouth of God'.*[13] It's a good job God's got such a chatty personality, or we'd all be starving.

---

[1]   Genesis 1:2–3.
[2]   John 1:1.
[3]   M. F. Unger, *Unger's Bible Dictionary*, Moody, 1957.
[4]   Psalm 42:7.
[5]   Hebrews 1:3.
[6]   W. E. Vine, *Vine's Expository Dictionary of Old and New Testament Words*, Thomas Nelson Inc., 1997.
[7]   1 Corinthians 1.
[8]   2 Corinthians 4.
[9]   2 Corinthians 5 and 6.
[10] 2 Timothy 4:18.
[11] Isaiah 49:4.
[12] Habakkuk 3:17–19.
[13] Matthew 4:4.

7
Revival in a Fortnight

The LORD is not slow in keeping his promise, as some
understand slowness. He is patient with you, not wanting
anyone to perish, but everyone to come to repentance.

2 Peter 3:9

The pace of change

Taking a close-up look at the nature of change, it's quite clear
that it can never be plotted on a straight line graph. Change can
happen quickly, change can happen slowly, but change rarely
happens predictably. In all the variety of human endeavour
under the sun, change will always take place in one of two
ways: evolution or revolution. Depending on our personality,
one or the other will have greater appeal. Steady, progressive,
incremental change suits many people just fine. Others are
driven to the point of blood-vessel popping annoyance if the
pace of change is anything less than full-throttle Bolshevik
madness! Eden is all about bringing positive change, to individual lives, to families, and to whole communities. In fact, the
buzzword most commonly used is 'transformation', which may

well have become the noughties' equivalent of the scary R-word touted so much from church pulpit and conference platform during the nineties.

If we look at the pace of change in the world of the Acts, there are some very appropriate lessons about mission, and some very clear and present dangers. Perhaps the most common mistake in reading Acts is the loss of a sense of time and space. Luke writes with such a wonderful flowing style that within the hour or so that it takes to read the 28 chapters we feel like we've physically been through the whole incredible journey of the early church. Thoughts unlikely to be in the reader's mind by the time we reach the words '*Boldly and without hindrance he preached the kingdom of God and taught about the Lord Jesus Christ*'[1] are, 'This church-planting business looks like a right pain in the neck,' or, 'Doesn't it take ages for God to do anything!' The book of Acts gets us revved up, full of faith, raring to go and change the world – but it did all take place over the course of 30 years, and there was a heck of a lot of blood, sweat and tears. Whilst '*the message of the Lord may spread rapidly*',[2] the transformation of the communities in its wake may take a bit longer.

War of words

A helpful little mini-story within the book of Acts is found in chapter 19, where Paul arrives in the great city of Ephesus. After correcting a few local issues of baptism and charismata, he gets on with the job of waging a war of words against the prevailing worldviews of the region. His strategy is reflective of the advice he later gives to the Corinthians:

For though we live in the world, we do not wage war as the world does. The weapons we fight with are not the weapons of the world.

On the contrary, they have divine power to demolish strongholds. We demolish arguments and every pretension that sets itself up against the knowledge of God, and we take captive every thought to make it obedient to Christ.[3]

Starting first in the synagogue, Paul takes on the stronghold of religious hypocrisy, arguing and persuading for three months until the Jews start getting personal about those following the way of Christ. Paul uses this as the trigger to move on to bigger and better things, getting fixed up with a residency at the lecture hall of Tyrannus, the Ephesian equivalent of the Ministry of Sound. Every bright spark and social influencer would be on the guest list and over the next two years they did Paul's culture-shaping job for him as he got into their heads and under their skin. Agitated by his radical message, they took his material out in their conversations, *'so that all the Jews and Greeks who lived in the province of Asia heard the word of the Lord'.*[4] Paul's war of words, authenticated by his daily campaign of works and wonders, had such a profound effect on the Ephesian society that the whole economy of the city was shaken.

The final snapshot we have of Paul in this context is his desperation to preach to the biggest crowd of his entire life – the baying mob packing out the 100,000-seater stadium. Living his life with an eye open for these opportunities, you can hear him say to the other disciples, 'This is it, guys. This is the big moment it's all been building up to. Let me at 'em!'

'Paul, mate, you're forgetting one small detail – they're not here for your stand-up show. They're here for your execution!'

'Oh.'

Who knows what would have happened if the guys had allowed him to seize that moment? Would it have been curtains for Paul or revival for Ephesus? We'll never know. Neither do we know how many people chose to become followers of Christ during Paul's time in Ephesus, or where the church met or what kind of programme had been established. All we know is that Paul's time there had brought transformation to just about every layer of life. In the educational institutions and in the economic structures the supremacy of Christ had been established. What Eden needs is people and churches who will take up that baton and run the race, understanding that it may be more of a cross-country slog than a quick lap of a slick track.

Revival mania

Eden was launched around the late nineties' peak of 'revival mania' – it seems that in a few short years the R-word is now only mentioned in hushed tones behind closed doors. In such a

---

REALITY BITES

The Curshams, on Eden from a family viewpoint.

We arrived as part of Eden on a grey February day and felt at the start of a major new stage of our lives. In the early evening there was a knock on the door by a child asking if our son wanted to play out. He was three at the time. Things were going to be different! We had been inspired by a book we had read some years earlier by Floyd McClung, saying that if God was calling us, he was calling our family too. We chose not to fear what those around us would say, especially about how our children's education may suffer; we chose to have faith in God's lead and call, mindful that God knew the needs of our children too. At the time we arrived in Wythenshawe we had one son and my wife was expecting – she gave birth to a wonderful girl two weeks later. Our son quickly settled in a local nursery, within five minutes' walking distance, and is now in Year 6 of the primary school. God is indeed good. When we moved to Wythenshawe

---

heady atmosphere you would expect a crazy idea like Eden to create a buzz. The Wythenshawe project had no shortage of applications from people wanting to join – recruiting staff and volunteers was like fishing in an aquarium. A team of about 20 people moved to Wythenshawe from September to Christmas 1997 and began to blitz the area with every kind of activity possible. They worked constantly, trying everything they could think of, from detached work to youth clubs, schools work, sports clubs, creative arts clubs, music clubs, big events, small events, cell groups, etc. Some activities worked well; others didn't and were stopped and replaced with new ideas. The team had no model to go by and had little idea of what problems they

---

we left behind friends and family, but feel repaid many times over, just as Jesus said in Luke 18:30.

The early days were busy, getting to know other people from Eden and the church as well as our new neighbours, who seemed surprised that people would want to move into the area from such a distance. With me working full time and having two young children, we found ourselves doing fewer youth activities than some others, but our home was a place where people could come and find rest. It was great to see local young people part of the youth groups and around at our often chaotic church meetings on Sunday mornings! It was good for them to see that the Eden team, and the wider church, had a whole mix of people, including families with children. It has been a blessing to see those who moved to the estate on their own to join the Eden team now married and having children, going to mums and toddlers groups and local schools, being teachers and school governors. And isn't that what we should expect? The Kingdom of God is, after all, like a mustard seed that grows to the largest tree in the garden.

would encounter. This initial period of experimentation was essential to the steep learning curve which future projects could also benefit from. A wealth of real experiences was gathered and the internal motivation of these crazy people who'd come to the inner city could be articulated with greater transparency. The way to become an effective agent of change and stay sane in the process had been mapped out for others to follow.

Towards the end of the second year of Eden Wythenshawe, the team (which had grown to 30 or so workers) found that they had worked so hard they were on the edge of burning out.

REALITY BITES

Not a great start for Jane in Failsworth.

What keeps me going is how obvious it is that cool things are by God's plans. For years I've lived with Jeremiah 29:11 running through my mind, *'For I know the plans I have for you, plans to prosper and not to harm you, plans to give you hope and a future … I will be found by you.'* It's a verse that's helped me through academic struggles at university, relationship break-down, job hunting, general strife and Eden. My first week on Eden was absolutely mad. I'd flown back from a post-finals summer in New Zealand on the Thursday, moved into Eden on the Friday (meeting my housemates for the first time ever on the doorstep) and started my new job on the Monday morning. The life I'd been praying for and looking forward to for years was about to start. This was the obvious fulfilment of God's plan – he'd been amazingly faithful and I was enjoying getting to know my team and the church. New job, new friends, new community.

They'd also suffered a wave of attacks, particularly car crime, vandalism and burglary, as well as a couple of scary gun-related incidents. Credit to them, they resolved not to give in to fear. This mad schedule of activity combined with the 'open house' nature of Eden left the workers with no time for themselves, no time actually to be part of their community and no time for each other. Eden had been treated like a year-round mission event, but that level of activity was unsustainable. The volunteers would be in Wythenshawe long term, and that

---

Three and a half weeks into my new life, I was involved in a really nasty car crash and ended up in hospital having my shoulder screwed back together. There followed two months off work recovering. Painful and crazy … but one thing it did give me was time. Time to pray about what I should be doing as part of Eden, time to study more of what God was saying through the Bible, time to get to know people in the church, time to think about (and one-handedly help set up for) the Kidz Club we were just launching, and time to get to know the kids – which is where God's faithfulness really shone. I love kids, but don't want to impose myself on them, if you get what I mean. I'd rather they initiated conversation. Well, after three and a half weeks of settling in but not really meeting as many kids as I'd have liked, I suddenly had tales of fast cars, flashing lights, broken bones, scars and screws with which to capture their imaginations! Barriers were broken and great relationships developed! I'm not saying the crash was God's idea, but I believe he used the aftermath to strengthen me and my position in the team, and especially to help me connect with the young people.

---

involved settling down, getting married and buying houses. They simply could not continue to keep up such a frenetic level of activity and live a 'normal' life at the same time. Eventually the team stopped a lot of the activity and took some time out. They took time to reflect seriously on what it meant to be an Eden worker and on the difference between an Eden worker and a regular youth worker. The team felt that their initial activity had been important in order for them to become established relationally within the community, but to move on to maturity the type of activity had to change. True incarnational living was agreed as being of higher priority than maintaining an exciting-looking weekly programme of service provision.

Facing the opposition

Jane's story of her car crash so soon after she'd moved in may cause some to think of the spiritual forces of darkness angered by the ministry of the teams coming into 'their area'. That may or may not be the right conclusion to draw; it's always tempting to try to find a demon under every banana skin. However, that said, it's not at all unusual for there to be suspicion of, and opposition to, the ministry of the teams in their community. In fact, it's pretty much a given, an everyday pressure to be factored into any plans and ideas, especially in the early stages of a project's life cycle. In the forgotten urban nooks and crannies that people only ever move out of, not into, the topsy-turvy laws of the Kingdom must appear quite baffling, and it makes the workers easy targets. Simply being there, in a place where they 'don't belong', may be enough of an offence to bring on direct confrontation with the local rogue elements. Coming home to find the house egged or graffitied is a common frustration, as is waking up to find your car window smashed or the tyres slashed.

It takes great grace to go on loving and giving in the face of all this. Often purely by physical location workers may get caught in the crossfire of an ongoing feud between warring families. Taking the role of peacemaker may not be immediately appreciated. And then there's the mess that comes with cranking up activities for the local youth. Who wants to do the door at the youth club if it means donning your waterproof jacket, not because it's raining but because you're likely to be spat on? Who wants to be the one to throw Terry the tearaway off the Eden bus while he's spewing out expletives and bile about how his brothers are going to come round and kneecap you? Whether caught in the spotlight of overt persecution or just suffering the leaching effect of a negative undercurrent, Eden teams must develop responses and coping strategies.

Solving these kinds of issues would generally involve a combination of the following approaches:

Prevention – Considering practical ways of limiting the occurrence or recurrence of an issue which is causing inconvenience or intimidation.

Prayer – Calling on the hosts of heaven to do the invisible work that we can't. Time and time again we've seen amazing reversals in impossible situations through the power of specific fervent prayer.

Partnership – Working with others – friends on the team, other neighbours or agencies active in the area – to reach those at the heart of a particular problem and to work at modifying their destructive behaviour.

Prosecution – Isolating the offenders using the strong arm of the law. Although most of the teams work in close partnership with the local police, legal action is generally only used as a last resort and when substantial evidence exists. Depending on the nature of the offence, taking this route may create as many problems as it solves.

Send revival – start with me

Tim and Charissa Cooke faced a difficult situation moving into the Swinton Valley Estate. The challenge wasn't really a cross-cultural one – still being fairly young themselves and sharing an interest in the urban music scene, they totally look the part. It was their council house that turned out to be 'hot property', but not in the *Location, Location, Location* sense. It had been derelict for some time before they moved in, and local youths had been using it as their drug den. Stories abounded about what had gone on in there. Tim and Charissa were faced with an issue of rights of 'ownership'. Some of these local nutters really did feel that the place belonged to them and so confrontations at the garden gate were quite usual.

Being located on one of the estate's most notorious intersections didn't help matters either. In this micro-community even the 'nice' families sell drugs. This seems to be *the* place where the gangs of local youth mass in the evenings to hang out. To get into some face-to-face youth work – it's the best of times; to enjoy a quiet night in on the sofa after a hard day's work – it's the worst of times. Any feelings of security Tim and Charissa felt were undoubtedly of divine origin, because night after night they were practically under siege. But God's destiny for them was clear and their response came straight out of the Gospels.

One night when Tim and Charissa's friends had been visiting, the local gang started kicking off. Tim was warned about his friend's car, which was parked quite vulnerably in the chaotic street outside. Venturing out to investigate, he found that its wing mirrors had been smashed, and very apologetically he suggested to his friends that they probably ought to leave before something worse happened. As well as breaking the wing mirrors of the car, one of the gang had thrown a bottle of barbecue sauce all over the front door of the house. With the gang still out on the street, Tim decided to clean the door. All sorts of verbal abuse was being hurled at him as he wiped away the sticky brown goo. Feeling fairly wound up and angry about the whole incident, Tim began to answer back with his own put-downs and one-liners. He remembers the voice of God rebuking him sharply: 'Shut up and pray!'

So Tim started praying as he cleaned, quietly under his breath, in English and in the language of the Spirit. The abuse quietened down as the ringleader of the gang, a shaven-haired lad of about 14, approached the gate. Tim turned and looked up at this angry kid, his boyish looks disguised by a hood, baseball cap and the yellow glow of the streetlight.

'Do you pray for me?' he asked matter-of-factly.

'Yeah,' replied Tim, stepping into the bizarre conversation.

'What do you pray?'

'That you'd realise how much God loves you.'

It was to be the first of many such small breakthroughs in the months ahead. The same lad would confide in Tim some weeks later, 'The council can make houses – but they can't make the stars. Only God can make them.'

Living in the old drug den, there was no way Tim and Charissa were ever going to remain anonymous. They are known throughout the estate for their compassionate work with the wildest young people. Their names aren't famous, but their

147

identity is. With hilarious regularity they will get consent notes from parents …

> To the Christians. Shanny can go to the bowling with youse tonight. Signed, Maggie.

… and umpteen variations on the theme. They are 'the Christians' to residents of the Valley who have seen God in action in all sorts of ways over the last five years. The 'Christian' label means something. One by one young people are beginning to experience what that identity means – and to want it for themselves. Like D, a well-built 17-year-old lad who takes full advantage of the breakdown of criminal justice on the estate. If ever a family deserved the 'neighbours from hell' title, it would be his. His mum is hopelessly dependent on alcohol, but is far too proud to accept any help. She and D often get into such violent arguments that between them they'll literally wreck the house. His 12-year-old sister will often be found just wandering around the little maze of local streets late into the night simply to avoid being caught in the crossfire.

REALITY BITES

Caroline, on relationship and ministry.

It's challenging being able to separate your relationship with God from your ministry. Your ministry comes out of your relationship with God, not your relationship with God out of your ministry, if you get me. Sometimes when your ministry, i.e. Eden, gets tough it's easy to view your relationship with God as tough as well just 'cos the two are so interlinked. It's also hard to remain

---

But Tim is determined to see God's love overtake D's life. Charissa has already had the privilege of leading his sister to Christ, and an amazing miracle of grace is happening in her little life. Without a hint of irony Tim will often give D a lift down to the Magistrates' Court to pay the latest instalment of the fine for the time he maliciously broke the window of the very car he's travelling in! When challenged about that particular incident by one of the other local lads, who asked, 'Why didn't you bang him out?' Tim replied, 'I won't do that, because I've forgiven him, because Jesus has forgiven him.' Stunned, this lad decided to broadcast this freaky new concept to the whole estate.

A job for life

On every Eden there are loads of examples of team members finding work in the community that adds real value to the ongoing mission of the project. Many will actually take up posts with other public sector agencies working in and around the focus area. An Eden volunteer may well also have a day job as a GP, a health visitor, a teacher, a Connexions youth worker, a Sure Start co-ordinator, or may take the flexible option and earn

---

hopeful when kids you've spent lots of time with, who seem to be really getting somewhere, end up falling away again, or you lose contact with them for whatever reason. It's hard not seeing immediate 'fruit', but you just cling to the promises of God – that one day *'every knee will bow',*[5] that there will be *'streams in the wasteland',*[6] and *'God's word never comes back empty ... it will accomplish what it set out to do'.*[7] Sometimes it just takes time – God's time – but that timing is perfect.

a crust shelf-stacking or checking-out in the local supermarket!

Across Manchester a number of Eden workers reaching out to local schools have been so impressive that the head teacher has hired them full time. Liz Askew of the Openshaw team is one of them and she is full of enthusiasm for her job. The high school she works in is well overdue for a revamp – the whole place is in a state of advanced dilapidation. Maintenance staff need to put buckets in the corridors when it rains to avoid the formation of little rivers running from classroom to classroom. The young people there have been trapped in a vacuum of zero aspiration, but Liz is doing her best to change that.

The first time Liz set foot in the school it was through the persistence of a helpful Christian librarian, who managed to get directly to the head. Initially the head was reluctant to allow a Christian group into school, perhaps because he feared an agenda of 'Bible bashing' or forcing religion onto pupils. My response to this has always been that it's hard enough to make a child put a chair under a table, so how could we force a religion on anyone? The first in-school Eden initiative was launched: an 8 a.m. breakfast club for hungry pupils where relationships could be built and motivation could be engendered. Next up was the commencement of literacy support and one-to-one mentoring, the stuff which Liz really excels in. Two noticeable findings became evident at this time:

1. If young people can be helped to appreciate the value of their education, they will achieve more.
2. Mentoring must not be reserved as an exclusive resource for young people with special needs or behavioural problems. There can be very high returns for investing a little bit of encouragement into the 80% of pupils who go unnoticed because they're at neither end of the scale – not acutely troubled or especially gifted.

Since taking on full-time employment with the school, Liz has developed an incredible mentoring structure which provides opportunity for 200 of the young people on the school campus. Every day her diary is absolutely chock-a-block with back-to-back appointments. Pupils will come to her office for a 15-minute session in which Liz will offer a word of encouragement and then agree learning targets for the coming weeks. She sees her role as helping them succeed at this thing called 'school'. Her ambition is that every one of the 200 young people she mentors will achieve at least five A–C grades at GCSE – and she's doing it!

The other staff have really accepted Liz, so much so that she's now almost part of the furniture. But they've never got to grips with the fact that Liz not only sees these young people at school – she lives with them as well. In fact, it would be fair to say, they think she's absolutely out of her mind. You *never* live in your catchment area, especially when that catchment area is the warren of terraced streets known as Openshaw. To Liz it's simple, it's the Jesus way, but they don't necessarily get that. Yes, there are drawbacks, like the sense of never really being 'off duty'. Often Liz will go home, change into T-shirt and jeans, then head off to serve drinks at the non-alcoholic bar in the Eden youth club. It's not unusual for the kids to get a bit confused too: 'Miss, can I have a Fanta?' A big plus, however, is the credibility and respect she's earned from parents. Down the road from Liz and her husband Pete is a family going through some real difficulties. The three kids are struggling to cope with school and so frequently truant. This physical closeness to the family has created unique opportunities to serve, support and intervene.

Pete, who works for children's agency Sure Start, sees every day that the crazy stuff some young people get up to is almost always a symptom of something else that's wrong. He sees the cycle that some families are in: long-term unemployment, often combined with very serious depression, never properly addressed and sorted, and so somehow 'modelled' and passed on to the next generation. Getting through to such families is really difficult, and this is often compounded by the size and complexity of the family network, which may criss-cross the neighbourhood from street to street.

Pete's passion is to reach the dads, particularly the young first-time dads, who are often still in their teens. These lads are just not prepared for parenting in any way, shape or form, but they would never step forward and ask for advice. By getting alongside them in the right way at the right time, before the birth, enormous good can be done. Accepting the privilege and responsibility of being a dad can be a massive force for change in a young guy's life. Pete has developed a really useful diary tool which dads-to-be work on as a project with Pete's support.

Pete and Liz exemplify the long-term commitment required to bring godly transformation to a community. They love Openshaw. They love the people. They get tired. They get criticised. Both sets of parents were cautious but ultimately really supportive. Other family members and friends, however, advised them that buying a house in the area was madness – even if it was only going to cost them less than a new Ford Focus! But they have a belief that they will see the community transformed by the gospel. It runs through their bones like the writing in a stick of Blackpool rock. And they're seeing that vision come to pass, one life at a time.

The Dean Street resistance

A rather ridiculous caricature which does get used every now and again is the impression in some quarters that Eden is here to 'save the day' in a triumphalistic, 'Don't panic, feeble community, we're here now!' sort of way. The reality is that even in the most ravaged of inner-city neighbourhoods there will generally be a sprinkling of people who really do care and really are prepared to do something about the numerous problems. They may be few and far between, they may be hard to find, they may feel discouraged and let down, but they will be there somewhere.

Hidden away behind a railway line, the residents of Dean Street in Failsworth had been all but forgotten. A large teenage gang led by a hardcore local troublemaker had been terrorising the area for years. Nathan and Steve, recruited to be the first Eden workers to move in, didn't have to wait long to receive the gang's welcome.

'Give us your car!' the ringleader bellowed at Steve.

'No,' replied Steve in his thick Bolton accent, to the amusement of the other cronies in the gang.

'Give us your car now or I'm gonna stab you!' threatened the angry ringleader.

'No! I'm going to the pictures. See ya!' And with a turn of the key Steve cranked the engine and coolly pulled away.

Chatting to some of his new neighbours, Nathan discovered that this kind of open lawlessness had become the norm. Parents were afraid to let their children play in the street. Pensioners were prisoners in their homes and nobody's property was safe. However, unknown to the gang, a resistance movement was forming behind the net curtains. Nathan discovered a nucleus of Dean Street mums determined to reclaim their street. Secret meetings were taking place with Oldham Council's new Community Safety Unit and a Christian police inspector who'd taken on the case as a righteous cause. It took the best part of a year to gather the full body of evidence, but the effects were almost instantaneous. The four central characters in the gang were given ASBOs[8] which restricted their activities massively. Any hint of foul language or threatening behaviour, even hanging out on the wrong side of the street, and these lads would be serving at Her Majesty's pleasure. Within a few more weeks, they were.

Team leader Nathan was very well positioned to make the most of the new safer atmosphere, and so when the local Labour councillor invited him round for a coffee he made diary space immediately. Nathan's Jesus-inspired approach was not exactly what the councillor had previously understood youth workers to be like – the local youth service seemed to pretty much ignore the residents' opinions and deliberately antagonise the police. Nathan explained his position: 'I'm a resident here … and I happen to head up a youth project … and I do have access to some resources. What can I do for you, councillor?'

This servanthood approach has been the key to Eden's huge success in Failsworth. Years of taking the rough with the smooth have earned the respect and acceptance of the residents and the authorities. Pass by Dean Street at 6.30 on a Thursday night, and you find an orderly line of about 30 young people standing exactly two feet from the edge of the pavement waiting patiently for the Eden bus to pay its weekly visit. And if anyone at a public meeting dares to question Eden's methods or motives, you'll hear the old-school Labour councillor emotionally testifying, 'These people live here, they work here and they walk the talk!'

The life cycle

By now you'll have realised that whilst the Eden teams share a vision of transformation and build on agreed cornerstones which are non-negotiable, they are actually quite different from one another in local expression. Different methods and models exist that are appropriate for a wide spectrum of community challenges. However, observing over time, The Message has noticed that each new Eden seems to follow a similar process from inception to maturity. It's a summary of recurring events, trends and milestones which can now help those feeling a bit deflated because revival didn't happen in a fortnight. This six-step 'life cycle' breaks each project into phases – Planning, Actioning, Establishing, Advancing, Transitioning and Maturity – with approximate timings. It goes like this:

Planning

Could take one, two, three years or more, until the time is felt to be right.

Criteria	Action
⇨ Need	Research
	State case / Objectives
⇨ Partner	Management structure
	Ownership / Accountability
⇨ Finance	Identify income sources
	Budgets
⇨ Agreement	Revelation
	Timing
	Written formal agreement with partners

- All the criteria must be met before the next stage.

- Create and action promotion and recruitment strategy.

Actioning

Six months to a year.

- Team leader moves in, official Eden start date.
- Team leader concentrates on networking – building relationships with police, schools, local churches, neighbourhood groups, etc.
- First team members move in.
- Team members do as much first-contact work as possible, e.g. detached work.
- Strong focus on early team building and training.
- Rumours and suspicion from community may begin.

Establishing

Another six months to a year.

- More workers move into area.
- Commencement of organised activities, e.g. youth clubs, cell groups, sports teams, Eden bus.
- Schools team created and sent into local schools doing lessons, clubs, assemblies, etc.
- Hold an annual mission week in schools using TMT evangelistic resources The Tribe, Blush or Xcelerate.
- Workers hit 'six-month wall' when faced with reality of long-term commitment.
- Begin to develop youth base if not already available.

Advancing

The next year or two.

- Team become established in roles and relationships.

- Specialisation – team are able to focus increasingly on their individual skill and gifting as experience and knowledge increases.
- Team either settle into long-term role, relationships and calling, or move on.
- Diversification of focus to encompass families and kids as relationships develop.
- Non-Eden fringe group develops – committed people belonging to the church but not full-blown Eden, i.e. may not actually live in the area.
- Eden/church relationship grows and the project's edges become blurry.
- Community influence and acceptance develops.

Transitioning

Any time from about three years into the project.

- Team members may get married or leave to do something else.
- Some team members enter church leadership structure.
- Team leader develops long-term sustainability plan with church, prior to the management change.
- After five years the relationship with The Message is 'deformalised', and the church takes over management.

Maturity

Difficult to achieve in less than five years.

---

1 Acts 28:31.
2 2 Thessalonians 3:1.
3 2 Corinthians 10:3–5.
4 Acts 19:10.
5 Romans 14:11.
6 Isaiah 43:19.
7 Isaiah 55:11.
8 Anti-Social Behaviour Orders.

8

Ten Ton Truck – Five Ton Bridge

We loved you so much that we were delighted to share with you not only the gospel of God but our lives as well, because you had become so dear to us.

1 Thessalonians 2:8

The 'B' of belonging

Driving into Manchester from the east, along the A662, you'll come to a busy intersection at the vast site of Sport City, location of the 2002 Commonwealth Games and the impressive City of Manchester Stadium, now home to Manchester City FC. Leaning over the lanes of traffic at a precarious angle is a breathtaking piece of public art – a gigantic exploding star spreading like the head of a cosmic dandelion 56 metres into the sky. The sculptor, Thomas Heatherwick, found his inspiration in a throwaway comment made by gold medal sprinter Linford Christie: 'I'm out of those blocks on the "B" of the "Bang"!' That finely tuned poise and readiness is not a characteristic often displayed by the church.

However, Eden seems to have found a remarkable gift for catching the 'B' of something far more important than the 'Bang' of a starting pistol. Eden has developed a knack of connecting with young people at the 'B' of belonging – the very first twitch of a yearning for some kind of spiritual connection. The value of this ability to reach the young people nobody else is able to reach is

---

REALITY BITES

Anna, on making a difference in real lives.

I met Dawn and Cathy six years ago through another young person in our Eden youth group. Dawn was 16 and had a little girl born the day I joined Eden. She lived with her friend Cathy, who was 17. Cathy was from a large Wythenshawe family whose reputation preceded them. They used to come round to the house and were curious about Christianity. We did a 'Get God' course at their flat, with screaming babies and dogs hurtling around, and over a few months, they grasped something, made a commitment and were baptised in Wythenshawe's swimming pool. One night, about half past midnight, there was a knock at my door. I opened it to find them both distraught and with all their worldly belongings in two plastic bags. They'd been evicted due to the behaviour of lads they knew who often came round to their flat. My housemates and I let them stay while we sorted out other accommodation for them. Dawn's baby and her mum also moved in. That made eight of us in a wee three-bedroom house! It was cosy, I can tell you. Her mum had mental health problems and it took me a while to find out that she had a supported flat, which we then helped her back into so that she could be better cared for. After a few weeks the girls were back in more appropriate housing. They couldn't believe we'd allowed them to stay. They were still being introduced to the extravagant love of God and it made a startling contrast to

---

not just recognised within Christian circles either. During one of a number of visits to Eden projects, a senior director of a huge Sainsbury's family trust commented, 'I have seen nothing as intimate or effective.' He's probably never come across the now-famous 'Belong, Believe, Behave' model, but no doubt if it was presented to him he'd recognise the parallel with Eden immediately.

some of their previous experiences. Church paid for them to come away on a weekend break with us and they were able to be children again – it revitalised them. I've remained in contact with them over the years.

Dawn found it hard to cope with her daughter and so I got her in touch with some local support groups and she's doing much better now. She's working and has a lovely flat. Cathy was pregnant when I first met her, but sadly she miscarried at eight months. Her church family supported her through that painful time. She had a period of time when she was struggling financially and briefly became a sex worker. We prayed and talked about this and she chose to stop. I see her often and she is a strong young woman now. She has two small children and a caring partner. The last time I saw her she was telling me how amazing it had felt when she was baptised and that she keeps her Bible under her pillow, 'because it keeps me peaceful'.

Often, young people recognise love through very practical actions. They appreciate commitment, consistency, grace and care. It's through these that they understand the character of God. I know both girls made a commitment to Christ and I know something in them changed for ever and that they wouldn't be the people they are today had they not heard some very good news. I also know they are not fully walking with God at the moment. But I, and the two of them, know about amazing grace and this will not be the end of their story.

Around the nation the owners and peddlers of today's regen-eration dictionary may talk about community cohesion and social inclusion, but few can offer anything nearly resembling the 3D relational architecture of Eden. So, what creates this relational depth? First, to cope with the roller coaster of missionary life, all team members must be securely strapped into a relationship with God. Secondly, to be of any use long term, they must recognise the nature of their relationship to the community around them, the whole 'married to the land' thing extrapolated from Isaiah 62. Thirdly, to offer any authentication to their mes-sage there must be evidence of grace in their relationships with

---

REALITY BITES

Matt, on going the extra mile in Wythenshawe.

We were still very much in the early team-building phase of the project. I'd certainly not been in my new home more than about three months, and probably every other week somebody new was moving into the area. It was around tea time and my new team mates had been trickling in through my front door for the last 20 minutes or so as we were all gathering to go out together to the pictures – *Titanic* had just come out and the girls were all up for a bit of Leonardo DiCaprio! There was another knock on the door and so I went over to do the whole welcome thing. As I yanked open the heavy front door, which had a habit of sticking in damp weather, I realised in an instant that this wasn't a new team mate stood on the step. An attractive mixed race girl in her late teens was standing there sheepishly – she was one of the local crew and I'd already had a number of run-ins with one of her younger brothers, a one-man crime wave. This was why she wanted to talk to me. He'd been arrested, trying to smuggle

---

each other – that old chestnut, *'all men will know that you are my disciples, if you love one another'*.[1] Like those intricately complex little cupboards full of wires that telecom engineers hover around, Eden is about connections. Every smile, every act of kindness, every word of forgiveness is like a fibre-optic cable transmitting a tiny ray of heaven from one life to another.

The hub of this relational network of people in partnership is the headquarters of The Message in south Manchester. While each project has its own staff locally, the essential core functions of recruitment, marketing, prayer support, fundraising, accounting and training happen here. Having this bird's-eye view of the whole Eden landscape across the city, patterns and

---

drugs in to his mate at the regional Young Offenders Institute. The phone call had come through earlier that afternoon from a police station near the prison, where he'd been transferred for questioning. As the lad was a minor, the questioning couldn't start without an 'appropriate adult' present – which would be her, at the ripe old age of 17. Why was she knocking on my door? Well, apparently I'd done or said something which had given her the idea that I might be able to help. She asked if I'd give her a lift to the police station, about 15 miles away, to enable her to negotiate his release, and then bring them back.

It wasn't a difficult choice really; this was exactly why God had told me to move in: to be available for young people on the estate at their times of need. The difficult bit was persuading the girls in the front room that one of them needed to come with me – even if this meant missing out on the cinematic event of the century. A fantastic level-headed youth worker called Kerry agreed to come along for the ride. I grabbed my coat and my keys, slammed the door behind me and set off on this

---

trends can easily be identified as they emerge. Probably the most glaringly obvious administrative challenge to appear was first highlighted in a Soul Survivor magazine article in 1998 entitled, 'Where are all the lads at?' The sad fact is that in the same way that 200 years ago the missionary movement was largely led by women, so is Eden. Statistically Eden has about 2.5 girls for every guy – some teams have 3, 4 or 5. (Yes, Eden romances, Eden marriages and now Eden babies happen regularly!) We've postulated all kinds of theories as to why the guys are so hard to find. Are they all mummy's boys? Are they all too concerned with the career ladder and material things? Are they more likely to be held onto by pastors who are

---

random rescue mission under the cover of the December drizzle. Taking Kerry was so the right thing to do, (a) because it meant I could keep within the protection of our Safe from Harm policy, and (b) because Kerry was a much stronger conversationalist than me and we found out more about the seedy underbelly of the estate on that half-hour journey than we had in the previous three months!

We sat around in the grotty police reception area for a couple of hours while the interview was conducted. Eventually the little family unit emerged from the secure section of the station, and then, somehow from the woodwork, two other mates who'd been there at the time of the arrest appeared as well – which was one too many people for my clapped-out Ford Orion. To be honest, by that stage it wasn't a big deal any more, we just needed to get out of there, so the back seat ended up being a bit squashed. On the way home we small-talked and one of the lads offered me a bit of loose change towards the petrol. I told him that it was no problem and tried to explain in a non-cheesy way that this was

---

grooming them for leadership? Are they less sensitive to the voice of God? Are they just disorganised and can't get round to filling out the application form? The guys we do get are amazing, but the guts, devotion and resourcefulness of the female Eden workers are worth special mention. *Rrrispek to the ladies!*

Building bridges

The approach to moving a team into an area has evolved quite a lot since the Wythenshawe model. With the benefit of hindsight, all involved now recognise some inherent flaws in that plan. Nick and Yvonne Carrington from King's Church bravely moved in with their kids because they knew that was what God

---

why God had brought me to Wythenshawe. I think I failed miserably and probably came across as a sandal-wearing tambourine-waver, but each of the guys did try to say thanks in their own way when I dropped them off.

You would not believe the ripples that went out from that simple act of kindness. As well as communicating something really important to the whole crew of local hooligans, it created a unique sort of access for me to speak into this lad's life in the future. I had opportunity to talk to him about what Jesus had done for him at the cross. I was able to challenge him about the way he was living his life, urging him to get out of the circle of drugs, crime and violence that he was involved in before it was too late. I wish I could say it worked. Maybe one day it will. About a year later his family were evicted and banned from coming back to the estate. Not long after that I heard he was sent down for a whole list of offences including a serious firearms charge. Maybe you could pray for him – his name's Tony. I think he's still alive, somewhere.

---

wanted them to do. Nobody had even thought about Eden at that point. When Dave and Colette moved in next door to them just prior to the launch of Eden, the whole thing was still under the radar of the other local residents, one helpful factor being the camouflage of their Manchester accents. Maybe a few neighbours noticed the novelty of these rather nice Christians appearing, and maybe they noticed that they seemed to know each other, but with anarchy ruling on the streets there were more important things to worry about. It was only when a dozen more people with 'out of town' dialects and dubious fashion sense arrived that things started to get tricky. When they accidentally created a Christian enclave by renting five houses in a row, the integration effort was somewhat undermined: how can

---

REALITY BITES

Chris, on a tricky situation in Openshaw.

I'd been part of Eden for a year and had just bought a house, contrary to the good advice of my parents. I arrived back from work one day and came through the door. Straight away I noticed my hi-fi on the floor. I then saw that my TV and video were missing and the penny dropped. I felt really sick and very angry. I'd never been burgled. It's one of those things you think could happen, one day, but it kinda leaves you speechless when it does. I thought that maybe I'd caught them in the act, so I ran around the house roaring like a lion! I was cacking myself, to be honest, but I thought that if I met them then this angry roaring man would scare them. In fact, they would have collapsed with laughter.

Fortunately for me, they'd gone. The back window had been

you witness to your neighbours when they're all on your team?

The most recent Edens have taken a steadier approach to the entry process. It's now accepted that the first person to move in will be the team leader. The team leader will normally be one half of a married couple, and it's essential that their spouse (and kids if they're around) is fully up for the challenge too. Their job is to begin to create a network of relational connections which can grow into a sphere of grace for the new project. A really cool book called *ChurchNext* mentions this from a historical mission perspective:

> The never-churched need to be enveloped by small communities of believers so that they can see the impact of the gospel in their relationships and experience some of the benefits through inten-

---

smashed and the back door was open. I couldn't see anyone so I went to the end of the alley, but no one was around. I saw a police car coming and frantically flagged it down. They stopped and I spewed some nonsense about, 'House … stereo on floor … think bad men still around!' They got the picture and came inside. I spoke to them in the lounge for a couple of minutes, telling them what I knew in a slightly more logical manner. They said they should go and look at the broken window, so I said I would go next door and see if the bloke there had seen anything. Immediately I noticed his door was open. I'd heard that sometimes burglars break into a few houses in a row and rob them all at once, so as a brave neighbour I thought I'd investigate.

I shouted 'Hello!' but got nothing, which reinforced my belief that he'd been burgled too. I kept shouting as I walked through the door into the grubby lounge. No one was home. I thought I should try the back room and shouted 'Hello!' up the stairs as I

---

tional spillover. Such was the dynamic that made the pre-Constantinian church so effective. Within the context of Christian communities, the disillusioned, cynical and uninterested are respected and accepted, are converted into 'awakened seekers', to employ John Wesley's significant description.[2]

Years on from those initial clumsy efforts at integrating with an existing community, the process might be slightly better understood but it hasn't fundamentally changed – the intention is still the same. Central to the relational methodology is the idea that relationships, like bridges, have a weight limit. You've seen the Indiana Jones movies where a flimsy rope bridge swings precariously in the breeze over a vast ravine. Will the ancient fraying cord hold the weight of our intrepid adventurers? Now

---

went. When I looked in the back room, there was my TV, my video, my microwave, my CDs and my coat! I shot back to my house and said breathlessly, 'It's next door. My stuff is next door!'

'Oh, we thought it might be him,' said the copper, not particularly surprised. What was I going to do? This was worse than that *Neighbours from Hell* programme. The police finished up and the forensics came and put black dust everywhere. The only things that were unaccounted for were my old Sega Saturn System and some chopsticks I had bought on a visit to China a few years earlier.

I spent a lot of time praying that week, mainly because I thought the guy was going to come back and beat me up. When I spoke to the other neighbours, some asked me what I would do to him, but most just found the whole thing a bit amusing. The neighbour, Paul, was a heroin addict, who had some fairly nasty mates who abused his hospitality. A few people offered to give me a hand if I wanted to give him a kicking.

apply that image to friendships you have with family, friends, colleagues. For each of your personal connections you'll have a subconscious warning sign which flags up a big 'WHOA THERE!' when a topic crops up in conversation which is going to put too much strain on that relational bridge and possibly cause it to give way.

For instance, maybe you're feeling pretty upset on the anniversary of your gran's death and your colleague notices that you're not your normal self. 'You okay?' she asks. And the 'WHOA THERE!' sign appears because this casual friendship can't deal with heavy goods like grief, so you reply, 'Yeah, fine.'

Now, it's important that we don't get too carried away with

God helped me to halt my anger and I just told people I was a Christian from the church down the road and none of that stuff would happen. The police came round and asked if I wanted to prosecute. I said that I did. Although I believe in a God of forgiveness, I also believe in a God of justice. On a deeper level God was helping me to forgive. I was determined that after all this I was going to be this guy's friend.

Paul didn't come back for a week, obviously lying low somewhere. It was the next Friday afternoon when I came back from work that I saw him, in his garden digging the weeds. He was a rather sickly looking guy with very yellow skin – this can happen with severe drug addiction. I spoke to him over the fence.

'Hi, Paul, how are you doing?'

'Oh fine,' he said. 'Just digging the garden while the weather is nice.'

Let's get this over with, I thought. 'Look, I got broken into last week. Did you know?'

---

this metaphor and get all scientific about the strength of our bridges and how they should or shouldn't be constructed. Joseph Myers, in his fantastic book *The Search to Belong*, explodes a whole load of widely held relational ideas, but the one that's really worth a mention here is 'More Time = More Belonging'.

> This is a pervasive myth. In reality, time has little to do with a person's ability to experience significant belonging. Many people tell of first-time, episodic introductions from which a spontaneous connection emerges. Have you ever said, 'I just met you, but it seems like I've known you all my life'?[3]

At the end of the day some people connect with each other and some don't. Some people seem particularly gifted at the art of

---

'Ooh yeah, I heard about that – terrible in't it?' he answered.

A little confused, but not wanting to let him off the hook, I pushed again. 'And we found all the stuff in your house, Paul.'

'Ooh yeah,' he said. 'Heard about that – terrible in't it?'

And that, it seemed, was a reasonable answer to the bloke you had just burgled and who was trying to get you arrested for it. I took a big gulp and said, 'Look, Paul, you know that I'm a Christian and I go to that church down the road. Well, because of that I believe in forgiveness and because of that there is not going to be any retaliation and I'm prepared to forgive whoever was involved.'

He denied any involvement or any knowledge.

I suddenly remembered my chopsticks, so I asked Paul if he had seen them. 'Ooh yes,' he said, 'they're on top of the telly.' And he went back inside, brought out my chopsticks and handed them back with a neighbourly smile over the garden fence.

connecting and others find it really difficult. The method of building a relational bridge with one young person may be completely different from the way that works for another. The point is that we ensure those bridges exist and that they are as strong as they possibly can be. When a bridge is only weak, the heavy goods of the gospel may need to be sent over in small packages of love, acceptance and forgiveness. Every time a parcel is sent over, the bridge is strengthened. This is the process which enables you to progress from first bumping into a young person on the street and being told to '@%!$ off!' to having them knocking on your door and asking for prayer.

A week later I came back from work to find Paul in my garden. He'd spent the whole day tidying it for me. He'd also taken a few cuttings from his garden and planted them in mine. It looked great. He advised me on what I could do with it and told me that he liked gardening and if it was OK with me he would do it for me each week. He kept to his word and we had the best-looking gardens in the street. Paul and I became good friends. We'd chat about what had been going on in the street and what he was thinking of doing with the garden. He didn't have a phone, so would occasionally knock on the door and borrow mine, but he never took advantage. We would do all the other neighbourly things like borrowing a bit of milk and sugar when we ran out. He'd always ask about my work and how the church and youth work were getting on. Ironically, he would also keep an eye on the house for me if I went away.

The police took a long time to get round to anything and couldn't get any fingerprints. As we couldn't place Paul at the

The gospel plus

The default Sunday school answer to any and every question of life is 'Jesus', right? And in our evangelism we need nothing more, and nothing less, than the gospel of Christ crucified, right? Okay, well, maybe a bit of apologetics comes in handy every now and again, tackling questions like 'What happened to the dinosaurs?' and 'How can a God of love allow such suffering?' And of course, if we're going to embark on any evangelism, it must be 'church based'; that's what we've been taught, right? We don't want any loose cannons on deck out there, saving people before they've planned their 'follow-up'! Ooh, heaven forbid! So are these crazy saints in council houses actually onto something that the church around the nation

---

scene, we couldn't prosecute. If it had gone to court there would have been a reasonable doubt, so the case was dropped.

Paul had health problems which meant that he was on dialysis each week. I went to spend some time with him in hospital and he told me his story. He had been born with a kidney problem, but contained it. He got into trouble as a youngster and also got into recreational drugs. He lived at home as a bit of a mum's boy till he was 28. He had a long-term girlfriend for five years and was thinking about getting married. Then within a year both his parents died and his girlfriend left him. He had no support and ended up back with his mates. He was very lonely and depressed, so had a lot of random people who came to stay with him who started using drugs in his house. He got into the drugs heavily himself, which aggravated his kidney problem and then infected his liver. The hospital gave him a transplant, which made him better for a bit, but as his lifestyle did not change the new kidney failed. Paul's life was a mess and he knew it, but he

should pay attention to? What could the average Jo Christian learn from Eden, without actually moving in? In the end, it may come down to this, recalled so clearly by the apostle Paul as he remembered his efforts to reach a community in Thessalonica:

> We loved you so much that we were delighted to share with you not only the gospel of God but our lives as well, because you had become so dear to us.[4]

'... not only the gospel of God ...' Eeek! So the approach taken by Paul, Silas and Timothy consisted of more than simply gospel proclamation: there was other stuff that came as part of the package, probably pretty important stuff if it gets mentioned in the same breath as 'the gospel'. And it's this important stuff, above anything else, that Eden has sought to put back into

---

didn't have the maturity or confidence to get himself out of that mess, and his so-called friends pulled him down again and again.

Paul went back into hospital in December 2002. He was refused a second transplant because the doctors felt it would be wasted. During his time in hospital I went to visit him every week. The nurse told me I was one of his only visitors. His brother visited him once in six months and his friends came in occasionally to ask about using the house for drugs. Once he got so depressed that he refused to eat; he knew that he would not get better and just wanted to die. One of the nurses, Hannah, was on the Eden team, so she told me and asked me to talk to him. I did, and he started eating again. I knew that I didn't have long with him, so I talked often about my faith. He had some good questions and sometimes I prayed for his health and that he would know God. He prayed with me once and I really hope that he gave his heart to Jesus. Paul eventually admitted to me that he had been involved in the burglary and we prayed a prayer of

evangelism – *'... our lives as well ...'* The gospel is the bit that God's already sorted, but here's the most controversial bit of this book, so get your pen out and get ready to write that howler: 999 times out of 1,000, the gospel is not enough.

Did you catch that?

Take a deep breath ... in ... out ...

It's a very rare event when someone, in complete isolation, with no frame of reference provided through a visible Christian life, simply reads the gospel, or has some kind of cosmic vision, and accepts Christ as Lord. Of course it happens, because the Holy Spirit's working all over the place touching lives without bothering to ask our permission first – in prisons and mosques,

---

forgiveness. I do know that Paul knew God lived in my life and he would talk about how he wanted God to change him. Paul was in and out of hospital for a year or so, and when I knew he was there I would try to visit. Hannah eventually came to tell me that he had gone in for the last time and died.

This isn't a happy story, but this is what our broken world is like – full of injustice, fear, despair and unfairness. I know God loved Paul and I know Paul knew that. I used to tell him often enough. I just hope that I will meet him again in heaven and we can sing together, praising God whose grace is sufficient for both of us. This is the most significant witness I had in Openshaw and I was constantly asked about it in the street. It was a great way to illustrate God's forgiveness. All I needed to do was live in that house and get burgled.

in drug dens and during moon landings, but there is absolutely no disputing the fact that God's number one way of enlarging his family is when an open life becomes available. It's a bit like logging on to amazon.com − your life is the 'user name' and the gospel is the 'password'. You need both to gain access. It's a truth that you won't get away from in this enlightening little letter. Paul has already taken time to establish the point in his opening shots, making a deliberate reference to what they'd had a chance to see of him day after day:

> ... our gospel came to you not simply with words, but also with power, with the Holy Spirit and with deep conviction. You know how we lived among you for your sake.[5]

This revelation is the golden thread that has run through every one of the 10 Edens so far, and it will weave through every new one too. It's not the thin end of some kind of 'social gospel' wedge, although the scent of that fear may waft around from time to time. Eden is really clear that people don't find eternal salvation through casually observing the good deeds of a few nice neighbours. If that were the case we'd have called the projects 'Ned'.[6] Eden presents the church-at-large with a working model of presence and proclamation, declaration and demonstration, of The Gospel Plus.

---

[1]   John 13:35.
[2]   Eddie Gibbs and Ian Coffey, *ChurchNext*, IVP, 2000.
[3]   Joseph Myers, *The Search to Belong*, Zondervan, 2003.
[4]   1 Thessalonians 2:8.
[5]   1 Thessalonians 1:5.
[6]   As in Ned Flanders, for those of you who were lost there for a minute!

9

The Innovation Gene

'... Perhaps the LORD will act on our behalf. Nothing can hinder the LORD from saving, whether by many or by few.'
'Do all that you have in mind,' his armour-bearer said. 'Go ahead; I am with you heart and soul.'

1 Samuel 14:6–7

Shiny disco balls

It took three or four of the burliest stewards to hold back the creaking door as the clock slowly counted the last few minutes to 8 o'clock. The fledgling Eden team's Sunday night youth event wasn't having a problem drawing a crowd – lots of loud music and a few crazy games was definitely a better option than hanging around on the street getting rained on. And of course there was always the possibility of copping off, or having a fight, or both if luck was really on your side. That's if you didn't mind these weird people in baggy trousers trying to mash your head about God.

In the last few weeks a fragile order had emerged. The hundred or so young people, aged from about 10 to 17, would surge into the tiny, dimly lit hall where the chairs were neatly arranged in rows facing the stage, which was impressively set with a stupidly huge PA system, disco lighting and a big video screen. The Eden team, acting like well positioned paddles in a pinball machine, could then deflect the hyped-up adolescents into their seats and attempt to settle them down with well versed welcome banter. However, within minutes of any calm being achieved, the whole place would erupt once again as the host introduced '... our resident band, The World Wide Message Tribe!'.

A weekly feature of these early youth events in Wythenshawe was the gospel appeal. There would always be a really punchy talk, carefully stripped of any cheesy Christian jargon, and in spite of the constant heckling and occasional Jarvis Cocker style stage incursion, an invitation to respond. And generally the response would be between 90 and 100%. So week after week the wildest tearaways in Manchester would be herded through the little door to the even tinier counselling room to ask Jesus into their hearts for the fourteenth time ... There was huge controversy about the event approach both inside and outside the team, and eventually it was cancelled and the energy poured into detached work. The detached work cost less, was simpler to organise and definitely helped develop relationships on 'their terms' and 'their turf'. Once the relationships were established, young people keen to have a great night out could be invited to a much larger and better organised event, 'Planet Life', where the same clear proclamation could be heard and a response made. Planet Life soon became Eden's maternity ward and its successor, the bi-monthly youth celebration 'SPACE', continues to perform this essential evangelistic function.

Innovation in action

October 1968, Mexico City. Something quite unexpected took everyone in the Olympic Stadium completely by surprise. A bloke called Dick Fosbury had appeared in the high-jump competition and proceeded to 'flop' his way through the opening rounds with some incredible jumps that confounded the opposition. Fosbury was racing towards the bar in a crazy arc, lifting off with his left foot, pivoting his right leg out and sailing over the bar, toes to the sky, in a bizarre levitation display. Using this radical new technique, Fosbury set an Olympic record of seven feet and four inches – a full two and a half inches higher than the 1964 Olympic record. Two and a half inches was an unprecedented amount of progress in the history of the sport. High-jumping would never be the same again. The event had evolved over many decades until Dick came along and revolutionised it with his new 'flop' technique. There's a lesson for us here: being switched on to the mechanics of innovation is important, because whilst you probably don't proudly wear an 'I love Dick Fosbury' T-shirt, you may well be one of the mass of people really hoping that their contribution to the world is going to make not just a small difference, but a really big one.

In the early chapters of the book we saw the way Eden came into existence. It was an innovation, a creative response to a difficult problem. That gene of innovation was somehow entwined as part of Eden's double-helix right from the start. It's a key strength of the ongoing work and an indicator of a bright future. Yet innovators are often awkward. Shell's Vice President Frank Douglas has found this out over years in business:

> Who wants to manage a rebel? They are a complete pain in the butt. They challenge you. They disagree with you. They break the

rules. The usual outcome is that one of you leaves. And, as they are the subordinate, it is usually them. But, the result is that your corporate immune system lives on, having rejected the invader that didn't fit in. So, if you are looking to change your organisational culture; if you are aware of the need to bring in innovation and innovators – change agents who do things differently, mavericks, whatever you want to call them – you have to be prepared for this: It is immensely irritating! Irritation is part of the innovation process. Recognise it – get used to being challenged – and find ways of accommodating it or any plans you have to change your culture and become faster-moving and more innovative will grind to a complete halt.[1]

Possessing the core competency of innovation is absolutely essential because:

- Connecting with young people is not always easy. In fact, a lot of the time it's really difficult. Gaining their acceptance and trust may require a variety of flexible approaches.

- Good youth workers will always seek to find the best, most appropriate ways of connecting and these may not be the immediately obvious options. Consideration of the varied forces and factors in play will often lead to the development of significantly improved modes of work.

- No environment is static, the world is constantly changing. Innovators will respond to changes and opportunities as they arise; indeed they will probably have seen them coming and are already prepared. As ice-hockey legend Wayne Gretzky famously said, 'A good hockey player plays where the puck is. A great hockey player plays where the puck is going to be.'

- Even the best ideas can get tedious and tired. What feels like freedom today often ends up feeling like a prison tomorrow. Innovation is a set of skills more akin to surfing than laying train tracks, and that's what inner-city youth work requires.

- Eden is breaking new ground and there is no textbook. Even this book is just a friendly travelling companion! A group of high-flying hobnobbers called the Inspired Leaders Network offer the following insight: 'Experience is only useful if the future is like the past. But, in times of fast-paced change, experience quickly becomes a liability that slows you down.'[1] That's why Eden application forms state that experience is helpful but not essential. The ability to innovate, however, is standard kit, like packing your toothbrush.

'Innovation' isn't really a Bible word; you won't find it in the Nearly Infallible Version, anyway. The gist of the concept is in there from front to back, though, expressed as the unique gift of creativity originating in God. It's a gift that sets us apart from the rest of creation and it must be one of the key characteristics referred to in the curious description, *'God created man in his own image ...'*[2] As the story of the world unravels, we get inspired by certain characters. One who displayed exceptional creative gifts was a guy called Bezalel, described as someone filled *'with the Spirit of God, with skill, ability and knowledge in all kinds of crafts – to make artistic designs for work in gold, silver and bronze, to cut and set stones, to work in wood and to engage in all kinds of artistic craftsmanship'.*[3] Bez had pretty strict orders when it came to working on the interior design of God's new mobile home, but you can be sure his kids had the most fancy go-karts in their clan for rocking down the slopes of Sinai!

It's absolutely God's intention for us to combine the passion of our hearts and the wisdom of our heads to create solutions to the challenges we face in life and ministry. Why do so many Christians think that every answer is going to be delivered as a fax from heaven? So often inertia can creep like ivy around our feet while we're stood still asking God what to do and where to go. Meanwhile he's tearing his hair out and yelling, 'I've given you authority to rule the planet, for crying out loud! Do I really need to tell you what colour bog roll to buy?' Here's a little tip, and this one's for free: if you ever find yourself in that sort of quandary, not feeling at all confident about what God's will might be, ask yourself this, 'What can I do that will bring God

---

REALITY BITES

Ruth, on home sweet home.

I thought life on Eden would be glamorous. I mean, I knew it sounded like hard graft, the thankless task of living in a shabby inner-city council house and working day in, day out with a bunch of people who, to be honest, couldn't be less like me. But it still felt kind of heroic – a 'Twenty-first-century Urban Missionary'. Nice job title, I thought.

As the sun began to set and the light faded, along with it went the shimmery effect of the 'Urban Missionary' label in my head. Reality hit me like a very big stick as I stood in a small, dark, cold, damp, seriously smelly hole that was to be my new living room. It was the kind of room that wasn't fit to keep a wild animal in. There were holes in the floorboards and bits of hideous old wallpaper trying desperately to cling on to the mould with their last shreds of adhesive.

With no electrics, gas, boiler or even water, I wondered what kind of state we could possibly get this house into in a week,

pleasure?' Why ask that? Because the Bible says, *'Thou art worthy, O Lord, to receive glory and honour and power: for thou hast created all things, and for thy pleasure they are and were created.'* [4] How do you know whether you've come up with the right idea to bring God pleasure? It will involve flexing your faith, because *'without faith it is impossible to please God'*.[5] Every Eden worker needs to have this problem-solving spirit, because every Eden worker is going to need to overcome obstacles if they're going to win the hearts of the young people of their neighbourhood for Jesus. The obstacles will come in all sorts of shapes and sizes, and they'll arrive on day one, guaranteed.

---

which was how long we had before moving in there permanently. A small group of new friends, still in good spirits, stopped work on the walls for a moment to discuss the fact that we were now freezing cold, starving hungry and it had gone dark so we couldn't see a thing. Time to give up? I set to work problem-solving – there had to be a way. First things first, I called the local pizza place to feed my wonderful volunteers. Despite being only two minutes away from the shop, I discovered that they wouldn't deliver to our estate as the pizzas, the money and the moped generally got stolen. OK, I thought, we'll collect it. Next, the cold. Not much could be done about this, so we just put our coats on. The dark – this would be the trickiest one. The only thing I had there was my car ... hold on, sudden brainwave! I pulled the car right up to the window and put the headlights on full beam. They shone into the living room providing light! We couldn't do anything but laugh as we sat on a pile of bits of old wallpaper. Su, my new housemate, looked at me, stuffed a whole piece of cold pizza in her mouth and garbled, 'Welcome to Swinton!'

A sphere of grace

Imagine in your mind's eye a transparent 3D football, or one of those molecule models your chemistry teacher might have had sitting on a shelf; that's what we're going to think about now. Eden's invisible tangle of human connections. This is the way we need to start thinking in our mission – beyond the visible. Have you ever thought about how much of the world is invisible? No, not just obscured from human view like the earth's core, but how much is *really* invisible? Many people dismiss faith by claiming, 'If I can't see it, I won't believe it!' What a load of twaddle. Imagine walking into a wedding. Can you see the love in the room? Can you see who's fallen out with whom over

---

REALITY BITES

Andy Lane, on taking the message to the schools in Salford.

I first got a heart for the Seedley and Langworthy area when I was in the youth group at Mount Chapel. On a few occasions we decided to go down Langworthy Road prayer-walking at ridiculous hours during half-night prayer meetings. The area was one that many people feared and would not enter alone because of the reputation for violence and crime that it had. One night as we prayer-walked through the streets I remember having to run away from a firework that had been fired through a drainpipe at my friend and me. The drainpipe provided amazing accuracy!

When I was 17, I and my brother and a couple of friends really felt that God wanted us to move into the area and live out a Christian life there. It was around the time that we were talking to Andy Hawthorne about the possibility of The Message starting an Eden project in Salford with us lot. We did and in 1999 I

---

the past 20 years? Can you see the memories that are present there of previous weddings at other times in other places? Can you see the heartache of those still hopelessly lonely but putting on a smile? Of course you can't. All that stuff is invisible, but it's all there, it all exists. You're hovering on the edge of one of life's infinite number of relational spheres.

Strategically, every idea Eden teams employ for connecting with young people should contribute to one objective: the growth and enrichment of the sphere of grace, where God's goodness touches lives. Team outputs will contribute to this end both quantitatively and qualitatively. Outreach activity such as schools work is a shop window for the grace available. Using

---

moved into the area. I somehow got the full-time schools worker's job which was going. It was scary but really exciting, as I've got a real passion to see the young people of Salford, my home town, transformed by the power of Jesus.

During the first few weeks of my new job we had three weeks of missions in the three local high schools with The World Wide Message Tribe (as they were known then). They took over every RE lesson in the week, plus assemblies. At the end of the three weeks we held a concert at the Maxwell Hall in Salford with about 200 young people coming along, of which at least 30 or 40 made a response. It was quite an amazing three weeks and for me it was a fantastic opportunity to get to know all the young people in the local schools. We went on to work heavily in one of those schools, Windsor High, which was a very needy place with many children coming from underprivileged backgrounds. God did lots of amazing stuff in there through our programme of breakfast clubs, lunch clubs, assemblies, RE lessons and

---

the Eden bus and detached youth work on the local streets is a grace-stretching exercise, and no-go areas feel the warmth of the sphere as new contacts are made. In these sorts of ways Eden teams across Manchester may be in touch with up to 5,000 young people a month. Nurture activities such as youth clubs can create atmosphere within the sphere, for good or for bad. Small groups and cell groups enrich the sphere with deeper levels of trust and honesty. All these Eden activities, and many more besides, are interlinked with many young people being part of the layers of Eden life. And just like Jesus explained, it's not our job to select who's in and who's out.[6]

---

working in the behavioural unit. There are loads of stories I could tell about this school, but I'll just focus on a few by giving you some excerpts from my newsletters of 2001.

We have recently done a lesson on Easter to all the classes in Year 9. We used something called the wordless book (a book of coloured pages from which you can explain the gospel using the colours) and in the 3rd lesson a girl came up to me and explained the gospel to me using it before I had even showed the class! Her friend had shown her it the day before! Non-Christian pupils witnessing to each other – Praise the Lord!

January 2001

All the regular stuff in Windsor is going well too, and we are seeing more and more young people wanting to come to cell groups! It's become a sort of positive peer pressure thing and young people (mainly girls) are saying things like, 'Why haven't I been invited to these groups?' and really wanting to be involved.

April 2001

186

In the last few chapters there have been vivid descriptions some of the external duress imposing upon the sphere of grace. There are, of course, also perils within. There would be little edification found in listing comprehensively every potential strain upon team life, but the top one or two do need mentioning. First and undoubtedly predominant is the 'tyranny of the urgent', when simple incarnational life is overtaken by a plague of busyness. Meetings start multiplying and that holy grail whose sacred name is 'The Free Evening' slips for ever out of reach. From time to time volunteers will ask for a bit of a break. The skill then for team leaders is to find a way to make this happen without adding to any existing stress the extra weight of guilt.

... about 130 kids came along to the concert and 30 made some sort of response to the gospel. I've been working in this school for about 2 years now and it was so good to see lots of the young people who I know well give their lives to Jesus. I was on the door for most of the evening with another Eden worker and we got talking to a girl called 'B' and a few of her mates. She said that during the week she had decided to live her life for God and that she wanted to change but couldn't understand how God could forgive her or accept her. It was so cool to see her make a response that evening and now she is in a cell group and coming to church! About 10 of those who responded are now in cell groups. I have known and worked for a couple of years with two of the lads who responded and have really been praying that God would somehow break through. It was well emotional to see them respond and now Carl and I are running a cell group for them and 3 others which is top. Praise the Lord! God is at work.

May 2001

The second danger is the development of a rut. The honeymoon's over, the bills need paying and sleep's not coming easy. It's so easy to get home from work, turn on the TV and ignore the knocks on the front door because your housemate's in and her job's not half as manic as yours. There are actually two problems rolled into one here. Maintaining a healthy state of mind is one, and failing to do so could have severe personal consequences, but the other problem may be even worse. In that sort of state, who is going to be there to seize the moment? Eden is so like that: plod, plod, plod, PZAZZ! An opportunity just comes out of nowhere. Maybe because these two dangers are related, they both get mentioned in the same breath by Peter and Paul, who insist on believers being both self-controlled and alert.[7]

The doorstep challenge

Living in the heart of the community brings all sorts of opportunities but also presents some big challenges. Creating a home that's safe from burglars but accessible to local youth who want to talk is quite a balancing act, especially when visitors could fit in both of those categories at the same time! Soon after launching the first project in 1997 it became clear that just opening the front door and welcoming the little cherubs inside for some fizzy pop, a Jaffa Cake and a Bible study – even a trendy Bible study with video clips and glossy workbooks – could be problematic. Young people in the inner city travel round in packs like laughing hyenas and before you can say 'Get God' the carpet's covered in coffee, the sofa's got cigarette burns, somebody's got a bleeding nose and half your CD collection is missing. Eden houses need clear boundaries to be established, and the most important boundary is the doorstep.

The Message has developed 'Safe from Harm' guidelines for the protection of the young people and the workers. There are expectations relating to level of supervision, gender issues, parental consent and lots of other variables. Unfortunately, it's not very helpful to get out the child protection policy and reference Section 9 point 3(d) when half a dozen bored adolescents are standing on your doorstep wanting something to do. So Jen Graves has come up with a genius invention – carpet. OK, so Jen didn't invent carpet, but she has developed a really clever way of connecting with the kids who were constantly knocking on her door. Rolled up in the hall she keeps a few feet of beige carpet. When there's a knock, out comes the Wilton and everyone can sit down on the doorstep! Being ready for the knock means Jen's kitchen must always be stocked with the necessary supplies of tea, biscuits and banana-flavoured hot chocolate. She comments, 'I've never seen young girls consume a packet of custard creams so quickly!' The hours drift by, as they sit on the carpet, chatting about life and school and family, talking about God and favourite Bible stories, while Roxy the dog sniffs around in that confused dog way when there are too many smells to cope with.

There are times when it's just not convenient to get the carpet out and get the kettle on, but Jen will always try to be gracious. If she's just stepped in from work, or if she's just getting ready to go out, she'll go to the door and explain. Over time she's learned that one thing she can't do is ignore the young people who turn up, otherwise the knocking will stop, the letterbox will squeak open and a shrill chorus of 'Jen … we know you're in …' will begin to echo around the house.

Unforgettable moment

The activities of the Failsworth Eden team had been successful in reaching a core of local girls with the gospel. These girls had really got it — a real passion for God had been born in their

---

REALITY BITES

Rachel, on unlocking star potential in Failsworth.

Three years ago we prayed for the young people in our area and God gave us a simple task and a long-term dream. We became inspired by the idea of setting up a Performing Arts School which would train up young people to reach their full potential, creatively and spiritually. Every dream starts with a simple step forward, and so the first thing was to set up a drama club. We decided to charge just £1 a week for our training, so as not to exclude anyone.

The first three weeks, we waited eagerly but no one turned up! We were a little disappointed, but we persevered. The fourth week, we had two young girls who were enthusiastic and got into it straight away. Within a couple of weeks, they were performing in church services and bonding with church members. Since then, our numbers have grown, as has the quality of our relationships with the local community. We work with 25–30 young people regularly (and have contact with over 50 others) and every term we put on a performance for the local community in church. It is so exciting to see a couple of hundred locals squashed into our church room!

We have always felt that Create should be about the performing arts, and although all of the leaders are Christians and we run Create with Christian values, we do not teach Christianity in our sessions. Because of this, we don't exclude the young people who love drama but don't want to know about God. We

---

hearts. The church was really revved up about this mini-revival and so when somebody suggested taking the girls away to a Youth Alive weekend event, where they'd be strengthened in their new-found faith, the approval was unanimous. Of course

---

run a girls' group and a lads' group after Create on Mondays, which is entirely optional, and is specifically for those young people who are interested in Christianity. The great thing is that most of the Create pupils come to girls' and lads' groups anyway! We have the great opportunity to disciple 30 young people each week, many of whom have either become Christians or are interested in God, and many attend church on a regular basis. We feel that God is raising up a 'new breed' of young person. They aren't stereotypical young people who come in late, sit at the back and disrupt the services. These are young people who, despite coming from non-Christian backgrounds, are totally in love with God, sit on the front row and recognise that they have the power to influence others positively!

God has multiplied everything we have given to him. Our motto at Create is 'Unlocking Star Potential', as we use drama, dance, music and media to encourage and build up the young people. They all have such God-given potential and we want to release them, train them and give them the confidence to be all they can be for God! One young girl, who started with us two years ago, grew so quickly in her skills and confidence that she became a trainee leader and taught a dance class to her peers. She has grown rapidly in God, and she has an incredible influence on her peers. She is able to reach young people in school, she helps girls who are struggling with their faith, she arranges girls' sleepovers and she runs a girls' day regularly where they take communion, pray and worship together. She has far greater opportunities to influence her peers where they are than we

---

there was no way that the girls would be able to pay their own way, though. The pastor, Paul Gibbs, agreed to take a special offering on a Sunday morning to cover the cost of the trip.

youth leaders do. We have learnt to invest in young leaders so that they can reach and disciple their friends.

One young lad has been with us for three years, yet he has always struggled to engage with the activities and gel with the rest of the group. He would always sit on his own and admitted that he had absolutely no self-confidence. We tried to find a way to engage with him but always struggled, until recently. One of our male leaders began a media project and asked this young lad to join in. Before long, he was performing in the starring role of a comedy film clip, and was the star of our summer perform-ance. Since then, his confidence has grown massively and he is getting on with his peers really well. His mum recently told us that she wished his school could see him at Create, because he has grown so much!

Finally, a young girl from a lapsed Catholic background joined us a year ago and warmed straight away to the leaders. She excelled in drama and was the lead in our summer show. One Monday after Create, she approached one of our leaders and asked if she could fully give her life to God. The leader prayed with her and since then she's been on fire. She comes to church twice on a Sunday without fail, she is on our welcoming team so arrives every Sunday at 9 a.m., she is a team leader at Create and girls' group, she helps with our kids' work, and she regularly shares testimony from the front at church. The other week she asked the other girls to pray for her in church to be filled with the Holy Spirit and it happened! Since then, she has said that she feels empowered, and she has invited people to church. She has even written a sermon, which she is looking forward to sharing with the church soon.

Imagine the scene in the church office as the offering was carefully counted and checked. 'There's too much money here, there's way too much!' Paul and Nathan deliberated about the situation for a while and came to the conclusion that the offering had been specifically given for the trip, so it would be spent on the trip. This weekend nobody would have to endure the wheezing old minibus: the group would travel by limousine! The church loved the idea of really welcoming the girls into their fellowship by creating this unforgettable moment for them. Screams of delight and surprise echoed from street to street as the sparkling white stretch Caddy pulled up at the door of each of the girls to take them on their weekend blast. Stunned parents gained a whole new perspective on their children, thrilled to bits that somebody was willing to invest in their future. What was that thing about a lamp on a stand?

Eden scores

If you happened to be walking past Holy Trinity Primary School at about 8 o'clock in the morning you'd be likely to see quite an unusual sight. At this early hour, before the car park is full of staff vehicles, before the playground has filled up with chattering kids, a solitary grown-up holds a football and the attention of a dozen 9- and 10-year-old boys. This is the breakfast club, developed by 20-year-old Lee Roberts from the local Harpurhey Eden team. It's not just about football … if it's a rainy day Lee will get out his 'wet weather pack' and have some fun with the lads in a classroom doing word-searches to help with their literacy, or talking about diet and nutrition to get them on the path to a healthy future. He's gained a contract from the school to be there five days a week, ensuring that the worst truants get out of bed, get a meal inside them and get motivated for the school day ahead of them. Tiny truants can easily be drawn into a life of crime by the older lads if they spend the day on the streets instead of in the classroom. Lee's ongoing efforts have ensured that 14 out of the 17 are now back in school working hard. God only knows what they've been saved from in the future.

Lee's a real character, proof of God's grace in action and a great example of what can be achieved when calling, gifting and willingness combine. When Lee became a Christian at the age of 14 the rest of his family thought he'd lost the plot. It would be true to say they do still struggle to comprehend his passion for the Jesus stuff, but they haven't stood in his way. Ever since the day his step-dad dropped him off with his bulging suitcase at the door of Xcelerate,[8] he's shown a determination to really make his life count. After completing his five months of urban evangelism training Lee felt it was right to invest another year being trained in a sports ministry specialism with a group called NRG, a dynamic outreach initiative set up by the legendary Dave Nuttall, whom we met in chapter 1. Shaped by the experiences and the discipleship gained on these programmes, Lee found his personal effectiveness massively enlarged.

Soon after becoming a member of the Harpurhey Eden team he got to meet a bunch of lairy local lads. They were always up for a game of football; in fact, between them the bare bones of a six-a-side team existed. Cocky and competitive, they hatched the idea of forming a team and entering the local under-19 league. Within a few weeks, though, their confidence wasn't quite so high, as they lost their first few games as badly as 15–0. Lee's ad hoc encouragement was about to get serious as they asked him to become their manager. He explained that things would have to change if they wanted to succeed; they'd have to start playing as a team for starters. Amazingly every one of them agreed to sign the 'players contract' that Lee introduced, which set out high expectations and a tight policy of discipline. These were some of the toughest lads on the block, but being in the team was really having a positive impact on them. By the end of the season the lads had won the league and come runners-up in the cup! Riding high on these achievements, Lee took the lads on tour – to Gloucester and Cambridge, where, in his own words, they 'stuffed the southerners'. Eden 2, Queen of the South 0.

---

[1] www.inspiredleaders.com.
[2] Genesis 1:27.
[3] Exodus 35:31–33.
[4] Revelation 4:11 (KJV).
[5] Hebrews 11:6.
[6] Check out the parables of the weeds and the net in Matthew 13.
[7] 1 Thessalonians 5:6; 1 Peter 5:8.
[8] Xcelerate is the name of our five-month residential training programme for young evangelists. It has recently been renamed Genetik. Details at www.message.org.uk.

10
The Next Generation

We will tell the next generation the praiseworthy deeds
of the LORD, his power, and the wonders he has done.

Psalm 78:4

The E and the N

Okay, it's the last chapter and it's time to come clean. Eden,
even though it sounds quite cool as the chosen tag for this
regenerative urban youth work strategy, and even though it has
atmospheric prophetic overtones, was at one time on the
drawing board as a cheesy acrostic. Isn't that upsetting? No,
please don't put the book down. You're nearly at the end now
and you need to get your money's worth! The E is Evangelism.
The D is Discipleship. The E and the N stand for Equipping the
Next generation. Of course Edeng isn't a word, so we won't
even go there ... Anyway, here, within the E and the N, lies the
ultimate unanswered question currently hanging just out of our
grasp: What would it look like if the young people of Britain's
inner cities and council estates began to reach their transformative potential *and* remained devoted to the streets where

197

they're needed most – instead of taking the traditional route of finding Jesus and as quickly as possible moving somewhere nice and safe? All we can do at the moment by way of answering that question is to apply the abilities of our spiritual senses. We can take a deep breath and try to detect any tell-tale scent on the wind. We can rub our eyes and look for signs of movement in the twilight.

School kids from Aberdeen to Yeovil will all at some point have sat back in their seats and yawned a deep yawn as the history teacher repeated in case they'd forgotten, '… and so, we study history to help us understand the present … and, maybe, the future?' with an eerie change of pitch to emphasise the final word. Unfortunately, although it may be boring, it's quite true. There's so much we can learn about where we're heading from looking at where we've come from. Perhaps at this point it's worth remembering that Eden isn't some kind of new invention. It's not the first time that Christians have recognised the biblical model of mission through incarnation and had a go at it for themselves. History, both ancient and modern, is littered with stories of both successes and failures, and everything in between. At present the UK is home to numerous networks of urban pioneers who have deliberately decided to move into the places where the church is either absent, or certainly far from vibrant. Right here in Manchester, at the end of the nineteenth century, when Ancoats, the world's first industrial suburb, was festering with every social ill under the sun, a wealthy philan-thropist called Frank Crossley sensed a call from the Lord to move into the squalor to shine the light of the love of Jesus. One of his many biographers, Edward Mynott, sums up the move:

> Until the 1890s Crossley's philanthropy had been to provide funds for an enterprise that was run by others, such as the rescue homes associated with the City Mission. Similarly, he funded the Salvation

Army to the tune of £100,000 allowing them to conduct their overseas missionary work. This earned him the title of 'The Paymaster' in Army circles. However, this pattern changed when Crossley made the decision not just to set up a new mission hall in the poor working-class district of Ancoats but to go and live there ... He was a member of the Downs Congregational Church in Bowdon and at one meeting, after the assembly refused his urgings that they should pray on their knees, he astonished everyone with his outburst: 'To some of you this place is sacred for its quiet, refined associations: you love it: as for me, I hate it all. Let us leave this respectable neighbourhood and go right down among the poor folks: this is where the church should be!' And that is precisely what he did.[1]

Maybe there's something in that Crossley style grace heritage which God has sovereignly chosen to reignite through Eden.

Small worlds, short horizons

Fairly regularly, when they feel relationships with young people and parents are up to it, and when finances will stretch to it, Eden teams will take out young people from their neighbourhood on day trips or residentials. It's at times like these that the poverty trap of many young people's lives becomes apparent. Although it may sound like a portrait of Frank Crossley's England, it is actually still the case in the twenty-first century that a youth group leader can take a group of teenagers from an urban housing estate into the countryside and half of the minibus will totally freak out because they've never actually seen a real sheep before. And the buzz to be had standing near the edge of a cliff with hardcore hooligans terrified because the greatest height they've ever known is peeing over the edge of the motorway bridge is fantastic! The fact is that for all the trendy mission books published about postmodernity and Gen-

eration X, Y and Z, young people on our urban housing estates
live within a social framework that is more medieval village than
metropolis. There are all the trappings of the information age,
interactive Sky TV, broadband, space-age shoes from the
planet Shox and weatherproof jackets Scott of the Antarctic
would have given his right arm for (literally). Except that's not

---

REALITY BITES

Jordan's hopes and dreams.

September 2001, Eden Harpurhey moved into my area and I
didn't know what they were here for. We got to know each other
and I started to develop an idea of what their exact mission was,
but couldn't actually see *why* God would call them to Harpurhey.
To be honest, I thought they were all lunatics for trying to get
their message across to this community. You see, I know what
the people round here can be like, and when it comes to
Christianity, they can be quite ignorant. I never would've thought
that three years on I would have become a Christian, wanting
the same things as the Eden team.

But somewhere along the way I did find myself wanting what
these people, who later became my true friends, had got. I
started out just concentrating on myself and God, failing to see
the bigger picture. Now though, I find myself always praying for
the area, my mates and my family, because they want 'something more' and don't know what that something is. But I do
know. I've found truth and freedom in God and I'm beginning to
understand the fact that it's for everyone, and God wants to use
me to show that fact to this area, my area.

It's funny how God speaks to you when you're not really
expecting him to, especially when what he seems to be saying

---

the point. Do you ever watch those naff American sci-fi series that seem to be two-a-penny on the minor channels? Intrepid explorers turn up in a distant galaxy and find a world inhabited by people who live in mud huts but have somehow developed laser beams … well, it's a bit like that, a strange co-existence of the past and the future.

is a scary thing to share. But this one time when I was praying with my mate Andy (a member of the Eden team), I felt God wanted me to say this: 'Andy mate, I mean no offence but I feel God is trying to tell me that it ain't you guys who've moved in to this area that are going to see a major change, but it's actually the people you have affected, like me, who will see it happen.'

The way God works is mad, because not only had God spoken to me about this, but also Andy had heard somebody else say the same thing only a couple of weeks before. He hadn't wanted to tell us in case we felt burdened. But instead of feeling burdened it felt like things inside me had balanced out and come together. I felt settled that God had spoken.

Now I feel like God wants me to be in this area to be his spokesperson to it. Because of this I have more heart to reach out to this community. I want to see it transformed in such a way that people can no longer say bad things about it, but that they can see it covered in the transformation that only Jesus can bring. And it's like a ripple effect, because when God speaks things happen, and that causes more and more things to start to change, for his glory.

Throughout our universe we know that two principal dimensions exist: space and time. Few people except the Hawking-type boffins really understand how they work, but that's not important right here. We're not about to go quantum, we're going to go urban. Spend any time living inside the labyrinth of the estate and you'll see an extreme limitation of these dimensions. In terms of space, young people growing up on the estates are likely to occupy extremely small worlds within which they may display an attitude of invincibility but outside of which they may feel extremely insecure. These worlds may be defined by just a few streets and landmarks, plus a certain bus route in and out. This goes some way to explaining why 'space invaders' like the Eden teams can have a really rough ride when they first move in. In the dimension of time, the same young people are likely to be equally restricted. Evidence of short horizons is all around. Living for the moment is the order of the day and future aspiration is rare. The ideas of cause and effect and of consequence would be quite foreign. Very little framework exists for extraterrestrial stuff like responsibility or guilt.

Can you imagine, then, what an amazing thing it is when all that changes as a young person comes to Jesus? Instead of the world being defined by the end of the street, it begins to swell out in all directions as the awareness suddenly dawns that there is a whole global family out there offering an open-arms welcome. Instead of the horizon being limited to how long it will be before I can score another eighth, the impact of a 2,000-year-old story flicks the switch of an eternal destiny, lighting up a whole new lifescape.

There's something massively encouraging about the way inner-city neighbourhoods are constructed here in the UK – not the bricks and mortar but the social ties, particularly the family connections. It's quite the opposite of the commuter belts, which have become more and more socially retarded with fewer people having any involvement in next-door's life. Anyone interested in trying out Jesus-style ministry straight from the pages of the Gospels would find immediate application. Take the example of when Jesus sends out the 72 in Luke 10. After his sort of reverse-motivational psychology bit, '*I am sending you out like lambs among wolves*',[2] he gets into some really smart network methodology. Quite deliberately he introduces a local character he refers to as the 'man of peace', which could probably be a woman or a man if Joshua 2 can be cross-referenced with that, or Acts 16:14 for that matter. The experience of seven years of Eden in 10 different locations has proved this point time and time again. God has been working by his Spirit preparing the heart of a key local resident before we ever arrived. They will have influence in the community by virtue of their extended personal network, perhaps a large family with branches here, there and everywhere. On moving in, the individuals who make up the teams need to be alert. Things will progress much more smoothly and much more quickly if they can connect early on with the 'man of peace'.

Panoramas and penicillin

After years of really hard graft with lots of regular encouragements but not much that really ticks the '*fruit that will last* '[3] box, Eden finally seems to have reached a special vantage point on its journey where the way ahead can be clearly seen. It's been just like climbing a huge hill, all the way up imagining what the view will be like on the other side. Eventually a moment comes when the mist begins to clear and the great plain below is seen as one huge panorama. What you see is what you'll be walking into in the future. We feel like we've seen it now. Maybe it's taken us a long time to get up the hill, maybe we could have done it quicker, but as Martin Luther King famously said, '… that doesn't matter now, my eyes have seen the promised land!'

What we see stretched out before us now is neither new nor radical – it's quite basic, quite obvious. Other people have stood on this hill and they've seen this vision too. But right now we're on the hill, and we're looking at it, right there before our eyes. It's not just in our imaginations any more; it's real and it's breathtaking. From the toughest homes in the toughest streets

---

REALITY BITES

Gemma (19), passionate about Salford.

Now that I've completed five months' training on Xcelerate I'm joining Eden Salford as a volunteer worker. The moment I was saved in August 2001, God gave me a passion to reach out to the young people in Manchester. When I look at the youth today, I don't see troublesome, out of control 'wasters' but instead I see gifted, talented people with God-given potential who have the ability to do amazing works.

I can understand why certain young people act in the way they do, why they feel the need to fit in with the crowd and by doing so become caught up in all kinds of trouble. I know how Christianity can be perceived and I fully understand why young people see it as boring and irrelevant. Like many of these teenagers, I've been in that situation and I can relate to them. However, through God's amazing grace and through the work of Eden I have discovered an incredible, relevant, exciting life in Jesus. He has given me hope and a future and I know that I am called to share this hope with the young people of Manchester.

I have been praying into this for some time and God gave me this verse:

---

of the toughest neighbourhoods we have seen the birth of the next generation, and with increased regularity we continue to see new spiritual babies born. For nearly 20 years The Message has seen decisions, thousands of them, and many are still going for it with God, but this just seems like something different. A lot of the stuff we saw in the first few years of Eden might be described as 'Close Encounters of the God Kind' – but this is not the same. There is a strong sense in our hearts that these few new disciples are the first generation of a whole new

> *This is how we know what real love is: Jesus gave his life for us. So we should give our lives for our brothers and sisters. Suppose someone has enough to live on and sees a brother or sister in need but does not help. Then God's love is not living in that person. My children, we should love people not only with words, but by our actions and true caring.* (*1 John 3:16–18 NCV*)

I have my salvation, my hope and my future rooted in Jesus, but loads of other young people haven't. If I don't help them, then the Bible says I don't have God's love inside of me. This verse has motivated me to help the young people in whatever way possible.

I have been reached by the work of Eden, been discipled by Eden, and now I will go back into the community as an Eden worker myself. Whilst on Eden I hope to study social work or a youth and community degree at university. I believe that this degree will enable me to have a full-time career in youth work in the future.

My vision for Eden is that one day it will be run by the young people who are currently being reached ... that they will see God's heart for them, discover their own potential, respond to Jesus and to God's calling on their lives and then reach back out into their own communities with the life-changing word of God.

strain of Christianity, genetically engineered by the Holy Spirit in Manchester's sink estates. Wasn't penicillin created in a sink, from the leftovers of a bungled experiment? Could God be doing an Alexander Fleming outside the sterile conditions of the lab? Will these young people go on to be the antibiotic their communities so desperately need?

Even the most sceptical, cynical and critical observers all have to concede that the twentieth century was a time of unprecedented success for the Christian church around the globe. Okay, Western Europe had, and is still having, a pretty rough time of it – but on every other continent ordinary women and men, girls and boys have been choosing to follow Jesus. In their millions. How did it happen? By halfway through the twentieth century the major missionary movements were pretty much out of steam. Many were beginning to concede that there was nothing more they could do. It was even forecast that within 30 years the flame of Christian witness would likely flicker helplessly and then die out.

The flaw in their terminal prediction was its lack of acknowledgement of the hardiness of the gospel seed planted into the generational heart-soil of the populations in which their missionaries had served so faithfully and patiently. The supply of professional expounders and expositors of Christian doctrine might have been drying up, but God had a 'latter rain'[4] in store. From barely visible lives, sprinkled throughout the earth's great continents, he would form dynamic teams of apostles, prophets, evangelists, pastors and teachers who would turn their nations upside down. Similarly, Eden expects to see the real

big-time changes taking place when the next generation – the young people currently being reached by the imported teams – take the lead themselves. It's absolutely essential that, whilst some of those reached may find their lives so transformed that they want to move on out and explore all sorts of possibilities in the big wide world, many more must stay and devote themselves to the communities in which they've grown up and that they know so well.

Multiplication principles

By now you'll sense that Eden seems to have shifted up a gear. Lots of images could be employed to describe this; ultimately our assessment is that the movement has been transitioning from a process of addition to a process of multiplication. It's no great secret that multiplication is at the heart of God's promises. Through Scripture's recordings of God's successive revelations to successive generations we see the word cropping up again and again. The principle of multiplication is found at the heart of God's promises. If you know your King James Version, which is a bit of a long shot, you'll find 107 references to multiplication. It's everywhere, especially at the critical covenant-making moments. Let's take a quick skim through. Way back in the beginning there was the original commission given to the first family:

> And God blessed them, and God said unto them, Be fruitful, and multiply ...[5]

Then, at another really critical moment, when the world has gone a bit pear-shaped and God has decided to make a fresh go of it, he reinforces that word:

> And God blessed Noah and his sons, and said unto them, Be fruitful, and multiply, and replenish the earth.[6]

If twice wasn't enough to make us pay attention, God rams the point home again after a few more generations have gone by, this time to the father of our faith:

And when Abram was ninety years old and nine, the LORD appeared to Abram, and said unto him, I am the Almighty God; walk before me, and be thou perfect. And I will make my covenant between me and thee, and will multiply thee exceedingly.[7]

And fortunately the multiplying theme doesn't grind to a halt with the end of the Old Testament. Jesus, in his stories of life in the new Kingdom, expresses the principle through parable:

... the man who hears the word and understands it ... produces a crop, yielding a hundred, sixty or thirty times what was sown.[8]

And of course our whistle-stop tour wouldn't be complete without taking note of the growth seen in the early days of the church:

... when they had prayed, they laid their hands on them. And the word of God increased; and the number of the disciples multiplied in Jerusalem greatly.[9]

There's no mistaking the favourite button on God's calculator, and it's not add, subtract or divide!

Multiplication can be interpreted as meaning two specific things for the future of Eden. First, rather than perpetually importing missionaries from around the nation, Eden is beginning to produce its own evangelists. In the early days of Eden a prophecy was brought to the leadership which revolved around the concept of a 'Gideon's army for the inner city'. That word shaped the strategy of calling a fearless army of 300 to stand and fight for the freedom of the land. Lately, however, this seems to have been overtaken by a greater revelation which has been referred to already but may have escaped your attention. The word of the Lord to Ezekiel, recorded in chapter 37 of his book, describes the way in which a vast army is formed by a miracle performed with a collection of scattered bits of human skeletons. Rather than the army of Gideon, which was a gathering of related tribes, this new army is the product of a resurrection miracle brought about by co-operation with the breath of the divine. Whether or not the term 'army' is actually a helpful image in today's climate of religious extremism is debatable, but the point is not the image but the dramatic leap of expectation between the two revelations. The mindset of the first word is bounded by the finite resources of the existing tribes. The new revelation has infinite possibilities because the raw material is visible all around, for those with an eye to see it and faith to believe it. It is now a stated goal that Eden teams themselves must not be a 'closed shop', their inner workings must become more and more transparent and accessible to local young leaders-in-the-making. Teams must be ruthless with any evidence of 'missionary compound' mentality. The number one priority from here on in is the creation of straight clear paths on which young people can travel to their full God-given destiny. Year on year now we may see a net reduction in the numbers of people we have to relocate into the inner city as the rate of multiplication increases within.

From Manchester with love

The second way in which Eden is expected to multiply in years ahead is through a multiplication of project partnerships. The most recent target of 10 projects in the Greater Manchester area has been reached, so what happens now? The first horizon remains fixed within the boroughs of our beloved sprawl. Eden is working in five of them at the moment. It would be great to see Edens multiplied out to Bolton, Bury, Rochdale, Stockport and Wigan – the lessons learned in Manchester, Oldham, Salford, Tameside and Trafford are definitely transferable. Whilst working in lots of different local authority areas brings added complications, there are great churches in all those areas who may well sense God's call to the wild and express a desire to partner with us.

Beyond that local horizon there is a truly awesome opportunity to see Eden multiplying throughout the nation. Behind the scenes in trustees' meetings at The Message there has been a growing sense that God has been allowing us to incubate the Eden model, but that he has much greater plans for it in the earth. For the first time there is a unanimous agreement that when we are approached in the future by groups from other towns and cities serious about taking on the Eden model we need to start going the extra mile. We feel privileged to offer the world not simply a bunch of mad ideas but a tried and tested model. In fact, Eden is more than just a model: we have an incarnational mission process that has been observed not only in the lab but also in the field. We've cross-bred various strains of the same plant to see which are the most robust, which have the greatest ability to thrive and reproduce in wild inner-city conditions. You could say that Eden is genetically modified! Some of the 'experiments' didn't quite turn out the way we expected, but everything that has taken place, good or bad, has brought valuable learning into Eden's corporate memory.

So, whilst this is the end of the book, it isn't the end of the story. It may be that as you've been reading these pages over the last few days God has been whispering in your ear. You may be sensing the call to join us reaching the wild. If you are, drop us a line. Our Manchester-based projects would love to hear from you. Perhaps you want to explore the possibility of Eden in a troubled neighbourhood in your part of the world. Great, we'd love to hear from you too. Here in Manchester we've just had the privilege of looking after this baby during its infancy; we've given support and encouragement and watched it grow. We do feel that it's our baby, but we know it's been growing up fast. To be honest, we do feel very protective and we're really scared about what will happen if we open the garden gate, but there's no denying it, Eden has a destiny beyond Manchester and beyond us. It has all the potential to grow bigger, go further and live longer, and it probably will.

Finally, throughout the book, you may have detected a certain reserve, particularly if you're familiar with any of the regular material published by us guys at The Message! Well, would you permit a bit of indulgence in this last paragraph? If the truth be told, we're flipping excited about what God is doing right now. When, after years of emptying ourselves into young inner-city lives, we see dominating oppressive powers crushed by the cross, we kind of like to celebrate that! When the ones and twos become threes and fours, and the threes and fours become fives and sixes, and the fives and sixes become multiplied by ten projects, and the ten projects start doing that Revelation 22 thing and 'yielding fruit every month', it's not long before the R-word that we mentioned at the opening of chapter 7 starts sounding like it might be possible after all.

---

[1] Edward Mynott, 'Frank Crossley – Saint or Sinner?', *Manchester Region History Review 1997*, Vol. XI, pp. 52–59.
[2] Luke 10:3.
[3] John 15:16.
[4] No reference intended to Latter Rain movement.
[5] Genesis 1:28.
[6] Genesis 9:1.
[7] Genesis 17: 1.
[8] Matthew 13:23.
[9] Acts 6:6.

Appendix

Eden believes that even the hardest-to-reach young people, when centred on Jesus and given opportunity to fulfil their God-given potential, will be transformational within their communities.

Eden – Our Cornerstones

1. Rooted in a local church.
2. Focused on the toughest neighbourhoods.
3. A large team of people establish their homes in the heart of the community.
4. The first priority is reaching youth to see their full potential unlocked.

Eden – Our Cornerstones expanded

1. *Rooted in a local church*

Rooted in a supportive local church, we seek to impact our community positively by the consistent witness of our presence and our proclamation. We desire to be a blessing to, and enjoy fellowship with, the whole body of Christ.

2. *Focused on the toughest neighbourhoods*

That is, communities widely recognised as suffering from multiple deprivations, such as high crime, poor health, low educational achievement, dilapidated environment, broken families and few opportunities for young people.

3. *A large team of people establish their homes in the heart of the community*

Devoted individuals with a recognised calling to live an incarnational lifestyle of integrating with the community. Dozens of such people join together in a missional team dynamic and make themselves available long term for the benefit of their community.

4. *The first priority is reaching youth to see their full potential unlocked*

Young people of high school age are seen to be a key part of the transformation of the whole neighbourhood. Our goal is to help them to achieve all their God-given potential, introducing them to Jesus by creating repeated and varied opportunities for them to hear, experience and respond to the gospel.

About the Author

Working for the Message Trust as EDEN Partnerships Director, Matt Wilson has the privilege of serving and encouraging the amazing people who form the Eden teams. As one of the first of those who 'made the move' he is able to write with empathy, honesty and poignant insight.

Survivor books . . . receive as you read!

Survivor Books came out of a desire to pass on revelation, knowledge, experience and lessons learnt by lead worshippers and teachers who minister to our generation.

We pray that you will be challenged, encouraged and inspired and receive as you read.

The Survivor Book Sampler: only £1
Sample all 21 Survivor books, including money off vouchers!

survivor

www.survivor.co.uk

God on the Beach: Michael Volland (£6.99)

Newquay: the UK's infamous summer party capital. The town heaving with young clubbers and surfers, each one desperate to live life to the full, eager for experience, ready to ride the waves and hit the heights. Into this caotic carnival dropped Michael Volland, DJ, surfer, and team member in a beach mission 21st century style. There was just one problem, Michael was not at all sure that God would turn up.

City-Changing Prayer: Debra & Frank Green (£6.99)

Imagine a regular city-wide gathering of Christians united and focused in prayer. Imagine a church that serves local institutions, and asks nothing in return. Imagine the crime rate falling; teenagers praying; people beginning to believe that there's something in this thing called prayer. Frank and Debra Green have seen all this and more over the past ten years. They have learnt lessons about how to foster mutual trust and spiritual fruitfulness, overcoming the obstacles both inside and outside the church family.

Diary of a Dangerous Vision: Andy Hawthorne (£6.99)

This is the story of Andy Hawthorne's dramatic conversion and the adventure of an ever-growing group of Christian's set to take Christ into the most tough urban areas. Reading this book will leave you challenged and inspired.

survivor

www.survivor.co.uk

Rad Lad Livin: Mark Bowness (£6.99)

The perfect manual to help any lad move forward in God, tackling issues ranging from lust to identity, from brotherhood to homosexuality – this book is practical in its nature and real in its content. Mark has grappled with biblical issues in order to present them in a real and relevant way, then sprinkled it with stories of past and present, making this a challenging, interesting and significant book for any lad to read.

Wasteland: Mike Pilavachi (£6.99)

With honesty and wit, Mike helps us to understand – and even relish – those difficult times in our lives when our dreams are unrealised and our spirituality feels dry and lifeless. Drawing from characters in the Old and New Testament, he puts together a biblical survival kit for the journey so that hope shimmers on the horizon like a distant oasis.

The Truth Will Set You Free: Beth Redman (£5.99)

With insight and humour, Beth helps young women to find God's answers to the big questions and struggles in their lives. Thousands of teenage girls have come to trust Beth Redman's powerful and relevant teaching through her packed seminars at Soul Survivor.

survivor

www.survivor.co.uk

Passion for Your Name: Tim Hughes (£6.99)

Timely and timeless advice for today's leader. If you want to be more involved in leading worship in your church, or become a more effective member of the band, then this book is a great place to begin. Tim Hughes looks first at the reasons why we worship God, and why we need to get our hearts right with him, before moving on to the practicalities of choosing a song list, musical dynamics, small group worship, and the art of songwriting.

The Air I Breathe: Louie Giglio (£6.99)

For some it's the office. For others, the mirror. "When you follow the trail of your time, energy, affection, and money" says Louie, "you find a throne. And whatever is on that throne is the object of your worship!" Learn to give your life to the only One worthy of it.

The Unquenchable Worshipper: Matt Redman (£5.99)

This book is about a kind of worshipper; unquenchable, undivided, unpredictable. On a quest to bring glory and pleasure to God, these worshippers will not allow themselves to be distracted or defeated. Matt uses many examples from the Bible and draws on his own experience as a worship leader, to show us how to make our worship more meaningful.

survivor

Facedown: Matt Redman (£5.99)

"When we face up to the glory of God, we soon find ourselves facedown in worship". Matt Redman takes us on a journey into wonder, reverence and mystery – urging us to recover the "otherness" of God in our worship.

Heart of Worship Files: Compiled by Matt Redman (£7.99)

A mixture of creative biblical insights and hands-on advice on how to lead worship and write congregational songs. Contributors include: Mike Pilavachi; Tim Hughes; Graham Kendrick; Darlene Zschech and Matt Redman. This book will encourage and inspire you to new heights of worship, giving practical advice for worship leaders, creative advice for musicians and perceptive insights into the theology of worship.

Inside Out Worship: Compiled by Matt Redman (£6.99)

Outside-in worship never works; true worship always works itself from the inside, out. A love for God, which burns on the inside and cannot help but express itself externally too. Purposeful lives of worship exploding from passionate and devoted hearts. Guidance from some of today's most seasoned leaders and lead worshippers, including Darlene Zschech, Robin Mark, Tim Hughes, Chris Tomlin, Brian Houston, Terl Bryant and many more.

survivor

www.survivor.co.uk

Red Moon Rising: Pete Greig (£7.99)

24-7 is at the centre of a prayer revival across the globe and this book gives a fantastic insight into what God is doing with ordinary prayer warriors. Read inspiring stories of people finding a new depth of heartfelt prayer and radical compassion.

The Vision & the Vow: Pete Greig (£6.99)

Has your faith become a chore where once it was a passion? Are you tired of the self-serving mentality of our culture? Join Pete Greig on the adventure of a lifetime in this inspiring and beautifully illustrated book; unlocking God's ultimate vision for your life and your community.

24-7 Prayer Manual (£9.99)

People are praying 24 hours a day, 7 days a week in countries around the world, with as a many as 20 prayer rooms running concurrently. This concise but detailed guide will help churches, youth groups, Christian Unions and groups of churches set up prayer rooms for one day, one week or one month. The book gives an introduction to the ethos of 24-7 and a step by step guide to setting up a prayer room. It's full of creative, low cost ideas that will help make the life changing prayer room experience accessible to everyone. Includes CD Rom.

survivor

www.survivor.co.uk

Salvation's Song: Marcus Green (£6.99)

Worship changes us. It changes our views of God, of the world, and of ourselves. . .at least it should. Marcus Green takes us on a journey through some of the big issues of Christian faith, making some exciting discoveries about the liberating nature of true worship. Jesus died so that we can worship God. That's the good news. That's the gospel.

The Shock of Your Life: Adrian Holloway (£6.99)

Dan, Becky and Emma have one thing in common. . .they just died. Were they ready? Do heaven and hell really exist? Are you a red-hot Christian? A lukewarm Christian? Or maybe you've never even considered Christianity. . .well, this book is for you. Read it for yourself and be shocked to the core.

Aftershock: Adrian Holloway (£6.99)

Dan is back. Back from the dead. Now there'll be trouble. Dan was the sole survivor of an accident that propelled three young people into the afterlife. Now he's back, ready to convince his friends and family that Jesus is their only hope before they face judgement after death. Adrian Holloway gives readers and youth leaders a powerful weapon in their spiritual armoury.

survivor

www.survivor.co.uk

Jesus Freaks II: DC Talk (£11.99)

Rarely has a book captured the attention of Christians of all ages as Jesus Freaks has with its stories of Christian martyrs. Featuring testimonies of revolutionaries who took a stand for Christ against the culture of their day, along with new stories of martyrs through the centuries. DC Talk challenge readers to pray for the persecuted church around the world and openly stand for Jesus.

Studentdom: Matt Stuart (£7.99)

In addition to study and exams the university years bring a new freedom, character development and the building of what may become lifelong friendships. But they can be daunting too, particularly for Christian students who may worry about fitting in or about misusing their new-found freedom. Matt Stuart provides a comprehensive guide to all aspects of university life, including areas such as relationships and debt management.

Prices are correct at time of going to press but may change.

survivor
www.survivor.co.uk